*A Garland Series*
# Foundations of the Novel

*Representative Early*

*Eighteenth-Century Fiction*

A collection of 100 rare titles
reprinted in photo-facsimile in 71 volumes

# Foundations of the Novel

compiled and edited by
Michael F. Shugrue
*Secretary for English for the M.L.A.*

with New Introductions for each volume by

Michael Shugrue, *City College of C.U.N.Y.*
Malcolm J. Bosse, *City College of C.U.N.Y.*
William Graves, *N.Y. Institute of Technology*
Josephine Grieder, *Rutgers University, Newark*

# The Prince of Carency

by

## Marie Catherine, comtesse d'Aulnoy

with a new introduction
for the Garland Edition by
Josephine Grieder

Garland Publishing, Inc., New York & London

*1973*

The new introduction for the

Garland *Foundations of the Novel* Edition

is Copyright © 1973, by

*Garland Publishing, Inc., New York & London*

All Rights Reserved

Bibliographical note:
*This facsimile has been made from a copy in the
Beinecke Library of Yale University
(Hfc39 50)*

Library of Congress Cataloging in Publication Data

Aulnoy, Marie Catherine Jumelle de Berneville,
   comtesse d', d. 1705.
   The Prince of Carency.

   (Foundations of the novel)
   Reprint of the 1719 ed.
   Translation of Histoire de Jean de Bourbon, Prince
de Carency.
   1. Bourbon, Jean de, d. 1458--Fiction.  I. Title.
II. Series.
PZ3.A924Pr5  [PQ1711.A85]     843'.4    70-170541
ISBN 0-8240-0542-2

*Printed in the United States of America*

# Introduction

The Prince of Carency, *by Mme d'Aulnoy, is a translation of the 1692* Histoire de Jean de Bourbon, Prince de Carency. *The French original was not as popular as the authoress' previous* Histoire d'Hypolite, comte de Duglas, *though between 1704 and 1729 it did go through at least five editions. The English translation of 1719 here reprinted reappeared in 1723 and 1724 — evidence of a modest popularity which may give pause for reflection to the thoughtful critic, curious about the reading public's literary taste and sophistication. For the book is a farrago, and yet not unentertaining; much less skillful and unified than* Hypolitus Earl of Douglas,[1] *and yet not lacking in a kind of how-will-the-characters-get-out-of-this charm.*

*Like* Hypolitus, *it is a hybrid of baroque heroical romance and the novel as "history."*[2] *With the latter genre it shares an exact historical setting, not too far distant in time; linear construction (though occasionally flashbacks are provided to explain a character's unexpected presence); characters acting as private persons rather than public figures (though the Queen of Fez does participate in political intrigues); and an interest in emotion and sentiment. Like the former genre — and it is far more baroque than* Hypolitus *— the novel features exotic locales and extravagant coincidences. In fact, it is not unfair to say that the plot (which is unsummariz-*

## INTRODUCTION

*able) places great demands on the reader, both on his memory (Carency and Casilda each assume two pseudonyms for purposes of disguise, Leonida and Abelhamar one) and on his credibility (at least four characters presumed dead later turn up quite alive).*

*The mainspring of this tumult of activity is love, and Mme d'Aulnoy holds firmly to the concept already developed in* Hypolitus, *that of the all-consuming, fatal passion that drives men, heedless of difficulty, to pursue their beloved over land and sea and women to remain rigorously constant to their lovers in spite of temptation and tribulation. "Oh Love," cries a friend of the Prince, "will you never cease persecuting us? You alone cause all our Misfortunes, and never grant a Favour that is not preceded by a Thousand Disappointments. Ah! Why have we no Fence against your Power?" (p. 275). Yet the Prince replies that he cannot forget Leonida: "alas! how is it possible? Fortune may be inconstant, but my Heart can never change" (p. 277).*

*But — and it is precisely at this point that the novel becomes curiously interesting — Mme d'Aulnoy is betrayed by the elaborateness of her plot into dealing with situations whose complexity she evidently does not understand and thus cannot definitely resolve. The reader approaches with her a grey area, a sort of subliminal inquietude as he encounters circumstances which seem at variance with her doctrine of the power of love. Whether the ambiguity is due to intent or simply to lack of skill, it provokes the reader to a little extra psychological inquiry.*

# INTRODUCTION

*Take, for example, the question of the Prince of Carency's passion. Once he has encountered the beauteous Leonida, he cannot rest until she is restored to him; this is indeed consonant with the overpowering passion he feels. But the fact is that she is not the only but the third woman he loves: the first being the fair benefactress who ransoms him in Nicopolis and whom he never knows except through her two letters; the second being Olympia, who, mistaking him for her lover La Vagne, overwhelms him with caresses and dies when she discovers her error. Yet he and his friend take this amorous predicament quite seriously.* "You love a Lady at Nicopolis, *whom it is likely you may never see;* Olympia *you have seen, and lov'd her at first Sight, she is now no more: I must own that all the Circumstances of your Adventures are fatal; but,"* counsels the friend, *"if you call Reason to your Assistance, it will tell you, that your Love is only due to* Leonida *[his official betrothed, whom at this point he has not seen]" (pp. 37-38).* "Alas," *moans the Prince,* "is it in my Power to love whom I please, and forget two Objects that so entirely possess my Soul? Love, without consulting Duty, takes Possession of our Inclinations." *His friend says no more, choosing* "rather to pity the Prince, than condemn those Sentiments which were too passionate and confus'd to be easily conquer'd" (p. 38).

*Casilda is placed in similar but more complicated circumstances. Finding a portrait which Donna Blanca has let fall by accident, she becomes immediately enamored of the unknown young man and simultane-*

## INTRODUCTION

*ously jealous of Blanca: "But (said I a Minute after) is it possible that in such a little Time, Love cou'd have made so great a Progress? . . . and I have form'd a Rival without having a Lover" (p. 62). She at last meets Henriquez and coaxes him away from Blanca by inventing a tale about his mistress's infidelity. When Leonida reproaches her for such perfidy, Casilda protests, "you little know the Effects of a violent Passion; every Thing is allow'd to Lovers, when they are in pursuit of a Heart" (p. 77). Henriquez deserts her; and upon experiencing the pleasures of Carency's company, she decides to solace herself. "Whatever Trouble a new Inclination may give me, thought she, it can never be equal to the Pain I endure. . . . I am resolv'd to be favourable to him, whatever may be the Event: Love is a pleasing Torment" (p. 105). And to the end of the novel she pursues Carency as rashly as he pursues Leonida.*

   *Casilda's dual passion, and her lapse from love's code, is to a degree explainable, for she is a villainess (in addition to the deceit she and her brother practice on the Prince, she stabs and nearly dispatches Leonida) and therefore perhaps to be regarded as morally aberrant. But what can one say of a hero who has not one but three inamoratas? And in fact even that statement is not accurate. In the French original, Leonida dies of Casilda's wound, and the Prince sadly returns to France, where he marries Catherine d'Artois, who helps "effacer un peu le précieux souvenir de sa chère Leonide" (II, 326).*[3] *But the English translator frankly admits that he has altered the ending, "since it seems unreasonable, . . .*

# INTRODUCTION

*that the Prince of Carency, who was so passionately in Love with her [Leonida], shou'd, after her cruel Fate, conceive tender Sentiments for any other Lady, a Character not becoming a Hero."*

The other curious element in The Prince of Carency is the ambiguity, not to say amorphousness, of sex and of identity. In two cases women disguise themselves as men, and the disguise is accepted without question.[4] To liberate Ramire, Inea poses as a young man and unwittingly becomes the confidant of the jailor's daughter, who has fallen in love with the Don. Casilda pretends to be Don Sanche, her brother's young page, and after Carency kills the brother in a duel, he takes Sanche into his household to protect him. That Inea's and Casilda's sex should go unrecognized may perhaps be explained away by the lack of occasion for familiarity on either side. But what of the case of Abelhamar, who, disguised as Eugenia, insinuates himself into the queen's harem and lives for some time in intimate proximity with his beloved Leonida and Inea? How is one to take the fact that Leonida finds Eugenia's companionship and caresses so agreeable, though she had shunned Abelhamar's attentions? And how can one interpret Eugenia's profession, as she attempts to persuade Leonida out of her passion for the Prince, that "although we are of one Sex, I must tell you, I take delight in gaining the Affections of a young unpractis'd Heart, who is unacquainted with Sentiments so destructive to our Peace" (p. 237)?

The ambiguity of sex, which permits one to become

# INTRODUCTION

*the other, undetected, is paralleled by an amorphousness of identity that is equally suggestive. The Prince of Carency is the double of the Count of La Vagne, as he learns when Olympia mistakes him for her lover. Taken in half dead by the compassionate Leonida and Casilda (themselves disguised), the Prince becomes La Vagne to conceal his identity. Leonida falls in love with him under this guise; and when in Fez the real La Vagne turns up as the sole survivor of a shipwreck, she cannot help being astounded by his total indifference to her. Toward the end, Carency-La Vagne metamorphoses a third time into the handsome Moor Assimir. This disguise is penetrated by Casilda and the Queen of Fez, who know him to be Carency, and Leonida, who believes him to be La Vagne. Carency is less perceptive: he recognizes Leonida immediately (as a lover ought); discovers, thanks to a friend, that the Queen is his unknown benefactress from Nicopolis (though he once loved her); and learns only as he stabs Don Sanche that this is Casilda (although he has seen her more often than Leonida).*

It may justly be argued that fictional transvestism was a long-established literary convention accepted unquestioningly by the reading public and that frequent disguises are simply plot devices to provide suspense and mystery for the reader's amusement. But both elements indicate profoundly the vacuity and the bankruptcy of this type of literature. These fictional creations have no palpability; their identities — and sex — are so amorphous that even their fellow creations cannot readily

# INTRODUCTION

*distinguish one from another. That passion justifies their metamorphoses is belied by a love which can fix on two or even three objects in succession, which seems to come into existence in and of itself, selfishly unconscious of and indifferent to the possible antipathy of its choice. A work like* The Prince of Carency *is not unentertaining for the reader willing to accept its superficialities. The more serious reader can only be glad that future novelists realized the bankruptcy of its suppositions and turned away to explore more promising areas.*

Josephine Grieder

## NOTES

[1] *Reprint ed., New York: Garland Publishing, 1973.*

[2] *See Henri Coulet,* Le Roman jusqu'à la Révolution *(Paris: Armand Colin, 1967), pp. 208-215 and 286-291, for a discussion of the development of these two genres.*

[3] *This appears to be a vague gesture towards historicity by Mme d'Aulnoy, for the real Jean de Bourbon did in fact marry such a lady.*

[4] *A similar event occurs in* Hypolitus, *when the Marquise of Becarelly falls in love with Julia, disguised as the pilgrim Silvio. This incident is particularly piquant because the Marquise begs the now-revealed Julia to dress herself once again as Silvio – and when Julia obliges, is so overcome by her passion that she retires to mourn in a convent.*

# THE
# Prince of *Carency*;
# A
# NOVEL.

Written in FRENCH
By the Countess D'AUNOIS,
Author of the *Lady's Travels into
Spain.*

Translated into ENGLISH.

LONDON:
Printed by *W. Wilkins*, for J. PEELE,
at *Locke's - Head*, between the *Two
Temple-Gates* in *Fleet-street*. 1719.

# THE
# PREFACE

HIS Translation was at first design'd as an Amusement, without any Intention of making it publick; the Translator not presuming to succeed in the Delicacy and Politeness of a Dialect peculiar to Heroism; but as the Countess D'Aunois is the Author of this Piece, and as most of her Works have had the good Fortune to meet with a favourable Reception, he was induc'd to hope it might obtain the like Success: Besides, he wou'd not have ventur'd to deliver it to the Press, had he not consulted with some judicious Persons, who had read the Original in French, and were pleas'd to honour it with their Sanction.

It must be own'd at the same time, that this is not a Literal Translation; for tho' in the

## The PREFACE.

the French, the Characters are well drawn, and the Adventures agreeably related, it was thought proper to retrench some surperfluous Repetitions, which are frequently remark'd in Stories, of this Nature, written in that Language.

As to the last Incident, which is the Murder of Leonida, succeeded by the Marriage of the Prince of Carency to another Lady; that Circumstance with the Conclusion is entirely alter'd; and it's presum'd, that those, who shall take the Trouble of comparing this with the Original, will approve the Design, since it seems unreasonable, that Leonida, who was a Perfection of Virtue and Beauty, shou'd die a tragick Death; and that the Prince of Carency, who was so passionatly in Love with her, shou'd, after her cruel Fate, conceive tender Sentiments for any other Lady, a Character not becoming a Hero. However, if the Publick shou'd censure this Opinion, the Translator must then submit to their unquestion'd Judgment; and he humbly hopes, that in Consideration this is his first Essay, they will out of their Candor and good Nature, pardon whatever Fault they find in the Attempt.

# THE
# Prince of CARENCY.

HE Dutchess of *Lancaster*, Daughter of Don *Pedro*, King of *Castile*, cou'd not, without the greatest Concern, see Don *John*'s Accession to a Throne where she shou'd have been plac'd, were not her Father's Misfortunes the unhappy Cause. She very much follicited the Duke her Husband to declare War against him, which he was inclin'd to, only waited for a favourable Occasion of making an Alliance.

At this Juncture, *Ferdinand* King of *Portugal* (who often had Differences about Matters of Interest with the King of *Castile*) gave the Duke of *Lancaster* an Opportunity of declaring his Intentions, and sent to him, desiring he wou'd join with him in the Conquest of their common Enemy: The Duke, without delay, set out with a considerable Number of Forces,

Forces, and took with him his Wife and Three Daughters: Thefe Ladies were very beautiful, and the Youngeft, whofe Name was *Catherine*, being the only Daughter of his fecond Marriage, had Pretenfions to the Crown of *Spain* by Right of the Dutchefs her Mother, who was Heirefs to that Dominion.

The King of *Caftile*, finding that two fuch potent Enemies had declared againft him, apply'd to his Allies, but more particularly to *Charles* the VIth King of *France*, to whom he already owed many Obligations. That Prince fent him Men and Money, and Fortune declaring in his Favour, he defeated the *Englifh* and *Portuguefe* in feveral Engagements. The Sicknefs produc'd by the Climate, was even more deftructive to them than his Arms; but having weighty Reafons to wifh for Peace, and knowing that the Duke of *Lancafter* had left the King of *Portugal* with fome Difguft, he fent the Prior of *Guadalupe* to him at *Bayonne* with confiderable Offers, and a Propofal of Marriage between his Son *Henry* Prince of *Afturias*, and the Princefs *Catherine*, Daughter of the Duke, which he reprefented to be the only Means of placing her on the Throne of *Spain*; and at the fame Time promis'd he fhou'd have fufficient Reafon to be fatisfied with their Alliance.

The Duke receiv'd with Pleafure this Overture of Peace, being in all refpects agreeable to his Intereft; and the King's Ambaffadors perform'd the Ceremony of Marriage at *Bayonne*.

The Dutchess of *Lancaster* left *Biscay* to conduct her Daughter to *Medina del Campo*, where the King receiv'd them with all the Magnificence imaginable. She there presented him in the Name of the Duke her Husband, with a Crown of Gold embellish'd with Jewels, and told him with a majestick Air, that since she had yielded to him the Right she had to the Kingdom of *Castile*, it was but just he shou'd receive the Crown from the Duke her Lord. The King answer'd, that he only accepted of it with a Design of putting it on the Princess's Head, as soon as his Son shou'd be of Age; the young Prince being then but Ten Years old.

The Duke of *Lancaster* remain'd all this Time at *Bayonne*, tho' he passionately wish'd to see the King, that he might endeavour to disingage him from the *French* Interest: But the *Spanish* Monarch was too sensible of the Services he had receiv'd, to have any wrong Proceedings with the King of *France* in such a Conjuncture, therefore declined the Interview which the Duke desired; and being indispos'd at *Burgos*, took Leave of the Dutchess in that Place.

*Charles* the VIth, being inform'd of the King of *Castile*'s Conduct in what related to him, thought himself so highly oblig'd, that he chose *John* of *Bourbon* Count of *La March*, his Kinsman, as Ambassador to that Prince; who had Orders to tell him, that he shou'd ever embrace all Occasions of expressing his Gratitude for the Value he was pleas'd to set on their Alliance. The Count of *La March* was more capable than any of making known the Sentiments of his King, being of the firſt Rank by his Birth and Fortune, and by his great Qualities eſteemed one of the fineſt Gentlemen of *France*.

After having acquitted himſelf of his Commiſſion to the King of *Caſtile*, he contracted a Friendſhip with Don *John* of *Velaſco*, who had married a *French* Lady, Daughter of *Arnauld* of *Solier*. She had for her Fortune the City of *Vilalpendo*, which is one of the greateſt in *Caſtile*. *Velaſco* by his Birth, yielded to none but Princes of the Blood, and his Merit was equally great. Dona *Maria* his Wife, preferr'd the *French* to all other Nations, and inſpired her Husband with the ſame Sentiments. The Count of *La March* had already ſo great an Eſteem for them, that conſidering their vaſt Fortune was to be inherited by an only Daughter, he reſolv'd to propoſe a Marriage between her and *John* of *Bourbon*, Prince of *Carency*, the youngeſt of his Sons.

Having meditated ſometime on this Affair, he viſited Don *John* of *Velaſco*, and among other things told him, He had three Sons, that the King his Maſter had provided for the Two eldeſt, and that the Youngeſt was ſtill at his Diſpoſal. I am ſatisfy'd, ſaid he, I ſhou'd have no reaſon to complain of his Fate, were he deſtin'd to your Daughter: Therefore, if nothing oppoſes our Alliances, I ask her for him.

*of* CARENCY. 5

him. Your Proposal, my Lord, (reply'd Don *John* of *Velasco*) is so obliging, that I have room to believe you sincerely wish it. She is yet but Four Years old, and the Prince your Son but Eight; to what End can we dispose of the Destiny of Persons, so little advanc'd in Years? That ought not to be the least Obstacle (said the Count) we can sign the Contract of Marriage, and I will send the Prince to you, that you may form him for *Leonida*. I don't question but you will like him, he is a fine Youth, and his Sense exceeds his Years. You will be under no Difficulty (interrupted Madam *Velasco*) to persuade us into an Opinion of your Son's Merit; it is sufficient that he is of your Illustrious Blood. By what you are, my Lord, we judge what he may be; and I thank Heaven, that you have such favourable Dispositions for *Leonida*. From her Birth, I design'd her for one of my Country, which is still dear to me: and Don *John* sets no less a Value on it than I. It is true (reply'd Don *John*) I have a great Veneration for the *French*, and am very sensible of their Desert. Judge then, added he, with what Pleasure we accept the Offer you make *Leonida*, which is as much above our Hopes, as her Merit. This Conversation ended with all the Assurances of a perfect Friendship, and the Articles of Marriage were drawn. The Count of *La March* sent his to the King of *France*, Don *John* carry'd his to the King of *Castile*, and each consented to the Agreement.

Don

Don *John* made his Daughter's Fortune very confiderable, and the whole Court was pleas'd with the Match.

Some time after, the Count of *La March* preparing for his Return into *France*, ask'd Don *John* of *Velafco* and his Lady, whether they were willing he fhou'd fend his Son to them? No, my Lord, (faid they) Let him remain in your Hands, as a Token of our Love and Efteem; the Education you will give him, will make him an accomplifh'd Prince; and we hope you will not part with him till he has taken a perfect Impreffion of your great Example. The Count promis'd he wou'd take all the Care imaginable to render his Son worthy of being ally'd to them; then took his Leave.

The King of *Caftile* acquitted himfelf by the Count, of the many Acknowledgments he owed *Charles* the VIth. And writing to that Prince, told him, He cou'd not fufficiently praife the Merit and Conduct of his Ambaffador. The Count had not been long arriv'd at the Court of *France*, when News came of the King of *Caftile*'s Death by a Fall from his Horfe, and his Son Don *Henry* fent an Account of it by Don *John* of *Velafco*. The Count of *La March* took that Opportunity to do him all the Honours of a Court, where he held a confiderable Rank, being nearly related to the King. He prefented the Prince of *Carency* to him, whom he found to be a finer Youth than he imagin'd; and from that Time, conceiv'd

ceiv'd as great an Affection for him, as if he had actually been happy in the Possession of *Leonida*. The Peace and Tranquility which *France* then enjoy'd, was soon after disturb'd by an Accident that happen'd to the King; who being struck with Terror and Surprize at an Apparation, fell into a Delirium, which continued for some time.

At this Juncture there was a very nice Negotiation to be carried on in *Spain*; and the Dukes of *Berry* and *Burgundy*, Uncles to the King, having taken upon them the Administration of Affairs, look'd on the Count of *La March* as the most capable Person to manage it. The seeming Pretence of his Embassy was, the usual Compliments to the King and the Infanta his Brother on their Marriage; the one being lately marry'd to the Princess of *Lancaster*, and the other to the young Countess of *Alburquerck*, who was one of the richest Heiress's in *Europe*. The Count of *La March*, at his Arrival in *Spain*, found Don *John* of *Velasco* in great Favour at Court; the King having made him High-Steward of his Houshold; and *Leonida*, tho' not above Nine Years of Age, was made one of the Maids of Honour to the Queen, and bred up in the Palace.

Madam *Velasco* was extremely pleas'd to see the Count again; and her Satisfaction was so much the greater, when he declar'd, he had never seen any thing comparable to the Beauty of her Daughter. He was so surpriz'd when he saw her, that he cou'd not at first express his Admiration; her Hair was black and her Complexion as fair as poſſible. It may be generally ſaid of the *Spaniſh* Ladies, that they have much finer Eyes than thoſe of other Countries. *Leonida*'s were ſo full of Life and Spirit, that one cou'd hardly withſtand their Brightneſs; yet they retain'd all that Air of Sweetneſs and Modeſty which becomes her Sex ſo well. In ſhort, the Beauties of her Mind were as perfect as the Charms of her Perſon; and the Count of *La March* was ſo taken with her, that had not his Glory, and the King's Service call'd him back for *France*, he willingly, for her ſake, wou'd have ſtay'd longer at that Court. Some time after his Return, he was ſent againſt the *Engliſh*, over whom he had the good Fortune of getting ſo many Advantages as oblig'd them to wiſh for Peace, which ſoon after was happily concluded, with Propoſals made by King *Richard*, of a Marriage with *Iſabella* of *France*; but the Count of *La March* had not the Satisfaction to be at the Concluſion of it, being forc'd by his Indiſpoſition to retire to *Vandome* for ſome Relief; and finding there, that his Illneſs increas'd, he did not doubt but he was very near taking Leave of the World, therefore ſent for the Prince of *Carency*, and in a feeble Voice, thus ſaid to him: The Condition I am in, my dear Son, wou'd give me great Concern, had I not procured a Father for you in Don *John* of *Velaſco*. I am perſuaded you will find no difference betwixt his

Houſe

House and mine, therefore perform the Promise I have made for you; marry *Leonida*, it is your dying Father's Command. Tell your Brothers how dear they have been to me, and that I recommend them to the Care of Heaven. Do not render your selves unworthy of your Name. Prefer Honour to Life, and never omit what you owe to God, or your King. I had rather see you dead, than survive a Disgrace owing to ill Conduct. And as for you, my dear Child, it is a great Consolation to me in dying, to believe your Inclinations will answer the Advice I now give you. The young Prince filled with Grief, fell at his Father's Feet, and in spite of the Sobs, which prevented his Utterance, he endeavour'd to express himself in Terms so moving and generous, that the Count of *La March*, after so great a Satisfaction, had little Regret in dying.

The Year following *Sigismund* King of *Hungary*, sent Ambassadors into *France*, to desire *Charles* the Sixth to assist him with Troops, being resolv'd to engage *Bajazet*. Those Ministers gave the King an Account, how that the Emperor *John Palealogus* had call'd that Enemy of the Christians to his Assistance, against the Despote of *Bulgaria*; and that *Bajazet* making use of the Advantages he had obtain'd, wou'd not leave a Country where they had so imprudently let him enter. The King concern'd at the Condition of *Sigismund*, permitted most of the Youth of *France* to make

make an Expedition in his Favour. The young Count of *Nevers*, who was then but Twenty Four Years old, put himself at the Head of the young Noblemen, who were very numerous; among others, *James* of *Bourbon* Count of *La March*, highly diſtinguiſh'd himſelf. The Prince of *Carency* his Brother, made this Campaign with him; and it is impoſſible to expreſs the Joy he receiv'd at having ſo early an Opportunity of proving his Courage.

The Particulars of this Expedition I refer to the Hiſtorian, and ſhall only ſay, there never was a more unhappy Campaign. *Bajazet* having defeated the Chriſtian Troops, made a horrible Slaughter amongſt the *French*, and with much difficulty, conſented to Ranſom Five or Six. The Count of *La March* and his Brother were dangerouſly wounded, and made Priſoners before *Nicopolis*. The Prince of *Carency* was ſo afflicted at the Diſaſter of his Brother, that in his Confinement he neither thought of the Danger of his own Wounds, nor his loſt Liberty. When the Count of *La March* was recover'd, and able to take Care of his, and his Brother's Fortune, he heard with mortal Diſpleaſure the Reſolution *Bajazet* had taken, of putting all the Priſoners to the Sword; and many were executed in that cruel manner. When the Count of *Nevers* preſenting his Head to receive the fatal Blow, an old *Turk* famous for his Predictions, cry'd out, (addreſſing himſelf to *Bajazet*) Spare that young Prince, for
he

he will deftroy more Chriftians than all your Arms. Thefe Words preferv'd the Life they were going to deprive him of, and the Event anfwer'd the Prophefy. The Prince of *Carency* appear'd in his Turn, and the deplorable State he was in at fo tender an Age, did no ways leffen that noble Air, which diftinguifhes a Man of Birth and Courage from a common Perfon. He was fo perfectly handfom, that *Bajazet* himfelf was under fome Surprize, and irrefolute, whether he fhou'd put him to Death, or be contented with his Ranfom: But after fome Sufpenfe, the happy Deftiny of the Prince triumph'd over the natural Barbarity of the other; and Life was granted to him and his Brother, upon Condition, that a confiderable Sum fhould be paid for their Ranfom: They writ to their Brother the Count of *Vandome* about it; but while they were expecting an Anfwer from *France*, they heard that the Count of *Nevers* had paid his, and was preparing to return.

One Night the Prince (not having a mind to retire) as he was walking very difconfolate on the Leads of the Tower where he was a Prifoner, heard the Whiftling of an Arrow, which fell at his Feet: He thought at firft, that fome Perfon had a Defign upon his Life; but ftooping to take it up, perceiv'd a Letter tied to it, which contain'd thefe Words, written in *Lingua Franca.*

*WHEN*

## The PRINCE

WHEN you appear'd before the Sultan loaded with Chains and in expectation of immediate Death, did you think you cou'd move any thing but Pity? You inspired at that Time more than you can imagine, Love hid in your Eyes, from a Captive render'd you a Conqueror. Alas, I saw you, my dearest Prince, and from that fatal Moment my Heart rebell'd against my Reason, and forced from me numberless Sighs. Methinks I see you; I imagine I speak to you; and all my Thoughts are of you. I almost persuade my self, that my Sentiments make a deep Impression on you, and that our Souls already united, flatter us with a perfect Felicity. But alas! that wou'd be too great a Happiness. I dare not hope nor even desire it, and shou'd sooner resolve upon Death, than make these Sentiments known to you, were not I persuaded you will never know who I am: And far from taking any Advantage of my Weakness, you will leave Nicopolis without seeing me. Oh! how unfortunate am I, to find Consolation in being distant from the Object I love! Consider this Extremity, and if you cannot love me because Unknown, at least do not refuse me your Pity. I assure you, it shall not prevail with me, for I will soon put it in your Power to leave this Place. I know your Ransom is not come with that of the Christian Prince, and that he is preparing to go without you: But do not afflict your self, all Things are possible to Love. Write to me to Morrow at the same Hour you receive this, convey it by the same Messenger to the Foot of the Tower, and learn betimes

*times to be secret.* Oh, of all Mortals you are the moſt amiable! Why have I ſeen you? And why muſt I never ſee you more?

The young Prince was not a little ſurpriz'd at what he read. It ſeem'd to him ſo tender, that he felt an extream Deſire to ſee the Perſon who expreſs'd ſo extraordinary a Paſſion for him, and expected with the greateſt Impatience, the Time that he was to return an Anſwer. He went as he uſed to do, to the Top of the Tower, and there made a Signal to the Meſſenger, who was waiting for it; then flung his Letter over, which was written in theſe Terms.

*Y*OU *are the firſt that ever made me ſigh, and the Sacrifice I offer you, Madam, of the firſt Motions of my Affection, ought to give me ſome Place in your Favour. I thought till now, it was impoſſible to love what one never ſaw; but the Uneaſineſs I feel, and the ardent Deſire I have to ſee you, convince me you are already too dear for my Peace. You render me the moſt unhappy of all Mankind, if you deny me the Means of making my Retributions, and entertaining you with my Tranſports. Is it poſſible you can refuſe me that Favour, and at the ſame Time expreſs ſo real a Paſſion for me? What, Madam, can you conſent I ſhou'd go from a Place where you are? Oh! rather leave me in my Priſon, ſince I am deſtin'd to wear your Chains.*

It was very late before the Prince retired, in hopes the fair Unknown wou'd have sent him a second Letter the same way he receiv'd the First, but was disappointed. He went again the next Day upon the Tower, where every Thing appear'd so silent, that he had no room to flatter himself with what he so much wished. Is it possible, (said he to his Brother, who was Prisoner in the same Place with him, and to whom he had told this Adventure) Is it possible, that the Person who writ this Letter, sought only to divert her self at my Expence? The oftner I read it, the more reason I have to believe it sincere; for I am persuaded there is a Smypathy in Hearts, and therefore it is impossible to be so touch'd with what is counterfeited. I am convinc'd of what you say, (reply'd the Count of *La March*) and have my self experienc'd it, which inclines me to think some other Reason obliges your Unknown not to write. They pass'd the greatest part of the Day on the Top of the Tower, entertaining each other after this manner, till at last, Night coming on without any hopes of a second Letter, they retired. The Prince return'd to his Chamber more melancholy than ever he had been; but he was no sooner enter'd, when he saw on a little Cedar Table, a Toilet richly embroider'd with the Cypher of his Name woven in Gold: The Work was perfectly fine, it cover'd a Scymiter embellish'd with Jewels and a little Casket with golden Plates, which he open'd with great precipitation, and found

a

a Letter in it, with a Sum that far exceeded his Ranfom. Here is what was wrote in the fame Hand with the firſt.

*GO young Prince, go far from a Place where my Paſſion may prove fatal to you. Expect no more Letters from me: This is the laſt you will receive. Oh Heavens! I am going to loſe you, and loſe you for ever. Why have not I power to follow you, and render my Fortune inſeparable from Tours? I ſhall never more know your Sentiments: You will forget me before it is poſſible for me to think of any Thing but you, or ceaſe to love you. My Wiſhes ſhall ever attend you. Pity me, dear Prince, ſince I muſt paſs my ſorrowful Life in bemoaning your Abſence, and my Misfortunes.*

The Prince of *Carency* admired the Proceedings of this generous Lady, and his Gratitude was of ſuch a Nature, that the moſt tranſcendent Paſſion cou'd not have made a deeper Impreſſion; for when he conſider'd he was to loſe even the hopes of ever ſeeing her, his violent Diſpleaſure took place of all the Joy he ought to have felt, at being in a Condition to pay his Ranfom, and return to *France*. He bid one of his Guards go and tell the Count of *La March*, that he wanted to ſpeak with him; but firſt took care to hide the magnificent Preſent he had juſt receiv'd.

The Count came immediately to him, and ſaw in his Eyes an extraordinary Air of Grief.
As

As soon as they were alone, the Prince flung his Arms about his Brother's Neck. I want your Confolation, dear Brother, (faid he) for I can receive it only from you. See! (continued he, fhowing him the Casket and Letter) fee! what I owe to my Unknown, and the Neceffity fhe impofes on me to go away without feeing her. Can any Thing be more great or noble? Or can there be any Thing more foft or moving, than the Words fhe imploys to bid me Adieu? Oh! how fatal will her Generofity be to me, fince I muft even lofe the Hopes of knowing who fhe is. Here he was filent, but after having meditated fome Time: She loves me, faid he, and I burn with a more than equal Paffion for her. Why muft I then leave *Nicopolis:* In remaining here, I may difcover the Perfon to whom I am fo highly indebted, and, if poffible, obtain the Happinefs of feeing her: For Love certainly is too good a Guide to forfake me in fo fair a way. The Count of *La March*, who loved his Brother entirely, was of Opinion that fo magnificent a Prefent could not come from any one but a Perfon of the firft Rank, and that if he expos'd himfelf by making an Enquiry after her, and penetrated into a Myftery that perhaps ought not to be difclos'd, he might create himfelf Enemies, which would be of a very dangerous Confequence in a Country where neither his Birth nor Merit could protect him, and where the Name of a Chriftian was a Crime great enough to deferve Punifhment. Full of thefe Thoughts

Thoughts, he conjured his Brother in the moſt engaging Terms, not to perſiſt in a thing which lay under ſo many difficulties; and repreſented to him, that he might not only ruin himſelf, but alſo be the Occaſion of undoing the Perſon whom he ſo dearly loved. Cou'd you ever forgive your ſelf, ſaid he, ſo Imprudent an Action? The Lady loves you, and were it poſſible for her to ſee you without Danger, ſhe wou'd have found means to favour your Requeſt. Therefore, dear Brother, let us go away with the Count of *Nevers,* and embrace the favourable Diſpoſition *Bajazet* is in at preſent: His Capriciouſneſs is ever to be fear'd, and ſhou'd he change his Mind, what wou'd become of us?

Altho' the Count of *La March*'s Arguments were very weighty, the Prince was unwilling to ſubmit to them, having a ſtrong Deſire to find out by what means the Casket and Scymiter were convey'd into his Chamber. He might eaſily imagine, that one of his Guards had been bribed; but as it was hard to diſcover the Perſon (fearing he ſhou'd apply to the wrong Man) he thought fit to be ſilent; ſo took his leave of *Nicopolis,* without knowing to whom he owed the higheſt Obligations.

The Prince of *Carency*'s Thoughts were conſtantly imploy'd on his generous Unknown; and after his Arrival at the Court of *France,* he found a ſecret Conſolation in making her the Subject of his Diſcourſe, with the Counts of *La March* and *Vandome,* who equally admired

mired a Paffion fo difcreet, and a Generofity without hopes of any Return. Moft Women that are in Love and make Prefents, faid they, have generally fome View, that tends to their private Satisfaction: They endeavour to gain a Heart by Gratitude, when they cannot conquer it by their Beauty. But this Illuftrious Foreigner, faid the Prince, aim'd at nothing but procuring my Liberty, fince fhe even commanded me to quit the only Place where I cou'd have feen her. He ufed to talk fo often of her, that the Count of *La March* feared he had fome defign of returning to *Mifia*, in order to difcover who this Charmer was. This made him entreat the Prince to write an obliging Letter to *Don John* of *Velafco*, to put him in Mind of their Contract, and affure him, that he only expected his Commands to go for *Spain*. The Prince having yielded to this Requeft: Confider well, faid he to his Brother, the Violence I do my felf. Shall I not be for ever unhappy in Marrying a Perfon for whom I have no Inclination? You know very well, that my Heart is fill'd with another Object. It is true, reply'd the Count, you love an unknown Perfon, who probably you will never fee: You do not even know her Name, and perhaps fhe is no longer at *Nicopolis*. Remember, Brother, that *Leonida* muft crown your Felicity, fhe is a great Fortune, and very Beautiful. How eafy it is, interrupted the Prince to advife others, and imagine that a Heart ought always to fubmit to Reafon: But alas!

alas! it too often rebels, and never suffers greater Torments than when it is forc'd into an Engagement by the Choice of others. The Count of *La March* was doing all his Endeavours to inspire other Sentiments in his Brother, which he hoped time might effect.

The Prince of *Carency* continued extreamly melancholy till he receiv'd Letters from *Don John*; wherein he assured him, that his Daughter should never be dispos'd of to any one but himself; but that being very young, he desired the Marriage might be defer'd for some Years, and advis'd him to imploy that time in Travelling. This last Request gave no small Satisfaction to the Prince; and as the Mareschal of *Boucicault* was going then to take Possession of *Genoa*, which had surrender'd voluntarily to the King of *France*, he embrac'd that Opportunity, and went along with him to see that great City, which passes for one of the finest in *Europe*. As so many have given a Description of it, I shall only pursue my Story.

The Mareschal did not make a long stay at *Genoa*, being commanded to go from thence to *Constantinople* with a fresh Army, which became dreadful to *Bajazet*. The Prince of *Carency* acquainted the Mareschal with the Design he had to accompany him in that Expedition; but the latter being inform'd by the Counts of *La March* and *Vandome* of the Passion he had for an unknown Lady at *Nicopolis*, and knowing that he was contracted to *Leonida*, spoke to him in obliging Terms, and represented how much his Honour was concern'd in the Performance of his Promise to a Person of so considerable a Rank; declaring at the same time, that if he insisted on going with him he wou'd be forc'd to inform the Court of it. These Reasons oblig'd the Prince to remain at *Genoa* in the Senator *Grimaldi*'s House, which had been offer'd to him in a most civil manner.

One Night the Prince being more melancholy than usual, went alone to the Mole, which affords a fine Prospect, and continued his Walk along the Shore, till he insensibly found himself a great way from the City. How unhappy is my Fate, said he sighing! I love and am belov'd, but know not the Object of my Passion: I can hear nothing concerning her Fortune, nor give her any account of mine; neither can I tell where to find the Lady, whose Generosity has only serv'd to destroy my Peace. He was lost in these melancholy Thoughts, which were succeeded by others of a more tormenting Nature. Why, continued he, did my Father sacrifice me to one whom I can never think agreeable, since I adore another! yet something tells me it is a Crime to disobey him. Oh, too Charming Unknown! cry'd he, were you but inform'd of the State I am in, you wou'd recal me to you; but what do I say? That is a Happiness I dare not hope, she paid my Ransom and commanded me to go; it is possible she now loves me no more or strives to forget me, and in either of the two, I find but Subject to torment me.

These

These different Reflections were perplexing the Prince, when of a sudden Night came on, with Rain and terrible Thunder, which oblig'd him to direct his Course along the Wall of a Park, where he found a Door that led him through a long Alley of Orange-Trees to a fine Pavilion; here he obferv'd a low Parlour, the Pannels of which were gilded, and the Roof finely painted. As the Weather was excessive hot, the Windows were open, and there being Lights in the Room, they gave him an Opportunity of seeing one of the most beautiful Persons in the World leaning on a Couch: She seem'd asleep, holding her Handkerchief in in her Hand, a mourning Veil cover'd half her Neck; and in this Posture she inspired both Love and Respect.

The Prince stood some time at the Window, and perceiving that every thing was silent, went into the Parlour, and kneeled by her the better to consider her Charms; she appear'd pale and dejected, and tho' asleep, fetch'd deep Sighs, which were follow'd by Tears, that found a Passage thro' her clos'd Eye-Lids. Who merits this Grief, said he, from so lovely a Creature? Is it a Husband or a Lover you deplore? He stop'd here, and reflected on Chance, that had conducted him to a Place so dangerous to his Liberty. Then he continued; Who can deserve those Sighs, and Tears? He looked with Admiration on the exact Proportion of her Features, the Whiteness of her Hands and Arms, the Beauty of her Neck, and Colour of her Hair:

His Eyes, fix'd on so Divine an Object, had already betray'd his Heart; and he had not well recover'd the first Effects of his Surprize, when the Lady wak'd, who appear'd to be seiz'd with Fear, which had like to have thrown her into a Swoon. He attributed this, to the Custom observ'd by the Ladies of *Italy*, never to see Men in their own Apartments, and thought she might be marry'd to some jealous Husband, who finding a Man in his House so late, might have some Suspicion, which wou'd prove of a fatal Consequence to a Person for whom he had already conceiv'd so great a Passion. I am extreamly concern'd, Madam, (said he) at the Disorder I have occasion'd, but will retire with Regret from a Place which gives me so much Pleasure. No, no, (reply'd she) my Dear Lover, (flinging her Arms about his Neck) do not leave me; I love you too well to be frighten'd, tho' my Astonishment is great. Be Witness of the Tears I shed for your Loss. Ah! dear Shade, why did that terrible Engagement part us? The Prince comprehended nothing of this obscure Speech, yet thought himself happy in the Caresses he receiv'd; and as the Name of a Lover pleas'd him, that of a Shade surpriz'd and afflicted him. The Sensibility he had shown on this Occasion might have convinc'd this fair Creature, that he was not one of the other World; but her Mind was so possess'd with his being dead, that she spoke to him as to a Ghost; which oblig'd him to say in a melancholy Accent; I find, Madam, you

are

are deceiv'd in favour of some Resemblance, and I protest, were I dead and deplor'd by you, I should think my self much happier than living and indifferent to you. Alas! I am not the Object of your Love. Who then, my Dear, reply'd she with Precipitation? What Sorrow could be equal to mine, when I heard you were lost in returning from *Nicopolis*, and that after having escaped the Fury of *Bajazet*, it was your Misfortune to perish by your Ship's being blown up in an Engagement? I own to you, as I cou'd not believe you safe, after so probable a Relation, I gave my self up entirely to Grief. Am I not very unhappy (said I) to have procured him his Liberty by paying his Ransom, since it has forwarded his End: But Oh Heavens! Can any Joy or Surprize be equal to mine? You are living, my dearest Lover, and your Eyes tell me you live for me; read the Motions of mine, they will convince you I live for you alone.

These Words were so moving, that the Prince cou'd not doubt any longer but this Lady, who entertain'd him so tenderly, was his Unknown of *Nicopolis*, and this Opinion occasion'd a Joy, which he cou'd neither conceal, nor express, but thought he shou'd die in Ecstasie at his Mistrifs's Feet; he look'd upon it as a Miracle of Love and Fortune, that he shou'd unexpectedly find so surprizing a Beauty, and he the Object of her Passion: He fix'd his Lips on her Hand, and kiss'd it with such Transports, as he had never felt before. Their Discourse

Difcourfe had no more Coherence, but their Sighs exprefs'd enough the State of their Souls. The Night was far advanc'd, when they were interrupted by one of the Lady's Women, who came to give her Notice that her Father was juft arriv'd. We muft part, my dear Lover, (faid fhe to the Prince,) return to *Genoa*, and in Two Days come here again, the fame Way, and at the fame Hour; I fhall expect you in this Place. Muft I leave you, Madam, (cry'd he with a dejected Air) no, I cannot refolve it; Oh! rather confent I fhou'd remain here, no Danger can alarm me where you are prefent. What you ask, faid fhe, is impoffible Go my Lord, all I can do for you, is to give you my Picture, which I fat for with a Defign to fend to you when you were in Confinement. Here it is, (continued fhe, taking it from off her Arm, and tying it on his) Let nothing in the World make you neglect fo precious a Pledge of my Affection. He threw himfelf on his Knees, and wou'd have exprefs'd his Acknowledgments to her; but fhe left him, fearing they fhou'd be furpriz'd by her Father.

She was hardly gone, when the Prince abandon'd himfelf to all the Reflections that cou'd attend fo extraordinary an Adventure: Love, cry'd he, what have I done for thee to merit thefe Favours? Is thy Goodnefs lafting, and may not I apprehend, that by fome fatal Turn thou wilt deftroy a Profperity fo little expected? Day began to appear, when
he

he perceiv'd he was still in the Parlour; and fearing his staying longer there might be of some Prejudice to his adored Mistress, he left the Place with Precipitation, and return'd to the Senator *Grimaldi*'s.

As soon as he arriv'd he threw himself on his Bed, but cou'd not sleep, his Mind was so much imploy'd on the Thoughts of his Charming Unknown; he had his Eyes continually fix'd on her Picture, and fancy'd in her Absence, he cou'd not have a Companion more dear. He rose very early, and the Senator hearing he was dress'd, came to wait on him, and wonder'd to see in his Countenance more Gaiety and Satisfaction than he had ever remark'd before. My Lord, said he, (with an obliging Air) tho' I have been in the greatest Uneasiness about you, not knowing what Accident might have detain'd you a whole Night alone, in a Country where you have so few Acquaintance, I no longer doubt, but you have met with some agreeable Adventure; for I find you so different from what you commonly are, that I cannot help congratulating you on it. The Prince, tho' a little surpriz'd at what the Senator said to him, (having naturally so much Discretion, as not to be capable of disclosing a Secret relating to Love) excus'd himself as a Man of Gallantry wou'd do on such an Occasion, and turn'd the Conversation on another Subject, when there came one who interrupting them, told the Senator, that the Count of *Fiesque* was come to see him;

him. He rose up, and said to the Prince, This Gentleman, my Lord, is of a Birth and Merit so distinguish'd, that nothing can be added to the Sentiments of Esteem and Consideration we all have for him: He has lost a Brother who was not inferior to him, and who resembled you extreamly. In finishing these Words, he went to his own Apartment to receive the Count of *Fiesque.*

In a little Time after the Senator return'd with the Count, and presented him to the Prince, who received him after so polite a manner, that he could have no reason to be displeas'd at his Visit; and during their Conversation, he look'd at the Prince with such Marks of Astonishment, that he perceiv'd the Count had found in him the Resemblance which the Senator had just spoke of. You look at me so attentively, my Lord, (said the Prince) that I shou'd think my self happy, cou'd the Motive that engages you to it acquire me your Friendship. That can be of no Service to a Person of your Distinction; (reply'd the Count with great Civility) it is impossible to see you, my Lord, and not have a particular Esteem for you; but I own that so perfect a Likeness affects me very much, and that if I were not well assured of my Brother's Misfortune, I shou'd have sufficient reason to doubt it in seeing you. They afterwards turn'd their Discourse on other Things, and parted with true Sentiments of Esteem for each other.

The

*of* CARENCY. 27

The Prince of *Carency* pafs'd the reft of that Day and the next, in making Vifits; and as he defign'd to ftay at *Genoa* fo long as wou'd be agreeable to his Unknown, he was defirous of being acquainted with Perfons of the greateft Confideration there. The Senator *Grimaldi* approving his Defign, propofed to wait on him to *Brancaleon Doria*'s, who for his eminent Qualities, was highly refpected in the Republick. It is not long, faid he, fince he return'd from *Sardinia*, where he went to fuccour the King of *Sicily*, whom, on this Occafion, he generoufly ferv'd; having acted contrary to his own Intereft, in regard to fome particular Pretenfions he had on that Kingdom. The Senator gave the Prince a true Character of this Lord, and added, that Signora *Doria* his Lady (who was a Perfon of great Merit) was ftill at *Cagliari:* If you pleafe, my Lord, (faid he) we will go and make him a Vifit at his Country Houfe; I am fure you will be charm'd with the Beauty, and Wit of his Daughter, which may induce you to ftay fome Time in this Place, for no Body can fee her with Indifferency. If fhe be fo dangerous as you reprefent her, I fhou'd avoid feeing her, faid the Prince; but I confefs to you, continued he fmiling, that the prefent fituation of my Heart puts me out of her Power. I left a Miftrefs at *Nicopolis*, who entirely poffeffes my Thoughts. I believe you, my Lord, (reply'd the Senator, fmiling in his Turn) but am a little afraid you were not fo faithful laft Night, as you fay, in

the

the Remembrance of that amiable Stranger.

As the Prince's Appointment was at Night, he hasten'd to Signor *Doria*'s, that he might return home time enough to obey the Commands of his Unknown: The Senator upon the Road told him, the young Lady's Name was *Olympia*, that she was passionately in love with the late Count of *La Vagne*, and that the Houses of *Fiesque* and *Doria* had a mortal Aversion for each other, which hinder'd her Father from consenting to their Marriage; that altho' they were reduc'd to Despair, yet the Obstacles they met with, serv'd only to increase their Affection; and that the Count thought by absenting himself from *Genoa* for some Time, Signor *Doria*'s Hatred might diminish; but this Departure prov'd fatal to him, for soon after News came of his Death. *Olympia*, far from concealing her Grief, yielded her self up entirely to it, which was fear'd she cou'd not out-live. The Prince knowing by Experience, that of all Passions Love had the greatest Empire, he extreamly deplor'd the Fate of this fair Lady. It is a great Unhappiness indeed, said he, to be separated for ever from the Person we love: In finishing these Words, they found themselves near the House they were going to, so that he cou'd not help interrupting himself, by praising it; he had sufficient Knowledge in Architecture to know a well finish'd Building, and in this he found Order, Magnificence, and a fine Situation.

The Senator *Grimaldi* introduc'd the Prince to Signor *Doria*, who gave him a Reception equal to his Rank; and during their Conversation said, he had never seen two Persons so like each other, as the Prince and the Count of *La Vagne*. This gave the Senator an Opportunity of desiring Signor *Doria* to present him to *Olympia*. I cou'd hardly dispense with my not answering your Request, reply'd he, but that I am assur'd, the Presence of the Prince will renew her Sorrow, and only serve to inspire us with Pity: He ask'd them to walk into a Garden joyning to his Apartment, from whence they saw a vast number of Fountains playing, whose Waters seem'd to pierce the Clouds, and made by their Fall a pleasing Noise, that inspired agreeable Thoughts; from thence they went into a Labyrinth at the End of the Garden, and through a little Alley of Jessamine, he led them into a Grotto, but was not a little surpriz'd to find his Daughter there, who had retir'd to be more at Liberty to indulge those Ideas that were most pleasing to her.

How astonish'd was the Prince when he saw *Olympia*, and knew her to be the same Lady he found asleep in the Parlour, and for whom he had already conceiv'd so great a Passion: And how great was her Surprize, when she saw her supposed Lover with her Father, who seem'd to have no longer an Aversion for him. She look'd with some Disorder at the Prince, whose Confusion increas'd at the Thoughts of what he had just heard of the Count of *La Vagne*.

The Condition of their Souls was equally painted in their Eyes, and the Senator *Grimaldi* began to penetrate into part of the Myſtery, when *Olympia* (advancing towards her Father) flung her ſelf at his Feet. Oh, Sir! ſaid ſhe, Oh my Father! Is it poſſible that you have at laſt pity'd our Sufferings, and that you your ſelf reſtore me my Lover? At theſe Words the Prince cou'd no longer be unacquainted with his Misfortune; he turn'd pale, and trembling ſupported himſelf againſt a Pyramid of Pebbles; but his Affliction being ſuperior to his Courage, he had like to have expired on the Place. Signor *Doria*, who was poſſeſs'd of nothing but *Olympia*'s Error, thought only of undeceiving her. My dear Daughter, ſaid he, the Prince of *Carency* whom you ſee here, is a Prince of the Houſe of *France*, who does not know you, nor did you ever ſee him before; you are deceiv'd by the Reſemblance there is between him and the Count of *La Vagne*; I wiſh that too unfortunate Gentleman were not loſt, I wou'd no longer oppoſe your mutual Deſires. Theſe Words were Daggers to her Heart; ſhe turn'd her Eyes on the Prince, and fix'd them on him a great while without having Power to ſpeak, then changing her Colour fainted away, and remain'd without any Senſe of Life. Signor *Doria* ran for help, whilſt the deſpairing Prince gathering new Strength from his Paſſion, took her in his Arms, and preſſing her tenderly, ſaid in a low Voice, (interrupted with Sighs) Have not I given you my Heart, Madam?

Cou'd

Cou'd the Count of *La Vagne* love you more than I? Who cannot think myself undeserving of the Declaration you made me, since I adore you with too much Ardour ever to change; and I hope my Constancy will make some Impression on you. While the Prince was speaking thus, without being heard by *Olympia*, Signor *Doria* and the Senator brought some Water from a Fountain that was near, and having sprinkled a great deal on her, she recover'd; but finding her self in the Prince's Arms; Ah! leave me, my Lord, said she (looking at him with a languishing Air, and endeavouring to disengage her self) you have deceiv'd me and interrupted my Grief, but Death shall soon repair an Error which was not voluntary. It is impossible to express the State the Prince was in, who found himself distractedly in love without any hopes of a Return; he heard his Mistress regret her Mistake, and retract the Professions she had made him; he secretly reproach'd himself for having been inconstant to his Unknown of *Nicopolis*, but cou'd not be enough surpriz'd at the fatal Likeness between him and the Count of *Vagne*, and the Similitude of their Fortunes; they being in the Campaign of *Misia* both taken Prisoners by *Bajazet*, sent to *Nicopolis*, and ransom'd by their Mistrisses: Every thing had so strange an Affinity, that the Prince had Reason to think himself the most unhappy of all Mankind.

*Olympia*'s

*Olympia's* Women being come, they took her from the Prince, who followed her into her Apartment; she was laid on the Bed, which he approach'd; but as soon as she perceiv'd him, she turn'd her Face from him and abandon'd her self to Grief. What have I done, Madam, said he, to deserve your Disdain? You have render'd your self Mistress of my Heart, and prevented me declaring my Sentiments to you, by generously confessing yours in Terms so obliging, that I was transported; yet you now hate me, you even deny me a Look; and what ought to influence you in my Favour, incurs your Displeasure. *Olympia* made no Answer, but with a feeble Hand push'd him from her. Signor *Doria* cou'd not guess at the Meaning of this Discourse, not knowing that the Prince of *Carency* had ever seen his Daughter. The Senator *Grimaldi* suspected something of the Matter: But thought it very extraordinary, that so Infant a Passion shou'd already have the force of the greatest Engagement.

The Illness of this divine Creature increas'd, and the Prince's Despair was equal to it; It is impossible to represent two Objects more worthy of Compassion. Signor *Doria*, distracted at his Daughter's Condition, desired the Prince to retire, because his Presence augmented her Pain, and nothing less cou'd oblige the other to withdraw; but before he retired, he approach'd her in Opposition to what they cou'd say, and kneeling by her Bed: See, Madam, the Affliction I am in, (said he, with broken Sighs

Sighs) own at least, that I deserve your Pity, if you are cruel enough to deny me your Esteem: Oh! What have I done within these two Days to render me so odious? I love you, Madam, to such a Degree, that I am too well assured if you disdain me, I cannot live; but what am I saying? If the Life of a Man you no longer seem to value, is a Sacrifice worthy of you, I shall prefer it as a happy Fate. No, my Lord (said she, endeavouring to answer him) I wou'd not have you participate of my Ruin, only wish that after the irreparable Loss I have receiv'd, Death may terminate my Misfortunes; I cannot help confessing the greatest Concern to see your Condition. But as I am the Cause of it, continu'd she, it is just I alone shou'd suffer; live, my Lord, live I conjure you, forget my Weakness, and let me dye. In ending these Words, she desired her Father, and the Senator to carry the Prince away; they told him, that as it was *Olympia*'s Request, she ought not to be disobey'd. Overcome by these Persuasions, he left the Chamber, but so disorder'd, that they were forc'd to support him. Signor *Doria* led them into a magnificent Apartment, and excus'd his being oblig'd to leave them, his Daughter's Illness requiring his Presence: The Senator stay'd with the Prince, who, after being silent some time, ask'd him if *Olympia* had been at *Nicopolis*, and whether it was there she had paid the Count of *La Vagne*'s Ransom? He answer'd, she had not been there, but that the Count, being taken Prisoner by

D *Bajazet*,

*Bajazet,* writ immediatly to his Miſtreſs, and his Brother, defiring the latter to ſend him a Supply; that ſome Affairs of Importance having at that time oblig'd the Count of *Fieſque* to go to *Rome, Olmypia* fear'd his Abſence might detain her Lover the longer in his Confinement, and for that Reaſon ſold ſome of her Jewels, which ſhe cou'd difpoſe of unknown to her Father, and ſent the Value of them into *Mifia* for his Ranſom; that as he was coming back in a ſmall Veſſel, it was attack'd by a Pyrate, and whilſt they were fighting, the Powder took Fire, and both Ships being blown up, all thoſe who were on board periſh'd. This News was brought to *Genoa* with ſo many Circumſtances, that there was no Room left to doubt it.

The Prince heard this Relation with a great deal of Concern, and after being a while without ſpeaking, he lifted up his Eyes to Heaven: I can hardly believe, ſaid he, there is a Mortal on Earth ſo wretched as I am. Give me leave to tell you, Sir, that I was but Eight Years of Age when my Father ſign'd a Contract of Marriage for me with *Don John* of *Velaſco*'s Daughter, and on his Death-Bed, commanded me expreſsly to marry her; ſome Years after I was taken Priſoner at *Nicopolis,* where I was uncertain of Life, or Death, having Reaſon enough to fear the worſt from *Bajazet*'s unequal Temper, who at laſt conſented to receive my Ranſom, which I expected from *France,* when a Lady, who is yet unknown

to

to me, made my Safety her care; she wrote to me, and sent me a Sum, which much exceeded my Ransom; and I must own, her Wit and Generosity inspired me with so perfect a Passion, that I believe, I cou'd not have lov'd her more, had I been acquainted with her. Being thus set at Liberty, I came to the Court of *France*, where I made but a small Stay; my Mind was continually distracted with the Idea of my Unknown, which determin'd me to come here with the Mareschal. Oh! certainly it was the Fatality of my Stars, that conducted me. You have been Witness since my Arrival of my excessive Melancholy; and as it was not in my Power to conceal it, rather than trouble my Friends, I endeavour'd to find out the most unfrequented Places to be more at Liberty to indulge it. Here the Prince recited his Adventure with *Olympia*, but the Thoughts of so cruel a Disappointment oblig'd him to be silent some time; then recovering a little, he continued his Discourse: Oh! Sir, said he, think how great is my Misfortune; she whom I adore at *Genoa* is not the same I lov'd in *Misia*; this charming Lady, who flatter'd me with her Heart, is now dying for another; the Tragedy is before my Eyes; I have by my Presence been an Addition to her Torment, and it is probable, she is this Minute expiring, whilst I am reflecting on the Cruelty of my Fate. He rose up, and was going out with Precipitation; but the Senator imagining he had a Mind to go to *Olympia*'s Apartment, stop'd him, representing,

senting, that such a Behaviour wou'd highly displease her, and that he ought rather, by his Absence, to procure some Ease to her disturbed Mind. The Prince was obstinate, but while they were disputing, they heard the Cries of many Women, which gave the last Alarm to the Prince. Oh Heavens! the Work is done, said he (flinging himself upon a Couch) It is done! She is now no more; I have lost her for ever! His Tears wou'd not permit him to continue his Complaint. The Senator seeing the melancholy Condition he was in, extreamly pitied him, neglecting nothing, that he thought cou'd allay his Grief, which was too violent for any thing to mitigate.

Some of the Servants came and told them, *Olympia* had just breath'd her last in her Father's Arms. It is hard to imagine the Agonies the Prince was in when he heard this dismal News; and as he cou'd not doubt the Certainty of it, it flung him into the deepest Despair. Oh! in what tender Language did he deplore her Loss? and with what Compassion did he move those, who saw him in his desolate State, which time it self cou'd hardly alter? He was going away without seeing Signor *Doria*, which Proceeding might appear irregular, did not one enter into his Afflictions; for he look'd upon this unhappy Parent as the Cause of his Daughter's Death. The Senator *Grimaldi* represented, that Civility oblig'd him to condole with Signor *Doria* on the Loss he had just receiv'd: Say rather (reply'd the Prince with some Passion) on) that I ought to load him with Reproaches. Barbarian as he was, to oppose *Olympia*'s Marriage with the Count of *La Vagne*, which occasion'd the Cruelty of his Fate, and has been the Source of my present Misfortune. But, my Lord, (said the Senator) do you reflect, that if she had been happy in the Count, she wou'd not not have met with this unfortunate Adventure. It is probable I might never have seen her, said the Prince, (interrupting him) or if I had, I shou'd have known who she was, and consequently not have taken her for my Unknown; and my Gratitude for the one, wou'd have protected me from the Charms of the other; but alas! it is no more in my power: Let us go, said he, let us go, Sir, I have done my last: His Tears and Affliction oblig'd him to be silent, so they return'd to *Genoa*.

The Prince spoke but little on the Way, and what he said, only related to the Unhappiness of his Destiny. Oh! Night! Oh! fatal Night, cry'd he, what Pleasures did you not promise me? This Minute I shou'd have been with that divine Creature according to her own Appointment: Alas I shall see her no more! her beauteous Eyes are shut for ever. These Cruel Reflections made him very thoughtful, and the Senator took that Opportunity to speak to him: Cou'd you follow my Advice, my Lord (said he) you wou'd endeavour to conquer two Passions which torment you at once; for you love a Lady at *Nicopolis*, whom it is likely you may never see; *Olympia* you have seen, and lov'd lov'd her at firſt Sight, ſhe is now no more: I muſt own that all the Circumſtances of your Adventures are fatal; but if you call Reaſon to your Aſſiſtance, it will tell you, that your Love is only due to *Leonida*; ſhe is deſtin'd for you, and I am inform'd, ſhe is a Perfection of Virtue, and Beauty: Why then, my Lord, ſhou'd an Unknown, or a Perſon that is no more, deprive her of the Right ſhe has to your Heart? Why? reply'd the Prince; alas, is it in my Power to love whom I pleaſe, and forget two Objects that ſo entirely poſſeſs my Soul? Love, without conſulting Duty, takes Poſſeſſion of our Inclinations; he promiſes a thouſand Pleaſures, and will ſometimes grant ſmall Favours: But oh! what Bitterneſs has been mix'd with thoſe he has hitherto beſtow'd on me? The Senator perceiv'd by the Warmth of his Diſcourſe, that his Advice, tho' very reaſonable, was ill tim'd, therefore choſe rather to pity the Prince, than condemn thoſe Sentiments which were too paſſionate and confus'd to be eaſily conquer'd.

*Olympia*'s Death was generally lamented at *Genoa*, being a Lady endow'd with many Excellencies: The Count of *Fieſque* was extreamly touch'd at it. Nothing cou'd give more Luſtre to my Brother's Merit (ſaid he to his Friends) than the Sacrifice of this fine Creature, who deſpiſing Fortune that perſecuted them, wou'd not ſurvive his Fate; no leſs than ſo great an Example cou'd perſuade me, that a Paſſion does not expire with the loſs of its Object.

The

## of CARENCY. 39

The Prince of *Carency* (who spoke of her with great Concern) soon made his Passion known to the World: his Affliction was so deep that it appear'd in his Countenance, and tho' he was deny'd to all Company, yet he cou'd not refuse seeing Don *Fernand Benavidez*, who was a Nobleman of *Andalusia* lately arriv'd from *Spain*; and appear'd to be so fine a Gentleman, that he easily gain'd the Friendship and Confidence of all who were acquainted with him. He was at that Time distractedly in Love with *Leonida*, whom he had often seen by the Means of his Sister *Casilda*, who was also Maid of Honour to the Queen of *Spain*, and was Mistress of so many agreeable Turns of Wit, that *Leonida* prefer'd her to the rest of her Companions. The perfect Friendship that was between these Ladies, gave *Benavidez* an Opportunity of declaring to his Sister, the Sentiments he had for *Leonida*, which engaged her to speak often to the young Lady in his Favour, but without the least appearance of Success. As he knew she was contracted to the Prince of *Carency*, who was then at *Genoa*, he was seiz'd with so immoderate a Fit of Jealousy, that he resolv'd to make that Voyage on purpose to see his Rival; and sometime before his departure, conversing with *Casilda*, he said to her, It is possible, Sister, I may discover some essential Defect in his Person or Humour, which being made known to Don *John* of *Velasco* and *Leonida*, will give them such an Aversion to him, as may induce them to break a

D 4 Match

Match that is not yet so far advanc'd, as to destroy all my Hopes: But if in this happy Rival, I can spy no Fault, I shall then apply to the only Remedy I have left; he must die by my Hand, or I by his, and in either of the Two I shall think my self much happier than in my present Condition. *Casilda*, who lov'd her Brother entirely, was surpriz'd and griev'd at so violent a Resolution; You need not go to *Genoa*, said she, with a Design to discover any Imperfection in that Prince; I have seen those who know him, and have no Interest in speaking his Praise, yet agree they never saw a more compleat Gentleman; besides, his high Birth greatly distinguishes him, and Don *John* is a Man of too much Ambition, not to promote a Match so glorious to his Family; therefore depend upon it, you will never prevail with him: I advise you to make your Passion known to *Leonida*, before you venture on any other Attempt: The Affection she has for me, may induce her to be favourable to you. Love is capricious, and there are no Measures to be taken with it. Chance often decides the strongest Passions, and if you can meet with that Sympathy which produces the Union of Hearts, you need no other Means to make you happy. Ah! my dear Sister, (reply'd *Benavidez*) do not flatter me, I have not Resolution enough to follow your Advice; if my Confession offends her, she will forbid me ever seeing her more, which must soon put a Period to my Life; therefore I will try all other Ways before

I

I speak to her. *Casilda* seeing her Brother so firmly resolv'd, took no further Trouble to perſuade him to the contrary.

Thus he set out on his Journey, and being arriv'd at *Genoa*, went to visit the Prince. He could not have recommended himself better, than by speaking *Olympia*'s Praise, and deploring his Misfortune in her Loss; but one Day in Conversation, he said to him designedly, You are not so much to be pity'd, my Lord, as you imagine, since Donna *Leonida* is destin'd to be yours. I believe (continu'd he, endeavouring to discover the Prince's Sentiments) you may find such Perfections in her, as will make you forget your other Disappointments. These Words rather afflicted than consol'd the Prince. You see my Grief, reply'd he, and as you are my Friend, I must own to you, the Engagement my Father has laid me under, gives me a mortal Displeasure: Were my Destiny in my own Power, I wou'd entirely lay aside all thoughts of Marriage; for at an Age that others are hardly capable of receiving the first Impressions of Love, I have indur'd all its Torments, without being bless'd with any of its Pleasures.

Whilst the Prince was speaking, *Benavidez* had time to divert the confus'd Thoughts which tormented him; he extreamly rejoyc'd to hear the Prince declare the Indifferency he had for *Leonida*; but that Joy was often interrupted with those Fears which generally attend great Passions. Here he resum'd the Discourse, and express'd expreſs'd himſelf with ſo unaffected an Air, that the Prince did not ſuſpect the leaſt Deſign. I participate with you, my Lord, (ſaid he) in your Trouble, which is too well grounded. The moſt agreeable Marriage, Time may render indifferent. Conſtant Society diſcovers many Failings, and it is very rare to find any Happineſs in an Alliance contracted without Inclination; but theſe are not the only Reaſons that induce me to pity you. Here he ſtop'd, and ſeem'd in a ſort of Diſorder, as a Man who had ſaid more than he wou'd willingly have done: The Prince taking Notice of it, I penetrate your Thoughts, Don *Fernand*, ſaid he, why ſhou'd you conceal any Thing from one who has no Reſerve to you; pray tell me what you know of *Leonida*. I know nothing prejudicial to her Honour, reply'd *Benavidez*; but I muſt own, my Lord, I am ſo particularly acquainted with her, that I fear you will be very unhappy if ever ſhe is yours; her Humour is inconſtant and ſuſpicious, the Haughtineſs of her Mind is inſupportable to all that know her; and, in ſhort, ſhe is become ſo ridiculous at Court, that ſhe wou'd meet with many Affronts, were it not for the Rank her Father holds there.

Oh Heavens! what do you tell me? (cry'd the too credulous Prince) is it poſſible that all thoſe who ſpoke of her, have endeavour'd to deceive me in, ſaying ſhe was the moſt accompliſh'd Creature they had ever ſeen. They only ſaid it to ſoften your Grief, my Lord, (reply'd

*of* CARENCY. 43

(reply'd *Benavidez* with an indifferent Air) and I think my felf very imprudent for having treated her with fo much freedom. You know me not, my dear *Benavidez* (faid the Prince, taking him in his Arms) do you think me capable of receiving ill fo generous a Confidence: No, I proteft, I am extreamly oblig'd to you, and what grieves me moft is, that I cannot make the right ufe of it; my Fate is decreed and there is no declining it. What, my Lord! do you then intend to marry her? reply'd immediately *Benavidez:* Alas! what can I do, faid the Prince? it was my Father's laft Command, and I will not deferve the Reproach of having difobey'd him. For my part, cry'd *Benavidez*, I fhou'd for ever upbraid my felf, if I fuffer'd you to proceed any farther in this Affair; as I profefs my felf one of your moft zealous Friends, I will fooner give my Life than fee you unhappy. You carry your Friendfhip too far, generous *Benavidez*, (reply'd the Prince) it is not reafonable that my Indifference for *Leonida* fhou'd make her Relations your Enemies; therefore I am refolv'd to offer my felf a Victim to my Father's Will, without thinking any more of what I may have to fear in the Society of a Perfon fo difagreeable. *Benavidez* began to apprehend, that if he continued to oppofe the Prince in his Defign, it might give him fome Caufe of Sufpicion, fo took his Leave in the moft violent Defpair. How unfortunate am I? (cry'd he) what muft I refolve on? I adore *Leonida*, and can never flat-

ter

ter my felf with a Return, whilft the Prince of *Carency*, who loves her not, is going to poffefs all her Charms. No, I cannot bear the Thoughts of it; I muft facrifice this happy Rival before he fees his Miftrefs, or lofe my Life. He pronounced thefe Words with a menacing Air; and like a Man almoft diftracted, was tempted more than once, to return and ftab the Prince; but after having been fome Time in this Diforder, his Spirits became more calm. What! faid he, can I with Juftice hate him, fince he is my Rival againft his Will? Ought not I rather to open my Breaft to him, implore his Pity, and conjure him to yield *Leonida* to me? No, this Expedient will never do, cry'd he again, I cannot repofe this Confidence in him: What would he think of me, fhou'd I confefs a Paffion for her, after having defcrib'd her as a Perfon undeferving of him, and advifed him againft her; he muft then believe me the greateft of Villains: But let him think what he will of my Sentiments, I had rather fubmit to every Thing, than be depriv'd of the Object I love: I fhall tell him the Reafons which induc'd me to fpeak of her as I did: The Force of my Paffion will excufe me to a Perfon who is fo well acquainted with the Effects of Love, and has no other Motive to marry than Obedience. But alas! my Happinefs is not in his Power: *Leonida*'s Father is the firft Grandee of *Spain*, Conftable of *Caftile*, and the King's Favourite; and fuppofe all his Engagements with the Prince were intirely

tirely broke off, he wou'd defign a Match for his Daughter much more confiderable than I could pretend to be. Thefe melancholy Reflections ferv'd to perfuade him, that to facrifice the Prince, or implore his Aid, wou'd be equally of no Effect, and that he ought to find other Means to procure himfelf the only Thing on which depended his Felicity.

 *Benavidez* ftay'd fome Time at *Genoa*, and the Prince propofing to go on his Travels, in hopes that changing of Places might divert his Grief, ask'd him whether he was willing to go along with him? He accepted of the Offer, and the Senator *Grimaldi*, who was perfuaded that the Prince's Affliction was exceeding great, refolv'd alfo to accompany him to *Rome*, being generoufly inclin'd to partake of his Troubles, fince he cou'd no ways remove them: He had a mighty Refpect and Friendfhip for the Prince, whofe Merit and diftinguifhing Qualities made fo ftrong an Impreffion on thofe who knew him, that they cou'd not help admiring him. *Benavidez* had now laid a Defign, whereby he expected to break the Prince's Meafures; and in order to fucceed he wrote to his Sifter, that Chance had conducted him to *Genoa*, where the Prince of *Carency* was deploring the Death of *Olympia Doria*, with whom, at firft fight, he had fallen paffionately in Love. Upon this he gave an agreeable Turn to his Letter, which render'd it very diverting, but fo ridiculoufly characteriz'd the Prince, that he wou'd have had all the reafon imaginable to refent it, had he known any Thing of the Matter. *Be-*

*Benavidez* defired his Sifter, by a private Note, not to neglect fhowing his Letter to *Leonida*, which fhe as exactly perform'd as he cou'd have wifh'd. One Day as they were both taking the Air, *Cafilda* told her, fhe had receiv'd a Letter from her Brother, wherein her Name was often mention'd. He has been fome Time abfent, faid *Leonida*, does he not talk of returning foon. He is at prefent imploy'd in your Service (reply'd *Cafilda*, malicioufly) fince he is confoling a Prince for whom you ought to be concern'd; and if you will promife me to be fecret, I can tell you fomething in Confidence, that may be of Ufe to you. I know you are always diverting your felf with one Raillery or other, faid *Leonida*, (who really thought it was nothing but a Jeft) neverthelefs I promife you to be fecret, if that will do. Take this Letter then and read it, reply'd *Cafilda*, you will fee I am in earneft, and that the Prince of *Carency* in giving you his Heart, will prefent you with nothing new. *Leonida* read with fome kind of Eagernefs, what *Benavidez* had written to his Sifter; then looking on her fmiling, I muft confefs, faid fhe, I am no ways alarm'd to hear of the Prince's Paffion for a fine Woman, and am vain enough to flatter my felf, that when he fees me I fhall have it in my Power to deface the Impreffion fhe might have made on his Heart; I am perfuaded a dead Rival can prove no ways dangerous; and provided I have no other to fear, I dare be affur'd I fhall live in perfect Tranquility.

lity. *Cafilda* was extreamly confus'd to see in what manner *Leonida* had taken a thing, that she imagin'd wou'd have vex'd her, but conceal'd her Disorder. You are in the right, my dearest Companion, (said she, embracing her) to promise your self every Thing from your incomparable Charms; they have Power enough to eclipse the strongest Ideas of any Love, but that which you inspire. *Leonida*, whose Modesty was parallel to her Beauty, wou'd hear no more of these Encomiums, so interrupted her, desiring she wou'd chuse some other Subject for their Conversation. I wou'd willingly oblige you, reply'd *Cafilda*, did I not think my self bound in Friendship to represent to you the Advantages you have over the Prince of *Carency*, and how unfortunate you will be if you marry him: Reflect a little on what my Brother writes: Can any Thing be equal to the Weakness of a Man who falls distractedly in Love with a Person at first sight, knowing at the same Time he was destin'd to be Yours? It is easy to judge of his Character by such a Proceeding; indeed, (pursu'd she, sighing) it grieves me, that you shou'd be promis'd to One who so little deserves you. I am sensible of the Marks you give me of your Affection, my dearest *Cafilda*, (reply'd *Leonida*) and am not less touch'd at the Misfortune you have made me foresee; were I Mistress of my Destiny, I cou'd make a Choice different from that which is allotted me: I wish my Father wou'd consult my Sentiments on that Subject,
and

and not so entirely follow his own; but let what will happen, I am resolv'd to obey him, and will not even endeavour to make him change his Resolution: If I am unhappy in a Person I do not like, it shall only affect my self, being determin'd never to give him any Reason to complain of my Conduct. *Casilda* made no Objection to so reasonable a Disposition, fearing *Leonida* shou'd perceive some underhand Design, but thought she had made a good Progress for the first Attempt, in discovering from her own Mouth, that she not only look'd on the Prince with Indifference, but had already conceiv'd an Aversion for him, which flatter'd her, that Time wou'd procure some other Opportunity of practising such Artifices as she was capable of framing.

The Prince at this Time was at *Rome*, and being inform'd of the Emperor *Vendisla*'s Journey to *Rheims*, where the King of *France* was preparing to give him a Reception, believ'd, on this Occasion, the Court wou'd appear in its greatest Lustre, and that it might be taken ill if he were not present; therefore propos'd that Tour to the Senator and Don *Fernand*, who readily consented to accompany him to the Solemnity.

Upon his Arrival at *Paris* he order'd a fine Equipage to be made, and from thence went to *Rheims*: The pretext of the Emperor's coming there, was a Treaty of Marriage between the Duke of *Orleans*'s Daughter and the Marquis of *Brandenburg*, tho' some ascrib'd it to

other

*of* CARENCY. 49

other Motives. The young Princes and Lords who attended the Emperor and the King of *France* to this Meeting, left them to treat by themselves, and pass'd their Time in Pleasures agreeable to their Age; as Tournaments, running at the Rings, and Balls, which daily succeeded each other with so much Order and Magnificence, that all the Nobility of *France* endeavoured to be Spectators of this triumphant Season.

The Prince of *Carency* amidst these Pleasures, was extremely melancholy; his Unknown of *Nicopolis,* the Death of *Olympia,* and his Aversion for *Leonida,* were equally a Torment to him, and *Benavidez* entertain'd him constantly in all these Dispositions.

Soon after the Emperor and the King of *France,* having agreed on what they came to treat of, took leave of each other; the latter being then inform'd that a Rebellion had broke out in *England,* sent over a Number of Troops under the Command of the Count of *La March:* The Count of *Vandome* and the Prince of *Carency,* who were desirous of acquiring Glory, embrac'd that Occasion, and accompany'd their Brother in this Expedition. The Senator *Grimaldi* took his Leave here of the Prince, and return'd to *Genoa,* but Don *Fernand Benavidez* went over with him for *England,* where they met with so little Success, that they were soon forc'd back. At their arrival at the Court of *France,* the Prince of *Carency* perceiving that the Princes of the Blood, his near Relations,

E were

were in Conteſt relating to the Regency, thought he cou'd not well remain there without engaging in their Quarrel, ſo reſolv'd to return to *Rome* ; and having told his Deſign to *Benavidez,* who was willing to go with him, took leave of the Court, and ſet out on his Journey.

The mean while, *Leonida* and *Caſilda* were made Ladies of Honour, which allow'd them more Liberty than before ; and as they waited on the Queen whenever ſhe went abroad, many People who had never ſeen *Leonida,* were ſo charm'd with her, that ſhe ſoon paſs'd in *Spain* for a ſurprizing Beauty. This Opinion did no ways intitle her to the Friendſhip of her Sex ; for tho' the Ladies at Court cou'd not diſown her extraordinary Merit, yet it invited them all to envy her. *Caſilda* uſed to talk very much to her in favour of her Brother, ſaying Things at the ſame Time entirely to the Prince of *Carency*'s Diſadvantage : It is true, that what ſhe cou'd ſay in behalf of the one, made but a ſlight Impreſſion on *Leonida*; but then the ill Character ſhe gave of the other, perplex'd her extremely : ſhe began to think her ſelf very unhappy in the Choice her Father had made for her, of a Prince, who had no other Recommendation but his Birth. I cannot imagine (ſaid ſhe one Day to *Caſilda*) why the World will attribute ſo many fine Qualities to a Man who is far from poſſeſſing the leaſt of them, and how thoſe who have ſeen him, can ſtudy to deceive me in his Favour. That is the Character

racter of the Age, reply'd *Casilda*; the Prince is consider'd as a Man of an eminent Rank and great Fortune; and such Persons as know he is contracted to you, will certainly set him off to the greatest Advantage: I am even surpriz'd at the Sincerity of my Brother, who I fear will have Cause to repent hereafter of what he has done: It is possible you may one Day tell the Prince what he writ to me about him, and your Disdain will be his only Reward for the Intention he had to serve you. Ah! know me better, cry'd *Leonida*, and do not think me guilty of Ingratitude; I am too sensible of my Obligation to your Brother, ever to expose him to the Prince's Resentment; and I declare to you, my dear *Casilda*, that after having consulted my Inclinations, I am at last resolv'd to make good use of his Advice: I will throw my self at my Father's Feet, and represent to him my Aversion for the Prince in so feeling a manner, that my Prayers and Tears shall prevent his concluding our Marriage. *Casilda* was extreamly pleas'd at this Declaration, and encourag'd *Leonida* in that Design, not omitting to put her in mind of the Misfortunes which attend an Alliance made out of political Motives; and not to give her Time to change a Resolution so agreeable, she conducted her to Don *John*'s Apartment, and there left her, in order to go and write to *Benavidez*: Her Letter was in these Terms;

*R*Eturn, *dear Brother, return, every Thing an-ſwers your Deſires*; Leonida *believes the Picture you ſent her of the Prince, is a true Copy of the Original, and that Love has no Share in what you write. Oh Heavens! how happy ſhou'd I be, had I as much Reaſon to be contented with my Deſtiny as you have with yours! But the ungrateful* Henriquez *has relapſed into his firſt Paſſion, in ſpite of all the Care I took to prevent it; he has ſeen Donna* Blanca; *conſider then the State I am in. I impatiently wait your Return to tell you my Trouble, and beg your Conſolation, ſince nothing elſe is capable of giving me any.*

    *Benavidez* was arriv'd at *Rome* when he receiv'd this Letter, which gave him inexpreſſible Joy: *Caſilda*'s Affliction had not Power to interrupt the Pleaſure he had conceiv'd at the Thoughts of *Leonida*'s being diſpos'd to favour his Paſſion: He went to viſit the Prince, who no ſooner ſaw him but perceiv'd ſo great an alteration in his Countenance, that he could not help inquiring into the Cauſe; *Benavidez*, ſaid he, you muſt have receiv'd ſome agreeble News, for your Eyes ſeem to own it. I will not keep any Thing a Secret from you, my Lord, (reply'd he) I come rather to make you my Confident. Speak then with an entire Confidence, ſaid the Prince, you cannot do me a greater Pleaſure. I am in Love, continu'd *Benavidez*, and have ſome Reaſon to flatter my ſelf with an obliging Return. You muſt know, that my Miſtreſs having unjuſtly ſuſpected my

Con-

*of* CARENCY. 53

Conſtancy, by the falſe Inſinuations of ſome of my Enemies, wou'd not ſo much as hear me in my Juſtification, but forbad me her Preſence; and the Care ſhe took to avoid me, had like, with my Life, to have ended my Misfortunes. I left the Court very diſconſolate and retired to my Country Seat, where I found, that Solitude only augmented my Grief; therefore to remedy this Ill, I reſolv'd to Travel, ſo took leave of my Siſter the moſt diſtracted of all Mankind. She extremely pity'd my Condition, and promis'd, in my Abſence, to uſe her utmoſt Endeavours to make my Peace, which at laſt ſhe has done with the moſt obliging Circumſtances. My Miſtreſs recals me, and now impatiently deſires my Return; but in ſpite of my Paſſion, I am ſenſibly affected, my Lord, with being oblig'd to leave you; for I have felt ſo real a Satisfaction in your Company, that I cou'd wiſh I had never known you, or that I were never to part from you.

The Prince, at theſe Words, embrac'd him with great Tenderneſs, which ſhew'd, that his Departure touch'd him to the Heart: I was in hopes, ſaid he, you wou'd have gone with me to the Court of *Navarre,* where my Brother is to marry the King's Daughter, and has deſired me to attend the Ceremony. What Violence muſt I do to my ſecret Pain, in a Place, where nothing but Pleaſure will be thought of? I cannot abandon my ſelf to my Melancholy, neither do I believe I can be ſo good a Counterfeit, as to conceal it from Perſons ſo diſcern-

E 3  ing;

ing; and if I speak of my torment to my Brother, I fear he will not think it worth his Concern. Judge then, my dear *Benavidez*, what Consolation your Company wou'd be to me, since you not only deplor'd my Fate, but soften'd my Misfortunes, and in all Respects have appear'd the best of Friends: Oh, how necessary wou'd your Assistance be in this Juncture, and how extremely shall I regret your Absence! But these Considerations are too weak to oppose what your adorable Mistress commands, and your Inclinations invite you to obey. Go then (continu'd he sighing) go and taste those Pleasures which are prepar'd for you. He finish'd these Words with so dejected an Air, that it wou'd have created Pity in any one but a Rival; for when once we adore an Object, we conceive an Aversion for those who are Obstacles to our Happiness, and have no longer Power to be just, even to the Merit of any other Votary.

The Nuptials of the young Princess of *Navarre* were celebrated with a Pomp and Magnificence equal to the Occasion; all manner of Diversions were given at the King's Expence, to make that Solemnity as fine as possible; but in the midst of these Pleasures, the Prince appear'd lost in a Distraction of Mind, which was too great for any thing to alleviate; however he affected a Gaiety which he was so little us'd to, that the Counterfeit was easily perceiv'd. What makes you so very melancholy, Brother? (said the Count of *La March* to him one Day)

I

*of* CARENCY. 55

I fee the Violence you do your Inclinations when you are in the beft of Company: It wou'd be better for you to break off with your Friends, and give your felf up entirely to your own Humour. You make me an indifferent Return, interrupted the Prince, for the Care I have taken to conceal my *Chagrin*; but I proteft to you, that it is of fuch a Nature as cannot be conquer'd; therefore, dear Brother, I will take your Advice, and in banifhing my felf from a Place where my Prefence is difagreeable, avoid Reproaches, which very much affect me. Thefe Words made the Count of *La March* fenfible, that to rally him upon his Grief, was a certain Way to augment it; and as he lov'd the Prince dearly, and found many fhining Qualities in him, he embrac'd him with the greateft Marks of Affection. What, dear Brother, (faid he in an obliging manner) is it poffible you fhou'd take a Thing fo ferioufly, which was only defign'd as a Jeft? Do you think, that for fo flight a Matter your Company cou'd be difagreeable to me? No, do your felf more Juftice, and never fufpect mine. So unfortunate a Man as I am, reply'd the Prince, has ever room to fear, and if you knew what it is never to have feen one Miftrefs, and to lofe another as foon as you had conceiv'd a Paffion for her, you wou'd not add to my Pain. The Count cou'd not help fmiling at the Fantafticalnefs of thefe different Adventures. You do not pity me then, faid the Prince, nor comprehend how one can fuffer fo much with fo

little

little reason; you think it ridiculous in me to sigh for a Person I do not know, and for one that is now no more; but Oh! these Two Things are the principal Cause of my Melancholy. The Count of *La March* pity'd him extremely, and omitted nothing afterwards that cou'd console him.

By this Time *Benavidez* was arriv'd at *Madrid*, where he found a great Alteration, the King being dead, and the Care of his Son Don *John*'s Education (who was then but Twenty Two Months old) left to Don *Diego Lopez* of *Cuniga*, and Don *John* of *Velasco*; which Mark of the King's Esteem for these two Lords, in reposing so great a Trust in them, gave a mighty Addition to their Fortunes and Power. The Court was very much divided at that Juncture; the Infanta Don *Fernand*, Brother to the late King, having a considerable Party, was offer'd the Crown, but he generously declin'd it, and had the young Prince proclaim'd King; which was perform'd to the great Satisfaction of the Queen, who (after her Son was settled on the Throne) retired to *Villa Real* for the Benefit of the Air, and agreeable Situation of the Place.

It was here that *Leonora*, Wife to Don *Diego Lopez*, introduc'd her self into the Queen's Favour, and had so great an Influence over her, that whatever she ask'd, was immediately granted; she had a great deal of Wit, but of so dangerous a Nature, that those who sincerely espous'd the Queen's Interest, began to lose their Credit by her malicious Insinuations,

which

which made them in a little time conceive as great an Aversion for the Sovereign, as for the Favourite.

Thus was the State of Affairs when *Benavidez* came to *Villa Real*, where he staid some Time before he cou'd find an Opportunity to speak with his Sister; because, during the first Days of Mourning, it is the Custom in *Spain*, not to admit any Person into the Palace except the Family; but as soon as the Queen cou'd be seen, he was introduc'd into her Apartment, where he found *Leonida* and *Casilda*. It is impossible to express the different Agitations he was in at the Sight of *Leonida*, who might have discover'd his secret Thoughts, had she perceiv'd his Disorder.

After having satisfy'd the Queen in some Particulars relating to his Travels, he hasten'd to his Sister's Apartment; but was agreeably surpriz'd, when passing through a Gallery of Paintings, where *Casilda* had designedly invited *Leonida* to walk, he met them, and saluted *Leonida* with much Respect. Give me leave, Madam, (said he) to acquit my self of the Commission I receiv'd from the Prince of *Carency*, who charg'd me to assure you, that he will be soon here, in order to conclude a Marriage to which you are destin'd, tho' unknown to each other. It is an equal Misfortune to us both, (reply'd *Leonida* with a dejected Air) and the Particulars you writ to *Casilda* relating to the Character of that Prince, have so tormented me, that I have omited nothing ever since,
which

which I thought cou'd perfuade my Father to change his Refolution; but he fo ftrictly regards his Word, that hitherto my Prayers and Tears have had no Power to move him. *Benavidez* fetch'd a deep Sigh, and after a Moment's Silence; The Prince defired me, Madam, (faid he) to fend your Picture to him, and I muft confefs it wou'd be a Trouble to me to fee him receive that Favour, had he not a Profpect of being happy in the Poffeffion of the Original. I cannot difpofe of my Picture, interrupted *Leonida*, without my Mother's leave, therefore it depends on you to ask it of her, but in my Opinion, it is entirely unneceffary: The Prince will fee me too foon for his Peace or mine. I am not amiable enough to efface the Objects which poffefs his Heart, but I will try, by my Obedience, to deferve his Efteem. Madam! faid *Benavidez*, fince you confent to it, I will tell Madam *Velafco*, that it is the Prince your Lover's Requeft. Speak to whom you pleafe of it, reply'd *Leonida*, with an Air of Contempt, but do not call fo fantaftical a Perfon my Lover; I can never like a Man that falls in love with all he fees, and even with thofe he never faw.

As fhe had finifh'd thefe Words, Madam *Velafco*, who was going to the Queen's Apartment, enter'd the Gallery: She knew *Benavidez* had been a great while with the Prince of *Curency*, which made her fuppofe there was an intimate Friendfhip between them; and as her Concern for a Prince who was contracted to her Daughter cou'd not indifferently affect her, she immediately enquired after his Health, and express'd a great Impatience to see him in *Spain*. *Benavidez* told her he had left *Rome*, and was going to the Court of *Navarre*, to be at the Solemnity of his Brother the Count of *La March*'s Nuptials, with the Princess *Beatricia*, Daughter to the King; that the Prince passionately wish'd for *Leonida*'s Picture, which he had promis'd to ask for him, and therefore address'd her for that Favour. Madam *Velasco* was very much pleas'd at the Zeal *Benavidez* seem'd to have for his Friend, and told him, She wou'd do any Thing that might be agreeable to the Prince; that her Daughter shou'd sit for her Picture, and desired he wou'd take Care to send it to him. *Benavidez* found that his Hopes as well as Passion augmented, and flatter'd himself that the Plot he was framing wou'd have its desired Effect; he left Madam *Velasco* and *Leonida* to go with his Sister into her Apartment, and after giving each other Proofs of an entire Affection; I have something to say to you, Brother, said she, come into my Closet: She took him by the Hand, and sitting down, cou'd not help shedding a shower of Tears. You weep, my dear *Casilda*, (said he, embracing her) have you any Thing to say to me concerning Don *Henriquez*? Ah! Brother, (said she) he is the ungrateful Object that troubles my Peace, and remembers no more the Obligations he owes me: I shall find some Ease in relating to you all that has happen'd, happen'd; and as a difappointed Paffion is lefs difcreet than a fuccefsful one, I am going to inform you of what you know but very imperfectly.

Don *Henriquez* was on Board the Fleet with the Admiral his Father, when one Day as the Queen was hunting, and we all attending her, Donna *Blanca*'s Horfe ftarted, and not knowing how to manage him, ran away with her: Several Cavaliers rode after her, who were invited to ferve her, either by Inclination or Intereft, fhe being perfectly handfome, and Daughter to *Leonora*, who was then the Queen's Favourite. As I am naturally politick enough, I endeavour'd to reach her before the reft, when I faw her from the rifing Ground I was on, fall in a Valley; I rid as faft as poffible to her Affiftance, where I no fooner came, but the firft Thing that ftruck my Sight, was a Cafe fet with Diamonds, which drop'd out of her Pocket when fhe was thrown off her Horfe; I took it up, and had no other Reafon for not returning it inftantly, but the Curiofity of feeing what was in it. Donna *Blanca* was in a Swoon when the reft of the Company came up; they immediately gave her what they thought wou'd reftore her to her Senfes, being ftun'd with the Fall; and as foon as fhe came to her felf, fhe perceiv'd fhe had loft her Picture-Cafe, which was fought for, but in vain. I took notice of all her Motions, and her Uneafinefs increas'd, with the fear of not finding what was fo dear to her: This gave
me

## of CARENCY. 61

me the greater Inclination to keep it, with the only View to mortify her, being one of the finest young Ladies of the Court, and Daughter to the Favourite.

As she had receiv'd no Hurt, she went up to the Queen, but appear'd so melancholy, that her Mother express'd much Concern. I was impatient to be alone, that I might see what was contain'd in the Case; but how can I tell you Brother, or at least in telling you, ought I not to dye with Shame? I had but just cast my Eyes on the Picture, which was inclos'd, when I found such Motions in my Heart as surpriz'd me, being what I never felt before. I was charm'd with the noble Air and Youth of a Gentleman, whose Features were so admirably well drawn, that I cou'd no ways doubt but it very much resembled the Person whom it was design'd for; I gaz'd at it with Delight, and, tho' unknown to me, I thought it was impossible to see any Thing more lovely. I did not consider at first, how dangerous my Curiosity might prove, so imploy'd some Hours in admiring this fatal Picture, whose Idea it was not in my Power to deface: It threw me into such Reflections as generally succeed excessive Transports. Oh! unhappy *Casilda*, cry'd I, what subtil Poison hath seiz'd thy Heart? Art thou so tired with thy Liberty, that thou must lose it this Day? I know not who this is that seems so Charming; I am well inform'd that he is in Love, and is belov'd, since Donna *Blanca*, who is so beautiful,

tiful, is the Guardian of his Picture, which she show'd by her Uneasiness to be very dear to her. What hopes then can I have of any Relief, and to whom must I apply my self? Shou'd not my Birth and Modesty be sufficient to impose Silence on me? What! cou'd I pronounce the Word I love, and pronounce it in Favour of a Man, who knows not the Value of so great a Sacrifice: No, my Eyes shall sooner be Witness of my Rival's Victory, and I will die before I expose my self to the Shame, which must needs succeed such a Confession: But (said I a Minute after) is it possible that in such a little Time, Love cou'd have made so great a Progress? I am forc'd to lay a Command on my self, not to speak of my Weakness, and I have form'd a Rival without having a Lover.

I confess to you, Brother, this caus'd so great a Change in me, that I began not to know my self: I was continually Thoughtful, and Solitude was the only Thing I courted: I fear'd to discover my Pain, or seek for Means to know the Author of it. If I show this Picture, thought I, Donna *Blanca* will be inform'd I have it, and then I shall be oblig'd to return it; she is belov'd, and in so great Favour, that I dare not declare my Sentiments, much less contend with so dangerous a Rival.

Two Months were over before I cou'd hear any Thing relating to this Affair; I sometimes enquired what young Lords were absent; among others, they named Don *Garcia*, Don *Pedro d'Avilas*, *d'Avilas*, and Don *Frederick Henriquez:* How cou'd I know whether the Man that poſſeſs'd my Thoughts, was either of them. I endeavour'd to be acquainted with their Character; but thoſe, who were ſo complaiſant as to deſcribe them to me, inſtead of giving me ſome light in the Matter, left me more in the dark and in greater Deſpair. I made it alſo my Buſineſs to diſcover, whether Donna *Blanca* had not a known Engagement, which I was perſuaded was the only Thing cou'd ſatisfy me; but they told me, ſhe was too imperious to receive the Addreſſes of any of the Grandees. I knew the contrary, tho' I was not at liberty to declare it; ſo that I languiſh'd between ſmall Hopes and cruel Fears. Donna *Blanca* was taken ill of the Small-Pox at this Time, and there was a Neceſſity for her leaving the Court. I cannot help confeſſing that I was extreamly pleas'd at my Rival's Misfortune. Heavens! cry'd I, juſt Heaven! make her as ugly as poſſible, that the Paſſion of her Lover may turn to a mortal Averſion. The Thoughts of this gave me ſome Eaſe, tho' I look'd upon my being in love with a Perſon I did not know, as the greateſt Unhappineſs that cou'd poſſibly attend me. How wretched wou'd be my Fate, ſaid I to my ſelf, if this Picture with which I am ſo charm'd, ſhou'd only prove the Painter's Fancy, and that I ſhou'd never ſee its Original. I reflected at laſt on which wou'd give me the moſt Uneaſineſs, to ſee Donna *Blanca* ador'd by him I lov'd, or

never

never to have hopes of seeing the Object of my Passion. These, in my Opinion, were two cruel Extremes; for I cou'd not determine my self on either, and therefore concluded I was the most unfortunate Person in the World.

My Mind was in this Situation, when in the Queen's Apartment, thinking of the Odness of my Adventure, I went to the Window, from whence I saw two Noblemen, follow'd by many Attendants; the youngest of the Two so perfectly resembled the Picture, that I did not at all doubt but he was the Original, already so dear to me. In the first Motions of my Surprize I fetch'd such a Shriek, and threw open the Sash with so much precipitation, that every Body took Notice of it; and tho' the Queen did not seem to mind it, the first Lady of the Bed-Chamber did, and reprimanded me severely. I recover'd the Disorder I was in, as soon as possible, and told her, I was deceiv'd by taking the young Lord for my Brother, whom I impatiently expected. The Affair pass'd in this manner, and I did all I cou'd to supprefs the Agitation, which might attend the first Sight of a Cavalier, whose Shadow had so much disturb'd my Peace.

In spite of all the Reflections I had made, I was seiz'd with such violent Emotions when the Admiral and his Son enter'd the Queen's Chamber, (for it was they) that I had like to have swooned. Don *Frederick Henriquez* appear'd so thoughtful, that I was griev'd to the Soul. I ought not to flatter my self, said I, that

that Donna *Blanca* is indifferent to him; In his Looks I read my Misfortune: He sympathizes with her in the Condition she is in, and thinks none here worth his Notice. Oh Barbarian! (cry'd I to my self) you think of nothing but your Mistress; cannot you turn your Eyes on me, and see the deplorable State of wretched *Casilda*? But, Brother, I am asham'd (said she, interrupting her self) I am asham'd of unveiling my Weakness to you, and exposing to your Censure, Thoughts so offensive to the Modesty of my Sex. I shall only tell you, that the Queen came out of her Closet, and the Ladies made a Circle about her, when the Admiral gave her an Account of her Naval Force: I resolv'd at that Instant on a Thing that will appear to you no less bold than precipitate, which was to write to Don *Henriquez*; therefore without consulting Reason, or considering the Consequence, I took out my *Tablettes*, and address'd him in these Terms.

*AFfairs wherein the Heart is concern'd, ought not to be defer'd; I deplore the Condition of yours. Give me an Opportunity of speaking to you, and you shall be indebted to me for your Peace. Let Secrecy be the Proof of your Gratitude. At Night I shall expect you on the Terrace-Walk under the Window by Dian's Statue: I there shall acquaint you, my Lord, with some Circumstances in which you are particularly concern'd.*

When I had finish'd my Letter, I was at a less how to convey it to Don *Henriquez*; at
F      last

last, I resolv'd to trust the young Count of *Oropez* with it; his Post of being first Querry to the Queen, gave him (as you know) an Opportunity of entertaining us often: He had a great deal of Wit, and having on several Occasions observ'd his Discretion, I made a Sign to him, and he came to me. I have assured one of the young Ladies (said I to him) that you can keep a Secret, and hope you will answer my good Opinion of you. There is nothing in my power, Madam, reply'd he, that I wou'd not do, to convince you, I am not undeserving your generous Sentiments. It is not my Secret (said I blushing) I am going to intrust you with, but that of my particular Friend, who has a mind to perplex Don *Henriquez*: She has just writ on my *Tablettes*, I desire you will find an Opportunity to make him read it, and do not forget to return them to me. I shall never neglect, Madam, the least of your Commands (reply'd he smiling) tho' I cannot say, you have charg'd me with so obliging a Commission as you wou'd have me think. One Word more, said I, be assured, I am not concern'd in it; but notwithstanding, shall ever acknowledge the Favour you do me in obliging my Friend. *Oropez* left me immediately, and acquitted himself of what I wish'd with great Address; while he was with Don *Henriquez*, I was extremely uneasy at this imprudent Step, but was not long so, for *Oropez* came back with my *Tablettes*, where at the End of my Letter, I found this Answer.

*I*

*I* *Never cou'd flatter my self that any Person was interested in the Concerns of my Heart, but now I am happier than I imagin'd. Your Commands shall be exactly obey'd. I assure you of Secrecy; and as for Gratitude, it is the least Return I can make so much Generosity.*

These Words so agreeably flatter'd my Imagination, that I long'd for Night with the greatest Impatience; in the mean Time, I made a thousand Reflections which gave me hopes, and entertain'd me till the appointed Hour. The Night was very dark, and hearing some Body approach the Window, I threw up the Sash, and ask'd in a low Voice; Don *Henriquez*, is it you? Yes, Madam, (said he) it is the Man in the World who is most indebted to you; but at the same Time I cannot help saying, that the Advantage you have over me is too unequal, since you know me, and I am not only unacquainted with you, but even a stranger to what induces you to favour me with this Interview. I will satisfy you presently (said I, in a trembling Voice) and that you may not suspect I sent for you hither on a frivolous Subject, know that I am *Casilda Benavidez*; therefore, my Lord, do not use any Dissimulation, but tell me, upon Honour, whether you are still in Love with Donna *Blanca*; if you will not be sincere in this Confession, I have nothing farther to say to you. Don *Henriquez* seem'd very much surpriz'd at the Question, and having paus'd a while, made me this Answer;

swer; Donna *Blanca* is so charming, that her Chains are glorious; and since you believe I am her Captive, I will not scruple to own it. These Words threw me into a very great Confusion. What! do you love that perfidious Creature, reply'd I, who has made a Sacrifice of you, and even dispos'd of your Picture to convince your Rival how indifferent you are to her? With that I took a Light, which I had hid for fear of being discover'd, and obliging him to come nearer, I shew'd him his Picture, and look'd at him so tenderly, that he might have read my Thoughts. Don *Henriquez*, after having view'd it, turn'd his Eyes on me, and I perceiv'd the Surprize was agreeable to him; but as what I had told him was very unexpected, he ask'd me how I came to know that he lov'd Donna *Blanca*, and by what Misfortune he had forfeited her Esteem. I can easily satisfy you both these Questions, reply'd I; your Absence having banish'd you from your Mistress's Heart, Don *Diego Cuniga* made his Addresses to her, and was favourably receiv'd: His Father, you know, is one of the first Grandees, and she being very ambitious, easily conceiv'd a Passion for him, of which she cou'd not have given a greater Proof, than sacrificing your Picture to him. His Vanity was satisfy'd, but his Love, instead of increasing by the Assurance he had of a Return, made him slight her, and even discontinue seeing her, which she resented so much, that it had like to have been the Cause of her Death: He endeavour'd vour'd to perfuade me, I was the Occafion of it; for that if he had not feen me, Donna *Blanca's* Impreffion wou'd never have been effac'd: But as I had no Inclination to believe him, and did not give him fo obliging an Audience as he us'd to receive, to alter my Difpofition towards him, he brought me your Picture, told me every thing that pafs'd when fhe gave it to him, and beg'd I wou'd accept it as an Evincement that he never more wou'd renew his Addreffes to her.

Altho' I look'd on him as an unthinking young Gentleman, I took the Picture, and I proteft to you my only Motive for fo doing, was to undecive you in relation to your ungrateful Miftrefs; for tho' I had no Acquaintance with you, I frequently heard fo much in your Praife, that it gave me no fmall Concern to fee you thus betray'd by a perfidious Woman, and therefore I refolv'd to do all in my Power to diffuade you from ever thinking of her more. I will take your Advice, Madam, (faid he, in a great Paffion) and Don *Diego Cuniga* fhall find at his Return from *Sevil*, that if I am not a dangerous Rival, I am at leaft a troublefome Enemy; but, Madam, (continu'd he with a milder Voice,) I hope you will affift me in my Revenge on Donna *Blanca*; you have been pleas'd to acquaint me with her Perfidioufnefs, and I fwear, I am already difpos'd to have an Averfion for her: Were you but concern'd in my Intereft, I fhou'd certainly be reftor'd to my felf, which happy State I only defire, desire, that I may be the more able to lay my Heart at your Feet: I dare assure you, Madam, that Constancy has ever been my Virtue, and I am so well acquainted with Love, that you will find in me a Passion, if possible, equal to your Beauty. It is too late (reply'd I smiling) to answer a Proposal which you wou'd not have made me, had you less reason to be piqu'd; but as I am inclin'd to wish, that your Words were sincere, it will be a Pleasure to me, when I find your Conduct engages me to determine in your Favour: In the mean Time, be very secret in regard to what is past; your Compliance in this will be an easy way to establish you in my Esteem.

I did not give Don *Henriquez* Time to make me an Answer, but parted from him with so much Satisfaction, that I wou'd not have chang'd my Destiny for that of a Queen: My Mind was all that Night imploy'd on pleasing Ideas. Donna *Blanca* is sick and absent, thought I, and will not appear at Court of a long Time; it is possible her Sickness may deface her Charms, and a Mistress who is suspected to be inconstant, having lost that Attractive, will find it a hard matter to justify her self: Besides, I have admirably well succeeded in my Stratagem: Don *Henriquez* is inclin'd to like me, and thinks he has Cause enough to break off with her. What have I then to fear? I shall have made the Conquest of his Heart before ever my Rival can be able to come and dispute it with me.

I

I appear'd the Day following at Court in a rich Dress, which every one admir'd, having a particular Interest in adorning my self to the best Advantage; and I dispos'd every Thing so well, that Don *Henriquez* came and assured me, he had no reason to complain of his Mistress's Proceedings, and that he was so entirely pleas'd at the Discovery I had made him, that it lay wholly in my Power to render him the most constant of Lovers. This Declaration was attended with all the Courtship that cou'd be expected from a Man passionately in Love. How great was my Felicity in those Days! I was bless'd with all, that Love and Gallantry cou'd inspire. But, Oh Brother! I am ready to die when I call these Things to mind, and have nothing now remaining but mortal Grief. Are you entirely disengag'd (said I sometimes to him) and cou'd you resist Donna *Blanca*, shou'd she endeavour to regain your Heart? You must needs suspect my Sentiments, reply'd he, to question what I wou'd do in such an Occasion: I take Heaven to witness, charming *Casilda*, that were she as constant as I cou'd have wish'd her, and more beautiful than ever she appear'd to me, I shou'd no longer confess her Power. Tho' his Protestations transported me, yet I had room to apprehend, that when he saw my Rival, a Discovery might be made in which I shou'd prove very unhappy. I secretly reproach'd my self with my Perfidiousness, and fear'd some Punishment wou'd attend it, which was sufficient to make me uneasy; therefore

fore I press'd Don *Henriquez* to follicite his Father's Consent to our Marriage, that they might afterwards join in their Request to the Queen about it; which being once granted, I shou'd have no longer reason to fear: He represented to me the fantastical Humour of the Admiral, but promis'd he wou'd apply himself with the greatest Care and Address, in order to prevail with him. These Assurances extremely flatter'd me, and I was expecting the Effects of them, when one Day the Queen went to take the Air in the Forest of *Javalles*, attended by her Ladies who were riding by her open Chaise; but we were hardly got to the Height of a little Hill, when we discover'd in the Plain some Men on Horse-back which we knew to be *Moors*: They were engag'd with *Spaniards*, whom they charg'd so vigoroufly, that we thought them in the greatest Danger: We saw at the same time a Lady at the Foot of the Tree, appearing to us in a Swoon, with several Women about her, who, by their Actions, express'd much Concern.

The Queen stop'd at some distance, and saw this Engagement with great Uneasiness; but Don *Henriquez*, who had follow'd us, came up to her, and desired leave to go and succour the *Spaniards*; which her Majesty having assented to, and commanded some of her Guards to attend him; he attack'd the *Moors* with so much Bravery, that the Scene was chang'd in an instant, and they being no longer able to oppose him, were oblig'd to fly for Safety. All this while

while my fearful Thoughts were imploy'd on the Dangers he was expos'd to; I was praying for his Succefs, tho' already Conqueror; and as I obferv'd all his Actions with a watchful Eye, I faw him approach the Ladies, who were ftill frighten'd, tho' their Enemies were fled.

Don *Henriquez* had fcarcely turn'd his Eyes towards them, when fpurring his Horfe, he rid full fpeed from the Place; but perhaps he confider'd, that fo great a Slight to the Lady (who was Donna *Blanca*) might difpleafe the Queen, fuppofing fhe took Notice of it; therefore his Politicks, or rather my inevitable Misfortune, forcing him to return, he went up to her, and alighting, faluted her very coldly; but what he faid what fo fhort and confus'd, that in fpight of her Attention, fhe cou'd not comprehend it. I owe you my Liberty (faid fhe) my Lord, for which I fhall think my felf eternally oblig'd to you, tho' I am perfuaded you knew not in whofe Caufe you fought. No, Madam, (anfwer'd he) I was a Stranger to whom I render'd this Service: I proteft, that had I known how far you were concern'd, I fhou'd have had Occafion for all my Generofity to fupport me, in fighting for the moft perfidious Perfon in the World. And for my part (reply'd Donna *Blanca* with an Air of Pride) I retract my Obligation, fince you confefs your felf unworthy of being my Deliverer. She faid no more, becaufe one of her Women was near, (from whom I had this Relation) but call'd for her Chaife, and went

went to meet the Queen. Don *Henriquez* left her, and came up firſt to give her Majeſty the Particulars of what had paſs'd, and to let her know that it was Donna *Blanca* he had reliev'd, who had like to have been carry'd off by the *Moors*. At this Name I was Thunder-ſtruck, and my Imagination contriv'd a thouſand Ways to torment me, repreſenting all I had to fear from ſo fatal a Rencounter. Can any Misfortune be equal to mine, ſaid I? Donna *Blanca* taken by the *Moors*, was going by her Captivity to deliver me from all the Alarms her Return cou'd be capable of giving me: She is reſcu'd from this Danger, and owes her Safety to the Arm of Don *Henriquez:* I have now every thing to apprehend; he is juſt come from her, and I doubt has diſcover'd my Treachery. I know not whether I deceive my ſelf, but his Looks tell me he loves her ſtill. The Thoughts of her being inconſtant might have cured him, but nothing can do it, if he is once convinc'd of her Innocence: I ſhall appear a Monſter to him, and become the Object of his Averſion. Heavens! what ſhall I do, if what I dread ſhould happen? Whether Don *Henriquez* would not talk to me for fear of being taken Notice of, or that he had no mind to it, I cannot tell, but he did not ſpeak to me all that Day. Donna *Blanca*, who had not ſeen the Queen ſince her Recovery from the Small-Pox, took that Opportunity to kiſs her Hand. I was inconſolable to find her as handſome as ever, and her Praiſe the Subject of every one's Diſcourſe,

whilſt

whilst I, as silent as Death, was observing Don *Henriquez*, who I thought did a Violence to his Inclination, in not approaching her. They appear'd both in some Confusion, yet their Eyes seem'd to express more Love than Anger. None but a Rival cou'd have known the Cause of these different Motions; but Oh! nothing escap'd my penetrating Jealousy: I read in their Looks (as I imagin'd) my eternal Ruin.

The Queen was return'd to *Villa Real*, and I in her Apartment before I knew where I was, or even which way I came: I was lost in Melancholy, and thought it was very cruel in Don *Henriquez* not to shew the least Concern for me. What! (said I) is his Passion come to this? He who has render'd Donna *Blanca* so essential a Service, and knows I apprehend nothing more than a Relapse; does he thus neglect giving me Assurances of the contrary? I pass'd all that Night in the greatest Anxiety; and tho' I found my self indispos'd in the Morning, I rose early, and went to the Queen's Apartment, fearing something might happen there prejudicial to my Interest.

Donna *Blanca* appear'd at Court that Day finely dress'd, and so beautiful, that all but *Leonida* yielded to her. Don *Henriquez* was just by me when my Rival enter'd the Chamber. Heavens! Madam, said he, how handsome she is! What Pity it is she is false. Why shou'd her Falsity affect you, my Lord, (reply'd I) since at present she ought to be indifferent to you. It is true, Madam, (answer'd he sighing) fighing) but I only deplore the Misfortune of those who wear her Chains. You are very charitable, said I, and the Publick is much indebted to you. Here such a Crowd of various Thoughts presented themselves to me, that I was at a loss how to continue my Discourse; and Don *Henriquez*, without enquiring into the Cause of my Silence, had his Eyes fix'd on Donna *Blanca*. What's this! cry'd I? you appear to me different from what you were Yesterday; Do you repent of having chang'd your Mind, and are you still Slave enough to love that perfidious Creature? Don't you remember that she sacrific'd you to a Man of no Merit, which made me blush for her, as much as I do now for you? At this he interrupted me, and said, Indeed *Casilda* you must know me very little to frame such injurious Suspicions: There is not a Man in the World who resents an ungenerous Usage more than I; and let me assure you, that after I have loaded her with Reproaches, equal, if possible, to the Offence, I will not only show an Indifferency for her, but even despise her to such a degree, that you shall have no reason to complain of my future Conduct.

He pronounc'd these last Words so faintly, that I was confounded. What! said I, do you want to come to an *Eclariciffement* with Donna *Blanca*; you cou'd do no more were she a Pattern of Tenderness and Constancy? I suppose, added I, you wou'd have no Value for such a Mistress. But give me leave to tell you, my

*of* CARENCY. 77

my Lord, that if you speak to her, I will never see you more. He was surpriz'd at these Words, and look'd at me a great while, endeavouring to penetrate into the Cause of this Resolution. He call'd to mind what Donna *Blanca* had said to him, which gave him Suspicion enough to increase his Curiosity; and tho' he promis'd to comply with my Commands, he did it with so indifferent an Air, that I could no ways doubt of my Misforfortune.

I went from the Queen's Apartment into my own, and flung my self upon my Bed, half dead and drowned in Tears. Soon after *Leonida* came into my Chamber, who saw my Concern and Distraction, which wanted very little of Despair, and sitting by me, did all she cou'd to soften my Grief, without knowing the Cause of it: But to disburden my Mind of part of its Depression, I gave her an Account of what had pass'd : As she had never been in Love, and consequently unacquainted with what one in that State is capable of, she cou'd not help condemning my Treachery to my Rival. Oh! *Leonida*, said I, you little know the Effects of a violent Passion ; every Thing is allow'd to Lovers, when they are in pursuit of a Heart: Say rather, reply'd she, that we often allow to our selves many Things which are very blameable. If I have committed a Crime, said I, my Punishment is near. Alas ! I was not mistaken : Don *Henriquez* had found an Opportunity to speak to Donna *Blanca*; his Impression was not
quite

quite effac'd, whatever reason she might have had to complain of his Behaviour. They accused each other, and by that means discover'd the Part I had acted. I leave you to think, Brother, whether they were not reconciled at my Expence. I was not long before I knew my Fate; for *Henriquez* came, and upbraided me with my Perfidiousness. I wou'd have persuaded him he was still captivated by Donna *Blanca*, and that by her artful Insinuations, she had prevail'd, and impos'd on him; but the ill Opinion he had of me, prevented his believing it. As I knew his Temper, I thought I cou'd not do better than confess the Motive which had incited me to make him quarrel with his Mistress. Judge the Condition I was in, dear Brother, when I own'd that Love was the Occasion of my Guilt, and expos'd my Weakness, which I was then sure wou'd meet with a fatal Return. I sought for Reasons to excuse my Crime, by painting my Passion in the most lively Colours, and my Tears convinc'd him of the Truth of what I said. He heard me without the least Interruption, but at last look'd at me with attention, and assuming an imperious Air; I think my self sufficiently reveng'd of your Treachery, said he, since you love me, and I have no Thoughts of you but what are despising; in finishing these Words, he left me. The Anger, Shame, and Grief which divided my Soul, had like to have immediately ended my unhappy Life; but *Leonida* came to me at that Time and us'd her Endeavours to

console

console me, without the least Success. I was meditating the Ruin of Donna *Blanca* and *Henriquez*, and felt in my self such a disposition for a desperate Undertaking, that nothing but the natural Sweetness of my Friend's Temper cou'd moderate my Rage. My Rival, tho' victorious, wou'd not resolve to pardon me; she complain'd to her Mother, who was weak enough to enter into her Sentiments as a Confident, and ever since they have watch'd all Opportunities for Revenge. I have, by their means, forfeited the Queen's Favour, and meet every Day with so many Subjects of Grief, as would deprive me of Life, cou'd any Thing be capable of it, but the Loss of the ungrateful *Henriquez*. I heard Yesterday, that *Leonora* had prevail'd with the Queen to propose a Match to the Admiral between Donna *Blanca* and his Son, and that he had given his Consent to it: I shall soon see her triumph: judge then —— Here *Casilda* cou'd no longer restrain her Sighs and Tears, which oblig'd her to be silent. *Benavidez*, who was extremely touch'd with her Affliction, told her, he wou'd fight Don *Henriquez*, and neglected nothing which he thought cou'd lessen her Pain; but as that which affects the Heart is very different from any other, so it requires more Time for its Cure. We shall find notwithstanding, in the Sequel of *Casilda*'s Story (despairing as she was) that many Years were not expired before she found Consolation.

*Benavidez* gave his Sister an Account of what had pass'd between him and the Prince of *Carency*, and told her, he must needs have *Leonida*'s Picture, for he had thought of an Expedient to make her have a great Aversion for her Lover; but that he wou'd not declare his Passion to her, till he was assured she had some Confidence in him; for which reason he beg'd *Casilda* to sollicite his Interest, who promis'd to act for him to the utmost of her Power: Accordingly she desired Madam *Velasco* to let her Daughter sit for her Picture, which, in Opposition to the young Lady, was immediately granted, and given to *Benavidez*; who caus'd another to be drawn, but with so aukward an Air, that none could see it without having a disdain for the Original. This was the Picture he sent by an Express to the Prince, with a Letter at the same Time, telling him, that that Piece wou'd show how charming the Person was whom Fate had decreed him, since it was her perfect Likeness; and that he had entertain'd her with his Merit, but she hardly wou'd have Patience to hear any thing on that Subject; which convinc'd him, her Thoughts were imploy'd on some other Object.

The Prince, who gave too much Credit to *Benavidez*, was struck with such Confusion at the sight of this Picture and Letter, that he immediately wrote to him, and without any Caution, confess'd the Cruelty of so unhappy an Alliance, and his Aversion for *Leonida*. But as she had some reason to be persuaded that her Picture wou'd produce a contrary Effect; she often ask'd *Benavidez*, out of a Motive of Self-love, whether he had heard from him, and what was his Opinion of her; therefore, as soon as he had receiv'd the Prince's Answer, (which was writ in such Terms as overjoy'd him, being that nothing more disobliging cou'd be added) he contriv'd, that *Casilda* shou'd show it *Leonida* with such an Air of Secrecy, as if he were no ways consenting to it. The thing was carry'd on as he had design'd it. *Leonida* read the Prince's Letter, at which she was so offended, that she immediately went and threw her self at her Mother's Feet, and conjured her with Tears to break off a Marriage, which wou'd render her the most unfortunate Creature in the World. I will not pretend, Madam, to disobey you in any thing, said she, but is it possible that you your self wou'd occasion my Ruin? Tho' I have but little Experience in the Sentiments one ought to have for a Husband; yet it appears to me, that without mutual Love nothing but continual Torment can be expected; for how can I value the Man you have chosen for me, since he has not only conceiv'd an Aversion for me, but thinks me ugly and despises me? Cannot you change my Fate, Madam? Oh! rather let me never marry, or if you are not pleas'd I shou'd live with you, send me to a Monastry; I will sooner embrace that State of Life, than be united to a Prince for whom I have no Inclination. Madam *Velasco*, mov'd at her Daughter's Complaint,

plaint, took her several Times in her Arms, and endeavour'd to confole her in a moſt tender manner. If it wholly depended on me, my deareſt Child, (ſaid ſhe) I wou'd ſoon eaſe your Mind; but your Father is my Lord, and we are both ſo far bound in Duty to comply with his Pleaſure, that I cannot promiſe you any thing till I know what are his Intentions. As ſhe had ended theſe Words, Don *John* of *Velaſco* enter'd the Chamber; the Mother and Daughter flung themſelves at his Feet, and with Prayers and Tears, conjured him to break off with the Prince: They ſhow'd him the Letter he had written to *Benavidez*, but all wou'd not do; Don *John* was determin'd to keep his Word with him, even at the Expence of his Daughter's Happineſs. He anſwer'd them, that the Contract was ſigned, and nothing ſhould ever make him revoke a thing he had concluded with the late Count of *La March*; ſo *Leonida* withdrew in the greateſt Affliction, and having inform'd *Caſilda* of her Father's Sentiments, told her, ſhe was reſolv'd to retire into a Monaſtry. That will be no effectual Relief to you, (reply'd *Caſilda* maliciouſly) for a Man who hath ſo much Power as Don *John*, will eaſily oblige his Daughter to quit a Place, wherein ſhe had thrown her ſelf without his Conſent: But, my dear *Leonida*, your Grief is ſo moving, that I have already propos'd Means to give you ſome Comfort. My Brother, who is entirely devoted to your Service, and in whom you may faithfully confide, has a fine

Houſe

House near *Carmona*; it is an agreeable Retirement, surrounded with spacious Woods. I will go and live with you there. What, my dear *Casilda*, (interrupted *Leonida*) is your love for me so great as to quit the Court? I cou'd make you a greater Sacrifice (reply'd *Casilda* sighing) you know the reasons I have to hate this fatal Place: The false *Henriquez* will soon be marry'd to Donna *Blanca*; I shall have nothing before my Eyes but what will increase my Despair; and in spite of my Pride and Reason, I cannot cease loving that cruel Man, tho' he glories in my Weakness. Absence is the only thing that can efface his Idea; let us go, charming *Leonida*, (continued she) let us fly the Man I love, and him you hate. My Fate is more deplorable than yours, reply'd *Leonida*, your Absence will procure you some Ease, and no Body will pursue you; but as for my part, I shall be pursued, and perhaps discover'd, and brought back to my Father's House, where I shall meet with very severe Usage. Ah! how little do you know the sad Condition I am reduc'd to, cry'd *Casilda*, do you think it a Consolation to tell me, that no Body will pursue me? That is the chief Cause of my Grievance: I cou'd wish the perfidious *Henriquez* wou'd abandon all, and follow me; Heavens! how transported shou'd I be! If you propose to enjoy a perfect Tranquillity, reply'd *Leonida*, do not harbour any Wishes so contrary to your Peace. Alas I know not what to wish (said *Casilda*,) then let us go; Solitude and

and Abfence may chance to give fome Eafe to my Mind. Young *Leonida*, who had but little Experience, and did not forefee the fatal Confequences of fuch an Undertaking, confented to the dangerous Propofals of her Companion: She embrac'd her a thoufand Times, and confefs'd in a moft tender manner, her Obligation for the confiderable Service fhe was going to render her. They afterwards agreed on a Day and Hour to execute their Project, and imploy'd all their Thoughts in taking fuch Meafures as cou'd make it fucceed.

This was the State of Affairs when they were inform'd, that the Count of *La March* was arriv'd at *Seville* with a magnificent Attendance, and a Body of Eight Hundred Men to fuccour the Infanta Don *Fernand*, who was then at War with the *Moors*. The Virtue and eminent Qualities of this illuftrious Prince were foon publifh'd in *Spain*, and the Prince of *Carency*, his Brother, had no fmall Share in the general Applaufe: He had accompany'd the Count to *Seville*, from whence he intended to go to *Villa Real*, in order to marry *Leonida:* but Fortune was preparing long Torments for him, inftead of thofe Pleafures he wou'd have tafted, in the Poffeffion of a Lady fo charming and virtuous.

The Prince wrote a Letter to *Benavidez*, to acquaint him with his departure from *Seville*, which he immediately communicated to *Leonida*. She now thought it Time to be gone, and without farther Confideration, trufted her

felf

self (with *Casilda*) to the Conduct of *Benavidez*, who over-joy'd and full of Hopes, omitted nothing that was necessary in this Affair. They left *Villa Real*, and he accompany'd them some part of the Way; but fearing his Absence from the Court at the Time of their disappearing, might give some Suspicion of his having a hand in it, he desired *Leonida* and his Sister to accept of one of his Friends, who shou'd wait on them to their Journey's End, being a Man whose Fidelity was so well known to him, that he ran no Risque in trusting him with his Mistress and Sister.

*Benavidez* express'd much Concern in parting from *Leonida*, who might have easily perceiv'd it, had not her Thoughts been imploy'd otherways. He took his leave of them, and they continued their Journey with all the Diligence and Secrecy possible. When they were arriv'd at *Benavidez*'s House, where no Body knew them, they chang'd their Names; *Leonida* call'd her self *Felicia*, and *Casilda* took the Name of *Beatricia*, saying they were Sisters, and of the House of *Leon*.

The Gentleman who had accompany'd them, return'd to *Villa Real*, and gave an Account to *Benavidez* of their successful Journey, whilst the young Ladies were taking the innocent Pastime of an agreeable Solitude.

*Benavidez*, notwithstanding the Impatience he had to see *Leonida*, appear'd at Court with a counterfeit Air of Gaiety. But Heavens! in what Affliction were Don *John* of *Velasco* and his

his Lady, when they perceiv'd their Daughter was gone: They believ'd at firſt, that ſhe and *Caſilda* were retired to a Monaſtry, and *Benavidez* ſeem'd to believe the ſame, ſaying, That that was the only reaſon, which prevented him from ſearching all *Spain*, in order to find his Siſter. Don *John*, who had greater Cauſe for Uneaſineſs, imploy'd all Means to diſcover the Place where *Leonida* might be; but his Enquiry being to no purpoſe, he was almoſt in Deſpair. *Benavidez* the mean while was propoſing to himſelf no ſlender Share of Happineſs in the Succeſs of an Enterprize he had manag'd ſo artfully; but the Queen being then inform'd that ſome Grandees of *Spain*, who were diſſatisfy'd with the Government, were carrying on a traiterous Deſign, and had reſolv'd to deliver up ſome conſiderable Towns to the King of *Granada*, ſhe order'd, that *Benavidez* (who was Governour of one of thoſe Places, and had been impeach'd, tho' Innocent,) ſhould be taken up. This unexpected Blow, threw him into a deſperate Condition; he fear'd, it had been diſcover'd that *Leonida* was at his Houſe, and that he was arreſted on that Account; but when they told him that it was for High Treaſon, he thought himſelf too happy, and ſeem'd leſs mov'd for the Loſs of his Life, than the loſing of *Leonida*; however, his being prevented from going to ſee her, increaſ'd his Grief to ſuch a Degree, that he cou'd not conceal it from his Guards, which made them conclude him guilty.

The Prince of *Carency* arriv'd at this time at *Villa-Real*, and did not know what to think of the many Reports he heard. The flight of *Leonida* and *Cafilda*, *Benavidez*'s Imprifonment, and the diftracted Condition of *Don John* of *Velafco* and his Lady, as well as his Concern for a Perfon to whom he was contracted, and the Neceffity he was under of ufing his utmoft Endeavours to find her, together with his Indifferency for her; all thefe united, perfectly confounded him. He made an ineffectual Attempt to fpeak to *Benavidez*, who was fo ftrictly guarded, that he judg'd the Affair he was accus'd of wou'd meet with no Favour, if once convicted, unlefs the Queen's Goodnefs wou'd prevail with her Juftice. He heard that *Leonora* was her Favourite, and having a ftrong Inclination to be ferviceable to his Friend, he made his Court to this old Lady, who, tho' as proud as great, cou'd not but conceive a particular Efteem for the Prince. *Don John* and his Lady were fo charm'd with him, that their Satisfaction wou'd have been compleated, had not his Prefence renew'd all the Grief which the Lofs of *Leonida* occafion'd; fo that nothing cou'd moderate the Affliction of thefe difconfolate Parents.

The Prince of *Carency* was prefented to the Queen, who received him with a Refpect equal to his Birth and Merit. Donna *Leonora* ufed to fpeak fo often to her of his fine Qualities, that fhe foon perceiv'd her Favourite look'd on him with an obliging Eye, and that he triumph'd in her Esteem over the other Princes and Grandees of the Court. He constrain'd himself as much as possible to oblige her, being invited by no other Motive than to serve *Benavidez.* Oh! had he known, that he was working for the greatest of his Enemies, and one who was endeavouring his Ruin, he wou'd have left him to his evil Genius.

One Day as the Queen was walking in the Palace-Gardens, attended by most of the Court, Donna *Leonora* affected to keep at some distance, which the Prince of *Carency* perceiving, he went and saluted her; she receiv'd him very graciously, and ask'd him if he wou'd go with her into a green Arbour that was not far: After he had return'd her Compliment, he led her to the Place, where being set down, she spoke to him in this manner. Do you take this Opportunity I give you, my Lord, of entertaining me, as a Favour I seldom grant to any? Your Youth, Wit and Quality are sufficient Motives to make you admired; but as I have no Inducements to create a Passion, be so kind as to tell me, from whence proceeds the desire you have of conversing with me. Is it the Effect of a Sympathy, that is frequently found between two Hearts, and for which no reason can be assign'd? The Prince was very much surpriz'd at what he heard, but still had a mind to obtain her Favour on the Account of *Benavidez,* without intending to make any Declaration that might distinguish a Lover from a Friend. He look'd at her some time as

one

one aftonifh'd, which entirely confounded *Leonora*. You ought, Madam, (faid he) to be convinc'd, that you have highly oblig'd me in condefcending to this Interview; which is an Honour I have this long time wifh'd for; but if you will give me leave to improve this Occafion, let it be in behalf of the unfortunate *Benavidez:* I know the Queen has fo juft an Opinion of your good Senfe, that fhe will readily affent to any thing you are pleas'd to promote: Grant him your Protection, it is the greateft Favour I can ask. Your Petition is not very great (reply'd *Leonora*, in an angry Tone) when you imploy for another the Opportunity you ought to embrace for your felf: Is it poffible, my Lord, that you can think of your Friend's Intereft, and neglect your own? Oh! I fee too well, that I am deceiv'd: there can be no Paffion where there appears fo much Indifferency. This embarafs'd the Prince more than ever any Thing had done, yet he try'd to conquer himfelf, and taking her by the Hand; You know very little, Madam, (faid he) the Language of my Eyes, when you form fo ill a Judgment of my Sentiments, as to doubt of my Paffion: Your Charms are the only Subject of my Contemplation, and the Fear of offending you was the Caufe of my Silence. This obliging Confidence, my Lord! reply'd fhe, equally flatters my Vanity and Love; for I cou'd not think my felf fo happy in your Favour: I am infinitely pleafed at the Confeffion you have made me,

and

and since you wou'd have me serve *Benavidez*, I promise you to do it effectually; whether he be innocent or guilty, he shall be set at Liberty. The Prince made his Retributions to her in so grateful a manner, that she was perfectly charm'd with him: but as he was tired with this disagreeable Conversation, he impatiently rose up and took his Leave.

When he was alone, he abandon'd himself to those Reflections which were most painful to him. Heaven, just Heaven! cry'd he, what am I reserv'd for? I find my self intangled in an Amour with the ugliest of Women, and who is the only one that ever gave me a favourable Audience. Oh! I love my Unknown at *Nicopolis*, and *Olympia*'s Memory is still dear to me. *Leonida*, prevented by some Fatality, has chosen rather to fly her Father's House, than yield to his Commands. Now must I, to serve my Friend, counterfeit a Passion for this Favourite, who is an Object fitter to inspire Aversion, than a more obliging Sentiment.

Tho' he reproach'd the Cruelty of his Fate, yet he did not omit paying his Devoirs every Day to *Leonora*, whose Passion rose to that Violence at last, that she determin'd to marry him, which was the thing in the World he least thought of. She sent to him, and desired he wou'd come to her; which having obey'd; my Lord, said she, if in the Profession you have made me there is more Truth than Complaisance, and that you are touch'd as much as
you

you wou'd perfuade me, you cannot give me a greater Proof of it, than by uniting your Deftiny with mine. I will not trouble you with a Detail of my Birth and Fortune, all *Spain* can inform you of both; but fhall content my felf with affuring you that you will find in me fo good a Friend in becoming your Wife —— My Wife! have you fuch a thought (cry'd the Prince, interrupting her.) Here he was filent, but perceiving his Miftake, he endeavour'd to recover it, and affuming a tender Air; fuch an Alliance, Madam, faid he, wou'd infinitely pleafe me, if I were not engag'd to *Leonida*, and you know it is not in my Power to retract my Promife. No, cruel as you are: I know nothing; (interrupted *Leonora*, in a furious manner) I faw your Surprize and Horror at a Propofal you are not worthy of; you have not only deceived me, but have alfo deceiv'd your felf. Know, Sir, that in this Kingdom, you muft not dare to offend a Perfon of my Quality unpunifh'd, efpecially one who has as much Power as the Queen: *Benavidez* fhall be my firft Victim, and take care (perfidious as you are) that you be not the Second. In finifhing thefe Words, fhe gave him a menacing Look, went into her Clofet, and fhut the Door with great Violence, leaving the aftonifh'd Prince in her Chamber.

He immediately went to Madam *Velafco's*, and without any Referve, acquainted her with all that had pafs'd. You may be well affured, Madam, faid he, that were I not even contracted

tracted to *Leonida*, I wou'd fooner chufe to dye than marry a Woman, who by her Cruelties, is become odious to all *Spain*. I know her Birth and Fortune are equally great, but I defpife them both; therefore give me your Advice, Madam, and tell me, what Meafures I muft take to deliver my felf from this Monfter, without expofing the Life of *Benavidez*. That is a harder Task than you imagine, (reply'd Madam *Velafco*) the violent Temper of this Woman has already facrific'd many, and I tremble for you: The Queen loves her to fuch a degree, that fhe will blindly condefcend to all her Defires. Alas, my Lord, why are you in *Spain*? Or why are you not the Husband of *Leonida*? With this fhe burft out into a Flood of Tears. You weep, Madam, faid he, and I have reafon to believe you are concern'd for me. Do you think this Affair will have any other Confequence, than my being oblig'd to quit *Villa Real*? I am no Subject of *Spain*, neither is a Man of my Rank to be infulted without Revenge; and I am affured, that if *Leonora* fees me no more, fhe will foon forget me. Then prepare to depart, my dear Son, (reply'd Madam *Velafco*, embracing him tenderly) I will take my Daughter with me into *France* if fhe is living, and nothing fhall alter the Refolution I have taken to make her eternally yours.

Tho' nothing cou'd be more obliging than the Affurances Madam *Velafco* gave the Prince, yet he did not extremely wifh for the Performance:

mance: He was in hopes, that either *Leonida* wou'd not be found, or that her Aversion for him wou'd continue; in which Case, the Marriage of Course must needs break off, and he wou'd be no longer under the Obligation of executing his Father's Commands. He immediately took leave of Don *John* of *Velasco*, being resolv'd to go away the same Night, in order to join the Count of *La March* (his Brother) who was waiting at *Seville* for the Infanta Don *Fernand*, to march against the *Moors*.

He retired early to his Apartment, and gave Orders, that all things shou'd be ready for his Journey; but *Leonora* (who had Spies over the Prince's Actions) was soon acquainted with his sudden Resolution; and seeing she had no Means left to prevail with him, ran and threw her self at the Queen's Feet, conjuring her with Tears in her Eyes, to take pity of her Weakness. The Prince of *Carency* is parting, Madam, said she; he abandons me, and I shall be the wretchedest Creature in the World, without your Majesty is pleas'd to protect me. The hopes of being his Wife, (flatter'd by his Assiduity and faithless Protestations) made so deep an Impression on me, that it was not in my Power to decline a Passion, which wou'd have united our Destinies: But the Traitor has deceiv'd me, and I am going to lose him for ever, unless you give immediate Orders to have him seiz'd. What Pretence cou'd I have to act in that manner, (reply'd the Queen, with that Complaisance which was usual to her) he is
con-

contracted to *Leonida*, and Don *John* of *Velasco* is in great Power : He has Friends and Relations in this Court, and shou'd I undertake to break his Daughter's Contract in favour of you, it wou'd be doing him the greatest Injustice. Besides, with what Authority cou'd I do it? I have no Power over that young Prince: Don't you know he is related to the King of *France*, and that a Man of his Quality is not to be dealt with like other People ; then consider, that the Count of *La March*, his Brother, is actually at *Seville*, and is Son-in-Law to the King of *Navarre*; all these Things are to be weighed with Deliberation. Ah Madam! reply'd *Leonora*, I do not intend to expose your Majesty when I intreat you to detain the Prince; you have a good Pretence to do it, without my appearing any ways concern'd. There is an intimate Friendship between him and *Benavidez*, and wou'd it not be sufficient to make the World understand, that the Prince has a Hand in the Rebellion ? Your Authority dispenses you from giving an Account of your Actions, and who dares inquire into your Conduct? The Prayers and Tears of this old Favourite prevail'd at last with the Queen, and she consented that a Captain of the Guards should go immediately, and put the Prince under Arrest; which was no sooner executed, but the Queen had him brought before her, and having order'd every Body to withdraw, spoke to him in these Terms; What, my Lord, said she, cou'd one have thought you capable

of

of betraying us; and that under the Notion of a Friend, you were privately confpiring with thofe, who intended to deliver up fome Towns of this Kingdom to the Barbarians? Don't pretend, Prince, to fay any thing in your Defence, for nothing can juftify you: I am too well inform'd of your Intreagues; fo prepare your felf to undergo the Punifhment you deferve: Your eminent Birth will not protect you without my Favour, and if I grant you your Life, it fhall at leaft be at the Expence of your Liberty. Donna *Leonora* loves you, my Lord, and has already interceded for Grace; if you will marry her, I may in regard to her, forget the pernicious Defigns you had form'd againft this Kingdom.

The Prince heard, with all the Refpect imaginable, what the Queen had to fay; then anfwer'd her with a noble and undaunted Air; My Heart is incapable, faid he, of forming fo mean a Defign, as that which your Majefty lays to my Charge, and I have too much Intereft in juftifying myfelf to confent that you fhould forget my Crime in Confideration of *Leonora*. No, Madam, I refufe the Mercy you offer me, and demand nothing but Juftice; which I have no Caufe to fear be it ever fo fevere. Go then, Prince, faid the Queen, you fhall be ftrictly guarded, and feverely punifhed if guilty.

He was conducted from thence, to the fame Caftle where *Benavidez* was Prifoner, and confin'd feveral Days, with Orders that no Body fhould should be admitted to him: However, this Affair could not be carry'd on with so much Secrecy, but that *Don John* of *Velasco* was informed how ill they used the Prince, for whom he had so great a Value. He address'd himself to the Queen about it in very warm Terms, and even threatned her with the King of *France*'s Resentment; but she was resolv'd to venture at all, and show no favour to him, unless he marry'd *Leonora*

This imperious Favourite (who was the only Person that had leave to see the Prince) came one Night into his Chamber, richly adorn'd with Jewels, but so frightful as to her Person, that he could hardly prevail with himself to look at her. Nothing shall be impossible to me (said she, my lovely Prince, taking him by the Hand) I have every thing in my Power, and if you will marry me, I promise to deliver you out of this horrible Prison; but if you are too proud, and despise me, be assured, you shall pass the rest of your Days here, or end your Life in a more tragick Manner. Ha! (continued she, perceiving in his Countenance a great deal of Anger mix'd with disdain) Do you conceive less Horror for the Block, than for my Person? I am not young I confess; yet such as you see me, I can make the Felicity of the greatest Princes in *Spain*, who daily offer me their Sighs and Vows, which with mine I sacrifice to you. See, my my dear Prince! See, what a shameful part you make me act; I blush in confessing my
Weak-

Weakness, and your Obligation to me ought to be the greater: I, who make all the Court tremble, am here before you, like a Victim, uncertain of Life or Death, waiting its Doom; say then, will you decide my Fate? You are the only Man that can make me happy, and without you, I am for ever wretched. Whilst *Leonora* was speaking, the Prince of *Carency* felt so violent an Aversion for her, that he cou'd hardly command his Passion; but having overcome it a little, he said, with a very indifferent Air: Are you not yet satisfy'd with what you make me suffer, and will you for ever persecute me with a Passion, to which I can make no Return? I declare, that in my Thoughts, the Misfortune of being belov'd by you, is one of the greatest that could happen to me; and since my Sincerity offends you, pursue your Rage, and let your Vengeance fall on a Man, who can reproach himself with no other Crime, but that of having given you room for some Time, to believe he cou'd like you. After these Words, he was silent, and whatever she cou'd say to him, he wou'd not make her any Answer.

She ran out of his Chamber like a Fury, threat'ning him with speedy Death, and from thence, went directly to see *Benavidez*, who was very uneasy (as one may well conceive) having been disappointed in his Design relating to *Leonida*, and not knowing whether she was still at his House, or whether, since his Confinement, her Father had not found her out, and marry'd her to the Prince of *Carency* ; besides, he cou'd not tell but the Crime he was accus'd of, tho' innocent, might coſt him his Life.

Theſe Reflections were tormenting him, when he ſaw *Leonora* coming into his Chamber; he cou'd not imagine the Cauſe of ſo unexpected a Favour, and juſt as he was going to make his Retributions to her, ſhe began in theſe Terms. *Benavidez* (ſaid ſhe, with a Voice that expreſs'd the Motions of her Soul) your Life or Death now depends on the beſt of your Friends; you are impeach'd, and believed guilty: The Prince of *Carency*, who loves you entirely, is actually a Priſoner with you in this Caſtle, and I am willing to let you know, that I have conceiv'd a particular Eſteem for that Prince ; you ſhall have leave to ſee him, and be ſure you uſe your utmoſt Endeavours to perſuade him to marry me, in which Caſe, I anſwer for your Liberty ; but otherwiſe, you will have Cauſe to fear both for him, and your ſelf; Farewel. Remember now, that your Intereſt and mine muſt be the ſame. After having ſpoke to him in this manner, ſhe gave him no time to make any Anſwer, but went away with great Precipitation.

*Benavidez*, who before was deſpairing, cou'd not hear this News without being extremely pleas'd: He reſolv'd to uſe his utmoſt Addreſs in perſuading the Prince ; and as he knew the Influence he had over him, he flatter'd himſelf
with

with easily overcoming all Difficulties. What a Happiness will it be, cry'd he, if he yields to *Leonora*'s Desires; I shall then be sure of my charming *Leonida*, and this Favourite, whom I shall oblige, will in Gratitude imploy her Credit to make her mine. I find, it is not, as yet, known where she is; my House has this Treasure still in its Possession, and assoon as I obtain my Liberty, I will go and visit her in her Retirement. After having imploy'd his Thoughts on so agreeable a Change of Fortune, he could not help reproaching himself with the treacherous Part he had acted towards his Friend and *Leonida*: No, said he, I shall never enjoy a real Felicity, since I must be oblig'd to deceive two Persons, who so entirely deserve my Affection, and will be inconsolable, when they come to know one another, to find their Destiny chang'd by my Perfidiousness. These Reflections gave him some Concern; but as his Love transcended his Friendship, he resolv'd to arm himself against all Remorse.

Whilst he expected, with great Impatience, to speak with the Prince of *Carency*, Don *John* of *Velasco* was using all his Endeavours to get him out of Prison. He at last brib'd one of the Guards, who having brought Ropes and a File, help'd to cut the Bars of his Window; and the Night being very dark, they both escap'd on Horses that were waiting for them.

But this could not be done so secretly, as not to alarm some of the Guards, who heard a Noise in the Prince's Apartment, which they enter'd, and perceiving his Flight, went immediately to give Notice of it to *Leonora*. This News made her furious. She order'd several Horsemen, who were all devoted to her Interest, to pursue him; and was so confounded, that without knowing what she said, she commanded them to take different Ways, and told 'em, that in case they overtook him, and cou'd not prevail with him to return, they shou'd kill him: But after they had left her, and the first Effects of her Passion were over, she reflected on the cruel Commands she had given, and did not at all doubt but they wou'd be too well executed by those Villains. What! cry'd she, am I going to be the Murderer of a Man, for whom I wou'd willingly lay down my Life; and do I convey the Poinyard to his Breast? Oh unjust Fate! Why are you not contented with taking from me the Object I love, without making me the Author of his Death? Being thus prepossess'd with dismal Thoughts, she was no more Mistress of her self; she sent immediately to countermand her inhuman Orders; but alas! it was too late, they had kill'd the Prince in spite of his brave Resistance, which was so great, that he wou'd not have been overcome but by a vast Superiority.

*Leonora* was saluted with this News at *Villa-Real*, which she receiv'd as one who already expected it, and had no other Thought, but that of dying. The Prayers and Tears of the
Queen

Queen were of no force. She tore her Hair and wounded her Face, and her extreme Grief soon forwarded her Death, which made some Atonement for the Barbarity she had just caus'd to be acted on one of the finest Princes in the World.

Don *John* of *Velasco* and his Lady were inconsolable for his Loss, reproaching themselves for not giving him a sufficient Guard; they regretted him as if he had been their own Child, and loaded with Imprecations the Memory of *Leonora*. *Benavidez* not being so strictly guarded as before, was soon inform'd of the Prince's Death; but his Love triumph'd over his Gratitude, which made him perfectly insensible of the Misfortune of a Person, who had lov'd him so entirely.

Whilst these Things were passing at Court, *Leonida* and *Casilda*, under the Names of *Felicia* and *Beatricia*, were strangely alarm'd in their Solitude; the Gentleman who had left them safe there, acquainted them with *Benavidez*'s being made a Prisoner of State, and accus'd of having a Correspondence with the *Moors*. *Casilda* at this News, was resolv'd to go back to *Villa-Real*, in order to intetcede for her Brother, and do him what Service she was capable of; but *Leonida*, who fear'd to remain there alone, represented to her, that as *Leonora* was not her Friend, and that through her means, she had already lost the Queen's Favour, her Presence instead of mending her Brother's Affairs, would make them worse; that besides, she wou'd have the Mortification of seeing *Henriquez* marry'd to Donna *Blanca*, which wou'd only renew her Grief: These Arguments wou'd not have prevail'd with *Cafilda*, had she not apprehended, that in leaving *Leonida*, who in the mean Time might return to her Father's House, *Benavidez* wou'd lose all the Fruits of her artificial Management; which Consideration prevented her Journey.

*Leonida* and *Cafilda* us'd often to walk in a Forest near their House; and one Evening, as they were sitting by the side of a Rivulet, a Horse ran by, in a full Gallop, which frighten'd them very much, seeing no Body on his Back; they quitted the Place hastily, and as they were in their Way towards the Castle, their Surprize was much greater, when they perceiv'd two Men lying on the Ground wounded, and cover'd with Blood; such a Sight was very frightful to these young Ladies, who believing they were dead, durst not approach them, but ran home, and call'd some of their Servants, with whom they immediately came back, in order to give Assistance to these two Gentlemen, if happily it were not too late.

The Ladies now having some Attendance with them, came up to these unknown Cavaliers, and found that one of them was already dead, and the other still breathing. *Leonida*, who had hitherto seen all Mankind with Indifferency, seem'd to have something more than Compassion for the Misfortune of this Stranger, whom one might judge, by his noble

ble Air and Dress, to be of the first Quality; and as *Casilda* appear'd to be equally concern'd, *Leonida* did not so much wonder at the Effects it produc'd in her.

Oh! what pity wou'd it be (cry'd *Leonida*, looking at *Casilda*) shou'd this Stranger die; but what hopes can one have of his Life? It is possible, he is now expiring. In saying this, she sprinkl'd Water on his Face, and laid his Head on her Knees, whilst *Casilda* caus'd a sort of Carriage to be made with the Branches of a Tree; at last fetching a Sigh, he open'd his Eyes, and perceiving *Leonida*, made an Effort to speak to her; but his Spirits being wasted, he fell into a Swoon, which gave them reason to believe his Life was in danger.

*Leonida* and *Casilda* (whom I must now call *Felicia* and *Beatricia*,) when the Carriage was finish'd, order'd their Servants to lay the Stranger on it, and thus they convey'd him to their House, in great Silence, being perplex'd with such a multitude of Thoughts, as wou'd not admit of any Interruption. As soon as they were there, they sent to *Carmona* for a Surgeon, who after having probed his Wounds, told them they were not Mortal: This agreeable News chang'd the Scene of Sorrow, into that of Joy. *Felicia* went to his Bed-side, and by this time he had recover'd his Speech, which he imploy'd in returning Thanks for her Generosity. I can no longer deplore (said he, in a feeble Voice) the dismal Adventure that had happen'd to me, since it gives me an Opportunity of knowing the moſt deſerving Perſon in the World; but I fear, Madam, my being in your Houſe may incommode you, which extremely leſſens the Satisfaction I ſhou'd have to be where you are: In ſaying theſe Words, he look'd at her with ſo much Admiration and Pleaſure, that had ſhe underſtood the Language of his Eyes, ſhe wou'd have eaſily gueſs'd at the Motions of his Heart. Do not be uneaſy, Sir (reply'd ſhe) you ſhall want for no Aſſiſtance, nor have reaſon to apprehend we ſee you here with Diſpleaſure; you are now in a Condition wherein Silence and Reſt are equally neceſſary, which Reaſon induces me to leave you: with that, ſhe retir'd, and left *Beatricia* behind her; who, as ſoon as *Felicia* was gone, approach'd the Bed, and ſaid to him; Tho' may Siſter hath aſſured you how deſirous we are to be ſerviceable to you, yet I muſt repeat the ſame, and conjure you, Sir, to have no other Thought but that of recovering your Health. It will be no eaſy matter, Madam, reply'd the Prince, to recover in a Place, where the Objects I ſee, may prove more Dangerous to me, than the Wounds I have receiv'd. *Beatricia* (who did not doubt but theſe Words were addreſs'd to her) ſeem'd not to comprehend their meaning; but taking leave of him, went to *Felicia*'s Apartment, and ask'd her what the Stranger had ſaid to her. She, without diſſembling, gave her an Account of their Converſation, which very much pleas'd *Beatricia*. I muſt confeſs, ſaid ſhe, he expreſs'd himſelf more o-

blingly

bligingly to me than he did to you: These Words gave some Uneasiness to *Felicia*, without knowing from whence it proceeded.

*Beatricia* (who was in a different Disposition of Mind) propos'd to her self, that the only means to banish Don *Henriquez* from her Heart, was to yield it to another. Whatever Trouble a new Inclination may give me, thought she; it never can be equal to the Pain I endure. The Man I love, is now in the Arms of Donna *Blanca*, and all my hopes on that side are vanish'd; but in placing my Affection on some other Object it may be kindly return'd. I had Cause enough to apprehend, that *Felicia* wou'd appear more beautiful than me, in the Eyes of this lovely Stranger, but his Words have convinc'd me of the contrary, and I am resolv'd to be favourable to him, whatever may be the Event: Love is a pleasing Torment.

The Prince of *Carency* continued ill some time; and during his Illness, receiv'd daily Instances of the Generosity of these Ladies, particularly *Felicia*'s obliging Behaviour to him (on all occasions) made him desirous to express his Gratitude. He began to think his Preservation was chiefly owing to her tender Care, and by Degrees fell desperately in Love, which threw into the following Reflections: How difficult a Task will it be, to make an Impression on that unpractis'd Heart? Her modest Looks, and the Blushes which cover her Cheeks, every time I cast my Eyes on her, evince

evince how little she his acquainted with Love; and dare I flatter my self with succeeding in such an Attempt? No, I must not hope for so great a Favour from Fortune. I was belov'd at *Nicopolis* by a Person I never knew; I no sooner became Captive to the Charms of a Lady at *Genoa*, but Death snatch'd the dear Object from me; and lately as I arriv'd at *Villa-Real* with a Resolution to marry *Leonida*, I was inform'd of her Flight and Aversion to me. Alas! my unkind Stars were not satisfy'd to afflict me with all these Misfortunes. They have sent me a greater one; *Leonora*'s Passion for me! Her desperate Rage caus'd me to be treated in this barbarous manner; and her Cruelty wou'd still threaten my Days with the greatest Dangers, were she inform'd that I had escap'd, and was now in this Place; but Oh! how can I resolve to leave *Felicia*, who is already more dear to me, than the Life I wou'd endeavour to preserve? All I can do in this distressed State, is to change my Name: I am inclin'd to believe, that as I was taken for the Count of *La Vagne* at *Genoa*, I may pass for the same here, where I am not known. If it be my good Fortune to render my Sentiments agreeable to this lovely Charmer, I shall never wish for a greater Blessing. I do not doubt but she has an Affection for her Sister, therefore I must address my self to her, and obtain Favour, if possible by her means. The Prince us'd often to entertain himself after this manner, betwixt Hope and Fear.

*Beatricia*

*Beatricia* one Morning rose earlier than *Felicia*, and went to see the Prince, who was awake, and had rested very ill all Night. Assoon as he saw her enter the Chamber, he thank'd her for so obliging a Care, and told her, he hop'd she had repos'd much better than he had done. I must confess, Sir, said she, I have felt some Uneasiness, which I must lay to your Charge, since it proceeds from the Curiosity I have to know who you are, and the Uncertainty I am in of being satisfy'd on that Subject. You judge very unfavourably of my Gratitude, Madam, reply'd the Prince, if you think me capable of not obeying your Commands. I am of *Genoa*, and of the House of *Fiesque*; my Title is the Count of *La Vagne*; I have been some Years in my Travels, and as I was riding thro' the neighbouring Forest, in my Way to *Seville*, I was assaulted by Robbers: I did my Endeavour to resist them, but their Number overpower'd me, and left me, Madam, in the Condition you saw me. I know your Family, my Lord, reply'd *Beatricia*, and cou'd have judg'd in seeing you, that your Extraction was illustrious. The Count of *La Vagne* (for now I must give that Title to the Prince of *Carency*) interrupted her, to enquire after *Felicia*, but with a kind of Impatience, which did not very much please *Beatricia*, who in a cold manner, made Answer, she had not as yet seen her. As she was speaking, the Surgeon came in to the dress Prince's Wounds, so she thought fit to retire. She went directly from thence to *Felicia*'s Apartment, who was
just

just rising. What, said she to *Beatricia*, dress'd already! How comes it, Sister, you are up so early! I can give you no other Reason, reply'd she, only I was asham'd to lie a Bed so fine a Morning: But will you believe I have been to visit the Stranger, and that I know his Name and Country. You may as well say, interrupted *Felicica*, that you know also the Secrets of his Heart. No, reply'd *Beatricia* smiling, I am very sincere, and can assure you, our Conversation ended with his acquainting me, that he is of *Genoa*, and is call'd the Count of *La Vagne*. As you are to visit him next, perhaps you may learn something more. I have not so much Curiosity as you imagine, reply'd *Felicia*, and I fancy I shall trouble him but very little with my Presence. Accordingly she did not go into the Prince's Chamber till late in the Evening, being then inform'd, he was very ill; for his Uneasiness at not seeing her all that Day, and the Pain occasion'd by his Wounds, had thrown him into a violent Fever. As soon as she approach'd his Bed, he look'd at her with much Tenderness, and said, I flatter'd my self more than I ought to have done, Madam, in thinking the Condition I am in, had mov'd your Pity, since I find at present, nothing touch'd you but the sad Aspect of a dying Man, pierc'd with Wounds, and lying in a Sea of Blood. You abandon me, charming *Felicia*, and take no Care to preserve the Life of an unhappy Wretch, who is indebted to you alone, for the small Share

he

he has left of it. I would not incommode you with a Visit, my Lord, reply'd *Felicia*, my Sister having told me this Morning, that in the State you are in, nothing was more necessary than Repose. No, no, Madam, (said he, interrupting her) you have not thought on me. Donna *Beatricia* did not hinder you from coming to see me; your Eyes convince me of the Truth, and you only wish my Recovery, to banish me your Presence for ever. He said this with an Air so moving, that she cou'd not help showing in her Looks more Affection, than Indifferency. You have been here so little a while, reply'd she, that I hardly have had time to consult my Inclinations, yet give me leave to assure you, that I find nothing in them to your Prejudice; and shou'd very much regret my having known you, if I thought in leaving this Place, you wou'd entirely forget me. She express'd these last Words blushing, and with some Fear, which charm'd the Prince, who was going to make his Retributions, when *Beatricia* enter'd the Chamber, in some Disorder: One of my Women, my Lord, said she, who is just return'd from walking in the Forest, found this Picture in the same Place where we first saw you. I suppose it is yours, and the Person it represents, is too charming, not to merit all your Affection. The Prince told her, it was true, the Picture had been recommended to his Care, and receiv'd it with a deep Sigh. It was that which *Olympia Doria* had presented to him. This gave much Uneasiness to *Felicia*, *tia*, who cou'd not help defiring to fee it, but had hardly turn'd her Eyes on it, when her Mind was fill'd with Trouble; which to conceal, fhe retired to her Clofet, where being alone: I thought, faid fhe, I had only *Cafilda* to fear; but alas! my Fate is much more fevere; for certainly the Perfon he loves is the moft beautiful Creature in the World, and his Paffion is return'd, fince fhe has given him her Picture. If he fhou'd ceafe to love her on my Account, it would be a Perfidioufnefs that might give me room to fear in my turn a refembling Deftiny; and if he is conftant to her, what can I hope? She yielded her felf up to thefe fad Reflections, and leaving them for others more tormenting: Oh! continued fhe, cou'd any thing be more fatal than this laft Adventure? I flew from the Prince of *Carency*, becaufe my Parents wou'd have me marry contrary to my Inclination. I thought my felf fafe in this Foreft, where I only apprehended to meet with wild Beafts; but thefe fierce Animals have done me no harm: It is a Stranger, a dying Man, that has deprived me of my Peace, and made me acquainted with Sentiments, I thought *Leonida*'s Heart incapable of receiving. A fhower of Tears attended thefe Words, and fhe refolv'd never more to fee this dangerous Cavalier; for which reafon fhe feign'd an Indifpofition, and confin'd her felf to her Bed; but cou'd not help enquiring after the Count, who was now extremely ill. His Fever was very much increas'd by his not feeing *Felicia*,

and

and his anxious Reflections so tormented him, that he thought of nothing but Death.

He was in evident danger, when *Beatricia* enter'd *Felicia*'s Chamber all in Tears. There are no hopes left Sister, cry'd she; the unhappy Count is dying. If you have a mind to see him before he expires, you have no time to lose. *Felicia* was not prepar'd for this disagreeable News, which had like to have thrown her into a Swoon; but being a little recover'd, she repented the obstinate Resolution she had made, to see him no more. She thought now she was going to lose him for ever, and that such a Loss wou'd make her the most unfortunate Person in the World. Ye Powers above (cry'd she going towards his Apartment) give me the Count of *La Vagne*, were he never to love me, shou'd he even hate me, let him live.

She ran into his Chamber whilst he was in a fainting Fit; his Eyes were shut, and he had neither Voice nor Pulse. She approach'd him trembling, and raising his Head, laid it on her Bosom, bathed his Face with Tears, and at that Instant was more to be deplor'd than him she lamented. At last he fetch'd a deep Sigh, and opening his Eyes, was transported to find his dear *Felicia* near him, and so touch'd at his Illness: He look'd languishing at her, and making an Effort to speak; Ah! divine *Felicia*, said he, is it you that gives me Assistance, and are you come to save me from Death? You need no longer fear, for a Life

I

I cannot lose, since its Preservation is become your Concern. My Lord, reply'd she, (low enough to be heard only by him) believe me, your Life is very dear to me, and I wish nothing more than its continuance. If you knew what you have made me suffer, you ———. Here *Beatricia* interrupted them by her Presence, so they cou'd not pursue their Discourse: But these few Words produc'd such wonderful Effects in the Count, that he daily recover'd.

How much were these Lovers to be pitied, not knowing each other? Chance had contriv'd to make them meet, yet it was their unhappy Destiny, not to enjoy a Blessing for which they wou'd have sacrific'd every Thing. Such is the Misfortune of some Persons, who purchase the most innocent Pleasures at the Expence of a thousand Torments. *Felicia*, accompany'd by her Sister, went often to see the Count, who observ'd the Care she took, never to be alone with him; but he could not desire *Beatricia* to give him an Opportunity of entertaining *Felicia*; for tho' of all Mankind he had the least Vanity, yet he perceiv'd by her Looks and Expressions, that she had some favourable Thoughts of him, and consequently an improper Person for a Confidant. But one Evening, hearing she was gone into the Forest without her Sister, he caus'd himself to be dress'd; and tho' he had hardly Strength enough to walk, yet went to *Felicia*'s Apartment.

She

She cou'd not help being very much surprized, when she saw the Count, who fell at her Feet without having power to speak one Word. He took her Hand and kifs'd it with such Tranfports, as exprefs'd the Motions of his Soul. *Felicia*'s diforder was not inferior to his. They looked at one another, as if they had met after a long Abfence; at laft the Count broke Silence: You have infpired me, Madam, faid he, with a Paffion fo tranfcendent, that you muft needs have perceived it in all my Actions, and I muft confefs, I thought you took fome Pity on me, but I have too much Caufe to believe the contrary, fince your Looks exprefs the utmoft Indifference. Oh! judge how uneafy I am at this cruel Uncertainty. I now come to know my Fate, and conjure you, adorable *Felicia*, to tell me what I muft expect. My Love is fuch, that nothing can ever make it change, and were I Sovereign of the Univerfe, I would lay it at your Feet: Here he was filent, and *Felicia* reply'd with as much Grace, as Modefty; My Concern was fo great whilft you were fpeaking, my Lord, that I did not confider you were on your Knees. I beg you will rife if you are defirous I fhould fay any thing to you. He obey'd her Commands, but fear'd to caft his Eyes on her, being like a Man, who expected to hear the Sentence of his Death. We are both in a diforder, faid fhe, which we might have avoided, had you not fpoke to me of your Paffion. I muft confefs, my Lord, to my Shame, that the same Inclination which engag'd you to entertain me, has prevailed with me to hear you. What more can I say of my Weakness (continued she blushing?) I discovered part of your Sentiments, and endeavoured in vain to conceal mine. I had never lov'd any thing before, and my Stars have decreed you should become agreeable to me? yet do not think to take any Advantage from so sincere a Confession, since I declare my Mind this time, with a Resolution never to speak to you more; but without having a desire to penetrate into the Cause, I cannot help telling you the Fear I am in, of being made a Sacrifice to another, whom, perhaps, you might love better than me. Oh Madam! cry'd the Count, (in a Rapture) judge better of a Man whom you have just loaded with your Favours, and do not suspect Ingratitude from a Heart, that bears your Image; be assured, a Person who sighs for you, can never think of any other Object. What have not I to fear, reply'd she, from the Lady, whose Picture you so much esteem. That shall never give you the least trouble, said the amorous Count, (presenting it to her) here it is; keep it as an Evincement of my Fidelity. *Felicia* was touched at so great a Proof of his Passion, and express'd much Satisfaction in receiving it, then desired him to retire, apprehending, that his being up so long, might do him a Prejudice, and whatever Violence he did his Inclinations, he could not refuse obeying her.

As

As soon as he was gone, she reflected on all that had pass'd. What! *Leonida*, said she, are you not content with hearing a Declaration, which you ought to have declin'd, but also have own'd to a Stranger that you could love him? You, who are engag'd to the Prince of *Carency*, can you be so easily captivated, and weak enough to confess your Affection for another? You have already shown your Jealousy, which is a certain Proof of a violent Passion; what Judgment will the Count form from such a Behaviour? You are going to lose his Heart, and become a disgrace to your Sex. Oh unfortunate Creature! what must you do to attone for a Fault, which seems of so high a Nature? These Thoughts gave her the deepest Concern, and her Face was bathed with Tears when *Beatricia* returned; but she took so much Care to hide them, that they were not perceiv'd.

The Count being retired to his Chamber, pass'd his time the most agreeably in the World, when he call'd to mind *Felicia*'s Generosity, but could hardly flatter himself with the Success he wish'd for. Oh Love! said he, will you at last change my Pain into Pleasure, and repair the Ills you have done me? Amiable *Felicia* has heard me, and protested I was not indifferent to her. Heavens! let us be for ever united, that our good or ill Fortune may equally affect us. Day began to appear before he could close his Eyes; he rose, and went to see *Felicia*, who was alone in her Closet, re-

flecting

flecting on that, which had rack'd her Imagination all Night: She received the Count with much Civility, but appear'd so melancholly, that he knew not what to think of so great an Alteration. What is my Crime, Madam, said he? Have I done any think to incur your displeasure? You seem unwilling to turn your Eyes on me. Are you concerned for having given me Room to think myself the happiest of Men, and do you already regret the obliging Terms, you imploy'd Yesterday to banish my Alarms? Alass! continued he, are you resolv'd to cast me at once into Despair by so cruel a Change? No, my Lord, reply'd she (looking at him with an Air, that might convince him of the contrary) I have us'd ineffectual Means to conquer those Sentiments I discover'd to you. I wish I could see you with Indifference; but I find it is not in my Power; do not then be uneasy; I alone ought to be so. The Count transported with Love and Gratitude took *Felicia*'s Hand, and kiss'd it with all the Marks of Passion and Respect, that could be express'd on such an Occasion. *Beatricia*, being informed they were together, entered suddenly the Chamber they were in, and surprized them, just as the Count was kissing *Felicia*'s Hand. How strangely was she amaz'd at seeing this. She chang'd Colour several times, and her Eyes were animated with an uncommon Fire, which they immediately perceiv'd, tho' she endeavoured to conceal her disorder.

Their

Their Conversation turn'd on a general Subject, and from that Hour, she us'd all possible Means to prevent their entertaining one another in private: These Proceedings extremely perplex'd the Count. Divine *Felicia*, said he to her one Day) pity my Sufferings, and consider how severe a Law I am forc'd to impose on myself, when I silence a Passion, which I have had the good Fortune to render agreeable to You. What Authority has your Sister to lay so cruel a Restraint on you? I see her Uneasiness, my Lord, reply'd *Felicia*, and to show the Confidence I have in you, I will own to you, she is not my Sister, nor even related to me; I would have let you sooner into the Secret, had I found a favourable Opportunity. Oh Madam! How obliging is this Declaration, reply'd the Count, and what Reproaches do I owe myself, for not having acquainted you with the Circumstances of my Life? The Hours I pass'd in your Company were so transient, that I chose to imploy them in confessing the Power of your Charms. We both of us have err'd, my Lord, reply'd *Felicia*, in neglecting to inform each other of some particulars, which are essential to our future Felicity; yet if I may judge of your Heart by my own, it had no share in this Omission, and I promise to give you a faithful Relation of all that has pass'd from my Infancy: You will then find it is not without Cause, that I sigh sometimes, and complain of the Rigour of my Fate; but you must prepare your self to overcome a great many Difficulties, if you perſevere in your Love for the unhappy *Felicia.* Oh Madam! reply'd he, no Difficulties can ever alarm me; I have Love and Courage to aſſiſt me, and if you eſpouſe my Intereſt, all Things will be eaſy to me: But, ſaid ſhe, ſuppoſe I were contracted to another, what would you do? At theſe Words, the Count changed Colour. What do you tell me, Madam, cry'd he, contracted! Oh Heavens! To what Misfortunes am I doom'd? Do not afflict your ſelf, my Lord, reply'd ſhe, I am yet Miſtreſs of my Deſtiny; can you think I would receive your Addreſſes, if I had an Inclination for any other? No, ſuch a Proceeding would render my Heart unworthy of you. Theſe Aſſurances gave ſome Eaſe to the Count's Mind, who was juſt going to expreſs his Satisfaction to his charming Miſtreſs, when *Beatricia* came and troubled them with her Preſence.

Her Jealouſy was now increaſed to ſuch a degree, that ſhe was even diſtracted, when ſhe ſaw them ſpeaking to one another, and aſſoon as ſhe was alone, ſhe abandon'd herſelf to the moſt violent Deſpair. I am not belov'd, ſaid ſhe, and I flatter'd myſelf, that I had inſpired the Count with ſuch Sentiments as would have been agreeable to me, but he is entirely devoted to *Felicia.* He adores her, and ſhe triumphs over my Weakneſs. What do I ſay, continued ſhe? (after having reflected ſome time) perhaps if he were acquainted with the Motions of my Soul, he would act

another

another Part. Ah! why did I not declare my Thoughts to him, and why should I accuse him of being the Cause of my Torment, since he does not know the Indisposition I am in? I must either inform him of what I feel, or resolve to see him constant in his Passion for my Rival.

After having pass'd the greatest part of the Night in Reflections of this Nature, she rose early and sent to the Count, desiring he would meet her in the Garden. This unexpected Message gave him some Uneasiness, notwithstanding he obey'd her Orders, and as soon as she saw him, her Mind almost chang'd in relation to the Subject, that induced her to send for him. He ask'd her obligingly what were her Commands, to which she answered in these Terms; your health, My Lord, is so perfectly recovered, that I fear we shall lose you soon; and as I have some reason to be convinced our Company is not indifferent to you, I take this occasion to assure you, how pleas'd we should be to see you remain here; yet I cannot help saying, I have endeavoured in vain to discover, whether my Sister or I have the Precedency in you Affections; perhaps this Question may show my Indiscretion, but I believe you a Man of too much Honour, to leave me in an Uncertainty; therefore let your Inclinations determine in favour of either of us; I will do you all the Service in my Power, and if you make me your Confidant, it shall no ways lessen my Friendship for you.

you. The Count (who was above any dissimulation express'd much Pleasure at the Opportunity she gave him, to declare his Sentiments. Nothing can be more generous than your Proceeding, Madam, said he, and I should be unworthy of your Goodness, if I did not repay it with Sincerity. I am in Love, it is true, and you would have been the Object of it, had I not feared my Passion might offend you: Young *Felicia* has captivated my Heart, and I conjure you to favour me in my attempt on hers; I shall in return, show my Esteem and Gratitude to you for so considerable a Service. *Beatricia*, at these Words, was Thunderstruck, and would have fallen down at his Feet, were it not for a Tree that stood by, which supported her; she made a vain Effort to conceal her Grief; her Colour chang'd, and the Tears which ran from her Eyes, discovered part of her Sufferings to the Count who said many obliging Things to her by way of Consolation, and protested, he would for ever do his best Endeavours to serve her; but all he could say was not capable of giving her Satisfaction; Love requires Love, and it is, an offence of the highest degree to offer any other thing in Return.

About this time Don *Fernand Benavidez* (who was innocent of the Crime, laid to his Charge, having no more *Leonora* for his Enemy) began, after the Death of this Favourite, to be heard in his Justification; he wrote the particulars to *Cafilda*, and withal, that he was in hopes of being soon set at Liberty after which he would immediately go to see *Leonida.* This she kept secret till she had penetrated into the Sentiments of the Count; but when she found all her hopes were destroy'd, she thought of nothing but tormenting these happy Lovers in their Amour. What! said she; shall I suffer this ungrateful Man to be bless'd with the sight of my Rival, and omit acquainting my Brother with an adventure, wherein he is so much concern'd? He doats on *Leonida* whilst she loves the Count of *La Vagne,* and is equally belov'd. My Brother and I, without doubt, must be the Victims of their Passion, and he will load me with eternal Reproaches, for having admitted so dangerous a Stranger into his House; I must sacrifice him to my Revenge, for what can I expect from his Cruelty? My Sighs and Tears, had no Power to move his Pity, and since nothing can prevail with him, I will punish his Barbarity. I have but this Remedy left, and cannot flatter my despairing Soul with any other relief.

Having tormented her self with these confused Thoughts, she wrote a Letter to her Brother, wherein she gave him the Particulars relating to what she knew of the Count of *La Vagne;* telling him at the same Time, that he had conceiv'd a Passion for *Leonida,* who return'd it with Sentiments so obliging, that she believ'd it wou'd be impossible to disengage them, unless he took very secret Measures. *Benavidez* was strangely affected with this

this News, which he receiv'd the Day the Queen had order'd his Liberty. What! (said he to the Gentleman, who had accompany'd the young Ladies to his Castle) have I depriv'd the Prince of *Carency* of the Possession of this excellent Creature, to yield her to the Count of *La Vagne*: I thought I had conceal'd her in a Place so retir'd, that she wou'd have escap'd the most penetrating Spy; yet the Cruelty of my Fortune has so contriv'd it, that she shou'd find in that solitary Forest, one of the handsomest Men in the World expiring, and prevent his Fate by making his Preservation her Care, which I fear has rob'd me of *Leonida*'s Heart: My Confinement cost the Prince his Life, whose Generosity engag'd him to make his Addresses to *Leonora* with the only View of procuring my Liberty. By what Fatality, continued he, does the Count of *La Vagne* live? Is not he the same whose Death *Olympia Doria* so much deplor'd, that her Grief terminated her Days? Has he so little Gratitude, after loving a Mistress who died for him, to make a second Choice? Her Impression ought to have been everlasting, but I will punish his Inconstancy to her, and his new Passion for *Leonida*, who has made me already commit too many Crimes to leave my Felicity imperfect: I must give some Ease to my bleeding Heart, by depriving this too happy Rival of his Life. These violent Reflections were follow'd by many others, for he thought that if he kept *Leonida* longer at his House, as Chance had

had made her acquainted with the Count of *La Vagne*, a like Accident might expose her to the sight of some Persons, who knew her, and wou'd inform Don *John* of her Retreat.

Love and Jealousy wou'd not permit him to stay any Time at *Villa Real*; he had no sooner seen the Queen, and return'd her Thanks for his Liberty, but went privately to *Porto Real*, in order to dispose every Thing for the carrying off of *Leonida* to *Morocco*, where he was sure to be in high Esteem, having several Relations of great Distinction in *Barbary*.

He there made an Agreement with a Captain of a Ship, then went to his Country Seat; but stop'd first in the Forest, and sent for his Steward, to whom he gave a Letter to *Casilda*, with Orders to deliver it into her own Hands: he was not long expecting an Answer, for he saw her coming with the Man he had sent. *Benavidez* went up to her, and after having embrac'd her tenderly, sought for the most conceal'd Place to entertain her: And here they took Resolutions so contrary to the Felicity of the Count and *Leonida*, that it had like to have depriv'd them of their Lives. Oh! how far were they from foreseeing their Misfortune? since at this Time they were making Protestations of eternal Love, and little thought that *Benavidez* and his Sister were proposing Means to disappoint them.

*Casilda*

*Cafilda* told her Brother she had sufficient Reason to be convinc'd, that the Count's Addresses to *Leonida* were favourably receiv'd. I will cross their Passion (interrupted *Benavidez*, with a furious Air) I am resolv'd to seize on *Leonida*, and carry her to *Morocco*; you shall go with us, but before we part, I must sacrifice the presumptuous Count of *La Vagne* to my Resentment. What, Brother! cry'd she, (almost distracted) will you not be content to possess your Mistress, without my going with you to a Place for which I have so great an Aversion. I do not intend to do any Violence to your Inclinations, said he, in making you this Proposal; but I suppose the same Motive which invited you to abandon the Count and enter into this Retirement, may engage you to go elsewhere; nevertheless, Sister, you are under no Constraint: The only thing I desire you will do for my Satisfaction, is to contrive a Way for me to be hidden this Night in the Count's Chamber, that I may have the Pleasure of striking a Heart that dares adore *Leonida*. Suspend your Design, Barbarian, (interrupted *Cafilda* in her first Transports) I am as little able to hear you as second your Cruelty; the Count's Life shall not be in your Power till your have taken away mine. What do you say, Sister, (cry'd *Benavidez*, extremely surpriz'd?) I can hardly believe what I hear. Is it possible, that you love this Stranger, and have already forgot *Hinriquez* ? Are you destin'd ever to make Choice of ungrateful

Men;

Men; remember how your firſt Lover treated you, and what you are to expect from this? Do you imagine, that after having a Paſſion for *Leonida*, and being belov'd by her, he can change his Mind in favour of you? This is very diſobliging, reply'd *Caſilda*, but I hope every thing, and flatter my ſelf with his Love, if he ſees her no more. Seize on her, fly with her and leave me here with him. Will it be conſiſtent with your Honour to ſtay alone with the Count, ſaid he? What will the Count think of it, if once it is known at *Villa Real?* They will think nothing to my Prejudice, re- ply'd ſhe; the Count muſt be mine, or I re- tire into a Monaſtry, ſo that I ſhall have but little Reaſon to be concern'd at the World's Opinion, whether good or ill Fortune attends me. Do you conſider, Siſter, ſaid *Benavidez*, that your Affection for my Rival, may put him hereafter in a Condition to diſpute *Leoni- da* with me? I wou'd have ſhown his Corps to her defac'd with Wounds, and her hopes being deſtroy'd by his Death, ſhe wou'd eaſily conſent to make me happy. What an Error it is, reply'd *Caſilda*, to ſuppoſe that ſo horrid a Scene cou'd introduce you into her Favour; ſhe wou'd ever reproach you of the greateſt Cruelty; yet if you believe his Death will ſerve your Deſigns, ſay you have kill'd him, tho' its uncommon to boaſt of ſuch a Fact, were it even true.

*Benavidez* perceiving his Siſter lov'd the Count too paſſionately to conſent to ſo cruel
an

an Action, in Compliance to her, as well as out of fear of her making any Discovery, wou'd no longer infist upon it. To shew my Affection for you, dear *Cafilda*, said he, I submit to your Pleasure, only oblige me in being secret. He had brought with him three Men devoted to his Interest, who he was sure cou'd carry off *Leonida*, without being discover'd; therefore having taken effectual Measures with *Cafilda*, the Design was soon executed to his Satisfaction.

That Evening his Sister invited *Leonida* to take a Turn in the Park, and by degrees led her into an Alley, which convey'd them towards the Forest; till at last, Night coming on, and *Leonida* hearing a Noise, was going to retire when she was seiz'd by *Benavidez* and his Men: In spite of the Fright she was in, she endeavour'd to disengage her self from them, and having sufficient room to believe it was a Plot against her, she cry'd out, repeating several Times the Count of *La Vagne*'s Name, and call'd him to her Succour; but alas, he did not suspect his *Felicia* was in danger, who was carry'd off, and gone a great way before he heard of her, or his own Misfortune. *Cafilda* took care the Count shou'd know nothing that Night of what had pass'd, to prevent his pursuing her Brother; but sent to him the next Morning, and desir'd he wou'd come into her Apartment, having an Affair of Consequence to communicate to him. As soon as he enter'd her Chamber, she affected to be melan-

melancholy; There is no Friendship, said she, but Love can dissolve: You were Witness, my Lord, of that between *Felicia* and Me: She is not my Sister, I must confess, yet I never cou'd have imagin'd she wou'd abandon me in such a manner. Read this Letter which she left on her Toilet; it was just now deliver'd to me; you will find it equally regards us. The Count in taking it, express'd as much Uneasiness, as if he had known it to be a Messenger of ill News; it was written in these Terms.

*THE Affection you have for your Brother, and your Fears of exposing him to any Danger, were the Motives that hinder'd me from acquainting you sooner, with his and my Design. You certainly wou'd have oppos'd it, had you known I am going away with him this Night. I cou'd wish, Sister, your Love for me wou'd invite you to come to us at* Jaën; *you may assure your self, I shou'd be over-joy'd to see you, and hear, that your Sentiments for the Count of* La Vagne, *have met with a kind Return. I leave him with you, so hope you will have no Cause hereafter to complain of his Indifference. As I have a particular Esteem for him, I desire you will inform him of what you know concerning my Affairs, that he may be convinc'd, it is no more in my Power to dispose of my Heart; and remember, my dear* Casilda, *that if I made my Resolution a Secret, you ought to forgive me, since Faults of Love deserve rather Pity, than Anger.*

This

This fatal Letter threw the Count into such an Agony, that he was like a Man who felt the Tortures of an approaching Death; he turn'd pale, and all his Senses abandon'd him. *Casilda* (who was prepar'd for this dismal Scene) took care that speedy Assistance shou'd be given him, and by the Help and Force of Remedies, he soon came to himself; he open'd his Eyes, and seeing several Persons about him, made Signs to them to withdraw; which they obey'd, and left *Casilda* with him in the Chamber: He look'd at her some time, without being able to utter one Word; at last, having recover'd his Speech, he said in a feeble Accent; It was unkind in you, Madam, to acquaint me with the greatest Misfortune that cou'd ever happen to me. No, my Lord, interrupted *Casilda*, I do not deserve a Reproach; it is but reasonable you shou'd be inform'd of *Felicia*'s Sentiments; after what she has done for *Benavidez*. Who is this you name, the Prince suddenly reply'd: I name Don *Fernand Benavidez* my Brother, said she, and the Lady who went here by the Name of *Felicia* of *Leon*, is *Leonida* of *Velasco*; her Father had contracted her to the Prince of *Carency*, who is highly distinguish'd by his eminent Birth and personal Merit; but having conceiv'd a tender Affection for my Brother, she preferr'd this Retirement to the Court, and wou'd not wait the unwelcome Arrival of a Person to whom her Father had destin'd her. We came away together from *Villa Real*, and ever since, she has

has continued a mutual Correspondence with my Brother; her going away with him last Night, is an Evincement of this Truth. The Prince, at these Words, broke out into so passionate a Grief, that it wou'd have mov'd the most inhuman Heart with Pity. O cruel Fortune! cry'd he, will you never cease to persecute me? Was it then *Leonida* I saw, and to whose potent Charms I yielded, only to make me more wretched, through her Inconstancy? The ungrateful Fair betrays and flies me; and that dear Friend too, that same *Benavidez* for whom I sacrific'd my self, he is the Man who has impos'd on my Credulity; he is in Love with the Woman to whom I am promis'd, and the Traitor describ'd her to me as a Monster, to make me conceive an Aversion for her. Is this all the Reward I must expect, after having ador'd *Leonida*, and so entirely lov'd *Benavidez*? *Casilda* was in the greatest Astonishment imaginable, to hear the Prince express himself in these Terms. She easily understood by his Discourse, that he was the same Prince of the House of *Bourbon*, whom the Count of *La March* his Father had contracted to *Leonida*; but her Surprize was the greater, because she thought the Prince, not finding *Leonida* at *Villa Real*, was return'd to *France*; and as she knew nothing of his Adventure with *Leonora*, she cou'd not well conceive, by what Accident he had been attack'd in the Forest, and why he had chang'd his Name: These different Circumstances wholly employ'd her Thoughts.

The Prince, on the other side, cou'd not moderate his Grief; he was like a Person depriv'd of his Senses; what with Sighs, Tears and Menaces, no Man ever appear'd in a more deplorable Condition.

What need you, my Lord, said she, express so much Concern for *Leonida* ? She never lov'd you : you see she has prefer'd *Benavidez*, and forgets even the Rules of Modesty, to follow her Lover: Why then will you suffer so much for an ungrateful Woman, who merits not your Consideration ? Oh, Madam! cry'd the Prince, I know not what I do; my Despair is so great, that I am no longer Master of my Reason ; my Misfortunes are not to be comprehended ; I find my self betray'd by a Person, who was contracted to me from her Infancy, and by a Friend to whom I had confided the Secrets of my Soul. *Leonida*, who seem'd to approve my Passion, has deceiv'd me, and added Contempt to her Ingratitude; she knew I ador'd her, yet the perfidious Fair receiv'd my Vows, only to sacrifice them to another. Just Heaven! revenge me of this perjur'd Beauty : But what do I say, continued he, a Moment after ? I have not Resolution enough to wish her the Punishment she deserves : She is dear to me in spite of all, and I will do my utmost Endeavours to regain her. Oh! I love her, and love her to Distraction. The Force of my Resentment must fall on the Traitor *Benavidez* ; his Blood shall attone for the Affront I have receiv'd. You might do what you say, my Lord,

Lord, interrupted *Cafilda*, if *Leonida* lov'd him lefs; but you have fufficient Caufe to believe by the Letter fhe left, and his Flight, that fhe is now marry'd to him; They are gone together to *Jaën*; Don *Alonzo*, who is Governor of that Town, and my Brother's Uncle, approves his Paffion for her, and will protect him; Believe me then, the Defign you form is impracticable. Do you think *Benavidez* wou'd have made fuch a Step, without taking all neceffary Meafures for it? Don *John* of *Velafco* is one of the greateft Men in *Spain*, and my Brother knowing his Power, has carry'd her to a Place where he defies his Enemies. His Precautions (interrupted the Prince) will be ineffectual againft me; I neither fear Danger nor Death, and if I revenge my Wrongs, I fhall die with Content.

Live, my Lord, (reply'd *Cafilda* blufhing) Oh! live for me, fince my Paffion for you is tranfcendent. Think with what Pleafure I receiv'd you into this Houfe; and tho' your Retributions were no Ways equal to the Greatnefs of the Favour, yet nothing cou'd prevent the Fatality of my Deftiny, which not only forces me to love you, but even deprives me of my Peace and Liberty. Ah, my Lord! can Sentiments fo tender make no Impreffion? My Fortune is great, and my Family one of the firft in *Caftile*; then let our Hearts be fo united as we may be for ever happy. I will leave my Friends and Relations to follow you to the utmoft Bounds of the World. While

*Cafilda* was thus declaring her Mind to the Prince, and flattering her felf with Succefs, he walked diftractedly up and down the Chamber with his Arms crofs'd, taking fo little notice of her Difcourfe, that he neither look'd at her, nor made any Anfwer; but like a Man in a violent Paffion, was leaving the Apartment, without knowing what he did, or where to direct his Courfe.

*Cafilda* (who cou'd not bear the Thoughts of lofing the Prince) had no longer Reafon in her Words or Actions, but ran and ftop'd him, with her Face drown'd in Tears. Will you go, Barbarian, faid fhe? What! will you fly me, and abandon a Woman that adores you, to follow perfidious *Leonida*? Leave her with my Brother; defpife her, and to compleat your Revenge, even forget her, fince by her Behaviour fhe has render'd her felf unworthy of your Love. My Quality is equal to hers, and what I have fuperior to her, is my Conftancy: But what do I fee? Oh Heavens! cry'd fhe (looking at him) with what Ingratitude am I rewarded? You leave me to expofe your felf to the greateft Dangers: you ——— She was going to continue her Difcourfe, when the Prince interrupted her. What wou'd you have me do, Madam, faid he? Can I love any thing but *Leonida*? and were I capable of a Change, cou'd it be in Favour of the Sifter of *Benavidez*? Ah! do you deprive me even of Hope, which is not deny'd the moft Unfortunate? (reply'd fhe, fhedding a Shower of Tears,

Tears, where Fury had no lefs a Share than Love;) but inhuman as you are, don't think to live in Peace with your Cruelty; I will find means to torment you, and make you repent the little Regard you have to my Sufferings.

The Prince did not ftay to make any Anfwer to *Cafilda,* whom he left in her Chamber, without either Strength to follow him, or Power to fpeak a Word; but was meditating on feveral violent Defigns, being divided between Love, Jealoufy, and Defpair.

After this Scene, it is not to be imagin'd the Prince wou'd remain in *Benavidez's* Houfe. He refolv'd immediately to go to *Carmona,* where he thought he might hear fomething concerning *Leonida*; and as that Town was in his way to *Jaën* (which was the Place mention'd in her Letter to *Cafilda*) he was in hopes, by a ftrict Enquiry, to difcover the Road *Benavidez* had taken. With this Defign he fet out, but cou'd not help complaining of the Adverfity of his Fortune. Can I ever flatter my felf, faid he, with the Poffeffion of a Heart, that has fo inhumanly betray'd me? What Motive cou'd induce *Leonida* to act in fo deceitful a manner? Was it only to facrifice me to *Benavidez*? No, I cannot harbour fuch injurious Thoughts of one, who appear'd fo modeft and virtuous. Then calling to mind, that fhe had told him fhe was engag'd; Why, cruel Creature, (faid he, as if he were fpeaking to her) why did not you entirely confide in me?

You are engag'd it's true, since I am the Man to whom you are contracted. We shou'd have known each other, and perhaps you might have lov'd me; but instead of acting sincerely, you have carry'd your Perfidiousness to an Extremity. You listen'd to my transcendent Passion, and flatter'd me with a Return only to make my Despair proportionable.

Had his Distraction been of a more moderate Nature, it is probable he wou'd have apprehended farther Consequences from the Fury and Resentment of *Leonora*, (for as yet he was not inform'd of her Death;) besides, he had no mind to go to *Seville*, for fear of seeing the Count of *La March*, his Brother, to whom he wou'd be oblig'd to relate his Adventure with *Leonida*, and the Error she had been guilty of, which he cou'd not resolve, being of a generous Temper, and incapable of saying any thing to the Prejudice of a Lady he lov'd so entirely.

These Obstacles at another Time wou'd have embarass'd the Prince, but in this Conjuncture, they did not in the least affect him, for his Thoughts were wholly imploy'd on the Measures he shou'd take to recover his dear *Leonida*. He arriv'd at *Carmona*, and tho' in a *Spanish* Dress, was presently known to be a Foreigner by the Fairness of his Complexion, and Colour of his Hair; he carry'd in his Countenance such Marks of Melancholy, that no Body cou'd see him without Concern. The Governour of that Place was soon acquainted with

with his Arrival; and as he had receiv'd Orders from Court, not to let any Stranger pass that Way, without Examination, hearing he was a Person of Quality and a Foreigner, out of a Compliment he paid a Visit to the Prince, who receiv'd him with so much Politeness and Grandeur, that after a short Conversation and many Offers of Service, the Governour invited him to accept of an Apartment in the Castle.

The Prince return'd his Civility in a most obliging manner, and desired to be excus'd, because his Affairs wou'd not permit him to stay above one Night at *Carmona*; but the other, unwilling to be deny'd, repeated his Importunities, and with much Difficulty, persuaded him to comply with his Request.

A noble Entertainment was prepar'd in the Castle for the Prince, who cou'd not suppress his violent Chagrin; which the Governour perceiv'd, but wou'd not enquire into the Cause. He understood by his Discourse, that his Design was to go to *Jaën*, and as he had a Son, who commanded a Company in the Citadel of that Place, and whose Name was Don *Gabriel d'Agular*, he told the Prince very obligingly, that if he approv'd of it, he wou'd write to him, in order to acquaint him with his Arrival there; and added, that if it were in his Son's power to serve him, he was satisfy'd he wou'd neglect no Opportunity of expressing his Readiness.

This free and gallant Behaviour of the Governour, engag'd the Prince to accept his Offer with the same Freedom. He knew no Body at *Jaën*; and as he wanted the Assistance of some Person in whom he cou'd confide, to enter privately the Citadel, where he thought *Benavidez* and *Leonida* were retired, he the more willingly embrac'd so favourable an Occasion. The next Day having made his Acknowledgments to the Governour for his extraordinary Favours, he took Leave of him, and left *Carmona*, but not without acquainting Don *John* of *Velasco* with what had pass'd, that he might act on his side for the Recovery of *Leonida*. Never was Surprize greater, than that which his Letters caus'd at Court; for Don *John* and his Lady were persuaded the Prince had been kill'd by *Leonora*'s Assassins. One may imagine how great was their Joy, when they heard Heaven had preserv'd him, yet it cou'd no ways alleviate their inexpressible Grief for the Loss of their Daughter. They immediately thought of means to get her away from *Jaën*, where they believ'd she was; but whilst the Prince is on his Journey thither, let us see what becomes of unfortunate *Leonida*.

As soon as Don *Fernand Benavidez* had brought her out of the Park, he sat her on Horseback before him, and held her with such Force, that all the Efforts she made to disengage herself, were in vain. She cry'd out, and implor'd Heaven and Earth for Succour. She call'd the Count of *La Vagne* to her Assistance, but her Cries and Tears had no Power. He led

led her through uncommon Ways, over Mountains and Rocks, where the Ecchoes answering her Complaints, rather augmented her Sorrow, than lessen'd it.

Whoever you be, said she to *Benavidez*, you are the most unjust of Mortals, to use this Violence with me. I never gave any One Cause to treat me after so cruel a manner. Why will you take Pleasure in disturbing the Peace of my Life? By what Authority do you act thus? If my Father has sent you, I am dispos'd to obey his Orders, without being under the Necessity of travelling all Night with a Troop of Men, as if I were a Criminal. Oh! let us stop (continued she, seeing he made no Answer) I conjure you, carry me back to the Place where you found me; you need not apprehend my Escape, since I am alone there with a young Lady, whose Brother is now Prisoner at *Villa Real*, and were he at Home, he has too great a Respect for my Family, to oppose my Father's Commands. Here her Tears interrupted her Complaint, and forc'd her to be some time silent. She began to be persuaded, these Men were come to take her away by the Order of Don *John*, who she thought had been inform'd of the Place of her Retreat, and of the Count of *La Vagne's* being there. She tenderly regretted the Absence of her Lover. If he knew (said she to herself) where they are carrying me, I shou'd have less reason to be uneasy; for certainly he wou'd soon find means to see me. His Birth and Merit

Merit are sufficient Recommendations to intitle him to my Father's Favour, who being once convinc'd of the Aversion the Prince of *Carency* and I have to each other, wou'd undoubtedly consent to break off the Match, and yield me to the Count. Thus she travell'd all Night, entertaining herself with Reflections of this Quality.

As soon as *Aurora* display'd her gilded Beams, *Leonida* endeavour'd to know the Person who was carrying her off; But Heavens! cou'd any surprize be equal to her's when she saw it was *Benavidez*? At first she had not power to speak, her Tears prevented her Utterance, whilst a Thousand different Ideas presented themselves to her Mind. She at last cry'd aloud, (no longer doubting of her Misfortune) are you become my Enemy Don *Fernand*? you who offer'd me your House to conceal me, and in whom I had that Confidence. Do you thus break through the Laws of Hospitality, and force me away in this manner?— Don't accuse me unheard, Divine *Leonida*, (said he, interrupting her) my Passion for you wou'd never have shin'd, had you been destin'd to the Prince of *Carency* by your own Inclination, as you are by the Will of your Parents. I saw with delight the Birth of your Aversion for him, which flatter'd me, that after procuring you a Retreat from the Persecutions of your Father, whose Authority and Resentment are not to be oppos'd, your Justice wou'd oblige you to turn your Eyes on me, and incline you to
think,

think, I was not so ardently devoted to your Service, without loving you to Distraction; but whilst I was an unfortunate Prisoner, depriv'd of all that cou'd give me Pleasure, you were entertaining the Count of *La Vagne*, whose Life you had sav'd: I was inform'd of his Passion for you, and of the favourable Reception you gave him. What! were all my Pains and Cares design'd for this Stranger; and did I expose myself for no other reason, but to procure him an Opportunity of declaring his Love to you? Was there ever a Destiny more unaccountable? I conjure you, Madam, to cease tormenting your self; you have no just Cause to grieve. It is not your Father's House you regret, neither is it the Prince of *Carency*, since your Disdain for him is so great, that you chose rather to quit the Court, than see him; but you sigh for the Count of *La Vagne*, his Absence occasions all these Tears; what Madam! ought you not to prefer me to him? Do me Justice; suspend your Resentment, and you will approve my Conduct. Ah! cry'd *Leonida*, your Offence is too great; you have behav'd yourself like a Traytor, and you must expect nothing but my Hatred, and that of my Family. If it be true you love me, as you say you do, use other means to gain my Favour: Restore me my Liberty, and let me have the disposing of my Destiny; you may afterward dispute your Title to me with the Count, and deserve by your Services that Precedency, which you apprehend

prehend I give him. You have one Advantage he has not, which is my being already under fome Obligations to you, and fo far I acknowledge my Gratitude; therefore I wou'd not have you forfeit the Efteem due to fo peculiar a Merit; but don't think you fhall ever prevail with me, by Force, or by a difrefpectful Behaviour; your prefent Conduct is a fufficient Motive to render you odious to me; yet upon Condition, you will obey me, I am willing to forget your Offence, and pardon the Rafhnefs of a Paffion, which perhaps you were not Mafter of.

I penetrate into your Thoughts too well, Madam, (reply'd *Benavidez*) to let my felf be deceiv'd by a Difcourfe, you wou'd not have made me, had you been at Liberty to declare your Sentiments. The Count has an indifputable Advantage over me; he has had the good Fortune to acquire your Favour, but as for my part, you ever look'd on me with all the Indifferency imaginable: Your Words bear more Policy, than good Nature, and your Heart fpeak's for my Rival; befides, do you think me credulous enough to believe, your Anger can be fo eafily appeas'd. No, I ought not to run the hazard of lofing a Treafure, I have already in my Poffeffion. Therefore Madam, for my Paffion's fake, pardon my not complying with your Requeft; refolve to be mine, fince by that means you can render me the happieft of Mankind. I will go with you to any part of the World, You fhall be Miftrefs tress of your Destiny and mine; then I will obey you for ever.

Ah! Barbarian, (cry'd *Leonida*, in a mournful Accent) I wou'd sooner sacrifice a Thousand Lives, if I had 'em, than consent to be yours. It is not without reason, you suspected my Words. I had no other Design in speaking to you, as I did, but that of retrieving my Liberty, and flying you as the cruelest of my Enemies. I see nothing can deceive a Man who is too great a Master of Dissimulation, not to dive into the Thoughts of others. You may easily judge, that as my Aversion for you is infinite, so is my Resentment of the Injury you do me; but you shall not glory long in your Treachery: I had rather cast my self into the Arms of Death, tho' never so dreadful, than live with you, ; yes, I can find the Way to die, and in dying, meet with too great a Felicity in my despairing Condition.

Having spoke these Words with much Anger and Emotion, she wou'd not say any more, nor even look at him, tho' he us'd his utmost Endeavours to appease her. This was the deplorable State she was in, when *Benavidez* embark'd with her at *Porto-Real*, in order to sail for *Morocco*, which Passage was then very dangerous, because the *Spaniards* having lately defeated the King of *Tunis*'s Fleet, the *Barbarians* were so enrag'd, that they swore they wou'd be reveng'd, and give no Quarter to any *Spanish* Vessel.

*Leonida* was hardly embark'd, when a handsome young Lady came to her in a respectful manner;

manner; her Features were very regular, and her Countenance so sweet and agreeable, that *Leonida*, tho' her Grief was inexpressible, fix'd her Eyes on her with a secret Pleasure. Her Name was *Inea*; she was Daughter to the Captain of the Ship, and shew'd an extraordinary Desire to be serviceable to our Distressed Fair, in her Affliction. I am extreamly oblig'd to you (said *Leonida* to her) for the Concern you express, but I beg you will give yourself no farther Trouble; The Condition I am in, neither lets me seek, nor wish for Relief: Oh! leave me to my Despair, since nothing but Death can ease me. I have no Design to displease you, Madam, reply'd *Inea*, but I think my self under an Obligation to serve you, in all that lies in my power. I can easily perceive your Trouble is exceeding, and that your Thoughts are entirely imploy'd on some great Disaster; but I am persuaded, we ought never to dispair, since the cruelest Fate may receive a favourable Change. Charming *Inea*, interrupted *Leonida*, (having heard her Name) I am almost without hopes. We are bound for *Africa*, and the Traytor who has forc'd me away, is carrying me into a Kingdom where he has great Power. Alas, who is it that will come to my help? Neither my Relations, nor Friends know any thing of my Misfortune; no body is acquainted with it, but a Woman, who is even as perfidious as himself. These Words made her call to mind *Casilda*; and so fatal a Remembrance, occasion'd her to shed a
Torrent

rent of Tears. O Traytress! said she, (as if she were present) what have I done to you, to deserve this from your Hands? 'Tis you that help'd your Brother to carry me off, and by your wicked Contrivance, I am now come to this Disgrace: You have ill rewarded the Affection I had for you. I hardly suffer'd the Count of *La Vagne* to make Professions of Love to me, because I knew you had a Passion for him, and cou'd I have dispos'd of his and my Destiny, I wou'd not have given you the least Uneasiness. You had no such generous Sentiments for me; it was by your means, your Brother knew the Affection I had for this Stranger, and at a time, that you pretended you were not deceiving me; by your false Caresses, you drew from me all my Secrets, which you have ungratefully abus'd, and only sought my Ruin by such a Discovery. She pronounc'd these Words with a Passion justly inspir'd, and thought by unloading her Mind, she might give some Ease to her over-burthen'd Heart.

*Benavidez* flattering himself with a successful Voyage, whenever he spoke to *Leonida*, entertain'd her with his Passion, and said, he hop'd that as she saw a Necessity of submitting to her Fate, she wou'd consent to make him happy. This Discourse she heard with Contempt, and had so little Regard for his Sighs, Tears and Menaces, that she never turn'd her Eyes on him, but was thinking how she cou'd escape the Hands of her Ravisher, which she
wou'd

wou'd have couragiously done by chufing Death, had not the Sentiments of Religion oppos'd fo cruel a Refolution. As *Benavidez* knew his Prefence was odious to her, he feldom appear'd; but was in hopes, time wou'd make an Alteration in his Favour, and propos'd, as foon as they were arriv'd at *Morocco*, to find means to make her obey him, if he was not fortunate enough to render himfelf agreeable to her.

The Wind being fair, they foon reach'd the Streights of *Gibraltar*, and enter'd the *Mediterrean*, where having fail'd fome time, the Seamen fhouted for Joy in feeing the Coaft of *Africa*, and did not doubt, but they fhou'd make the Land in a few Hours. *Leonida* at this News lamented her unhappy State; fhe went upon Deck, and cafting her melancholy Eyes over the vaft Ocean; I am looking into the Skies (faid fhe to *Inea*) to fee whether I can difcover any dark Cloud, or Sign of an approaching Storm; I wifh you were not with me in this Ship, then fhou'd I be the more willing to perifh here: But alas! how calm is the Sea, and how ferene the Air? We fhall foon reach *Africa*, and I have nothing left my wearied Soul, but cruel Defpair. Her Head was leaning on one of her Hands, and her Neck bathed with Tears that ran from her beauteous Eyes. In this Pofture *Inea* was endeavouring to give her fome Confolation, when fuddenly fhe cry'd, O Heavens here are too great Ships coming up to us under full fail; how unfortunate fhou'd we

be

be, if they were Enemies? These Ships belong'd to the Queen of *Fez*, and had discover'd by the Flag of *Benavidez*'s Ship, that they were *Spaniards*, which was a sufficient Motive to attack them, War being declar'd at that time between the two Nations; they came up to them, and tho' there was a great Inequality of Force, yet the Captain wou'd not surrender without fighting; *Benavidez* seconded him in his Defence with all the Courage imaginable. It distracted him to think, he was going to lose a Person he lov'd more than Life, and lose her in such a manner; since it wou'd either be by his Death, or her Captivity.

These dismal Thoughts made him believe, he shou'd have power enough to defend his Mistress; you shall see this Day, Madam, said he, whether I deserve to be preferr'd to the Count of *La Vagne*: I will sacrifice the last drop of my Blood to deliver you from the Danger, you are threaten'd with; but if I dye, Adorable *Leonida*, remember I dye for you; and that, had not my Passion been the Cause, I wou'd not have committed those Crimes, for which I have incurr'd your Aversion.

I don't think (said she, with an Air as full of Pride, as Coldness) that I am any ways oblig'd to thank you for what you are going to act in my Defence. I cannot fall into Hands more barbarous, nor more odious to me, than your's. *Benavidez* had no time to make her an Answer; he ran above Deck, and did such Actions as one wou'd have though incredible, had he

L.  burn'd

burn'd with a milder Paſſion; but this brave *Spaniard* was not long able to ſuſtain the overpowering Force of the *Moors*: Thoſe that cou'd have ſeconded his Courage, were already wounded; and as he was alſo pierc'd with Wounds, he was forc'd at laſt to yield, and let his feeble Body take Place among the Enemies, he had juſt ſacrific'd to his Rage.

The young Prince *Abelhamar*, who had juſt fought him, admiring his Courage, did not ſee his approaching End, without ſome Concern; he commanded that nothing ſhou'd be neglected to relieve him, and was going to ſpeak to him, when he was inform'd, that ſeveral Ladies were found in the Cabbin. *Leonida* appear'd among them like a Queen in the midſt of her Subjects; he was ſurpriz'd at her ſuperior Beauty, and tho' Fear was ſtill painted in her Face, and her Eyes had leſs Power than uſual, yet her Charms had ſo great an Influence, that the Prince from a Conqueror became almoſt a Captive. *Benavidez* knew her tho' dying, and made an Effort to riſe, and ſpeak to her. You are reveng'd, Madam, ſaid he, of an unfortunate Man, who never could have been capable of diſpleaſing you, had not his Paſſion for you been proportionable to his Offence. Don't envy me the Conſolation of believing, my Memory will not be odious to you, and that the Loſs of my Life may attone for my Crime.

*Leonida*, mov'd at ſo melancholy a Sight, and her own Condition together, cou'd not reſtrain
her

## of CARENCY. 147

her Tears. I pardon you, *Don Fernand*, said she, the Injury you have done me, and was never cruel enough to wish your Death; she said no more, seeing his Eyes were closing, and that Paleness had overspread his Face. This new Scene of Misfortunes afflicted her extremely, and gave her Room to fear, the Danger which now threaten'd her was far greater than that she had escap'd. She saw herself a Slave to the cruelest Enemies of the *Spaniards*, and was well inform'd, *Don John* her Father had once been a Terrour to those Barbarians, which made her believe, were she known, her Captivity wou'd be the more rigorous.

Whilst she was fill'd with these Reflections, young *Abelhamar* look'd on her, rather as a Divinity than a human Creature; and tho' the Admiral commanded in Chief, yet as Prince of the Blood he had all the Deference paid him, that was due to his Quality. He approach'd *Leonida*, whom he address'd in a most obliging manner, saying, she shou'd have no Reason to deplore her Fate, and promis'd to use all his Interest with the Queen of *Fez*, to restore her to her lost Liberty. He spoke *Spanish* very well, and *Leonida* return'd him Thanks for the Compassion he shew'd to her Misfortune.

Since the Condition I am in, my Lord, said she, inspires you with Pity, I beg you will let me know my Fate. You shall be obey'd, Madam, reply'd *Abelhamar*, as soon as you go on

Board the Admiral; for the miserable Objects, that present themselves to you here, only increase your Melancholy; he then gave her his Hand, and conducted her on Board the other Ship.

All the Women who were taken with *Leonida*, follow'd her, in hopes that by her means they might be delivered from the Captivity, which threaten'd them. As soon as she was in the Cabbin, *Abelhamar* spoke to her in these Terms; You seem uneasy, Madam, to know your Destiny; were it in my Power, I wou'd soon resign to you the Disposal of it, and esteem myself happy in serving you. I am sorry my ill Fortune obliges me to comply with the Admiral, who, I must inform you, has given Orders for us to return to *Sallee* the Capital of the Kingdom of *Fez*, where you will be presented to the Sultaness *Celima*: This Princess is my first Cousin; her Father had her brought up in a Castle by the Seaside, and one Day as she was walking on the Shore, attended only by her Women, some Corsairs, who were at a Distance, perceiving her, landed suddenly, and finding she was very handsom, took her and carry'd her to *Bajazet*, who rewarded 'em considerably for their Present.

This Emperor of the *Turks*, in spight of his natural Haughtiness, became distractedly in Love with this Princess, whose Charms were so transcendent, that she receiv'd the greatest Marks of Distinction from the proudest Prince in the World.

World. *Celima* made her Father acquainted with her Fate, who, taking Advantage of the Influence she had over the Emperor, prevail'd with him to lend him Men and Money, in order to dethrone my Father, who then poffefs'd the Crown by his Birth-Right, and the Laws of the Land; accordingly he not only fucceeded in the Enterprize, but even depriv'd him of his Life; and as my Youth cou'd give him no Apprehenfion, he was contented with keeping me confin'd in his Palace.

*Bajazet* carried his Arms into *Miffia*, and took *Celima* with him, who was Witnefs of the Advantages he gain'd over the *French* and *Hungarians*; but this Prince's Fortune met with a ftrange Turn; his Army was defeated by *Tamerlane* the Great, and Himfelf taken Prifoner in the Battle. *Celima*, notwithftanding his Overthrow, found Means to make her Efcape, and return'd to *Sallee*, where her Father receiv'd her with Joy proportionable to her Merit; fome Time after, he and his Son dying, the Crown fell to this Princefs, who took effectual Meafures to fecure it. It was thought at firft, fhe had a Defign to marry me, which wou'd have partly made Amends for the Wrongs I had fuffer'd from her Family, but fhe has folemnly declar'd againft Marriage, tho' Young and Handfome; and the melancholy Life fhe leads, makes People fufpect, fhe is affected with fome deep Concern, which cannot be attributed to the Captivity of *Bajazet*, fince fhe has often protefted, fhe wou'd rather be the Last of his Slaves, than the First of his Favourites; she seldom sees any Company, but has a great many beautiful Slaves, which are brought to her from all Parts of the World; and as she is extremely unwilling to restore them to their Liberty when she likes them, I very much fear you will acquire so great a Share in her Favour, that she will not part with you; I wou'd prevent this Misfortune were she less absolute, but she is so Jealous of my Actions, that shou'd I release you, it wou'd be sufficient to make her think me Criminal.

Alas, my Lord! interrupted *Leonida*, I am now too well satisfy'd, I shall pass the rest of my Days in an unhappy Captivity; yet I own, the Danger I have escap'd from the Power of him that forc'd me away, appear'd to me much more terrible. *Abelhamar* desir'd she wou'd acquaint him with her Adventure, which she related with all the Grace imaginable, but conceal'd *Benavidez*'s Name and her own, telling him, her's was *Felicia* of *Leon*, and so disguis'd her whole Story after the same Manner.

*Leonida* having entertain'd him some Hours, he order'd a Repast to be serv'd, then retir'd, leaving her with *Inea*, who was lamenting the Misfortune she had receiv'd by the Death of the Captain of their Ship, who had been kill'd in the Fight. Oh Father! said she, Why have I lost You, or Why did I not die with You? What are become of all my Hopes? They are vanish'd, and the Remainder of my Life will be be a continu'd Scene of Misery. I am now a Slave, and dare not flatter my self with any Relief from my Relations, who will never ranfom me: You were every Thing to me, and your paternal Love was my only Joy. Tho' *Leonida*'s Troubles were great enough, and she not in a Condition to comfort any One, her Natural Generofity and Tenderness wou'd not permit her to forget *Inea* on so sad an Occasion. She approach'd her, and embracing her said, my Dear *Inea*, do not indulge your self in these Complaints; you see I am as unhappy as you are, yet bear my Misfortunes with more Refolution. Ah Madam! reply'd *Inea*, you have less Reason to complain than I, or more Courage to support you. As to what regards me, every Thing has contributed to load me with Torments! my Father, pierc'd with Wounds, is represented to my afflicted Mind, and by his Loss, all my agreeable Hopes are for ever destroy'd. What have I not done, ye mighty Powers, cried she, to attempt this Voyage? I had at last compass'd it, and was flattering my self with Success; but you see, Madam, how little we must depend on Fortune, which binds me with Chains, at a Time that I expected to enjoy a perfect Felicity. In ending these Words, (which were often interrupted with Sighs) she turn'd her Eyes on *Leonida*, and seeing her Face was bath'd in Tears, did not doubt but her Discourfe had affected her, which gave some Ease to *Inea*. Alas! how generous you are, Madam,

dam, said she, to share my Troubles; I am so sensible of your Goodness, that I wish nothing more, than an Opportunity of giving you an Evincement of my Gratitude; you have this Day gain'd a Heart, Madam, which shall for ever be at your Devotion. The Compassion I have for you, *Inea*, said *Leonida*, you well deserve; and I protest to you, I shall much less deplore my Misfortune, if by its Means I acquire your Friendship. We are Both of us Captives, and as yet unacquainted with our future Destiny; but whatever happens, I hope we shall be together, that we may tell our Pain to each other, which is the only Thing can give Relief to the Unfortunate.

These melancholy Reflections led her into Those of a deeper Nature, to which she entirely abandon'd her self, and continu'd weeping bitterly most Part of the Night; then complaining, she cried; Why don't you come, my Dear Count of *La Vagne*, and deliver me from the Hands of our common Enemies? Oh! how agreeable shou'd I think such a Change of Fortune; after so considerable a Service, my Father cou'd not deny giving me to you, and the Prince of *Carency* wou'd be overjoy'd at having escap'd a Marriage, to which he had so great an Aversion: But alas! (continued she) How far am I from this happy State? My Infelicity is real, and I cannot acquaint you with it. I know not in what Manner the Queen of *Fez* may treat me; it's probable you will never hear of me, and Death only will ter-

terminate my Misery. She would have pass'd the rest of the Night in these sad Repinings, if *Inea* (who was much troubled for her) had not diverted her Thoughts. Pardon me, Madam, said she, for interrupting you, and let me intreat you to take a little Repose: They say, we are to land to Morrow at *Sallee*; Wou'd you appear before the Queen under so deep a Concern? Our Dependance is on your Perfections, and we believe, her Majesty will be so pleased with you, that by her Favour, you may soon contribute to our Liberty: But, Madam, were it only for your own sake, preserve those Charms, which I fancy have already touch'd Prince *Abelhamar*; fine Ladies may expect every Thing from their Beauty.

Oh! *Inea*, What do you tell me? (replied *Leonida*, fetching a deep Sigh,) How different are your Sentiments from mine? The unhappy Experience I have made of a violent Passion, gives me too just a Cause to fear the like Disaster; tho' if you consider well the Figure we shall make in the Court, where we are going, as being *Christians*, we must rather expect to be slighted by those *Barbarians*, and expos'd to their Cruelty; but there is nothing I wou'd not prefer to the Misfortune of being belov'd by *Abelhamar*. You imagin'd, my Dear *Inea*, that such a Conquest wou'd flatter my Vanity; yet for my own Satisfaction, I will sooner believe you misinterpreted his Meaning, and thought, what he acted out of Generosity, proceeded from some other Motive; however, since

since you desire it, I will endeavour to take a little Rest; in finishing these Words, she embrac'd *Inea*, and laid her self on the Bed.

Love had already made a great Progress in the Heart of *Abelhamar*, who was so taken with the Beauty of *Leonida*, (whom we must again call *Felicia*) that the Thoughts of losing her, when once presented to the Queen, gave him much Uneasiness. Is it possible (said he to *Mula*, who was his Favourite,) that I can deliver up this Divine Creature to the Power of my mortal Enemy? Why has Fate order'd, I shou'd be the Author of her Captivity? How shall I, after such a Conduct, evince her of my Sentiments? Will she not have Room to load me with Reproaches, which must be succeeded by her Aversion? He was now ruminating on a Thousand different Projects: First, he had no Mind she shou'd land at *Sallee*; then he thought how he might carry her off at his Arrival there; and after all, wou'd thus examine himself; From whence proceed these Motions? Sure I am not in Love? Have I had Time to conceive a Passion for this Fair Stranger? No, no, said he, it is only the Effect of Surprize and Admiration, which will have no farther Consequence, and I shall forget her in ceasing to see her; yet if she shou'd become dear to me, continued he, I can ask her of the Queen, who, I believe, will not refuse me One Slave out of so great a Number: *Celima*, in making me a Present of this Young Lady, whom I might have kept without her Consent, will

will think she highly obliges me, and I dare assure my self, she will be ready to give me such a Proof of her Goodness, at a Time that I have Pretensions to greater Favours.

This Opinion compos'd a little the Agitation his Mind was in, but its Calm was not long: Ah, *Mula*, said he, it is not *Celima* alone can oppose my Good Fortune; *Felicia* is the Person who must decide my Destiny. Can I flatter my self, that she is not already engag'd? If she has an Inclination for any One in *Spain*, I must not expect she will be favourable to me; I shall appear in her Eyes as a Tyrant, that forces her from the Arms of the Man she loves. *Mula* us'd all Arguments to perswade him into a better Conceit of his Personal Merit; but as in Affairs of Love, the least Uncertainty is a cruel Torment, he pass'd that Night betwixt Hope and Fear, without taking any Resolution.

At the first Appearance of Morning, he grew impatient to see *Felicia*, and hearing she was up, went to her Apartment: She receiv'd him with much Civility, but seem'd extremely dejected, which griev'd *Abelhamar*, who us'd many tender Words to express his Concern. After a short Conversation, she beg'd Leave to go upon Deck; he readily consented to her Request, being desirous to embrace any Opportunity of obliging her, and immediately order'd it to be spread with a Rich Carpet, and Cushions of Cloth of Gold, then conducted her to the Place that was prepar'd, and sat
down

down by her under a Magnificent Canopy. They were some Time without speaking to one another; for *Felicia* having turn'd her Looks towards the Coast of *Spain*, cou'd not forbear melting into a Flood of Tears, which threw *Abelhamar* into so deep a Melancholy, that he had no Power to interrupt her. At last she recover'd a little from that Excess of Grief, and broke Silence: The Respect that is due to you, my Lord, said she, ought to make me conceal my Affliction in your Presence, but your generous Compassion hinders me from laying so great a Violence on my Spirits; I must let my Sorrow take its Course, since it is the only Relief I can expect in my deplorable Condition. Here, forc'd away from my Friends, my Country, and a considerable Fortune, I am suddenly become Slave to a Queen, who perhaps will not grant me my Liberty at any Rate. Alas! my Lord, Is there no Means left to deliver me from this Misfortune? The Prince, no longer Master of his Passion, flung himself on his Knees, and taking her Hand, Divine Stranger, said he, judge better of your transcendent Charms: You are not yet arriv'd at *Sallee*, and 'tis in your Choice not to go there at all: I adore you, amiable *Felicia*, for it is impossible you shou'd not inspire something more than Love: If such Sentiments merit your Favour, here I lay my Fortune at your Feet; do not disdain the Vows of a Prince, who in Right ought now to be King of *Fez*. Oh, that I had a Crown in my

Pos-

Poſſeſſion, I wou'd place it on your Head, if you thought me worthy of wearing it with you; yet I have ſome Friends left, and a Sanctuary to go to; Come, Madam, then let us away, ſo that I poſſeſs you, all my Ambition will be ſatisfy'd. Ah, my Lord, (ſaid *Felicia*, interrupting him,) do not follow the Dictates of an Infant Paſſion, which may cauſe you to bluſh hereafter; conſider you are ſpeaking to a Chriſtian Captive, who has Gratitude and Generoſity enough, not to accept Offers, which might occaſion your Ruin: I am indebted to you, it's true, yet think what I owe to my ſelf. It wou'd be impoſſible for me to conſent to go with you, without being the Author of your Diſgrace, and my eternal Shame. The Difference of our Laws and Religion, the Inequality of our Fortunes, and our little Knowledge of each Other, all Theſe oppoſe ſuch a Deſign; and ſhou'd I leave my ſelf to your Care, you your ſelf wou'd tax me with the greateſt Imprudence. Continue, Madam, (replied *Abelhamar* with Impatience,) and rather ſay, you love ſome Perſon in *Spain*. Say, cruel Creature, you have an Averſion to me, which is the only Motive of your Conſideration. Ah *Felicia*! How eaſily might we overcome all theſe Difficulties, were you inſpired, like me, with a tender Paſſion? And how little wou'd you reflect on the Conſequences of an Engagement, which flatters us with ſo perfect a Felicity? But alas! I ſee too well, you prefer the Queen of *Fez*'s Chains to that Liberty

berty I now offer you. Here leaning his Head upon his Hands, he filently exprefs'd his Pain with Sighs that prevented his Utterance: *Felicia* continued fpeaking to him with much Sweetnefs and Prudence; but foon forgeting he was near her, fhe relaps'd into her former Affliction, at the Thoughts of her unhappy Deftiny. They were Both in this Situation, when the Admiral (who at a Diftance had obferv'd them fome Time,) approach'd the Prince, and ask'd him whether he was difpos'd to Eat; Who having recover'd from the little Diforder he was in, made Anfwer, it fhou'd be as *Felicia* pleas'd. This beauteous Lady, blufhing, faid to him, You do not reflect, my Lord, that I am a Captive here, who alas, has no Command. Ah, Madam! reply'd he, (fpeaking to her in a low Voice) you know too well the unlimited Power you have, where-ever I am, and no Body feels the Effect of it more than I: If your Empire is fo great in Misfortunes, what wou'd it be at another Time? In ending thefe Words, they were interrupted by the joyful Shouts of the Sea-men, who had juft difcover'd the Coafts of the Kingdom of *Fez*, which News ftruck *Felicia* with Confternation; for whilft fhe was at Sea, fhe had fome Hopes, that either a Tempeft wou'd arife, and caft them upon the Coaft of *Spain*, or that the *Spanifh* Fleet, which was then Abroad, wou'd retake 'em; but fhe was too well affured, that being once landed at *Sallee*, fhe cou'd not any more expect to be reliev'd.

*Abel-*

*Abelhamar*, on his Side, thought Death less terrible, than parting with this Young Lady, whom he wou'd soon be oblig'd to yield up to the Sultaness; and as he had not much Time to remain with her, he employ'd those Hours in representing his Passion to her in the softest Language, Love and Respect cou'd inspire; but she receiv'd his Addresses with so much Coldness, that he began to despair of meeting with an obliging Return.

They were now arriv'd at *Sallee*; and as *Abelhamar* cou'd not resolve to go himself, and present *Felicia* to the Queen of *Fez*, he told the Admiral he was indispos'd, therefore desired he wou'd excuse him to her Majesty for not waiting on her. He approach'd *Felicia* at the same Time, and said, it's you, Madam, that hinders me from making my Court to Day; for I cannot attend you to a Place where you go with so much Reluctancy; but be assured, that in Spite of your Indifferency, I shall not omit any Thing to deliver you from your Confinement. You are too generous, my Lord, reply'd she, in endeavouring to contribute to my Satisfaction, which will be purchas'd very dear, if it shou'd hereafter give you the least Chagrin.

*Abelhamar* retired exceeding melancholy, and soon after, *Felicia*, *Inea*, and the Rest of the Slaves, were set on Shore by the Admiral's Command, in order to be sent to the Queen. Alas! my dear *Inea*, said *Felicia*, (looking at her with a dejected Air,) we see our selves going

going into Captivity; and, till now, the civil Treatment of *Abelhamar*, prevented us from feeling the full Weight of our Misfortunes: This Prince now leaves us, and the fine Palace we see, is to be our Prison. At these Words, she cou'd not restrain the Course of her Tears, and *Inea* kept her Company in this dismal Scene, till they alighted at the first Court of the Castle, from whence they were immediately carry'd to the Queen.

They found her seated on a Carpet of Gold, beautify'd with Diversity of Colours, and round her were several embroider'd Cushions enrich'd with Pearl; she was dress'd in a *Turkish* Habit of Silver Brocade, Flower'd with Crimson, and Button'd with Diamonds and Emeralds; her Girdle, which was set with Precious Stones, girded a little Poigniard to her Side; Part of her Hair was tuck'd under a Muzlin Veil, strip'd with Gold, and the rest hung in Tresses down her Neck; her Eyes, which were Large and Black, tho' languishing, shin'd with irresistible Lustre; but in her Mein was painted so much Pride and Haughtiness, that it rob'd her of Part of her Charms, and render'd her awful to All that approach'd her.

*Leonida* (attended by the Women who were taken with her,) came and flung her self at the Queen's Feet, who thought her a surprizing Beauty; she chose her and *Inea* to be of her Chamber, and gave the rest to the Admiral to dispose of as he pleas'd. The Queen knew *Leonida* was a *Spaniard* by her Dress, there-

therefore speaking to her in that Language, ask'd her Name, and to what Part of the World she was going when they took her; to which she answer'd, her Name was *Felicia*, that a Gentleman had run away with her, who told her, he intended to carry her to *Morocco*; but that he had been kill'd in the Engagement, and she thought her self too happy in her Misfortunes, to fall into the Hands of so great a Queen. She finish'd these Words with so weak an Accent, that *Celima* easily perceiv'd she was under a great Affliction. She extremely pity'd the Youth of this Lady, whose noble Air perswaded her, she was of Eminent Birth. Be under no Concern, *Felicia*, said she, to her; I shall extend my Goodness to you; there are greater Troubles than those you are to undergo in this Palace: You must not judge of Felicity by Appearances, and I know not, after enquiring into your Condition, and that of some Sovereigns I have heard of, but your's is more Happy; for, I believe, added she, your Heart has prefer'd its Liberty, being uncommon for One at your Age to receive an Impression of Love. *Leonida* made no Reply, but looking on the Ground, chang'd Colour, and fetch'd a deep Sigh. *Celima*, who only spoke to her in this Manner to discover the Motions of her Heart, observing her Disorder, perceiv'd she was touch'd with a secret Passion, but did not take any farther Notice of it.

A little after, the Governess of the Slaves order'd *Felicia* and *Inea*, to follow her to that Part

Part of the Palace affign'd for their Ufe, where
fhe made 'em change their Cloaths; and as
they were to wait on the Queen, fhe gave
them very rich Stuffs for their Drefs: They
generally went Bare-headed, with their Hair
falling negligently on their Shoulders, and as
a Mark of Servitude, wore Golden Bracelets,
and Chains on their Arms; when they attended the Queen to any Place, they had large
White Veils of an extraordinary fine Stuff,
which cover'd their Head, and Part of their
Face.

*Felicia* appear'd as beautiful in this new Apparel, as in that fhe had juft put off, and her
Actions were accompanied with fo much Grace,
that nothing feem'd ftrange to her. They carried her into a Room, where they were teach-
ing the Slaves to fing, and play upon Inftru-
ments, which furpriz'd her extremely, not expecting to fee fo great a Number of Handfom
Creatures, as if *Celima* had the Privilege of
choofing them out of all the Courts in the U-
niverfe. Thefe Captives fhow'd no lefs Admiration in feeing *Felicia*; they all came up to
falute her, and amongft them, fhe obferv'd a
young Lady, whofe Air was fo Majeftick and
Charming, that fhe took a particular Delight
in looking at her; but what increas'd her Attention, was, the Fancy fhe had to have feen
her fomewhere before, and that fhe was not
unknown to her: They exprefs'd an extraordinary Civility to each other, and as there is
generally a greater Sympathy between unfortunate

nate Perſons than others, theſe Two Fair Captives mutually contracted a particular Friendſhip.

From thence, *Felicia*, in her new Dreſs, was carry'd to the Queen, but made no Stay in her Apartment. Soon after, *Abelhamar* (forgetting he had deſired the Admiral to make his Excuſes to *Celima*, for not paying his Court to her that Night,) ran impatiently to the Palace, and ſeem'd extremely uneaſy, when he perceiv'd *Felicia* was not with her. He did not preſume to mention any Thing concerning her, but the Queen ſaluted him in theſe Terms: You have brought me a lovely *Spaniard*, whom you ſhall ſee preſently in her Slave's Dreſs; I am perſwaded, you will not think her leſs beautiful than before; and I muſt tell you, I have learnt ſince your Departure, that ſhe who was taken in the Iſland of *Sardinia*, is the Daughter of *Brancaleon Doria*, her Name is *Olympia*, and—— here ſhe is, (continu'd the Queen, ſeeing her enter the Apartment) ſhe will inform you of ſomething particularly ſurprizing. *Celima* commanded her to entertain the Prince with her Story, which ſhe obey'd, and *Felicia* coming in at the ſame Time, approach'd *Olympia*, who began the enſuing Relation.

A young Count extremely Handſom, and of a Merit ſo ſhining, that he was univerſally admir'd, fell in Love with me; I made him no diſobliging Return, thinking my Father wou'd be very well ſatisfy'd to give me to a Perſon of his Quality, and one who had highly diſtinguiſh'd himſelf in the World. His Conſent, my Lord, was the only Thing wanting to make us Happy; but alas! we little foreſaw the Difficulties that oppos'd our Deſires.

My Father diſpleas'd with this Nobleman's Family, look'd on him, and all his Relations, as Enemies; however, for a long Time, his politick Reaſons oblig'd him to conceal his true Sentiments, which he diſcover'd, when my Marriage was propos'd to him; it was then we knew with mortal Diſpleaſure, that Time only cou'd relieve us; we both labour'd under all the Vexation, that ſuch a Diſappointment was capable of giving us; and as our Affection daily increas'd, we cou'd not deny our ſelves the Satisfaction of private Interviews; my Father was acquainted with our Proceedings, which being oppoſite to his Inclinations, made him ſo angry, that he told me in the greateſt Paſſion, he wou'd revenge my Diſobedience to him on the Object I lov'd. Theſe Menaces caus'd me to tremble for this young Lord, whom I conjured to abſent for ſome Time, and ſoon after, a glorious Occaſion invited him to go Abroad. *Bagazet* had conquer'd a great Part of the *Levant*, and the King of *Hungary* endeavouring to beat him out of it, apply'd himſelf for Succour to moſt of the Princes of *Europe*, who readily ſent him all poſſible Aſſiſtance. Tho' I conſider'd this to be a long and tedious Journey, and even apprehended all the Dangers the Count might
be

be expos'd to, yet through the Necessity of his Absence, I seconded the Desire he had of going to *Missia*.

We exchang'd Vows of eternal Constancy to each other, and the Grief we felt at parting I thought wou'd have cost us our Lives. The Event of the Campaign was very unhappy, the Christian Troops were defeated, and the Count taken Prisoner, which News I heard with a Concern, not to be describ'd; I sent him Money to pay his Ransom, and was expecting his Return with the last Impatience, when I receiv'd an Account of his Death. It is hard, my Lord, to imagine, how cruelly such a Loss affected me. I cou'd no longer restrain my Sorrow. I persecuted my Father with Reproaches, and wou'd not permit either my Relations or Friends to see me; I thought Life it self insupportable, and beg'd of Heaven to shorten its Date, that I might be eas'd of the Torment I then endur'd.

This was my melancholy Condition, when slumb'ring one Night, my Mind fill'd with my Misfortunes, I suddenly awak'd, and saw a Person near me, whom at first I took for the Shade of my Deceas'd Lover: Such an Apparition wou'd have terribly frightened me, had my Passion been less violent. I found afterwards by his Discourse, that far from being with a Phantom, I had Cause to believe he was the same lovely Man, so dear to me. At this Sight, I abandon'd my self to all the Joy, that cou'd attend such a Surprize, and shew'd to this Cavalier all poſſible Marks of Affection; he was cruel enough not to undeceive me, and I was not ſenſible of my Error till the Day following, when by Chance, my Father brought him into a Grotto, where I had retir'd to indulge my ſelf with the pleaſing Thoughts of the Count's being reſtor'd to Life.

I was then inform'd, this Gentleman, whom I had taken for him, had never ſeen me before, which ſenſibly touch'd me; I was ſo aſham'd of this Miſtake, that my Affliction had like to have put a Period to my Days. My Father was extremely mov'd at my Condition, and as I knew his Sentiments, I did not doubt but he wou'd oblige me in any Thing I deſir'd; therefore embracing the Occaſion, I conjured him in moſt preſſing Terms, to give out that I was Dead, and permit me to go to my Mother, who was then in *Sardignia*, which he readily aſſented to. I had not far from *Cagliary* an Aunt, who was Abbeſs of a famous Monaſtry, that lay in a Wilderneſs near the Sea-Side, where I intended to end my deplorable Life, conceal'd from the Sight of any Object, that might renew my Sufferings.

My Father, notwithſtanding the Chagrin this Separation gave him, diſpos'd every Thing for my Departure, and the News of my Death was ſpread Abroad, without any One's thinking it ſuppos'd. I immediately left *Genoa*, and my Voyage had nothing Remarkable in it; for I ſoon arriv'd in *Sardignia*, where my Mother receiv'd me, and without Deliberation
con-

consented to what I so much wish'd. She carry'd me to her Sister, who was the Depository of my Secrets, and having chang'd my Name, I led a Life so retir'd, that without being of the Number of the Dead, I cou'd not be reckon'd amongst the Living; but I us'd often to be alarm'd with Letters from my Father, pressing me to quit my Solitude in order to return Home, which made me apprehend, he wou'd use his Authority to compel me to it; therefore I went and flung my self at my Aunt's Feet, and conjured her to give me the Nun's Veil; that having once made Vows, my Relations might lose the Hopes of my returning again into the World.

She at first oppos'd my Request, believing she ought not to make such a Step, without the Advice of my Friends; but at last my Prayers and Tears prevail'd on her. She desir'd the Bishop of *Cagliary* to perform the Ceremony; and as it is the Custom in that Place, for the Person who takes the Habit of a Novice, to go with a Number of young Ladies, to hear the Prelate in a little Chappel by the Sea-Side, I went out dress'd in a long Gown, Brocaded with Silver, my Hair hanging loose on my Shoulders, and my Head crown'd with Flowers; my Companions were also dress'd in White, and in this Manner we form'd a Procession along the Shore.

It's now, said I, my Dear Count, that I am going to sacrifice to you the rest of an unhappy Life, which was destin'd to be your's.

Were you sensible in the Region where you are, of what I do for you in this World, you wou'd rejoyce to have inspir'd me with such Sentiments. I was lost in these Thoughts, when I heard a great Noise; the Cries of my Companions oblig'd me to look behind me, where I saw several Men following us with their Swords drawn. I endeavour'd to make my Escape, but two of them being come up to me, carry'd me off, with some of the young Ladies; and having forc'd us into a Boat, row'd immediately up to their Ship, where we were under Sail before any one cou'd come to our Assistance.

One may easily imagine, that such a Surprize terrified us extremely; but it was nothing to the inexpressible Grief which seiz'd us, when we found our selves in the Hands of a *Corsair* of *Algier*, neither our Prayers nor Tears had Power to soften him; all his Thoughts were fix'd on making the most of our Captivity. He soon lost Sight of *Sardignia*, and after having taken other Prizes, steer'd his Course towards *Sallee*, being sure to sell some of us to the Queen, who was pleas'd to chuse me (as you know, my Lord,) out of a Motive of Pity; for I was so very melancholy, that none cou'd see me without Compassion.

It never came into my Head to acquaint my Father with my Captivity, nor did I wish the Recovery of my Liberty, which I was going to offer as a Sacrifice, when the *Corsair* took me. It was equal to me, to be shut up in the Palace of *Sallee*, or in a Monastry; since I had

no

no other Defire, than that of leaving the World, and paffing the Remainder of an unfortunate Life without any Engagement.

In this State, were my Affairs, and I daily receiving new Favours from the Queen, when a Merchant of *Genoa*, who deals in Jewels, came to this Court. Her Majefty being defirous to fee what valuable Things he had to difpofe of, fent for him, and I was near her, when he enter'd the Apartment. He no fooner caft his Eyes on me, but feem'd aftonifh'd; for he did not doubt of my being Dead, as it was reported; yet in feeing me, he had Caufe enough to believe, I was *Brancaleon Doria*'s Daughter; fince he had fpoken to me too often at my Father's Houfe, not to know me again; and as he immediately perceiv'd I knew him, it fo confirm'd his Opinion, that he defir'd Leave to fpeak with me, which he obtain'd of the Queen. Is it poffible, Madam, you fhou'd thus neglect Writing to your Friends, who fo infinitely love you, and are lamenting your Death at *Genoa*, whilft you are Living, and a Slave at *Sallee*? Who bemoans me? (faid I, with a melancholy Accent:) Do you believe, that after the fatal Deftiny of a Perfon, who was dearer to me than Life, I cou'd find any Relifh for the World? No, as my Paffion was great, fo was my Sorrow; and no other Motive induc'd me to fpread Abroad my pretended Death, only to retire into fome Solitude, and there forever regret the Lofs of a Man I fo dearly lov'd. In finifhing thefe Words, I burft out in Tears, and the Jeweller fixing his Eyes on me with Admiration; you deserve a better Fate, Madam, said he, and I esteem my self happy, to have met with this Opportunity of assuring you, the Gentleman you actually deplore, did not perish as it was related; he arriv'd at *Genoa* a little after the Report of your Death, at which he was so touch'd, that his Trouble is not to be describ'd; he admitted me to see him often, but his Grief wou'd seldom allow him to speak, and whenever he broke Silence, it was with your Name; he afterwards fell dangeroufly ill, and as soon as he recover'd, went to Travel; but he is now return'd to *Genoa*, and I can give you Testimonies, Madam, of his eternal Love.

We were in a Place pretty distant from the Queen, who cou'd not hear our Conversation; but I was so transported at this News, that (without knowing what I did, or considering why,) I ran and flung my self at her Feet; at first I was not able to speak, my Eyes gush'd out with Tears, and I look'd at her in so moving a manner, that she ask'd me several times what was my Request? The Merchant being a Man of Sense, came up, and explain'd the Meaning of my Disorder; and as I had time to recover my self during their Discourse; Ah Madam! said I to the Queen, I entreat your Majesty to give me my Liberty; I am now willing to live, and wish my self at *Genoa*, since my Misfortunes are at an end. No Creature was more wretched than I, and now, none is more happy. I protest to you, Madam, I daily saw
the

the Light with Pain, having as I thought, lost the only Person that cou'd make my Felicity, and defir'd Death to terminate my Miseries, as it had done his. I cannot call to mind all I said to the Queen, who was pleas'd to hear me with a great deal of Condescension; and being inform'd who I was, as a particular Proof of her Esteem for my Family, she restor'd me to my Liberty, for which I return'd her Majesty repeated Thanks. I ask'd the Jeweller a great many Questions, and desir'd he wou'd procure me Conveniencies for my Passage in the next Ship that shou'd sale for *Genoa*; but after having made more serious Reflections, I thought it prudent, not to put my self into my Father's Power, till I had first consulted the Count, and taken Measures with him to succeed in our mutual Desires, without running any Risque of meeting with new Obstacles.

After these Considerations, I wrote to him by the same Merchant, who is return'd to *Genoa*, in order to bring him here: This is, my Lord, what has pass'd during your Absence, which the Queen commanded me to relate to you.

*Abelhamar* thank'd her Majesty, and afterwards *Olympia*, for whom he had always shown a particular Value. You have no reason now to complain, Madam, said he to her; *Hymen* is going to reward you for all the Pains Love has made you suffer: You'll soon see the Object of your Affection, and unite your Destinies. Ah! how happy is such a State? In ending these Words, he sigh'd and look'd languishingly

guishingly at *Felicia*, who turn'd her Eyes on the Ground, fearing they shou'd meet his; he also endeavour'd to speak to her, but she carefully avoided his Approach. This Proceeding so deeply affected the Prince, that he retir'd almost in Despair. The Queen, who was troubled with a secret Uneasiness, went into her Closet to indulge her usual Melancholy, and the Slaves repaired to their Apartment.

*Felicia* finding *Inea* in her Chamber, embrac'd her with as much Pleasure, as if she had not seen her of a long time. We have, said she, illustrious Companions in our Servitude; that fine Creature they call *Olympia*, is Daughter to the famous *Doria*; I have just now heard her Story, which she related to Prince *Abelhamar*. Oh Heavens! my dear *Inea*, how worthy of Envy is her Fate? she will soon see her Lover, whose Death was so surely believ'd, that after his Loss she determin'd to sacrifice the Remainder of her Life to Solitude; if you ever have felt a tender Passion, you may imagine how agreeable such a Meeting will prove to them: Her Eyes already shine with an unknown Lustre, and express the Motions of a satisfy'd Mind. Alas! continu'd she, how different is her Case and mine? I conceive, Madam, interrupted *Inea*, your Uneasiness does not proceed entirely from your Captivity; were I permitted to say more, I shou'd judge, your Heart was concern'd in the Sighs and Tears which sometimes you cannot restrain: Relieve your self in complaining, Madam, and if you

think

think me worthy of being your Confident, I dare assure you, I shall never forfeit that Honour by divulging your Secret. I am persuaded of your Sincerity, my Dear, reply'd *Felicia*, and think my self happy to have met with a Person, in whom I can confide; but if I relate my melancholy Story to you, I hope you'll oblige me with a Recital of yours, and believe, what I desire, does less proceed from my Curiosity, than the particular Interest I have in all that concerns you. I flatter my self with what you are pleas'd to say, lovely *Felicia*, reply'd *Inea*, and to shew how obedient I am to any thing you command, I will now give you a Relation of my Misfortunes.

### The Story of Inea.

I Am born of a noble Family of *Andalusia*, where my Father had a good Estate, and marry'd a Lady, who brought him no Fortune; he was ever thought a gallant Man, and being bred up to the Sea from his Infancy, the King gave him a Ship of War; he has left two Daughters, my eldest Sister's Name is *Mathilda*, who is very handsom. We us'd to see but little Company, according to the Custom of *Spain*; but my Father having receiv'd into his House a young Gentleman of a distinguish'd Family in *Toledo*, whose Name is Don *Ramire* of *Castro*, a secret Sympathy dispos'd his Heart and mine, to receive Impressions for each other. I was pleas'd at his gentle Air, his Wit, and
soft

soft insinuating manner, which engaged me unawares; and we were not long acquainted, before he declar'd, I had inspir'd him with the tenderest Passion.

He thought himself happy in wearing my Chains. His Fortune and Merit gave him such Advantages, that he had no room to apprehend any of my Friends wou'd oppose his Felicity, and I was of the same Opinion; for tho' I resisted the Infant Inclination I had for him, it proceeded only from the fear I had of its not being sincerely return'd. How unfortunate shou'd I be, said I to my self, were my Affection plac'd on a Man, who might receive it with Indifference? I ought, before it's too late, resolve to fly, and deny my Eyes the Pleasure they take in seeing him. The just Diffidence I had of my own Merit, oblig'd me to be very reserv'd to Don *Ramire*, and behave my self in a manner quite opposite to my Sentiments, which inclin'd him to believe, I had conceiv'd an Aversion for him; this Thought did not only afflict him, but made him so timerous, that he had not Power to speak to me. I examin'd all his Actions with great Care, and when we were together, he appear'd extremely pensive; I attributed this to the weak Impression I had made on him, which created in me much Uneasiness, and I did the greatest Violence to my self in not showing my Concern; but tho' our Minds were prepossess'd, yet our Eyes, meeting sometimes, cou'd not help confessing the inward
Motion

Motion of our Hearts. Ah! too indifferent Don *Ramire*, thought I, if you are really touch'd, in what manner wou'd your Looks exprefs it, fince without being fo, they fpeak the foft Language of Love ? He told me afterwards, he had conceiv'd the fame Idea of me, and difcover'd in my Eyes fomething which wou'd have flatter'd him, had I not given him too many Inftances of my Infenfibility.

My Sifter pafs'd fome time in ftudying our Looks, and was endeavouring to know whether we had a Paffion for each other, having her felf a fecret reafon to be inform'd of the Truth ; all the Care fhe took, ferv'd only to perfwade her, there was no Love between us, and that fhe might undertake what fhe pleas'd without Apprehenfion. Don *Ramire* appear'd as agreeable in her Eyes, as he did in mine ; but the Difference of his Proceedings with her was very remarkable : It came into his Head, firft to acquire her Friendfhip, that afterwards he might make her his Confident, and fo by degrees, engage her in his Intereft. Thus one may fee, how blind is Love, in fome of his Projects ; for there was very little Probability, that *Mathilda* wou'd act in fuch a Character. She was my Mother's Favourite, as my eldeft Sifter had a Right to be married before me ; therefore (Don *Ramire* being the only Perfon who then feem'd defirous to make an Alliance with our Family) it was thought but juft, fhe fhou'd have the Precedency.

I

I was not long, before I difcover'd her Intentions, and my Uneafinefs met with fo vaft an Addition, that it had like to have thrown me into Defpair. What (faid I, complaining of my Fate) am I already jealous? I who can hardly tell what it is to love, and muft I feel a thoufand different Pains, which ought to be unknown to one of my Age? Methinks, I cou'd approve his Paffion, were he difpos'd to like me; yet I have avoided him with the fame Caution, I wou'd have done the Man I hate; was ever Conduct like mine? My Sifter is taking Advantage of my Timidity; fhe is belov'd, and in fpite of that, I ftill harbour fuch Sentiments as ought to make me blufh, fince they will render me the unhappieft Creature in the World.

Don *Ramire*, whofe Perplexity of Mind was not inferior to mine, cou'd no longer be filent; and as *Mathilda* gave him all Opportunities of entertaining her, one Evening as they were walking together in one Ally of the Garden, and I in another, (unknown to them, and at too great a Diftance to hear what they were faying) I perceiv'd he was talking to her with a great deal of Emotion; at laft I faw him fling himfelf at her Feet, and taking her Hand, kifs'd it fo ardently, that I no ways doubted but he had juft declar'd his Paffion to her; which meeting with an obliging Reception, occafion'd thofe Tranfports in him. Oh Heavens! what a Sight was this to a Perfon in my Condition? I wou'd no longer obferve
them,

them, but went into an Arbour at the end of the Ally, not having Strength enough to support me, nor Power to resist the Course of my Grief.

There I threw my self on the Ground, leaning my Head on a Bench, and covering my Face with my Veil, I shed a Shower of Tears. Oh! how cruel is my Destiny, said I? Don *Ramire* and *Mathilda* love each other; she has heard his Declaration, and given him a favourable Audience, for which, he made his Retributions to her on his Knees, and I can never flatter my self with the Hopes of being dear to him. Here my Sighs and Tears made me perfectly asham'd, and I was as mad at my own Sensibility, as at his Indifferency; but had I known what was passing between him and my Sister, I shou'd have had as much reason to be pleas'd, as I thought I had for the contrary.

In fine, Madam, after a Conversation that turn'd on different Subjects, Don *Ramire*, urged by the Violence of his Pain, deliver'd his Thoughts to her in the following Manner: Charming *Mathilda*! I must intrust you with a Secret, on which depends the Peace of my Life; be pleas'd to hear me, and let me find in you those generous Dispositions, that may contribute to my future Happiness. As she believed he was going to disclose a Secret to her, wherein she was chiefly concern'd, she thought fit to keep him under such a Restriction, as not to allow him too much Liberty.

You ought, Sir, anfwer'd fhe, to difcover your Pain to a Perfon of more Wit than me; I have not Experience enough to give you any Advice, and there are certain Things I do not defire to know. Be affur'd, Madam, interrupted he, I have too great a Refpect for you, to fay any thing that cou'd give you the leaft difpleafure; moreover, you have nothing to fear, fince you are not interefted in this Affair. I am only going to tell you, I have a Paffion for *Inea*, whom I adore; I hope my Succefs from your good Offices, and conjure you to grant me your Favour in this Requeft. In finifhing thefe Words, he flung himfelf at her Feet, and his Thoughts were fo entirely taken up with what he was faying, that he took no notice of the different Emotions, which appear'd in her Looks. All, that Rage, Shame, and exceffive Love cou'd make one feel, join'd at once, to torment her. You love my Sifter, (faid fhe, after being fome time filent,) and you chufe me for your Confident, without confidering, that as I am the eldeft, my Fortune muft be fettled, before hers: I am fo offended at the Injury you do me, that were I more revengeful than I am, I wou'd inftantly punifh your Indifferency. Go, Sir, continu'd fhe, fpeak to her your felf; I fhou'd render you but a very ill Office; with that fhe left him, and no Man was ever feen in a greater Confufion. He walk'd fome time in the Ally, reflecting on what had pafs'd, and was now convinc'd, *Mathilda*, having difcover'd her

Weak-

Weakness to him, wou'd leave no Art unpractis'd to disappoint his Passion for me.

Don *Ramire*, perplex'd with these Thoughts, came into the Arbour, where I told you, Madam, I had retir'd, and was not a little surpriz'd to find me there. As for my Part, I knew not what Resolution to take, whether to go, or stay, when he put himself on his Knees by me, and intreating me to hear him, Adorable *Inea*, said he, the Condition I am reduc'd to, does not permit me to be any longer silent. I cannot doubt of your Aversion, since you not only debar me of your Conversation, but even turn your Eyes from me. I have us'd all possible Means to decline a Passion, which I fear will displease you: But as the Torment I endure is little inferior to Death, whatever Usage I am to receive from you hereafter, only think, I daily die for you.

I cou'd not imagine, Don *Ramire*, (reply'd I) you were so capable of Deceit, but your Conduct convinces me of the Truth. You try in vain to perswade me. This Dissimulation is worse than the Offence, and I know what I am to depend on. Go, Sir, I am resolv'd never to see you, nor speak to you more. Ending these Words, I ran from him, in spight of his Endeavours to prevent me, and left him with an Air, so full of Pride and Anger, that he told me since, he had like to have expired on the Place. His Despair was so great, that (being retired to his Chamber) he was taken ill with a violent Feaver, which oblig'd him to keep his Bed.

The mean while I went into my Closet, where being alone, I abandon'd my self to a thousand cruel Reflections. Were I only to contend with *Mathilda*, thought I, there wou'd still be hopes of obtaining some Advantage over her; but the Case now is such, that shou'd Don *Ramire* yield his Heart to me, methinks I wou'd reject the Offer. He is a Traytor, who tells me, he has Sentiments for me, which he has not. He says the same to my Sister, and loves neither of us; at least I have cause to complain, since he chuses me for the Subject of his Raillery. Oh! what Fatality deludes me, to love this perfidious Man? I fear he knows the Affection I have for him, which is a Misfortune, I cannot bear. These Thoughts forc'd a Flood of Tears from my Eyes, whilst I endeavour'd to banish him from my Heart; and I was thus depress'd with Sorrow, when my Mother sent for me: I went down to her Apartment, and appear'd so dejected, that my Sister (who examin'd every Motion of me) did not doubt, but I was come from Don *Ramire*'s Chamber, and that his Illness was the Occasion of my Melancholy; tho' at the same time, I knew nothing of the Matter, nor wou'd I enquire after him, thinking he did not deserve so great a Favour, therefore I return'd to my own Chamber again, without hearing his Name once mention'd.

*Mathilda* persisting in her Love for Don *Ramire*, told my Mother the Conversation they had together in the Garden, and desir'd, she wou'd wou'd be favourable to her, in laying her Commands on me, to ufe him with fo much Indifference, as might deftroy his Hopes of ever attaining to my Affection. This, my Mother promis'd her, and all fhe cou'd wifh on that Subject. The next Day, I heard the Condition he was in, who little thought, I had the leaft Concern for his Illnefs, tho' I muft confefs, it gave me much Uneafinefs, and Compaffion foon took place of my Anger; yet I wou'd not go to fee him, whatever Pain I fuffer'd, in denying my felf that Satisfaction.

Ah! how great is my Misfortune, cry'd I, not to have Pride enough to fupprefs a Paffion, which fo immoderately difturbs my Mind, and yet have fo much Refentment, as to deny my felf the only Pleafure this World can give me? How is it poffible, I can be fo cruel to a Perfon, whofe Idea is never abfent from me, and whofe Life I wou'd purchafe with my own?

By this time, his Feaver was fo violent, that the Phyficians were of Opinion, nothing but his Youth cou'd fave him. I was in my Mother's Apartment, when they came to acquaint her with the Danger he was in, faying, they believ'd him very near leaving the World. At this News, I was fo feiz'd with Grief, that all I cou'd do, was to reach my Chamber, where I fell in a Swoon, and continu'd fo almoft an Hour.

I had with me a young Servant, called *Tereza*, who lov'd me entirely; and as fhe was no Stranger to my Affection for Don *Ramire*, fhe help'd help'd me to conceal the Defpair I was in. No, cry'd I, (when I was a little recover'd,) I cannot let him die, fpite of his Ingratitude: I find the Prefervation of my Life depends on his. Heavens, (continu'd I, bath'd in Tears) fhorten my Days, and give Health to Don *Ramire*; for alas, without him, what can I expect, but unconceivable Pain? I proteft to you, Madam, I faid a thoufand diftracted Things, the Recital of which, wou'd tire you; for fure, no Sorrow was ever equal to mine. I was thus tormenting my felf, when my Mother came into my Chamber, and her Prefence fo furpriz'd me, that I had like to have related to her the Subject of my Grief. She had juft been with Don *Ramire*, who conjured her in a moft preffing Manner, to let me favour him with a Vifit; adding, that after fo great a Satisfaction, he fhou'd contentedly die: She told him, any thing he defired fhou'd be granted, then came to prepare me for this Interview, telling me how I fhou'd behave my felf. Don *Ramire*, faid fhe, is fo near Death, that what I am going to enjoyn you, I believe, is unneceffary; yet that I may have no Caufe to reproach my felf, I command you, *Inea*, to fhow him all the Indifferency poffible, in cafe he fpeaks to you of his Paffion. I fhall obey your Orders with Pleafure, Madam, reply'd I, tho' I am perfuaded, if he intended an Alliance in this Family, he never had a Thought of me. You make an unfeafonable Declaration (interrupted my my Mother, in a severe Tone) for I know he loves you to Distraction, and it was very imprudent in him, to chuse your Sister for a Confident; as being your eldest, she ought first to be provided for; besides, it's my Will, pray tell Don *Ramire* so, and that I had rather see you dead, than his Wife.

My Mother spoke to me with so much Heat, that I cou'd not dispute the Truth of what she said. I presently comprehended her Meaning, and instead of a Traytor, as I thought him before, I now found he was a Man of Honour, and the constantest of Lovers. This no ways soften'd my Pain; for tho' I was overjoy'd to know his Passion was sincere, yet on the other hand, I saw my self at the point of losing a Person, I then esteem'd worthy the Sentiments I had for him; and my Alarms continually persuaded me, nothing cou'd mitigate so real a Misfortune. The Impatience I had to see him, wou'd not permit me to say much to my Mother. I left her, and took *Tereza* with me to Don *Ramire*'s Apartment, which I had hardly enter'd, and approach'd his Bed, when he turn'd himself towards me, and reaching out his Hand, said in a weak Voice; Come, Madam, come and receive the last Breath of a Man, who never sigh'd for any one but you; tho' your Injustice accus'd my Heart with Deceit. The State you see me in, ought to convince you, there never was a Passion more perfect. It's for you I die, adorable *Inea*, (continued he, pressing my Hand,) it's you alone, who is the Cauſe; and ſince it was my Fate, not to deſerve your Eſteem, I think my ſelf happy not to ſurvive your Averſion. In finiſhing theſe Words, he look'd at me with Eyes drown'd in Tears, and fell into a deep Silence, which I did not preſently interrupt, being either in Diſorder, or pleas'd to hear him mention a Paſſion, I began to believe, and was willing to approve. At laſt I ſpoke to him; Ceaſe to reproach me, Don *Ramire,* ſaid I; ceaſe to complain, and think only of recovering; I am unfortunate enough already, and did not want this laſt Stroke to compleat my Ruin Muſt I lay aſide the Modeſty of my Sex, and in ſpite of Shame, confeſs I love you? Oh! conſider what a Sacrifice I make you, when I own thoſe Sentiments, I have ſo long endeavour'd to conceal. I thought you had an Inclination for my Siſter, which gave me much Uneaſineſs; all your Civilities to her, I us'd to attribute to Love; and what very much increas'd my Torment, was the Action you did ſome Days ago, when you flung your ſelf on your Knees before her in the Garden. I concluded, you were entertaining her with your Paſſion, which made me retire to the Arbour, where you found me, in order to indulge my Grief; that was the Cauſe of my upbraiding you; but now, Sir, you may be ſatisfy'd; for I have puniſh'd my ſelf ſeverely, and you are ſufficiently reveng'd. In finiſhing theſe Words, I burſt out in Tears, and this Gentleman, who before cou'd ſcarcely ſpeak,

speak, cry'd aloud, with Transports of excessive Joy, Ah charming *Inea!* why was my Happiness so long unknown to me? I was just going with my Despair to end my Life; but since you have deliver'd me from the Arms of Death, I am resolv'd to live, and live to serve you alone. Here I interrupted him, to acquaint him with my Mother's Intentions, which he protested, he never wou'd comply with. I represented to him the Necessity there was to affect an Inclination for *Mathilda*, in order to carry on our Amour the more successfully. He told me his Honour wou'd not suffer him to act such a Part, and that he thought it more prudent, to speak directly to my Father concerning our Marriage; but as I knew my Mother's jealous Humour, I was satisfy'd such a Conduct wou'd highly offend her, and that no Scheme wou'd succeed so well, as a feign'd Passion for my Sister; which Opinion I at last persuaded him to approve.

I cannot deny you any thing, Madam, said he, since my Life is your's. Dispose of my Destiny as you please, I am devoted to your Commands. In short, Don *Ramire* promis'd me to make his Addresses to my Sister in such a Manner, as might incline her to believe he design'd to marry her. As soon as I left his Chamber, I went to my Mother, and told her, what he said on that Point, which pleas'd her extremely; and as for my Sister, nothing could equal the Joy she express'd, at so agreeable a Change.

We us'd every Day to visit *Don Ramire*, during his Illness, and whenever I was alone with *Mathilda*, I constrain'd my self to exaggerate the Affection he had for her, which I really repeated so often, that sometimes I was afraid I spoke the Truth. Thus we manag'd Affairs till he recover'd; and my Family looked upon him as *Mathilda*'s Votary. About this Time, the Governour of *Porto Real*, (whose Daughter had been newly marry'd) gave an Entertainment, with a Ball at Night, to all the Nobility of that Place. We were invited to this Assembly, which was much greater than any we had ever appear'd at before. Don *Ramire*, who was to be of the Party, express'd some Uneasiness at my going thither, fearing my Charms, as he told me, wou'd create him many Rivals. Indeed, tho' I had no extraordinary Conceit of my self, I cou'd not condemn his Jealousy, but rather approv'd it, and thought I had Reason to return him the same Compliment. We said a great deal on that Subject, till at last, I took it into my Head not to go there at all, and was meditating on some Stratagem to favour my Design, when my Mother sent to let me know, she was ready, and only waited for me. I immediately went to her, but first made Don *Ramire* promise me, whatever happen'd he wou'd not leave the Ball, till he saw my Mother and Sister Home again.

We all went together to the Governour's; Don *Ramire* gave his Hand to my Mother, who

who was follow'd by my Sister; and as for my part, just as I step'd out of the Coach, I designedly fell down, and pretended I had sprain'd my Foot, so that I cou'd not appear at the Ball. My Mother (displeas'd at this Accident, which she did not know to be a Counterfeit,) sent me Home, and Don *Ramire* stay'd with them, very much surpriz'd at what I had done, being sensible, it was a Sacrifice I made him; he had not Resolution enough to stay by *Mathilda,* during all the Entertainment, but took an Opportunity, whilst she was dancing, to go and place himself in a Corner of the Room, and there wrote to this Effect on his Tablets.

*WHAT Torment does your Absence give me, adorable* Inea ? *Here you leave me, expos'd to the Smiles of a Woman I hate. How do you think it possible for me to be complaisant to your Sister, when you are not by? As soon as you were gone, my Thoughts like your Shadow, follow'd you. Alas, this Moment, absent from you, Who is more unhappy than I? And how fortunate shou'd I think my self, were I paying Homage to your beauteous Eyes ?*

*Mathilda* (who was naturally uneasy) not seeing Don *Ramire* by her, look'd every where for him, and at last perceiv'd him Writing on his Tablets: She went and took him out to dance the *Sarao,* which you know, Madam, was invented by the *Moors;* every Cavalier leads his
Lady

Lady with one Hand, and carries a Torch in the other. My Sister, as she was dancing, found it easy enough to take his Tablets away, unknown to him. The Dance being ended, she went aside, in order to examine them. You may easily judge, at reading what was wrote in 'em, how enrag'd she was, to find her self thus betray'd, and the Preference given to me; having so good an Opinion of her own Merit, as to believe, it wou'd have insured her from this Misfortune.

Nothing cou'd be equal to the violent Passion she was in; yet during the Ball, she endeavour'd to conceal it; and what help'd her most to dissemble, was, that (to do her Justice) as she is very amiable, Don *Sanche* of *Gusman*, Son to the Governour, who was a fine Gentleman, but extremely vain, addrefs'd himself particularly to her, and she thought, she cou'd not have a better Opportunity to cure her Passion, and be reveng'd of Don *Ramire*, than giving a favourable Reception to this Cavalier; therefore, she immediately gave him to understand, my Mother wou'd be willing he shou'd visit us: Altho' we are not fond of Company, said she, yet, Sir, your distinguish'd Birth and Merit intitle you to a Privilege, others cannot pretend to. This Invitation highly pleas'd him, inasmuch as he had already declar'd his Passion for my Sister, and cou'd not well expect a Return, unlefs he were admitted to pay his Devoirs to her.

*Mathilda* prepar'd my Mother to receive him, but did not mention the Adventure of the Tablets; she only told her, that as she was not very sure of Don *Ramire*'s Heart, a Rival might give him some Jealousy, and induce him to conclude a Marriage, he daily seem'd to decline. While she was studying Means to satisfy her Revenge, Don *Ramire* acquainted me with the Loss of his Tablets, which he fear'd were fallen into the Hands of my Sister: Tho' I take little Notice of her Behaviour towards me, said he, I observe within these few Days, she treats me with an affected Civility. I cannot well penetrate into the Cause, nor shou'd be any ways uneasy about it, only I apprehend, she is inform'd of what we had agreed shou'd be kept secret: If you will give me Leave, continu'd he, to declare my Passion to your Father, we shall soon know what to depend on.

I must confess, Madam, the only Motive I had to make a Mystery of it, was the Pleasure of being secretly belov'd by a Man, whom I esteem'd so worthy my Affection; therefore I desired he would stay some Time longer, before he discovered his Sentiments.

Consider, Don *Ramire*, said I, that our Condition is not so unhappy, as you imagine. We live together in the same House, and in Spite of the jealous Eyes, which continually observe us, we see one another every Day, and our Love is mutual.

Such as these were our daily Conversations, when we perceiv'd by Don *Sanche*'s assiduous Courtship to my Sister, that his Passion for her had receiv'd a new Addition. We thought she treated him with so much Distinction, as perswaded us he wou'd soon be happy in her Favour, which extremely overjoy'd us, for we waited nothing else to perfect our Felicity. How bless'd will be my Days, said Don *Ramire* to me, when without Opposition, I shall possess those Excellencies, I now adore? Ah! dear *Inea*, does your Heart sympathize with mine, and may I hope to find in you those Endearments, which none but tender Lovers can truly relish? If once I am so fortunate, as to obtain that Wish, continued he, no Thought of any other Happiness (for sure there can be none) shall ever dwell in this Bosom. My Vows shall be dedicated to you alone, and the Height of my Ambition will only be to merit your Love.

Alas, Madam! you may imagine, these obliging Assurances from a Man, I so entirely loved, made the Days pass like Hours; but will you believe, that while we were expecting the Conclusion of my Sister's Marriage with Don *Sanche*, her Jealousy increas'd to such a Degree, that it wou'd not give her a Moment's Peace. She was more taken up with the Thoughts of Revenge, than with the Care of pleasing a Person, who was proposing to her so advantageous an Alliance. I heard that one Day, Don *Sanche* having desired

Leave

Leave to speak to his Father about it, she suddenly chang'd Colour, and her Eyes express'd a more than ordinary Grief: I can no longer be silent, said she to him, in a Cause, wherein you are interested; since you confess a Passion for me, and seem willing to unite your Destiny with mine; let me tell you, Sir, you must first destroy the Hopes of a Rival, to whom I am already engag'd. Don *Ramire* has obtained the Consent of my Family, and impatiently expects an Answer from his, to terminate every Thing. Before I saw you, I was not averfed to him; but alas, I cannot now think of my Fate, without Horror. I do not doubt, but your Love and Courage united will releafe me from this Engagement, since nothing, except my Inclination for you, cou'd induce me to decline it. Here her malicious Tears interrupted her Discourse, and by this Stratagem, Don *Sanche* was easily perswaded to undertake any desperate Thing against Don *Ramire*. He assured her, he wou'd soon make him renounce his Pretensions to her, if he had Assurance enough to oppose him in a Place, where his Authority was great, and in an Affair, where his Heart was so particularly concern'd; adding to these Words, all that Love cou'd inspire.

This made *Mathilda* believe, Don *Ramire* wou'd rather yield her up, than engage in her Quarrel, or that if he answer'd the Challenge, out of a Point of Honour, he wou'd have a potent Enemy to contend with. She must
have

have been very revengeful, to enter into a Sentiment so opposite to those of her Sex; for she imprudently expos'd at once two Persons, who were very dear to her. Don *Sanche* impatient to come to a Decision with Don *Ramire*, writ to him that Night, in Terms which show'd an insupportable Pride. He thus address'd him.

*THE Passion I have for* Mathilda, *will not admit of a Rival. I am inform'd you are mine, tho' it little concerns me: You know who I am, and that you will be disappointed in contending with me; therefore I advise you to be secret in this Affair, and generously yield a Pretension, you cannot dispute without Rashness.*

Don *Ramire*, was highly provok'd at reading this haughty Billet; and tho' he knew it was a Plot of my Sister's, yet he wou'd not let me into his Resolutions, fearing I might oppose 'em; but immediately return'd Don *Sanche* an Answer, in these Terms.

*THE Indifference I have for* Mathilda, *cou'd not have engag'd me to dispute her Heart with any one, but your self. It's sufficient you admire her, for me to oppose your Pretensions; and in Return to your Liberty with me, I advise you never to see her more, unless you intend, with your Life, to satisfy my Resentment.*

As

*of* CARENCY.

As Don *Ramire* believ'd, so violent a Beginning wou'd have a suitable Consequence, he went the next Day to a Place, where he thought he might meet him, (as he effectually did.) Don *Sanche* no sooner perceiv'd him, but came up, and said in a low Voice, without the least Affectation; Well, Sir, are you dispos'd to measure your Sword with mine? I am dispos'd to punish your Insolence, reply'd Don *Ramire*, and shall expect you on the Strand by the Sea-Side, where no Body may prevent us. They separated on this, and Don *Ramire* went to the appointed Place.

He was hardly there, when he saw Don *Sanche* coming up to him with menacing Looks. They both immediately drew, and made several Passes at each other: Don *Ramire* parry'd those of his Enemy, and soon put him in some Disorder, till at last, he gave him a mortal Wound, which hardly left him Life enough to confess the Author of his Fate. As for Don *Ramire*, he returned Home, with so much Serenity in his Countenance, that it was to be admir'd: He did not even think of taking the least Care of his Safety, and seem'd as if some secret Charm detain'd him. Alas! I am perswaded, that fatal Charm was my self. He spoke to me with a Freedom, I cou'd not attribute to any thing, but the Greatness of his Soul; and I had no Room to suspect the Misfortune, which had just happened to him, when of a sudden, the Governour and his Guards,

Guards, surrounded my Father's House, and snatch'd him from my Arms, in Spite of all I cou'd do to oppose 'em.

Those Moments I cannot call to mind, without the greatest Concern. The Governour, who was perfectly distracted, as well as inconsolable for the Loss of his only Son, came himself, on purpose to sacrifice Don *Ramire* to his Resentment. I do not at all doubt, but as he was seconded by a strong Guard, he wou'd have kill'd my Lover before my Face, had not I prevented him by standing between 'em, and to save him, expos'd my self to all the Danger; for tho' I am naturally so timerous, that even the Sight of a drawn Sword strikes me with Terror, yet I assure you, Madam, on that Occasion, I behav'd my self with so much Resolution, that I am convinc'd, to be Brave, it is sufficient to be in Love.

Don *Ramire*, who saw with the utmost Despair, the Danger which threatened me, was like a Lyon, defending himself against a Company of eager Huntsmen; he wounded some, and avoided the Fury of others; but alas, his Courage, and the little Assistance I cou'd afford him, did not hinder them from seizing, and carrying him immediately to Prison.

I thought at that Time, my Soul wou'd have departed from its Habitation, my Blood turn'd so cold in my Veins. I would have follow'd Don *Ramire*, and shar'd his Misfortunes, had not my Mother and Sister prevented me. *Mathilda*, more like a Fury, than a reasonable

Crea-

Creature, loaded me with Imprecations and Reproaches. The Death of Don *Ramire*, said she, shall revenge me, as well as the Person whose Fate I deplore. The Traitor shall be a Sacrifice to the Governour's just Resentment, and my Heart can receive no real Pleasure, till the Day comes, that he is to lose his Life. The Violence of my Grief wou'd not permit me to make any Answer; my Eyes said enough, and I have well experienc'd, that excessive Affliction makes every Thing, but its Cause, indifferent to us.

Who can represent, the Torture I lay in, all that Night? As soon as it was Day, I sent to some of Don *Ramire*'s Friends, desiring they wou'd acquaint me with what they knew concerning his Fate. I was then inform'd, he had been examined, and the partial Judgment of the Court had already condemn'd him, the Governour being resolv'd, not to show him the least Favour; but as there was a Form to be observed in the Tryal, they had permitted an Acquaintance of his, whose Name was Don *Tiello*, to plead in Defence of his Life.

Far from sinking under this Misfortune, I receiv'd new Strength from its Extremity: It is no Time now to shed Tears, cry'd I; the Safety of my Lover, is what I must think on. *Teresa*, continued I, you were ever faithful to me, and are the only Person, in whom I can confide; go, run, and buy me a Suit of Mens Cloaths, for I am resolv'd to see Don *Ramire*: I can pretend I am Son to Don *Tiello*, who sends

sends me to inform him of what is passing in his Affair, and by that Means I shall be admitted to enter the Prison, where we may take Measures together for his Escape. Ah, Madam, take Care what you do, reply'd she; if you are known, what will become of you? I am not in a Condition, said I, that will permit me to apprehend any thing. We must endeavour to snatch Don *Ramire* from the Governour's Revenge, and when he is safe, I shall have Time enough to think on what relates to me. In ending these Words, I obliged her to get me the Cloaths, which I immediately put on, and fancy'd in that Dress I might very well pass for a young Cavalier.

Night being come, I ordered *Teresa* to take the Key of my Chamber, and give out I was ill in Bed; then went out in this Disguise, protected by none but my Guardian Angels. If by Misfortune, said I, Don *Tiello*, (who has generously offer'd to defend Don *Ramire*,) shou'd be with him, or perhaps come in, whilst I am there, what must I do, and how shall I extricate my self from such a Difficulty? Love, said I! oh Love, for whom I suffer unconceivable Torments, be favourable to me this time! you see my deep Concern for the Danger, which threatens my Lover; I have little Hopes, and every Thing to fear, unless his Safety becomes your Care.

When I was arriv'd at this fatal Prison, I hardly had Strength to support me; my Spirits were feeble, and I found my self in much

Dis-

Diforder. The firſt Perſon I ſpoke to, was the Jaylor's Daughter; I told her, I was Don *Trello*'s Son, Friend to Don *Ramire*, and was come to inform him of the State of his Affairs. At theſe Words, ſhe preſs'd my Hand, like a Perſon in ſome Concern, and ſaid, Ah, Sir, the unhappy Gentleman is loſt, if you do not take ſpeedy Meaſures to ſave him. I know more of that Matter than you, continued ſhe, and perhaps intereſt my ſelf as much. The Place we were in, was ſo dark, that I cou'd not ſee her Face, tho' I had a great Curioſity to know the Perſon who expreſs'd her ſelf ſo feelingly; but I ſaid in a trembling Voice, pray tell me, what you have heard concerning him. All the Judges, reply'd ſhe, are devoted to the Governour, and Don *Ramire* will be condemn'd without Appeal; I have endeavoured in vain to find an Opportunity of ſpeaking to to him, but never cou'd ſee him, ſince he was brought here, cover'd with Blood and Duſt; and in that diſmal Condition, he appear'd to me the handſomeſt Man, I had ever ſeen. Alas, how fatal was that Sight to me? I was ſo touch'd with his Misfortune, that all my Thoughts ever ſince have been employ'd on his Safety, and I am happy enough to have found an Expedient, which cannot fail.

Here ſhe was ſilent, but after a little Pauſe, aſſum'd her Diſcourſe; and ſince you are his Friend, continued ſhe, I ought not to conceal from you, the Diſpoſition I have for him; I muſt

must confess I love him, and my Affection is rais'd to such a Degree, that I am resolv'd to deliver him from hence, if in giving him his Life, he will dedicate the Remainder of it to me, and render my Fate inseparable from his. Tell him, how near the Danger is, since he will not have common Mercy shown him, and that if he can purchase his Life on these Terms, I am ready to serve him: I know he is a Man of Quality, and the vast Disproportion there is between us; but the Condition, I hope, will make me acceptable to him: I shall for his sake, expose my Family to the Governour's Resentment, who will believe my Father contriv'd his Escape, and perhaps, punish him accordingly. How often have I said to my self, *Laurea!* unfortunate *Laurea!* cease attempting a Happiness that meets with such Difficulties. What! has my Passion for a Stranger, Power enough to make me forsake my Parents? Alas, Sir, I have disputed with my self, till I am no longer Mistress of my Reason; I cou'd sacrifice every thing for him; he is dearer to me than Life, and the Danger he is in, affects me beyond Imagination. Assure him from me, that my Heart never receiv'd an Impression before. I am young, and tho' not beautiful, may pass for agreeable. Oh! how happy shou'd I think my self, if he did but like me? And cou'd his Passion proceed more from Inclination than Gratitude, I shou'd die transported: Yet, said she to me, as you are particularly acquainted with him, pray tell me, whether he is not already

en-

engaged; for in fine, as I do every thing for him, I also expect, he will make me an equal Return; therefore, go to him, I shall wait your Answer here, in order to undertake something in his Favour.

Tho' my Heart was so contracted with Grief, that I cou'd hardly answer her, after she had ceas'd speaking, I said to her, Madam, your Design in preserving a Gentleman, so deserving of Life, is truly generous. I am perswaded, he will not be ungrateful, and shall let you know his Sentiments, when I return. She left me immediately to tell her Father, I was Don *Tiello*'s Son, who desired to see Don *Ramire*. He made no Difficulty, but conducted me to the Place, where this unhappy Gentleman was shut up: Alas, Madam, where shall I find Words to express the Anguish and Trouble I felt at that Instant? What am I going to do, and what Advice shall I give him? said I. Must I deliver him up to my Rival? No, I cannot bear the Thought of it. He shall never know the Passion she has for him; then reproaching my self, for coming to such a Resolution; What, continued I! wou'd I thus see him perish, and deliver him up to the Fury of his Enemies? Oh! sure, I cannot be guilty of so much Cruelty, for rather than let him die, he shall be hers: I will with my own Hand give him to her, and since I am destin'd to be a Sacrifice, my Peace and Liberty shall be the Ransom of his Preservation.

Thus, Madam, I came to the Chamber where Don *Ramire* was confin'd, and being let in, the Doors were shut again. He was so extremely thoughtful, that he hardly turn'd his Eyes towards me, till I spoke to him; What makes you so dispirited, Sir? said I: Where is that Courage, which ever supported you? The Tone of my Voice, made me known to him, and opening his Arms; Oh, my Angel! cry'd he, the only dear Object of my Vows; Is it you I see here, in this frightful Prison? Are you come to share my Pains? At these Words, he took hold of my Hand, and kiss'd it with Transports of the greatest Passion. I sat down by him, and was some Time, before I cou'd recover my Speech, so many dismal Thoughts conspir'd to increase my Despair; at last, I made an Effort, and said, if you knew, my dear Don *Ramire*, what is contriving against you, my Presence wou'd not give you all this Joy. They are working your Ruin, and you cannot possibly avoid the Misfortune, you are threatened with, but by Marrying *Laurea*, the Jaylor's Daughter, who is in Love with you, and will do her utmost to save you. The Dress I am in deceiv'd her, and she has confess'd her Passion for you; she charg'd me to inform you of it, and requires your Answer, assuring me at the same Time, you will have nothing to fear, if once you consent to her Wishes; I conjure you then, by all our Affection, to embrace this important Occasion: Marry her, since there is no other Remedy left:

*of* CARENCY.

left: I had rather deplore the Loss of your Heart, than that of your Life. O fatal Resolution! added I, must I even lose the Hopes of ever being yours? But alas, what do I say? It is no time now to reflect. I cannot ballance your Interest with mine. You must live, Sir, tho' you live for another: Whilst unhappy *Inea*, (retired to some remote solitary Place) will be dead to you, and to the rest of the World.

Don *Ramire* heard me with Surprize, and made me this Reply; Do you think, Madam, I shall not always prefer Death to an inglorious Life, and that I am capable of making you the Sacrifice? No, unfortunate as I am, Love and Resolution are my Companions, and nothing shall ever make me change. Here, I cou'd not restrain my Tears, which he perceived, and said, cease weeping, my dear *Inea*; Why will you add to my Calamities? Oh! rather conceal your Trouble, since it is in vain to advise me to such an Alliance. Must I speak to you no more of it? (reply'd I, sighing) Are you then resolv'd on your Death, and mine, and will your Love and Courage, be of no other Help to you, than to let you fall a Victim to an incens'd Parent, whose only Son, you have destroyed? At least, strive to save your self; promise every thing to *Laurea*, and perform what you please. You know me very little, Madam, interrupted he, if you believe, I can be so perfidious: This young Creature will depend on my Assurances, and I cannot resolve to deceive her. Heavens! What
shall

shall we do then? cry'd I: Your tender Scruples, are very ill timed; Do you consider, how near you are the Danger, which threatens you, and that your Fate is almost inevitable? I beg of you, I conjure you to comply with *Laurea*, tho' you are dearer to me than Life. Alas! if I saw the least Ray of Hope, do you think, I wou'd defire you to act so contrary to my Peace? Oh my Dear! my eternal Love! continu'd I; don't facrifice your felf to our mutual Affection, but yield to my laft and earneft Requeft.

A Deluge of Tears follow'd thefe Words, and my Spirits were fo faint, that I cou'd hardly continue my Difcourfe. Ah! how fatal will your Pity be to me, cry'd he? Your Trouble pierces my Heart. Don't be fo dejected, charming *Inea*, Heaven will take care of us. Yes, faid I, Heaven wou'd take care of us indeed, if you did but fecond its Infpirations. Has not Providence fent you *Laurea*? Oh! name her not, reply'd he; I conjure you, by all the Powers of Love, never to mention her more. You are refolv'd to perifh then, faid I. I wou'd live for you, anfwer'd he, but if it be not poffible, I will at leaft die conftant, and be fatisfy'd with giving you the laft Proof of my Fidelity. Here in a deep Silence, he embrac'd my Knees, and moiften'd my Hands with his Tears, which gave a new Courfe to mine. My Breaft, was fill'd with Grief, and in this fad Moment a Thought came into my Head, which I fancy'd might be executed without much Difficulty. Don't

Don't be against all the Ways there are left to preserve your Life, said I, but swear by your Passion for me, that you will strictly follow the Advice, I am going to give you. It's unnecessary, you shou'd engage me by Oath, to obey you, reply'd he; you know I am devoted to your Commands, and tho' I cou'd not consent to deceive *Laurea*, you must not judge from thence, of what I am capable of doing for you. Well, said I, you shall have nothing to say to her; I will be with you about this time to Morrow, and we must exchange Cloaths; you shall go out in mine, and immediately repair to Don *Tiello*, who will have Notice of it: There are Vessels going out a Cruising, and as you have Relations at the Court of *Morocco*, you may find an Opportunity of going to a Place, where you will be out of the Power of your Enemies. What, Madam! cry'd he, and leave you here a Prisoner, in my room, expos'd to the Fury of your Relations, and the Governour's Resentment. Must you be sacrific'd for my Liberty? No, I had rather die before your Face. I am not base enough to resolve on any such thing. I see very well (said I to him, in an angry Tone) that I must use all my Authority to make you obey me. Since you compel me to it, Sir, I command you to prepare your self to go off, in the manner I told you; I protest if you continue to be obstinate, I never will see you more, I retract the Promise I made you of being yours, and dispense you
of

of all your Vows to me; fo that now being free, we may difpofe as we pleafe of our Deftinies.

Never was Man in a greater Confufion, than poor Don *Ramire*, when he heard me utter thefe Words, he flung himfelf at my Feet, and look'd like one diftracted: Are you then refolv'd, Madam, to hate me, and make another Man happy? faid he; what Crime have I committed to deferve fo many Misfortunes? I only refufe to fly this Prifon, becaufe I wou'd not leave you here; fure this Proof of my Paffion cannot be fo cruel an Offence? Why will you add one Torment to another? I muft be abfolutely obey'd, reply'd I, fince in leaving me here, I run no Rifque; *Laurea* will get me out, and it's with her, I fhall take Meafures for that Purpofe; therefore if you love me, do not oppofe my fetting you free. Alas, Madam! difpofe of me as you pleafe (faid he in a dejected Manner) I am wholly yours, and never wou'd have difputed your Power, were it not for the fear I was in, of expofing you to inevitable Dangers. I am now fatisfy'd, anfwer'd I; for be affur'd Don *Ramire*, if I lov'd you lefs, I fhou'd not have been fo difpleas'd with your Refufal: At thefe Words he paffionately kifs'd my Hand, and with tender Regret we feparated.

The Jaylor being told by a Soldier of the Guard, that I wanted to have the Door open'd, came and conducted me out, but I was uneafy, not feeing *Laurea*, who (having veil'd her felf) was

was standing in a dark Paſſage near the outward Gate, where on a sudden I heard her ſay, Hold, Sir, pray let me know what News from the Perſon you have juſt ſeen; he acknowledges your Generoſity with the higheſt Gratitude, Madam, ſaid I, and will make you Miſtreſs of his Fate, being reſolv'd to live only for you. I fear you flatter me, reply'd ſhe, for I am eaſily deceiv'd, but if you do, Heaven will puniſh you both. No, ſaid I, do not ſuſpect his Honour, nor mine, you ſhall never have reaſon to repent your generous Sentiments, but when will you ſet him free ? As ſoon as poſſible, anſwer'd ſhe; my Father, and the Soldiers who guard him eat together; I intend to put Opium in their Wine, and when they are aſleep, ſteal the Keys, ſo let him out. But what will become of us afterwards, continu'd *Laurea*? You ſhall embark together, ſaid I, and rejoyce at your good Fortune, far from *Porto-Real*; thus I left her, and ſhe ſeem'd highly pleas'd at the Aſſurances I gave her.

I was going towards home, when I thought it very neceſſary, Don *Tiello* ſhou'd be inform'd of what had paſs'd; therefore I went to him, and told him I had us'd his Name to be admitted into the Priſon, which I hop'd he wou'd approve; that I had been trying Means for my Friend's Eſcape, and as I did not doubt of ſucceeding, we had agreed he ſhou'd come to him as ſoon as he was free, being perſuaded he wou'd be ſo generous, as to take care of his Safety, till he had found a Ship to carry him

him to *Morocco*. The Circumstance is very lucky, said he, for my Brother lies now in the Road, and only waits a fair Wind to sail for that Coast; be assur'd I shall neglect no Opportunity of serving him. After this Answer, I desir'd him not to go the next Day to the Prison, because I was to be there, and shou'd pass for his Son; so left him without being known, and my Mind was more compos'd, than it had been ever since Don *Ramire*'s fatal Confinement.

By this time I was come home, where I found *Teresa* waiting for me. I related to her all that had pass'd; but when I recollected, I had advis'd Don *Ramire* to lay his Liberty at *Laurea*'s Feet, I thought, I cou'd never have been capable of acting so contrary to my Sentiments. What cou'd I do *Teresa*, said I, for were he as weak as I have been, and had Fear made him inconstant, by this time, I shou'd see him no longer mine; and on the other side, had I not us'd this Stratagem, in a few Days he wou'd be no more in the World.

I found some Ease in entertaining her after this manner most part of the Night, and representing to her his extraordinary Passion and Constancy, his Design of going to *Morocco*, and mine of meeting him there. I ought not to distrust, said I, the Promise he has given me, since he declar'd he rather wou'd chuse Death, than be contracted to his Deliverer; and if I can get my Jewels (which are in my Mother's keeping) nothing shall prevent my making this Voyage.

Voyage. *Terefa* told me, it was eafy enough to get into her Clofet, and if I wou'd carry her with me, fhe wou'd take upon her to get 'em, tho' fhe fhou'd hazard her Life for it. Her Affection to my Service fo fenfibly touch'd me, that I embrac'd her, and promis'd never to forfake her. You muft go out with me to Morrow Night, continu'd I, difguis'd in Men's Cloaths, for fear my Relations (perceiving my Flight, and the Lofs of the Jewels) fhou'd feize you; as Don *Tiello* is a Man of Honour, and in our Prifoner's Intereft, I will meet him before I go to the Prifon, and tell him my Refolution of ftaying in Don *Ramire*'s Place; I fhall defire him at the fame to protect you, and procure us a Ship to follow him. But, Madam, reply'd fhe, what will you do with *Laurea*, whom you intend to deceive, under the Notion of your being Don *Ramire*? She will follow your Fortune, and if fhe difcovers who you are, may give you a great deal of Trouble. This requiring fome Reflection, every thing I had to fear, prefented it felf to my Imagination all that Night, and tormented me a thoufand different Ways.

The next Morning I pretended I was extremely indifpos'd, to prevent my Mother's fufpecting I had any Defign; and as foon as it was Dusk of Evening, *Terefa* difguis'd, enter'd my Mother's Clofet, and took the Jewels, as we had propos'd it; then I went directly to the Prifon, where *Laurea* was expecting me, without any Light; I told her, I was refolv'd

to

to expose my Life for her, and Don *Ramire's* Service, assuring her, I wou'd carry them to a Ship which wou'd soon put 'em out of the Power of their Enemies. My Fate is in your Hands, reply'd she, and provided I am with him I love, carry me where you please: I am now endeavouring his Liberty, and do not doubt, but I shall succeed in what I undertake. I return'd her Thanks in the Name of Don *Ramire*, then hiding my self with my Cloke, went to the Jaylor, whom I complimented in few Words, and desired the Favour of seeing Don *Ramire*, as from my Father; you shall see him this Night, and no more, (said he to me, in a rough manner) for Orders are given, that none but Don *Tiello* shou'd be admitted, and if the Governour knew I suffer you to speak to him, he wou'd make me repent it. This unexpected Reception stun'd me: Alas! thought I, if we do not improve this Opportunity, we are all undone.

Don *Ramire*, as soon as I enter'd his Chamber, receiv'd me in his Arms, and saluted me with so much Tenderness, in his Words and Actions, that it show'd at once, his Love and Gratitude. Come, my Dear, said I, let us make good use of this precious Moment; put on my Cloaths immediately, and give me yours; cover your Face after the same manner, I did mine; and if you meet *Laurea* as you go out, tell her, Don *Ramire* depends entirely on her Friendship: *Teresa* (in whom I confide) is dress'd in Mens Cloaths, and waits at the end of a Street, to go along with you to Don *Tiello*'s, who is ready to receive you; as for my part, I shall stay here, till *Laurea* comes to relieve me. Alas, my charming *Inea*, reply'd he, how shall I resolve to forsake you? No, my only Dear, I cannot submit to a Command, so desperate. If I must perish, or lose you, I readily prefer the first. Ah cruel Man! said I, shall we then dispute for ever, and will you act both your own Destruction and mine? How can you be so obstinate? I beg you, dear Don *Ramire*, I conjure you, by all the Love you ever profess'd to me, and the Proofs I have given you of a Return, not to deny me this Favour; I fear every thing on your Account, but have little to fear on my own; obey me this Instant, and make no Reply.

Thus, Madam, I at last persuaded him, tho' not without much Difficulty, and having divested my self of my Clothes, I made him put 'em on. The Disguise seem'd favourable to him, and I was flattering my self with a successful Event, when the Hour of parting drew near. Our Sighs and Tears, were the Interpreters of our excessive Grief. Is it possible, I have Resolution enough, said Don *Ramire*, to act a Part, so contrary to the Sentiments of my Soul? Oh! think, that in obeying you this Day, I give you the greatest Testimony of an inviolable Passion. I regard it as a Proof of your Constancy, reply'd I, which will have its Reward; our Fortune may receive a happy Change, then we shall triumph over our ill Stars;

Stars; I even feel a secret Satisfaction in my present Misfortune, since it gives me an Opportunity of showing, how much I love you. In what a different State is my bleeding Heart, cry'd he? Can I ever be more unhappy, than to leave you in this frightful Place, and live some Days without you? But, continued he, be assur'd, my Body only will be separated from you; my Thoughts shall ever attend you; receive my Vows, divine *Inea*, and let this Ring be the Pledge of my Love; Heaven ordain, we may be so united, as never to be parted more. I accept your Hand, reply'd I; here, receive mine, and may the superior Powers be witness of our Promises. Adieu, my Dear, (continued I, embracing him, and bathing his Face with my Tears.) Farewel my Angel, said he, pressing me in his Arms, it grieves my very Soul to leave you.

Don *Ramire*, in this manner, was conducted out; and as soon as I had lost sight of him, all my Fears for him, and my own Conduct, came hurrying to my Mind. I know not, Madam, how it was possible, I cou'd bear with the Anxiety of my Thoughts; all that was dismal, and full of Terror, enter'd my Imagination, whilst I was uncertain of his Fate; but by the time I thought he might be out of Danger, my afflicted Mind receiv'd some Relief.

As I had pass'd but a very indifferent Night, I lay all the next Day on the Bed, which made the Jaylor believe I was sick; therefore whenever he came into my Chamber, he wou'd not interrupt

interrupt me, but leaving what was necessary by me, retired. I continued in this Situation, till the Evening, when I was agreeably surpriz'd with a Visit from Don *Tiello*, who brought me a Letter, and inform'd me of Don *Ramire*'s being happily embark'd; he highly commended the Resolution I had shown, in staying in his Place, with the hazard of my Life, to preserve his; but after he had been some time with me, he discover'd, I was not what I appear'd to be; the Tone of my Voice, my Complexion, and particularly the Emotion I was in, when I spoke of Don *Ramire*, with the Joy I express'd at receiving his Letter, and my Tears, every thing confirm'd his Suspicions; yet for fear of offending me, he wou'd not mention any thing of the Matter; protesting only, he wou'd do all, that depended on him to serve me, and that I cou'd not confide in a Person, who wou'd make a more generous return. After some Discourses of this Nature, he took Leave of me, wishing I might meet a Recompence, proportionable to so great and perfect a Friendship. I pass'd the rest of my Night in reading over, and over, Don *Ramire*'s Letter, which was the only Consolation I had, the five Days I was Prisoner; it was writ in these Terms,

*I* Have left you, my dear Inea, *in so frightful a Place, and with such melancholy Circumstances, that you may easily imagine, the Condition I am in, is not less deplorable than yours. I must confess, fefs*, I was juſt on the Point of returning to you, but the Apprehenſion I was under, of diſpleaſing you, prevented my giving ſuch a Proof of my Love. Oh! ought I not to be aſham'd you ſhou'd have ſurpaſs'd me in Generoſity, and that I cou'd be weak enough to ſuffer it? Yet do not interpret this to the Prejudice of One, who only conſented to fly, that he might preſerve himſelf yours; and ſince our good Fortune equally depends on my Life, I ſhall take care of it, as an Offering, no longer mine, but conſecrated to you. Come then ſpeedily, my Angel, and let us by our Union, taſte immortal Pleaſures. My leaving this Place, is defer'd no longer than the finiſhing this Letter. I am going, and ſhall expect you with Impatience, proportionable to the Happineſs of our next meeting: Adieu, my Soul, Adieu my only Dear; we ſhall have no Reaſon, I hope, to complain hereafter of Fortune, ſince our Paſſion ſurpaſſes every thing, that has ever been known in the World.

I muſt tell you, Madam, I had taken *Tereſa* with me to the Priſon, by which means I made her acquainted with *Laurea*, who ſuppos'd her to be a young Gentleman, and our intimate Friend. As they us'd often to meet in a Place, they had appointed for that Purpoſe, *Laurea* cou'd not help ſaying one Day to her, that ſhe was very uneaſy, concerning what ſhe ſhou'd act in favour of Don *Ramire*, and that ſhe had a mind to leave him in Confinement; for what can I hope from him? continu'd ſhe; I may depend on a great deal of Chagrin on account

count of my Father, who will be prosecuted for his Escape: I shall be the occasion of the Ruin of my Family, and how do I know, but I may be lost with them. It's true, I am promis'd every thing from Don *Ramire*, yet my Birth is so inferior to his, that nothing less than an extraordinary Passion, cou'd induce him to condescend to our Alliance; besides, he has never seen me; and when we are once embark'd together, instead of loving me, perhaps he may hate me. Oh! I think my self already abandon'd by him, and set ashore on some desert Island, where Death will be the Recompence of all my Pains. *Teresa* trembled at what she heard this young Creature say, knowing I cou'd only make my Escape by her means, so omitted nothing to bring her back to her first Intentions. Generous *Laurea*, said she, I am persuaded, if you knew the Person you propose to serve, as well as I do, you wou'd never change your Resolution; he has all the Sentiments of a Man of Honour, and I am sure, his Passion for you will be eternal: The Chimeras you frame to your self, have not the least Foundation; I therefore conjure you, to be constant in so important a Cause, which will undoubtedly contribute to your good Fortune, as well as his. *Laurea*, asham'd of having shown so much Inequality of Temper, made some Excuses, then resolv'd again on her first Design; I am willing to believe you, said she, and to convince you of the Truth, be here exactly at Two after Midnight;

I will bring Don *Ramire* to you; every thing is ready for his Escape, and you may take Measures for our Departure. *Terefa*, extreamly overjoy'd at thefe Words, left her immediately, and went to Don *Tiello* to tell him, Don *Ramire*'s Friend, whom he had seen in Prison, wou'd be that Night set free, and desired, he wou'd prepare a Sloop for their going off; but, continu'd she, how shall we disengage our selves from *Laurea*, who will do us all the Prejudice in her Power, if once she perceives we have betray'd her. When she comes aboard, said he, and finds it is not Don *Ramire*'s Concern, she will be too happy to return home, without discovering any thing, for fear they shou'd charge her with having an Hand in his Escape; and if some unforeseen Accident does not happen, I am persuaded, we shall manage this Affair to our Satisfaction.

As I cou'd not tell, what Hour *Laurea* had appointed to set me at Liberty, I began to be very much tired with my Confinement; but in the dead of Night, I was reliev'd of my Uneasiness, when I heard my Door open softly, and saw the Jaylor's Daughter; being wrap'd in my Cloak, I advanc'd towards her, with my Face almost hid, for fear she shou'd discover I was not Don *Ramire*: I embrac'd her with the greatest Marks of a violent Passion, but said little to her on the Score of my Gratitude; she was in such Disorder her self, that I believe it wou'd have been hard for her, to perceive the Deceit, had she even seen my Face.

Face. In one Hand she had a dark Lanthorn, and in the other a Bunch of Keys, so without saying any thing to me, she made me a Sign to follow her, which I did, and we pass'd all the Soldiers who were fast asleep, as she had contriv'd it, by putting Opium in their Wine. Thus we left the Place without the least Obstacle; but as soon as we were in the Street, she took hold of my Arm, as if she were afraid I shou'd fly her, cling'd to me so close, that I was hardly able to walk.

Don *Tiello*, and *Teresa*, were waiting for me in the Place they had appointed, from whence, we went together to the Sea-side, where we found the Boat belonging to the Ship, which was to carry me to *Morocco*. The Night was very dark, and *Laurea* made me a thousand Caresses, I cou'd but very ill return, being in pain to know, what wou'd become of this young Creature, after she had discover'd the Plot. We were not long a making up to the Vessel, and as soon as we came on board, Don *Tiello* carry'd us into the Captain's Cabbin; but, Madam, how shall I tell you the Surprize I was in, when I found this Captain to be my Father, who was no less astonish'd to see *Teresa* and me, after all the Enquiry that had been made about us throughout the whole City. Don *Tiello*, knowing he profess'd a great Friendship for Don *Ramire*, had trusted him with the Secret, and declar'd, I was that unhappy Gentleman's Mistress, who had resolv'd to follow his Fortune into *Morocco*, in Man's Difguife; he ftarted back three or four Steps, and not being Mafter of the firft Effects of his Paffion, was going to draw his Sword, when I flung my felf at his Feet: Oh Sir! faid I, forgive me; remember you are my Father, and vouchfafe to hear, before you punifh me. I embrac'd his Knees, and wet his Hand with my Tears. Tho' he entirely lov'd me, yet in this Occafion, he fhow'd his Refentment, by making me many Reproaches, and at laft, bid me fay what I cou'd, to juftify my felf.

I knew my only Remedy was, to confefs the Truth, which I did in fo feeling a Manner, that it mov'd his Compaffion. He was very well acquainted with Don *Ramire*'s Merit, and had been thoroughly concern'd for his Imprifonment; but being inform'd of his Efcape, he exprefs'd an entire Satisfaction. My Father left us to go into another Cabbin with Don *Tiello*, who was very much his Friend. I fee, faid he, you are furpriz'd, as well as me, at what has happened; you were certainly a Stranger to *Inea*'s Flight, and did not think, it was her you had put into my Hands. I proteft to you, reply'd Don *Tiello*, I am under a Confternation, which I cannot exprefs. I can't fay I have committed a Fault; for perhaps, it may turn to Advantage, that the Affair has pafs'd after this Manner; but if you will make me perfectly eafy, I beg you will grant me your Daughter's Pardon, whatever Reafons you have to be difpleas'd with her,

her. You see, she is contracted to Don *Ramire*, who is a Man of Birth and Fortune, and in my Opinion, you cannot dispose of her better, than uniting her Destiny to his. I agree with you, reply'd my Father; but his Proceedings to obtain *Inea*, without my Consent, highly offend me. I receiv'd him into my House as a particular Friend, and wou'd have willingly given my eldest Daughter to him; was it not a very ill Return, he made to so much Civility, when he engag'd this young Creature to disguise her self, and follow him like a Madwoman? If you remember what *Inea* has related to us, reply'd Don *Tiello*, she is alone culpable; yet of all Crimes, those which Love makes us commit, are most excusable, and especially in a young Person, who has so little Experience. Forgive her then, I conjure you, added he, and you will confer an Obligation on me, which I shall ever acknowledge. My Father, who was already dispos'd to favour me, embracing Don *Tiello*, said to him, I am considerably indebted to you, for entering so generously into the Interest of my Family, and will forget *Inea*'s Crime, since you desire it; if Don *Ramire* has a real Passion for her, I shall rejoice at the Match; and as a Proof of my Satisfaction, I will carry her to *Morrocco*, in order to compleat their Happiness.

This Conversation ended in my Favour, as you see, Madam, which I little expected; for I was in the Cabbin so extremely afflicted, that

that I may say, no Sorrow cou'd be equal to mine. What will become of me, (said I to *Teresa*) I am for ever unfortunate? I loose my Liberty, in the very Moment, I thought my self Miſtreſs of my Deſtiny, and I am now in the Power of a Father, who will have no Mercy of me. Alas! poor Don *Ramire*, I muſt never ſee him more; he will certainly think I am Dead, or Inconſtant, and either of the Two will drive him into Deſpair; I ſhall be deliver'd up to my Mother and Siſter's Severities, which is a Misfortune, I can never endure.

Whilſt I was ſpeaking, *Laurea* look'd at me with the Eyes of a Fury: Don't you deſerve the Fate you have met with, ſaid ſhe? Nay, even more than what ſeems to threaten you. You have deceived me, perfidious as you are, and improv'd my Weakneſs in Favour of your Lover. I have juſt delivered up my Family to the Governour's Reſentment, but don't think to eſcape me; you ſhall be my Victim, as I am your's. In pronouncing theſe Words, ſhe flung her ſelf upon me, and I do not doubt, but wou'd have ſtifled me, had not *Tereſa* come to my Aſſiſtance, as well as my Father and Don *Tiello*, who hearing a Noiſe, ran, and freed me from this mad Creature's Rage; I ſtood in want of their Help, for I did not reſiſt her, prefering Death to an unhappy Life.

Don *Tiello* ſaw very well, to what a Condition my Grief had reduc'd me, and neglected nothing to eaſe my troubled Mind; he beg'd

I

I wou'd no longer afflict my self. I have prevail'd with your Father, Madam, said he, and he has promis'd me to carry you to *Morocco*. I had not patience to hear any more, but upon these Assurances, went and flung my self at my Father's Feet, and embracing his Knees, express'd my Gratitude; he told me with a great deal of Goodness, that, as it was Don *Tiello*'s Request, he forgave me, and consented I shou'd marry Don *Ramire*. At these Words *Laurea* cry'd aloud, and made such Complaints, as wou'd move any one with Pity; I knew by my self what she suffered. Alas! (said I, to *Teresa*) were my Case like hers, how wretched shou'd I be? She loves Don *Ramire*, and was flatter'd with the Hopes of passing the rest of her Days with him, but now those agreeable Thoughts are all destroy'd. She loves him less than you imagine, reply'd *Teresa*, and if I had not done my utmost to make her pursue her first Intentions, I very much doubt the Performance of what she promis'd you. Here, *Teresa* related to us what had pass'd between them, as I have already inform'd you, Madam; and Don *Tiello* told *Laurea*, the best Thing she cou'd do, was to return to *Porto-Real* before Day, that her Father might not know of her having a Hand in the Matter; so he took his Leave of us, and carrying her with him into the Boat, they both went ashore.

I had but just Time to change my Cloaths, when you came on Board, and your Trouble, Madam,

Madam, interrupted the Pleasure I began to taste, at the Thoughts of seeing Don *Ramire*, who as yet has not heard of my Misfortune; he will leave *Morocco*, perhaps, in Hopes of finding me at *Porto-Real*; his Passion may make him forget the Danger, which threatens him at that Place, and I know not whether I shall ever see him more: I have also lost *Teresa*, who was so true to me; this poor Creature was snatch'd from me, by one of the Officers in the Admiral's Ship; my Prayers cou'd not prevent her being carried off by this Barbarian; and I assure you, Madam, had it not been for you, I shou'd have sunk under the Load of innumerable Calamities.

Here *Inea* endeavour'd to hide her Tears, but cou'd not restrain their Course. *Felicia* embrac'd her, and us'd many tender Expressions to soften her Sorrow. Alas, my Dear, said she, I my self am very unfortunate, and did you know the cruel Torments I endure, you wou'd own, you are not alone to be pitied; but I consider, it's Time for you to retire; I have kept you up too long. I am sensible, Madam, reply'd *Inea*, I have tired your Patience with the Recital of my Adventures, but that's a Fault which attends all unhappy Lovers, since the only Consolation they have left 'em, is that of lamenting their Fate. You do me Injustice, replied *Felicia*, if you have so disobliging a Thought; I am extremely pleased with your Compliance; and to convince you thereof, I will to Morrow, in Return, confide
the

the Secrets of my Life to you. In finishing these Words, she embrac'd her again, and *Inea* went to her Bed.

*Phœbus* had no sooner grac'd the watery Plain, but young *Inea* (impatient to hear *Felicia*'s Adventures) rose, and saluted her with a pleasant Morning: I wish, my Dear, (said *Felicia* to her,) I had not clos'd my Eyes all Night, for I have had a frightful Dream concerning a Person, I very much esteem; he appeared to me in the greatest Dangers, engag'd with the *Moors*, and vanquish'd. Oh, how my Soul is alarm'd! Your Mind is so possess'd with dismal Ideas, reply'd *Inea*, that you must not be surpriz'd, if they affect you in your Sleep; yet, Madam, Dreams are not to be taken Notice of. Alas, said *Felicia*, they wou'd make no Impression on me at any other Time; but what have I not to fear at present, being far from my Country, and from a Friend, whose Absence is the chief Cause of my Uneasiness? Tho' I own to you, *Abelhamar*'s Passion for me, is no small Addition to my Woes, since I must be continually on my Guard against the Pursuits of a Prince, who has so much Power in this Court. Unhappy Creature that I am! Were not my Misfortunes great enough? Why must the few Charms I have left, serve only to render them the more insupportable? Don't add to your Affliction, Madam, said *Inea*, the Prince has too much Respect for you, to use his Authority in Opposition to your Inclinations, and you may easily

easily imagine, as soon as your Relations are inform'd of your Destiny, they will employ all their Interest to relieve you. I shou'd be in the Wrong to doubt their Affection for me, reply'd *Felicia* weeping, tho' in their Opinion, my Behaviour merits no Favour. Oh! that I rather owed my Liberty to the Man, whose Presence now wou'd make me happy. I find you are in Love, Madam, (said *Inea*, interrupting her.) I confess it, reply'd *Felicia* blushing; and since you have given me so great a Proof of your Confidence, I promise you mine, and will inform you of my Weakness.

*Felicia* began immediately to relate her Story, from the time her Father had contracted her to the Prince of *Carency*, but her Discourse was often interrupted with Tears, which the Thoughts of her Misfortunes extorted from her; I am not only concern'd, said she, at my being separated from the Count of *La Vagne*, but inconsolable, when I think, how *Casilda* betray'd me, after having chose her for my Friend, and lov'd her sincerely. I condemn her, reply'd *Inea*, and wonder how any one cou'd be so perfidious, especially to a Person, who no ways deserv'd such inhuman Usage.

They were talking in this manner, when the Governess of the Slaves came, and bid 'em dress themselves, in order to wait on the Queen to the *Mosquez*, where they were oblig'd to attend, tho' Christians. *Felicia*, during the Ceremony of those Infidels, took such care to hide self in her Veil, that altho' *Abelhamar* sought

sought her with a great deal of Attention, he cou'd not distinguish her from the rest of her Companions; he did not doubt but this Affectation was design'd, which so sensibly griev'd him, that he retir'd to his Apartment, and wrote the ensuing Letter.

*WHAT Crime have I committed, lovely Felicia, to deserve your Aversion? You fly me, and even deny me the Satisfaction of seeing your beauteous Face. Can you be offended at a Passion, your Charms have created? What Violence have I not done my self, to suppress my Transports, rather than incur your Displeasure? Oh! treat me with less Severity; my Love is worthy a more obliging Return, since I am seeking Means to procure your Liberty, which I hope to effect, in spite of the Queen's Opposition.*

Celima being return'd from the *Mosquez*, order'd that some of the Slaves shou'd come and work by her; *Felicia* was of the Number, and as *Abelhamar* was watching an Opportunity to give her this Letter, he approach'd her, and slip'd it into her Lap, which he thought she had perceiv'd, and wou'd have taken care to hide it; but it happen'd otherwise, for the Queen (who was inform'd of the Prince's Sentiments for *Felicia*) seeing him put a Paper into her Work, found Means to take it, so was convinc'd of the Truth, and extremely pleas'd this young *Spaniard* made no Return to *Abelhamar*'s Passion. The Queen had

had a fecret Averfion to him, tho' his only Crime was that of being lawful Heir to the Crown fhe was in Poffeffion of, which was a fufficient Motive, to make him difagreeable to her.

That Evening, *Celima* took a Walk in the Palace Gardens, and as fhe had a Mind to fpeak with *Felicia*, fhe call'd her, as it were, to lean on her Arm, and advanc'd towards a Terrace-Walk, from whence one cou'd difcover the Sea-Side, with a moft delightful Profpect; there fhe fate down, and looking at *Felicia* with a graceful Air; Tho' you have not been with me long, faid fhe, I have a particular Kindnefs for you, and am willing to tell you, that if you have a Mind to merit my Affection, you muft entirely banifh *Abelhamar* from your Heart. I am inform'd of his Sentiments, and know part of your's; but it's to be fear'd, that a young Creature as you are, (having no other Engagement, and being flatter'd with the Hopes he gives you) might facrifice your Virtues to your Ambition; yet I cannot believe, you wou'd confent to be his Miftrefs; for that is all you muft expect from a Man, who certainly never will Marry you. I do not know, Madam, anfwer'd *Felicia*, (with a great deal of Modefty) who cou'd fpeak to you of the Prince's Sentiments; but if your Majefty is inform'd of mine, you are convinc'd I have receiv'd his Offers in fuch a Manner, as ought to deftroy all the Hopes, my Misfortunes might have given him; the Condition I am in, Madam, continu'd fhe, has not made

made any dishonourable Impression on my Heart, and I bless Heaven, to find your Majesty so oppos'd to a Thing, which I cou'd not think on, without the greatest Horror; for in my Opinion, it is more glorious to die, than live a Life destitute of Virtue.

What! said the Queen, wou'd you sooner chuse Death, than be Mistress to *Abelhamar*? Who wou'd not, as well as I, Madam, (replied *Felicia*,) and what other Thought cou'd enter into one's Head? This Resolution is my only Comfort, since I know it to be an effectual Way to deliver me from an infamous Passion. But if you have a Lover in *Spain*, said the Queen, do you consider, that in dying at *Sallee*, you never will see him more? Suppose there were any One, for whom I had an Inclination, replied *Felicia*, I shou'd be the more ready to die, as being the strongest Evincement I cou'd give him of my Constancy; for if it were my Misfortune, not to live for him, I never wou'd for any other. Ha, *Felicia!* said the Queen, smiling, What do you tell me; is it possible that *Cupid* hath already summon'd a Heart so young? But alas, there is no Age free from his Empire; in one Moment the fatal Dart is lanc'd. Ending these Words, she sigh'd, and remain'd some Time in a deep Silence.

All the Ladies who attended the Queen, were standing at such a Distance from the Place where she was sate, that she cou'd speak to *Felicia* without being heard; here, said she, (taking the Prince's Letter from her Bosom,) see what *Abelhamar* has wrote to you. I believe you are virtuous, therefore cannot suspect your Conduct: When you see him, take no Notice of my knowing his Sentiments; but advise him, not to persevere in his Design; for instead of procuring your Liberty, as he promises, perhaps he may lose his own for the rest of his Days. This she pronounc'd with a melancholy Accent, then rose, and return'd to the Palace.

*Felicia*, overjoy'd at what the Queen had said to her, join'd *Inea*, whom she desired to stay with her in the Garden, and they both went, and sate down in the same Place, which *Celima* had just quitted. Notwithstanding all the Misfortunes that afflict me, (said *Felicia* to her Companion) I have Cause to bless Heaven, for the Disposition the Queen is in; she forbids me receiving the Prince's Addresses; think, my Dear, how willing I am to obey her, and whether she had Need to use her Authority on this Occasion. I congratulate you, answer'd *Inea*, since it adds to your Comfort, but I cannot conceive out of what Motive she opposes a Thing, which ought to be indifferent to her, unless she has her self taken an Affection for him. I am apt to believe, said *Felicia*, her Thoughts are employ'd on some Object, and that her Heart is not entirely free from Love; for when she ask'd me, whether I had any Engagement, I perceiv'd she grew of a sudden so pensive, that it was some Time be-

before she cou'd recover her self; yet I cannot think she likes the young Prince, for as she is Mistress of her Destiny, I suppose she might make him her Husband if it were her Pleasure; I rather believe, she intends to keep him under an absolute Submission to her Will. Can she be so little acquainted with the Motions of a Heart, interrupted *Inea*, to imagine *Abelhamar's* Sentiments will receive Laws from a Sovereign, whom he has some Reason to hate? As for my part, I know it wou'd be impossible for me, either to Love, or not Love, by Command; I might so far prevail with my self, as to be silent, or to counterfeit an Indifference, and yet I cannot tell, whether I shou'd act that Part so well, as to please those who wou'd lay such a Duty on me. I shall not dispute with you on that Subject, replied *Felicia*; but between us, I esteem it a great Happiness, that my Inclination is so ready to comply with the Queen's Commands.

As she had finished her Discourse, she perceiv'd a Man near her, whom by the Light of the Moon, she knew to be *Abelhamar*, which not a little surpriz'd her; she rose in order to run from him, but he took hold of her, and said, Do not fly me thus, cruel *Felicia*; I am unfortunate enough, to have heard your Conversation with *Celima*, and cou'd wish my self dead, rather than give you the Displeasure of seeing me once more at your Feet. Here he was silent, but after some Time, continu'd in this Manner; What! did I think One, whom I look'd on a Divinity, wou'd approve of the unjuſt Queen's Barbarity, and reduce me to the laſt Deſpair, by an inhumane Uſage? Take Care, ungrateful *Felicia*, how you behave your ſelf towards me. I am not here among Strangers, and *Celima* (who wou'd fain diſpoſe of my Heart, as ſhe does of my Crown) may find, Fortune is not always conſtant, and that Uſurpers have ever Cauſe to fear. My Lord, replied *Felicia*, I perceive you heard what the Queen ſaid, relating to you; I muſt not concern my ſelf in Affairs of State, and ſince you know my Sentiments, I ſhall make no Diffiulty in confeſſing them. It is true, I was ſenſibly pleas'd to receive a Command ſo poſitive, and conformable to my Inclination, for I cannot love an Enemy to my Country and Religion. Why have I treated you like an Enemy? anſwer'd the Prince: What Advantage did I take of my Victory? Was it a Crime to love, and ſerve you? I am ſenſible of all you acted for me, interrupted *Felicia*, and my Gratitude is equal to your Favours; accept of it then, my Lord, as the only Return I can make, and it's even more than the Queen will conſent to.

The Prince falling into a violent Paſſion, lean'd himſelf againſt a Balliſter of Marble Pillars, which boarded the Terrace-Walk, and looking at *Felicia*, with Deſpair in his Countenance; I ſwear, ſaid he, by our great *Mahomet*, and by my Love, that if I don't enjoy you,

you, I will put the Kingdom of *Fez* into Desolation, pull down from the Throne the unworthy Princess who sits on it, and burn this magnificent Palace to Ashes. You shall see, *Felicia*, what such a Lover as I can do, when he finds himself despis'd. Your Eyes shall cause more Confusion amongst us, than any Revolution ever did. Oh Heavens, my Lord! cry'd *Felicia*; can any thing be more dreadful, than such Designs? What! for an unfortunate Slave, as I am, wou'd you disturb the Peace of this Nation? Are not my Woes great enough already; must you attempt to force me away from the Queen, after I have declar'd to you, that I will resolve on Death, sooner than consent to your Desires? My Lord, since I must confess it, I am in Love with One in *Spain*, and I will as willingly give my Life, as marry any other; Absence it self shall never lessen my Affection for him: I know the Way to be constant, and preserve my Heart for One, who—— No, I can hear you no longer, (said the Prince, interrupting her) you endeavour to distract me, with the cruelest Things, you can imagine; but in Time, I will be reveng'd on you, the Queen, and that dangerous Rival. Finishing these Words, he left *Felicia*.

Her Affliction was so great, that she had hardly reach'd the Palace, when she was seized with a violent Feaver, which continu'd all that Night. The Governess of the Slaves went next Morning, to acquaint the Queen of it, it, who sent *Olympia Doria* to stay by her. As soon as *Felicia* saw her enter the Chamber, she said to her, with a languishing Air; The Condition I am in, Madam, will only give you Uneasiness, and the Company of so unfortunate a Creature as I, can be no ways agreeable to you. I cannot tell, whether it be a Pleasure to you, to see me, answer'd *Olympia*; but I know very well, nothing can give me a greater Satisfaction, than being with you; and tho' I am in Expectation of the only Happiness, that can bless my Days, yet in quitting this Palace, I cannot help regretting the Absence of my charming *Felicia*. How obliging you are, my dearest Companion, (replied she) but alas! I shall have the greatest Cause to regret, when I see you no more. What Consolation wou'd it be me, were I going with you to *Genoa*; I have some Reasons to wish it. I will not presume to ask 'em, said *Olympia*, fearing you shou'd think my Curiosity too great; but if you will tell me, why you are so desirous of going that Voyage, I shall take it as a mighty Favour. I will grant your Request, replied *Felicia*, as soon as my Health permits me, and shall desire you also, to acquaint me with some Particulars, relating to a Person of that Country. Which *Olympia* promis'd her; and after having staid some Time with her, she went, and gave the Queen an Account of the Condition she was in.

The mean while, *Felicia* and *Inea* entertain'd each other with their Grief, whenever they found

found an Opportunity of being alone. Shou'd I inform the Queen of *Abelhamar*'s Menaces, (said *Felicia*, to her Friend) she wou'd take such Measures as might secure the Peace and Tranquility of her Kingdom, and by sending me for *Spain*, deliver me from his Violence; but (continu'd she, after a Moment's Pause,) what Reproaches shou'd not I deserve, supposing this young Prince was only urged by his Passion, to speak as he did, without having any Thoughts of executing so rash a Design, and that upon my Information, he shou'd be arrested; then his Disgrace, and perhaps the Loss of his Life, wou'd be owing to me? What an ungrateful Return shou'd I make, to the obliging Sentiments he conceiv'd for me, from the Beginning of my Misfortune? *Inea* approv'd very much her prudent Considerations, and represented to her, how willingly the Queen wou'd embrace that Pretence, to make a Sacrifice of *Abelhamar*, whose Passion she only oppos'd, with a Design to provoke him to use her with Disrespect, which wou'd consequently bring him to inevitable Punishment; and were it otherways, it wou'd not stand with Reason, that the Queen shou'd concern her self with any thing so much below her, as a Slave. *Felicia* was of *Inea*'s Opinion, and thought there was so much Probability in what she said, that she chose rather to be silent in the Matter, than make a Discovery, which might be the Cause of greater Disorders; so implor'd the Assistance of Heaven for her Deliverance. As for *Inea*, she had already writ the Particulars of her Voyage, to her Dear Don *Ramire*, and was impatiently waiting his Answer.

*Abelhamar*, whose Passion was grown desperate, retired from the Queen's Palace to his own, and there confin'd himself with his faithful *Mula:* Cease flattering me, said he, and don't make me hope any thing, from my Submission to the Queen, and *Felicia*. I now am too well inform'd, of what I must expect from their Cruelty. As I was walking in the Palace Garden, distracted and melancholy, I perceiv'd at a Distance, *Celima* follow'd by her Women; and to avoid paying my Court to her, I retired to a Grotto, under the Terrace-Walk, which I had just enter'd, when the Queen leaning on *Felicia*'s Arm, came, and seated her self in a Place, where I cou'd distinctly hear all they said; no *Mula*, it is not possible, to express the intolerable Aversion she has to me, and with what Disdain she speaks of me; she has given reiterated Commands to that lovely Captive, to fly and hate me, who (ungrateful as she is) not only receiv'd 'em with Pleasure, but even promis'd *Celima* more than she requir'd of her; and it was not long before I felt the Effect of it, for as soon as the Queen was gone back to the Palace, and I cou'd find an Opportunity to speak to this young Slave, she confirm'd with a most rigorous Air what I had already heard, and moreover told me, she was in Love with

One

One in *Spain*, and that nothing in the World fhou'd ever make her change: In a Word, I find there is no Time to be loft; I muft immediately adhere to the King of *Tituan*'s Propofals; that Prince extremely refents *Celima*'s Refufal; a flighted Paffion demands Revenge, and he looks on me as One, who is capable of affifting him. Before I had feen *Felicia*, I wou'd not favour his Defigns, thinking the Queen might chufe me to Reign with her: Now I fee my Error; fhe not only hates me, but even oppofes my Happinefs, where-ever I feek it.

If I may be permitted to give you my Advice, my Lord, (reply'd *Mula*,) I am of Opinion, you fhou'd fpeak to *Celima*, before you enter into the King of *Tituan*'s Intereft, and try whether you cannot bring her into a more favourable Difpofition for you; 'tis probable, fhe may make fome ferious Reflection, and for her own fake, not provoke you to act any Thing defperate. I am willing to make that one Step more, faid the Prince, tho' ever fo nice; but as I believe the Queen has a Defign to take me up, let us be prepar'd for the Worft: If I am put in Arreft, do you go to *Tunis*; tell *Ifmael*, the Number of Friends I have in this Court, and manage Affairs fo, as by his Affiftance, and theirs, I may obtain my Liberty, poffefs my Love, and be reveng'd.

It was late before *Abelhamar* had ended his Converfation, which prevented him from going the next Morning to the Queen's Apartment,

ment; and the first Thing he heard, was *Felicia*'s Illness. This News caus'd him to be extremely uneasy; he soon forgot all other Projects, and fix'd his chiefest Thoughts, on seeking Means to see the Person he lov'd; which met with some Opposition, *Celima* having given Orders he shou'd not be admitted into her Chamber; and as for the Governess of the Slaves, he cou'd not flatter himself with the Hopes of gaining her, being an old Woman, entirely devoted to the Queen's Will; so that he was almost despairing of Success in his Enterprize; but what is not Love capable of? It conquers all Difficulties.

The Prince, being young and handsome, resolv'd to disguise himself in Woman's Cloaths, in order to be presented to the Queen by a Captain of a Ship, with whom he was particularly acquainted. He was a perfect Master of the *Spanish* Tongue, and did not doubt, but he might easily pass for One of that Nation. He told his Design to *Mula*, who used his Endeavours to divert him from an Attempt, which might prove fatal to him; but his Arguments were of little Weight, where Love had so great an Influence. He order'd immediately his Physician to be call'd, and bid him give out every where he was dangerously ill of a Feaver, and that it was convenient he should see no Company. This News being talk'd of at Court, the Sea-Captain brought him to the Palace, among several other Slaves, which he had lately taken. The Queen took a particular Notice of *Abelhamar*, and ask'd him some Questions, which might have puzled him, had not his Wit been prevailing, and his Replies so ingenious, that they did not give her the least Suspicion of a Disguise. The Governess of the Slaves having ask'd his Name, he told her, he was call'd *Eugenia*, and that he was a Native of the Kingdom of *Castile*: The Queen order'd, she shou'd be conducted to *Felicia*, who perhaps might know her, and be much pleas'd to see One of her Country.

*Abelhamar* was sent in this manner to *Felicia*, who was in Bed, very much indispos'd. He no sooner enter'd her Chamber, but seeing her in this Condition, he turn'd pale, and seem'd so dejected, that it wou'd have pitied any One, that was present at this Interview. As *Felicia* and *Inea* believ'd, this new Slave's Affliction proceeded from her late Misfortune, they were no ways surpriz'd at the Disorder she was in, but endeavour'd by their kind Expressions, to soften the Rigour of her unhappy State.

The amorous Prince thus continu'd with his dear *Felicia*, and the oftener he saw her, the greater were the Effects of her Charms; which at last so potently influenced him, that he cou'd not resolve to quit the Palace, esteeming himself too happy in the Company of his adorable Mistress. He had so many Perfections, that it wou'd have been easy for him to make the Conquest of the Queen's handsomest

Slaves,

Slaves, had he made the least Pursuit towards it; but his Heart was entirely fill'd with *Felicia*'s Idea, and all his Thoughts were employed on the only Care of pleasing her.

She also very much contributed by her innocent Caresses, to detain him. Their Humours agreed so well, that she desired as a Favour, they wou'd let *Eugenia* stay with her during her Illness. There is a secret Charm in your Conversation (said she, sometimes to her) which gives me a much greater Pleasure, than any I can find in that of my other Companions. It is the Effect of my Love for you, beauteous *Felicia*, that inspires you with this Sympathy, replied the passionate Prince, and how bless'd shou'd I be, were I as dear to you, as you are to me! but, continu'd he, if you will give me Leave to tell you my Thoughts, I believe you are indifferent whether belov'd or not. Alas! how great wou'd be my Felicity, (answer'd *Felicia*, with a melancholy Tone) were I such as you represent me: You little know my Sentiments; they give me more Uneasiness, than my unfortunate Captivity. What, Madam, said the pretended *Eugenia*, is it possible, that after having wholly resign'd my self to you, you wou'd make any thing a Secret to me? If your Heart is touch'd with a tender Passion, will it not be a Comfort to you to make me your Confident? What shall I say to you, replied *Felicia*? I can only tell you my Weakness, and confess an Engagement, which is so dear to me, that
it

it fills my Soul at once with a Thousand different Motions. These Words cruelly affected the Prince, who cou'd not utter one Syllable, but turning pale, he fix'd his Eyes on her, and continu'd some Time in this Posture, as astonish'd at what she said, tho' she had already declar'd her Sentiments to him in the Garden: At last he endeavour'd to speak, and with a languishing Accent, said, I shou'd not be surpriz'd, so perfect a Creature as you were ador'd, yet, *Felicia*, I flatter'd my self, that far from having lost your Liberty, you were free from any Passion. This Opinion pleas'd me extremely, for although we are of one Sex, I must tell you, I take delight in gaining the Affections of a young unpractis'd Heart, who is unacquainted with Sentiments so destructive to our Peace. This made me conceive a particular Friendship for you; but I understand, your Disdain for some, is equal to your Weakness for others. Oh! what Shame and Disorder do you cause in me? (replied *Felicia*, covering her Face with her Handkerchief,) I expected in telling you my Secret, you wou'd have pitied, and consol'd me; alas! do you upbraid me, *Eugenia*? Your Severity will compel me hereafter to fear, and fly you. The unhappy Prince, at these Words, flung himself on his Knees, and taking her Hand, kiss'd and bath'd it with Tears; his Speech was suppress'd with Sighs, which wou'd have been sufficient to discover him, were it not that *Felicia* had a strong Opinion of his being of

her

her own Sex, and did not in the least take Notice of his passionate Expressions.

*Inea* enter'd the Chamber, whilst they were in this silent and melancholy Condition: What is the Cause of this Sorrow, said she? Is this the Way, *Eugenia*, you entertain our dear sick Lady? You have, without doubt, said something to her, which renews the Remembrance of her past Misfortunes. I have said nothing to *Felicia*, interrupted the Prince immediately, but what was agreeable to her, therefore do not accuse me; I wou'd undergo any Pain my self, rather than aggravate hers. Alas, *Inea!* said *Felicia*, here cruel *Eugenia* has been reproaching me with Sentiments, I have for a Person, whom she her self wou'd love, were she as well acquainted with him as I am. No (replied *Eugenia*) I am convinced of the contrary; I even have an invincible Aversion to this unknown, who perfidiously robs me of your Heart, which is a Crime not to be forgiven. This is no Subject to create a Dispute between you and I, said *Felicia*; the Affection we have for a Lover, or a Friend, is of so different a Nature, that the one does no Prejudice to the other. Give me Leave to tell you, cry'd the young Prince, that when a Heart is touch'd with a powerful Passion, it's incapable of receiving any other Impression. Then you don't believe I love you, *Eugenia*, interrupted *Felicia?* I know not what to believe, replied the Prince; but what I am assur'd of, is, no Creature can be in
greater

greater Despair. As he ended these Words, *Olympia* enter'd the Chamber.

It is given out in the Palace, said she, that Prince *Abelhamar*, having counterfeited a Sickness, is gone away secretly, in order to assist *Ismael*, King of *Tunis*, who intends to declare War against the Queen; which News has so much alarm'd her, that she has given Orders to search his Apartment, in spite of what his Physician says to oppose his being seen; and if it be possible to penetrate into the Queen's Sentiments by her Uneasiness, she is in a great Apprehension concerning the Consequence of this sudden Departure. The Queen's Thoughts and mine are as different as our Interest, replied *Felicia*; she is concern'd at the Prince's being gone, and I am overjoy'd at it. *Abelhamar*, who had not interrupted *Olympia*'s Discourse, cou'd not help looking earnestly at *Felicia*; that Prince is very unfortunate, said he, that his Absence shou'd give you so much Pleasure: I perceive the Love and Respect he has for you, meet with a very unkind Return. What is become of that Complaisance you show'd us at first, my dear *Eugenia*, replied *Felicia*; you equally blame me for having an Inclination, and for not having one. I think it wou'd not be reasonable for me to have any other Sentiments for *Abelhamar*; and I am even assur'd, that if I liked him, you your self wou'd condemn me. Try, Madam, continu'd *Eugenia*, strive to love the Prince, were it only to be reveng'd, and to punish me

for

for my Capricioufnefs; I promife you before it be lon g, I will renderhis Paffion very difagreeable to you. I fhall not give you that Trouble, replied *Felicia*, my Conftancy might then be brought in Queftion; it is dangerous to make fuch Tryals. Thefe Words fenfibly affected *Abelhamar*, whofe paffionate Looks exprefs'd fuch Emotions, that is was furprizing *Felicia*, *Inea* and *Olympia* fufpected nothing extraordinary under the Difguife.

But what Advantage did the young Prince receive from this Stratagem? He faw *Felicia*, and daily difcover'd fome tranfcendent Charms, which inflam'd him the more, and increas'd his Defpair, when he reflected on the Sentiments fhe had for him; for his Paffion was not only violent, but fo nice, that he wou'd not have been fatisfy'd with the Poffeffion of her Perfon, without that of her Heart; and as he knew he had no Share in her Affection, it threw him fometimes into fuch a deep Melancholy, as cou'd not be conceal'd. Befides, the Queen being inform'd of *Abelhamar's* Counterfeit Sicknefs, his going off, and part of his Defigns, gave Orders, that thofe Officers, who ferv'd him, and cou'd give her further Light into the Affair, might be taken up, and examin'd: She was alfo raifing Troops, repairing the Fortifications of the Town, and taking all Meafures neceffary to fecure her felf againft the Infults of an Enemy, whom fhe thought already with the King of *Tunis*, tho' every Day in her Chamber, and fometimes

times lying at her Bed's Feet; thus the amourous Prince elected his Felicity, in a Confinement, where he was expos'd to a Danger he did not apprehend, and good Fortune was so favourable to him till then, that his Disguise did not give the least Cause of Suspicion.

*Felicia's* Illness, tho' extremely violent, did not continue long; her Youth and good Constitution contributed very much to her speedy Recovery, and gave her Strength enough to walk in the Palace Gardens. The Court at that Time was so attentive on the Preparations of War, that the Slaves were not so strictly watch'd as usual. One Day *Felicia*, *Olympia*, *Inea*, and our Counterfeit *Eugenia* taking the Air, had turn'd their Steps towards a pleasant Terrace-Walk, which afforded a most agreeable Prospect; but the Weather changing, there suddenly rose a High Wind, succeeded by terrible Thunder and Hail, which oblig'd them to run for Shelter into a little Summer-House, that had a View on the Ocean.

*Felicia* and *Inea* were looking out of a Window, and had been some Time observing the Sea, which furiously came, and broke against the Rocks, making a horrid Noise, when they perceiv'd a Ship in the greatest Danger; she had lost all her Masts, and thus toss'd from Wave to Wave, was waiting the fatal Moment. These young Ladies were moved with Compassion at such a Sight, and concern'd for those who were on Board: They implor'd implor'd the Assistance of Heaven, and whilst they were making Vows for their Safety, the Wind decided their Destiny, for the Ship was driven ashore, and there entirely wreck'd. It was a most dismal Scene, to see how these unfortunate Wretches strove to save themselves, but their Efforts were fruitless; they All perished excepting One, who was happy enough to reach a little Rock, which lay at a small Distance from the Shore.

The Storm being allay'd, some Fishermen, who had seen the Shipwreck, took their Boat, and row'd towards the Rock, where they found the Man I mention'd in a Swoon, and as cold as Death; they took him and brought him ashoar, where they immediately lighted a Fire, and gave him all the Help they were capable of.

These Things happen'd so near the Summer-House, where our young Captives were retired, that they cou'd easily see the Condition this Stranger was in; but how great was *Felicia* and *Olympia*'s Disorder, when they knew him to be the Count of *La Vagne:* They wou'd have express'd their Satisfaction, were it not for the Fear they were in of his being Dead. It is he, (cried *Olympia* in her first Transports) it is certainly himself. *Felicia* on the other Side, (pressing *Inea* and *Eugenia*'s Hands) cou'd no more be Mistress of her Moderation; Oh Heavens! said she to them, my dearest Companions; there is the Man whose Absence has given me so much Displeasure; he appears

now,

now, juſt as he did when I found him in the Foreſt of *Carmona*, where he had been attacked by Robbers; the Picture of Death was painted on his Face: I was then in a Condition to aſſiſt him, but now alas, I am forced to ſee him periſh, without being at Liberty to give him any Help.

Whilſt ſhe was thus ſpeaking to *Inea*, and the diſguis'd Prince, *Olympia* left 'em, and ran to a Door adjacent to the Sea-Side, which ſhe caus'd to be opened without any Difficulty, and in a ſmall Time reach'd the Place where the Count was lying: As ſoon as *Felicia* perceived the Concern, and Care ſhe expreſs'd in aſſiſting him, ſhe knew not what to think. I am well perſwaded, ſaid ſhe, they are both Natives of *Genoa*, and perhaps Relations; but methinks her Affection is very great, ſince ſhe weeps as well as I, and embraces him in ſuch a paſſionate Manner.

The mean while *Abelhamar* (enrag'd and jealous) was acting the greateſt Violence on himſelf, in not diſcovering to her who he was, that he might reſolve on the immediate Sacrifice of this dangerous Rival. *Inea*'s Thoughts were alſo confus'd, and ſhe was hardly able to ſpeak a Word. The more ſhe conſider'd *Olympia*'s tender Concern for the Count of *La Vagne*, and the ſecret Conſolation ſhe ſeem'd to derive from his Preſence, the more ſhe ſigh'd, and ſent her Wiſhes to her faithful Don *Ramire*; in a Word, it is not to be conceiv'd, how tormented they all were by different Cauſes of Uneaſineſs.

finefs. But how was lovely *Felicia*'s Mind employ'd all this while, and what were her inward Motions, when she saw the Count recovered from his Swoon, who appeared in Transports of inexpressible Joy, at the Sight of *Olympia*? He kiss'd her Hand, and fix'd his Eyes on her's, as if Fortune had snatch'd him from the Arms of Death, only to lead him into perfect Felicity. Am I then betray'd, (cried *Felicia*, in a faint Voice) and can I believe what I see? Is the Count of *La Vagne* in Love with *Olympia*? You ought not in the least to doubt it, (answer'd *Eugenia*, who was very willing to confirm her Suspicions) and if you flatter'd your self with being belov'd, you are mistaken in the Heart of that Traytor; any one may see by his Actions, that he has a Passion for *Olympia*. Do not have so rash an Opinion of him, interrupted *Inea*; it's probable he has some particular Reasons for acting as he does; perhaps the Count is inform'd of Prince *Abelhamar*'s Passion for *Felicia*, and as he is come in order to ransom his Mistress, he thought it convenient to conceal his true Sentiments, the better to succeed in his Designs. What Pleasure you take in being deceiv'd, (cried *Eugenia*, who cou'd not bear to hear her express her self in this Manner;) have you already forgot that *Abelhamar* is suspected to be with the King of *Tunis*, and consequently there are no Measures to be observ'd with him? But the Count knows nothing of it, interrupted *Felicia*, and I am inclin'd to

be-

believe, *Inea* has interpreted the Sentiments of
his Heart. How great is our Weakness when
we love, said the Prince; we scarcely can credit our own Eyes, we are so inclin'd to embrace any Thing which flatters our Wishes.
Indeed *Eugenia,* replied *Felicia,* you always represent Things in the falsest Colours: What have
I done to invite you to take such Delight in
tormenting me. The Prince, who perceiv'd she
was displeased, said no more to her, but resolv'd in himself to make the Force of his Revenge fall on this happy Rival.

*Olympia* sent to acquaint the Queen, that
the Count of *La Vagne* was cast on the
Shoar, but had escaped Death, and beg'd
Leave to pay his Respects to her Majesty.
*Celima* (who was exceeding melancholy, and
apprehensive of the Consequences of *Abelhamar's* Revolt) declin'd seeing this Stranger, not
to let him be Witness of her Affliction; but
sent back to *Olympia,* to tell her, she might
bring him to the Palace, where she shou'd have
an Apartment prepared for him in One of the
remote Pavilions, having given Orders that
he shou'd be receiv'd with a Distinction equal
to his Birth; to this she added, how willing
she shou'd be to admit him, were she not indispensibly oblig'd to attend some Affairs of
the highest Moment. She gave Orders also,
that they shou'd supply him with all Necessaries, and several Slaves immediately brought
him Variety of rich Garments, that he might
please his Fancy. Whilst *Olympia* went to return

turn the Queen Thanks for her Favours, the Count was conducted through the Gardens to the Palace.

*Felicia, Inea* and *Eugenia,* were walking in an Alley, which had a View on the Sea-Side, when the Count of *La Vagne* came up pretty near to them; *Felicia* perceiving him, her Heart fluttered, and she grew so faint in an Instant, that had not *Inea* supported her on one Side, and the disguis'd Prince on the other, she would not have been able to stand; but the Count (who had no Cause to remark her Motions, tho' in Favour of himself) pass'd by the Ladies, and only saluted them with much Respect, without taking any particular Notice of *Felicia.*

As soon as he was gone far enough from her not to be heard; Oh Heaven! cry'd she, is it possible he can be so much Master of his Temper, as not to show some Tenderness in his Eyes? He looks as if he had never seen me: What means this Indifference, *Inea?* Are these his Transports? Oh! What must I think of his Passion? Madam! reply'd *Inea,* is not his coming hither to fetch you away, a sufficient Motive to convince you of his Fidelity? *Inea* only deceives you, interrupted the Prince, for I have seen many Persons in Love, and can assure you, that altho' they were in a continual Restraint, and obliged to be on their Guard in the Presence of jealous Observers, yet their Passion discover'd it self in their Eyes and Actions. Why (continu'd he, addressing him-

himself to *Inea*) do you really think the Count of *La Vagne* was overjoy'd to see *Felicia*? He did not so much as change Colour, nor even fix his Eyes on hers: No, no, his Passion is not so violent as you imagine; and if you continue speaking in his Favour, you only do it with an Intent to sooth our Friend's Pain. Don't torment me in this Manner, cruel Creature, cry'd *Felicia*; am I not unfortunate enough already? Why will you persist in saying such vexatious Things to me? Have you resolv'd on my Death? I take Heaven to Witness, reply'd the Prince sighing, that I have no such Intention; you wou'd certainly judge more favourably of my Sentiments, were they well known to you.

*Felicia* fearing it wou'd be taken Notice of at the Palace, that she had been so long Abroad, returned speedily to her Chamber, which she no sooner enter'd, but wrote to the Count in the following Terms.

*I Have now some Reason to flatter my self, that Heaven will soon put a Period to my Misfortunes, since Love and Generosity have invited you here to your* Felicia's *Deliverance. How shall I express my Joy, my Affection, and my Gratitude, and when shall I be at Liberty to entertain you with my tender Sentiments? Alas! what Violence did not I do my self in seeing you so near me, without speaking to you; but how was it possible, you cou'd pass by me with such an Air of Indifference? I must confess it very much affected*

R 4 *me,*

*me, and if I may tell you my Thoughts, I almoſt ſuſpected your Fidelity. I began to fear, you had devoted all your Tranſports to* Olympia; *this extremely augmented my Uneaſineſs, being an Effect of my Delicacy, which you muſt pardon. Let me know how I am to behave my ſelf hereafter in this Court, and don't neglect any Thing to procure us a ſpeedy Departure. I hope Fortune will influence the Intereſt of our Hearts, and crown our Sufferings with eternal Felicity.*

This Letter cou'd not be convey'd to the Count without ſome Difficulty. *Felicia* bid *Inea* read it, and conjured her to find Means to have it immediately deliver'd into his Hands. I cannot think on any Way, reply'd *Inea*, but to carry it my ſelf. Your ſelf! cry'd *Felicia*, how will you venture to do it? Leave that to me, Madam, anſwer'd *Inea*, I will run any Riſque to ſerve you. This is very generous, my dear Companion, ſaid *Felicia*; then thanked her for ſo obliging an Offer, and deſir'd her, ſince ſhe was willing to render her ſo conſiderable a Service, not to defer it.

*Olympia* was now in the Queen's Apartment, and the Count in his, but being extremely impatient to ſee his lovely Miſtreſs, he ſtep'd into the Garden in Expectation of meeting her; It was a fine Moon-light Night, and as he was walking with his Thoughts wholly employ'd on the Happineſs he promis'd himſelf, in the Poſſeſſion of a Lady, for whom he had ſo tranſcendent a Paſſion; young *Inea* (wrap-
ed

ed in her white Vail) accosted him, and said, read this Letter, my Lord; it comes from a Person who ought to be dear to you. The Count open'd it, and was surpriz'd not to know the Writing; after having read it over, and over, without conceiving the Meaning, it came into his Head, that it was a Jest O*lympia* had imagin'd to divert her self, so said to *Inea*, I desire you will tell the beauteous Lady, from whom I receive this Favour, that I intend my self to be Bearer of the Answer.

As *Inea* was going back, she perceiv'd a Woman at a Distance cover'd with her Vail, who was coming towards her, and fearing she shou'd be known by her, she pass'd on the other Side of the Pallisadoes, and went into the long Walk, where she found *Felicia*, who taking her under the Arm, said to her in a low Voice; you will think me very impatient to know what the Count has said to you, but that is not the only Reason which brought me hither. I was looking out of my Chamber-Window, waiting your Return, when I saw a Woman cross the Garden with great Diligence, and go, as it were, towards the Count's Pavilion: I must confess, my dear *Inea*, it gave me much Uneasiness, and I made all possible Haste to follow her. As far as I cou'd distinguish, she appear'd to me to be *Olympia*, and I believe it is her. Oh! *Inea*, how my Heart akes! and in what Torment is my Mind, for fear of losing the Object of my Love? Judge more favourably of the Count, said *Inea*, interrupting

terrupting her; he read your Letter with an extreme Attention, and addreſſing me in very obliging Terms, aſſur'd me, he wou'd anſwer it perſonally. It's very well, continu'd *Felicia*, but let us go on without making a Noiſe; we may perhaps, diſcover where that Perſon is going, whom I mention'd to you. In finiſhing theſe Words, they walk'd on, hiding themſelves behind the Palliſadoes; and hearing ſome Body talk in an Arbour, which was at the End of the Alley, they drew near.

The Count of *La Vagne* and *Olympia*, were converſing together in this Place; it is impoſſible, Madam, ſaid he to his Miſtreſs, for me to expreſs the Deſpair I was in, when I heard of your Death, and the Circumſtances which preceded it; they ſo intirely affected me, that even Life began to be odious to me, and never was Mortal in a more deſolate Condition. But how tranſported was I, at the unexpected Change of Fortune, when the Jeweller (who had ſeen you in the Queen's Apartment) inform'd me, that the ſame beauteous *Olympia*, whoſe Loſs I was deploring, was actually living, and at *Sallee*; judge —— I well conceive, my dear Count, ſaid ſhe, interrupting him, what might employ your Thoughts in Two ſuch different Occaſions; as our Affection is mutual, we ſympathize in all the Pleaſure and Torment, which derives from our good or bad Fortune; you may imagine after what I ſuffer'd for your ſuppoſed Death, how exceſſive was my Joy, when I heard of your Safety.

Safety. I have told you already, said the Count, that your illustrious Father has given his Consent to our happy Union, receiving my Proposals with such extraordinary Marks of Friendship, that I must confess, I shou'd have suspected so uncommon a Favour, were it not that my long Sufferings give me a Title to so great a Reward. Yes, continu'd he, most divine *Olympia*, you are now to be mine, and I for ever yours. As they were speaking in this manner, a doleful Voice interrupted them, which (repeating these Words, *I am dying,*) gave 'em to understand, that some Person very near the Arbour, was taken ill. This induc'd them to discontinue their Conversation, tho' ever so delightful, in order to assist the Lady, who was complaining so dismally.

They look'd on every Side, without perceiving any one, but hearing some Noise behind the Pallisadoes, they approach'd and saw *Inea*, holding in her Arms, *Felicia*, in a Swoon. Ah, my Lord! don't come near, cry'd *Inea*, weeping; your Presence wou'd become fatal to *Felicia*, and you, Madam! (continu'd she, speaking to *Olympia*.) I beg, as a Favour, she may not see you. What Aversion can she have to us? (reply'd they both at the same Time,) We do not know her, and it wou'd be strange she shou'd hate us without Cause. This is not a proper Time to explain Matters, answer'd *Inea*; all the Assistance I desire of you, is, to run to the Palace, and send us some Help.

*Olympia*

*Olympia* (without making any Reply, tho' extremely astonish'd at what she heard) went to give Notice to *Eugenia*, and some other of the Slaves, of the Condition *Felicia* was in, and the mean while the Count staid by her. No, said he to *Inea*, I cannot go from you, till you have unriddled this Secret to me; was it not you that just now gave me a Letter, which I do not understand the meaning of? One wou'd think by your Air and Words, that I had disoblig'd this Fair Lady; but alas! how cou'd I have done any thing, either to deserve her Anger, or your Reproaches? It's impossible, reply'd *Inea*, to dissemble better, and conceal with more Confidence, the horridest Perfidiousness, that Man cou'd ever act against a Lady of Birth and Merit. Don't expect, my Lord, that I will explain Things to you, which you know better than I. The Count of *La Vagne* cou'd not have help'd laughing at so odd and obscure an Answer, had not the Condition *Felicia* was in inspired him with great Compassion, and finding *Inea* seem'd displeas'd at his remaining there, he resolv'd to retire.

By this Time, several Slaves were come to *Felicia*'s Help, and among others, *Eugenia*, or the disguis'd Prince, who seeing her in a Swoon, express'd his Affliction in Terms so passionate, that his Counterfeit was soon discover'd. Unfortunate *Eugenia*, (cry'd he, in a doleful Accent) thou art going to be depriv'd of the only Object of thy Love. *Felicia!* my
dear

dear *Felicia!* to what a sad State are you reduc'd? Divinest Creature, if I lose you, my Death shall succeed your's, since I cannot live without you. Whilst he was talking in this manner, *Inea* and her Companions were throwing Water on *Felicia*'s Face, but as their Assistance cou'd not recover her, they carry'd her to her Chamber. The Prince, as you may imagine, surpass'd the rest in attending his sick Mistress; as soon as she was lain in Bed, he sate by her, and forgetting himself, his excessive Grief forc'd from him such Expressions, as were not becoming his Female Disguise.

The Governess of the Slaves, who watchfully observ'd every thing, took Notice of his Words, and examining earnestly *Eugenia*'s Features, discover'd Prince *Abelhamar*'s Resemblance. She ran immediately and related what had pass'd to the Queen, who was not a little surpriz'd at this unexpected Adventure. It was late at Night, therefore she wou'd not call a Council, fearing it might alarm the People, who were already under great Apprehensions from the King of *Tunis*'s landing, so defer'd, till next Day, taking any Resolution against the Prince.

He little knew the Danger which threaten'd him; all his Thoughts were then employ'd on the State *Felicia* was in, nor cou'd he reflect on any thing more tormenting. She scarcely recover'd her Speech, but lamented being restor'd to a Life, which at that Time, all Things render'd burthensome to her. *Inea,* apprehending

that

that the Violence of her Affliction, wou'd force her into such Complaints as ought to be conceal'd, told her Companions, who were present, that it was convenient *Felicia* shou'd be left to take a little Rest, and that *Eugenia* and she wou'd stay by her; the others hearing this, immediately retired.

*Felicia*, after they were gone, gave an entire Course to her excessive Grief; see, *Inea!* cry'd she, see, what Calamities I labour under! I am remote from my Country, out of Favour with my Family, become a Slave, and betray'd by a Man, who appear'd to me deserving of every thing; he is now in Love with another; 'tis *Olympia* he is come to deliver: This Lover, whom she impatiently expected, and receiv'd with so much Joy, is the same, on whom I bestow'd my tender Care, when in a most dangerous Condition, and my Solitude afforded him a Refuge from the Fury of his Enemies. He conceiv'd a Passion for me, engag'd me by a Thousand Promises to make a Return, and vow'd his Love shou'd be eternal. But Heavens! how perfidious has he prov'd? I remember now, as an Evincement, he sacrific'd *Olympia*'s Picture to me, which perswaded me, I had seen her Resemblance before. Oh! what a sad Object am I, of Fortune's Capriciousness? Here she was silent a long Time. Alas! what have I done, said she again, to deserve at so tender an Age, such a Series of Misfortunes: Yesterday I was deploring the Absence of the Man I lov'd;

lov'd; this Day I lament the Lofs of his Heart. Her Sighs and Tears interrupted her feveral Times whilft fhe was fpeaking, and at laft, fhe cou'd fay no more. The Prince flattering himfelf with fome fmall Hopes, took this Time to fpeak to her; if you were in a a Condition, to tafte the Pleafure of Revenge, faid he, you wou'd be foon fatisfy'd; my Arm fhou'd fecond your Refentment, for 'tis no longer in my Power, charming *Felicia*, to conceal, what my exceffive Paffion for you has made me undertake. See at your Feet, wretched *Abelhamar*, your Slave! Here I remain in this Palace for your fake, altho' I know, that were the Queen inform'd of it, my Life wou'd attone for my Crime. Compare this Proof of my Love, with that of my unworthy Rival's, whom you prefer, and then you will own your felf the moft unjuft Perfon in the World.

Oh Heavens! (cry'd *Felicia*) can I believe my Eyes? What new Fatality doth attend me? You here, my Lord! and an Enemy to the Queen? Have you been my Confident, and carefs'd me by fo many Days, without my perceiving the Deceit? Alas! where fhall I go for Refuge? What muft the Queen think of me? Will fhe not have fufficient Reafon to fufpect my Virtue? Can any one imagine, that without my Confent, you wou'd have made fo rafh an Attempt? Ah! nothing but Death can relieve me from my Misfortune. *Abelhamar's* Diforder was fo great, that he did not fay much in his Juftification; and as for *Inea*, who
was

was present at this Scene, she cou'd not deny them her Compassion. She endeavour'd to excuse him, and said to *Felicia*, the true Respect the Prince has for you, Madam, ought in some Measure to appease you, since no Body knows of his being disguis'd: Your Honour, which is dearer to him than his Life, and the inevitable Danger that threatens him, if the Queen shou'd be inform'd of what has pass'd, will engage him to keep secret an Affair of this Importance. You are very little acquainted with Mankind, interrupted *Felicia*, who glory in relating their Adventures, and never love so sincerely, as to make any Thing a Secret. Well, my Lord, (continu'd she, addressing herself to the Prince) you have made your last Efforts to augment my Miseries; I shou'd have dy'd esteem'd by Those who know me, but at present shall deserve their Contempt. You may go now to the Count of *La Vagne*, and tell him, that since he has sacrific'd me to *Olympia*, I have quitted him for you, and contriv'd this criminal Disguise to favour your Admittance. Know me better, Madam, reply'd *Abelhamar*; were not my Passion for you transcendent, I shou'd never deviate from the Rules of Honour, and what I owe you. No, my *Felicia*, you shall never find me guilty of acting any thing, that may incur your Displeasure; yet I cannot help saying, you ought no longer to deplore the Loss of a Man, so unworthy your Esteem, who without Dispute has deceived you; for 'tis impossible, if he

once

once lov'd you, he cou'd ever love another. Divine *Felicia!* be convinc'd of the Power of your Charms, and think, that I, who feel their Effects, can never change. The present Situation of Affairs gives me Hopes of a happy Turn in my Fortune. I may ascend the Throne on which my Ancestors were seated; but, oh *Felicia!* what Pleasure can it afford me to possess a Crown without you? I intreat you now to grant a Request, you cannot reasonably refuse me, which is, to forget your perfidious Lover, and receive the Vows of the most passionate, and most constant of Mankind: If you compare my Sentiments with his, you will do Justice to my sincere Passion; you shall be deliver'd from your Captivity, and shall give Laws to the Queen, whose Chains you now wear. Ah! my Lord, (cry'd *Felicia* in a dejected Tone,) I desire nothing but Death, therefore give me Leave to complain, and do not interrupt my Grief with Proposals, which I cannot accept. I have not Power to forget the Traytor, who thus neglects me: I love him still, spite of all the Reasons I have to hate him, and shou'd I be doom'd to sink under my grievous Woes, or even live to despise the Author of my present Pain, do not think that a Crown cou'd invite me, ever to believe perfidious Man again.

*Abelhamar* heard her with an unconceivable Anguish, and had not Strength to make a Reply, but look'd at her with the greatest Concern; and his Sighs interpreted the tormenting

menting Motions of his Soul. *Felicia* was not in a Condition to obferve the Defpair, this young Prince was reduc'd to, but renew'd her Complaints, and nothing cou'd reftrain the Courfe of her Tears. What are you doing, Madam, faid *Inea* to her? Is it poffible, that a Perfon fo charming fhou'd regret the Lofs of a Man, who even difowns you, and abandons you, to go away with *Olympia?* Is it thus he ungratefully repays the obliging Sentiments you have for him? Call Revenge to your Aid, Madam; forget a Man who forfakes you, and let your Difdain be the Reward of his Falfity. It is eafy, my Dear, reply'd *Felicia,* to give Advice on fuch an Occafion, I wou'd do the fame to you, were you in my Cafe, and I in your's: But do you think, it is in our Power to act as we pleafe, when Love has once render'd himfelf Mafter of our Inclinations? Ah! cruel Rival, what Torment do you give me? And you perfidious Count, fhall not I fee you punifh'd for your Ingratitude? Imploy my Arm, Madam, interrupted the Prince, and with your Confent, I will revenge you of your perjur'd Lover. I wou'd fooner refolve to die, faid *Felicia,* than yield to fo inhuman a Propofal; the only Favour I defire of you, my Lord, (which I conjure you not to deny me) is, that you will leave me; you are no longer *Eugenia,* you are a Prince whom I dare not admit at this Time of Night into my Chamber; my Peace and Honour depend on your Compliance: Think of the Danger you expofe pose your self to, for a Person who can make you no Return. That is the only Misfortune I fear, interrupted *Abelhamar*; every Thing else might be easily surmounted. Retire, my Lord, reply'd *Felicia*, I am extremely uneasy at your being here. The Prince, perceiving it was in vain to resist, withdrew, but not without assuring her, that altho' he were to suffer innumerable Torments, thro' her Indifferency, yet his Passion shou'd ever be the same.

*Olympia Doria*, all that Evening, had not found an Opportunity to speak to the Count of *La Vagne*, which made her pass the rest of that Night in such an Agitation of Mind, as troubled the Joy she ought to have receiv'd, at so agreeable a Change in her Fortune. What means, said she, *Felicia*'s swooning away, and *Inea*'s Anger; cou'd they have such Motions for a Stranger? Yet the Count pretends not to know them, and this Dissimulation seems to me very Criminal; how can I tell, whether in his Travels he did not come acquainted with this young Lady, and who can assure me, they do not love each other? These melancholy Thoughts tormented her cruelly, and the Count on his Side was not less uneasy, fearing *Olympia* wou'd let her self be deceiv'd by Appearances; for tho' he cou'd not penetrate into this Mystery, he saw enough to make him apprehend, it might give his Mistress some Suspicion; and as his Passion for her invited him to prefer Death to her Displeasure, he impatiently waited for Morning to undeceive her.

As they had an equal Defire to entertain one another, they rofe early, and met on the Terrace-Walk. *Olympia*, the better to know the Count's Sentiments, endeavour'd to conceal her Uneafinefs, but her Melancholy foon difcover'd her fecret Thoughts. The Count alfo appear'd fo dejected, that one might eafily imagine what pafs'd in his Soul: He broke Silence firft, and ask'd her, how fhe had repos'd? To which fhe anfwer'd with Indifferency, that fhe had refted very ill, without knowing the Caufe: Here *Olympia*'s Sighs interrupted her Difcourfe. Ah, Madam! (faid the Count, proftrating himfelf at her Feet) do not let me be long uncertain of my Deftiny; you are not the fame you were Yefterday; what have I done, to deferve from you fo cold a Reception? I have not Refolution enough to be filent, reply'd *Olympia*, tho' it was my Defign; it is unjuft to harbour Sufpicions of the Perfon one loves, without coming to an Eclaircifement. Tell me, my Lord, Do you ftill love *Felicia*? I fay ftill, becaufe after what has pafs'd, I have no Reafon to doubt, but you once had a Paffion for her. The Count wou'd not let *Olympia* perfevere in an Error, which was to the Prejudice of his Honour; he foon by his Proteftations perfwaded her of the contrary, then offer'd to go with her to juftify himfelf before *Felicia* and *Inea*. I believe you, my Lord, faid fhe, without fuch a Proof, fince I had much rather you fhou'd not fee 'em any more. The Queen has confented to our

our leaving this Place, therefore let us go, for the Approach of the King of *Tunis* terrifies me. It wou'd be very unfortunate fhou'd we find our felves befieg'd here, at a Time that my Father is difpos'd to favour us. Let us depart, reply'd the tranfported Count, there is nothing I wifh fo much; I have a Ship now ready to fail for *Italy*, and only waits for a favourable Wind; may Heavens protect our Voyage, and bring me to my long wifh'd for Happinefs; come, Madam, added he, difpofe all Things for your Departure; every Moment will feem to me an Age, till *Hymen* has crown'd my Love with the Union of our Deftinies.

Thefe endearing Expreffions highly pleas'd *Olympia*, who immediately went to the Queen, and obtain'd Leave to embark; *Celima* at the fame Time reftor'd to their Liberty the young Slaves that were taken with *Olympia*, then prefented her with her Picture, fet round with Diamonds of great Value, and repeated to her, what fhe had already faid in Behalf of the Count of *La Vagne*; withal, that at another Time, fhe fhou'd have been very glad to fee him. *Olympia*, having return'd her Acknowledgments in a moft refpectful Manner, went into the Slaves Apartment, where fhe chofe the Ladies I mention'd, and took her Leave of the reft, who by their Tears and Careffes fhew'd the particular Affection they had for her. As fhe doubted whether it were proper to fee *Felicia*, fhe defir'd the Governefs of the

Slaves to acquaint her with her Departure; but at the Name of *Olympia*, and the News of her going away, she fetch'd a Shriek, and made such Complaints, as wou'd have infpir'd the hardest Heart with Pity: *Olympia* hearing this, wou'd not aggravate her Pain by her Prefence, and tho' she paffionately wish'd to entertain *Felicia*, that she might know from her, whether the Count of *La Vagne* was fincere in what he had told her, yet she was no ways willing to fatisfy her felf, at the Expence of fo amiable a Perfon.

The Count was expecting *Olympia* with Impatience, when she came to tell him the Favours she had receiv'd from the Queen, who order'd fome of her Officers to accompany them to the Ship. The mean while, *Felicia*, oppref'sd with Sorrow, continu'd lamenting with *Inea*; I have no Hopes left, faid she to her; my Fate is decreed; the ungrateful Count of *La Vagne* is now going off, and I shall lofe him for ever; he flies me, and carries with him the Object of his Love; the Barbarian cou'd fee me dying without being touch'd; nay, he even deny'd me his Pity; and the deplorable Condition, that perfidious Man has reduc'd me to, has not coft him a Sigh. Ah! leave me, and let me die with Grief, and Shame! Don't indulge your Affliction, Madam, interrupted *Inea*; think only, that he who leaves you, is unworthy of the Tears you fhed; reflect on his Ingratitude, and it will be an effectual Way to forget him. You are deceiv'd,

*if*

if you believe it, said *Felicia* sighing; when one is inspir'd with a Passion, the Loss of its Object wholly employs our Thoughts. I protest to you with some Confusion, that all the good Qualities I knew in that inconstant Lover, appear to me now with greater Lustre, tho' I can no longer doubt of his Infidelity, or my Misfortune; and to let you see more of my Weakness, I have a pressing Desire to write to him, in Hopes my Reproaches might move him. What, Madam! interrupted *Inea*, cou'd you receive his Devoirs again, after such an injurious Proceeding? Alas, reply'd *Felicia*, what are not we capable of acting to recall a Heart, whose Possession is dear to us? Then don't add to my Pain; I too well comprehend what you think, and blush to see my Honour concern'd: But consider, I am an unhappy distracted Creature: My Dear, I conjure you, in the Name of your faithful Don *Ramire*, to find some Person, that will deliver a Letter to the Count of *La Vagne*; you cannot confer a greater Obligation on me. *Inea*, who was very willing to serve *Felicia*, left her immediately, in order to make an Attempt; but soon after she return'd, and told her, it was impossible to send any Body to the Port, that the Queen had either receiv'd News of *Ismael*'s Approach, or that something extraordinary was passing at Court, since she had commanded the Guards of her Palace to be doubled, and the Gates to be shut, that none might be admitted without her Order.

Then I must lose all Hopes, (cry'd unfortunate *Felicia*,) for I can neither stop him, nor follow him. Just Heaven! revenge me on that perjur'd Man! punish his Perfidiousness! punish the Cause of this last Misfortune! may the angry Waves swallow them up, and let me hear the News of their Loss, soon after that of their Departure! But alas, am I capable of forming Wishes so contrary to my Inclination? No, I have lov'd the Count too well ever to hate him; then let him live and be happy. All my Fury ought to be turn'd against my self, for I deserve the Miseries I now linger in. Had I, instead of leaving my Father's House, submitted to his Commands, I shou'd not at present have the cruel Mortification, of reproaching my self with an imprudent Conduct, which I never shall be able to justify to the World. While *Felicia* is thus deploring the Cruelty of her Fortune, we must return to the Prince of *Carency*.

*Cafilda* had maliciously perswaded him, that *Benavidez* was gone with *Leonida* to *Jaen*, where he wou'd be sure (as she said) of the Governour's Protection. A Man must certainly have as much Valour, as Love, to attempt any thing against a Person, who was protected by the Governour of so considerable a Place; but the Violence of his Passion, and Extremity of his Despair together, wou'd not permit him to reflect, even on the greatest of Dangers.

Where-ever he pass'd, People observ'd something extraordinary in him and tho' his Eyes express'd much Grief, his Noble Mein carry'd Marks of the Highest Distinction. He made the strictest Enquiry after *Felicia* of *Leon*; whom sometimes he call'd *Leonida* of *Velasco*, but when he describ'd her to those he apply'd to, he was so lavish in her Praise, that they easily discover'd he was her Lover.

Notwithstanding all his Care and Diligence, his Pursuit was in vain, for she had not pass'd that Way, nor cou'd any one give him the least Intelligence concerning her. He began to be very uneasy, and hurrying from one Thought to another, his Mind was fill'd with his past Misfortunes, till he came to *Jaen*, where he arriv'd exceeding melancholy. He look'd on the Citadel of that Town as a Place, where his Life and Disasters were to be terminated. Here, said he! here, I expect to see the ungrateful Beauty I adore, and before her Eyes, I will attack the ungenerous Man, who next her self had the first Place in my Heart. What a strange Destiny is this, cry'd he? My Mistress and my Friend equally betray me, and to satisfy my Resentment, I must destroy the One, to wound the Other. It is probable, they are this fatal Hour contriving my Ruin, and giving each other fresh Assurances of eternal Love; but my Death must confirm their Felicity, for whilst I am living, they have a cruel Enemy, who will endeavour to defeat their Projects, and ever trouble the Happiness they propose. At

At his Arrival, he had a mind to go directly to the Citadel, for (as I told you before) he had accepted of a Letter from the Governour of *Carmona*, to his Son Don *Gabriel d'Aguillar*, by whose Interest he was sure of an easy Entrance into the Place; but he thought it was better first to send to him, and the mean Time inform himself of what pass'd there. As he was going thro' the Town, he met a *French* Chevalier of the House of *Boucicault*; his Name was *Alphonso*, a Person of an obliging Temper, who came to *Seville* with the Count of *La March*. What do I see? Is it you, my Lord, (cry'd he, coming up to the Prince, with a great deal of Joy and Respect;) are you living, whom we so much lamented with the Prince your Brother, believing you were assassinated near *Carmona*, as it was reported in *Spain*, and for which we were meditating a proportionable Revenge? I shou'd have been happy, my Dear *Alphonso*, (said the Prince) had my Enemy's Designs been effected, but I am reserv'd for greater Calamities; yet I desire my Name may be kept secret, for important Reasons, which engage me to conceal it, and you can be very serviceable to me. I am in love, and betray'd, and must revenge my self on my Rival and my Mistress. Oh! how I shall load *Felicia* with my just Reproaches? She is now in the Citadel with him. What you say is true, my Lord, interrupted *Alphonso*, I know it from Don *Gabriel d'Aguillar*, who is one of my particular Friends:

*Feli-*

*Felicia* is confin'd againſt her Will, in an Apartment where ſhe ſees no Body, but by the Means of the *Spaniſh* Captain I have already mentioned; one Night, without being perceiv'd, I ſaw her ſadly deploring her Fate. Oh! my Lord, how Young and Handſom ſhe is; I muſt confeſs, I extremely pity her.

Do you pity her, ſaid the Prince with a deep Sigh? Have you any Compaſſion for her? Ah! you are little acquainted with her Perfidiouſneſs; but tell me, what means that manner of Confinement? Did not you ſee her come here with Don *Fernand Benavidez*, the Governour's Nephew? No, reply'd *Alphonſo*, the Perſon you name has not appear'd here ſince my Arrival, for as I am every Day at the Citadel, I ſhou'd probably have ſeen him; yet if he be there, he certainly keeps himſelf conceal'd. Ah, the Traitor! cry'd the Prince, he is only hid for *Felicia*'s ſake, and without doubt has deſir'd a Guard to protect him from my Reſentment. The Villain has ſufficient Reaſon to fear me; it is dangerous to inſult a deſperate Man who does not value his Life. This Thought made the Prince fly into ſo violent a Paſſion, that *Alphonſo* beg'd of him to retire from the Place where they were ſtanding, for fear they might be obſerv'd.

The Prince ſaid to him, if you will prevent my committing any Extravagancies, you muſt ſecond the Deſire I have of ſeeing *Benavidez*, and *Felicia*. I have a Letter for Don *Gabriel d'Aguillar*, who I am glad to hear is your Friend;

Friend; you will oblige me extremely in sending inftantly to him, that we may take neceffary Meafures for that purpofe. *Alphonfo* promis'd the Prince every thing that depended on him, even at the Hazard of his Life, then left him to execute his Orders.

Whatever Enquiry *Alphonfo* and Don *Gabriel* made, before they came to the Prince, they cou'd learn nothing fatisfactory; thofe to whom they apply'd concerning Don *Fernand Benavidez*, told 'em, they believ'd he was at *Villa-Real*, but that he was not Nephew to Don *Alonzo Fajardo*, and that no body had feen him at *Jaen*, where hardly any one knew him. When they brought this Account to the Prince, he cou'd not believe 'em. Since *Felicia* is in the Citadel, interrupted he, 'tis a certain Confequence *Benavidez* is not far; do you only contrive that I enter her Apartment; it is likely he will come there when every body is retired. Don *Gabriel* told him he fhou'd be obey'd; then went to receive Orders from the Governour, who named him for *Felicia*'s Guard; at Night he came back to the Prince, to conduct him and *Alphonfo* to the Citadel.

Now can any Mortal imagine the Trouble this amorous Prince was in, when he thought, he was fure to fee the Object he ftill ador'd; he refolv'd his Rival fhou'd perifh, tho' he himfelf were to fall with him; which violent Reflection made him figh deeply, efpecially when he confider'd that this fame *Felicia* was

was *Leonida* of *Velasco*, to whom he was so strictly engag'd, that his Honour wou'd not suffer any other to carry her off.

He was in this Confusion of Thought, where Love and Revenge were equally concern'd, when Don *Gabriel* conducted him through several Courts, till at last he brought him to the Tower, where *Felicia* was conceal'd in a low Apartment; the Windows were bar'd with Iron-Grates, and the Weather being excessive hot, she had obtain'd leave to walk on the Leads of the Tower for the Air; the Prince took that Opportunity to enter a Closet, which was only shut with a Glass Door, and there hid himself behind the Window Curtain, from whence he could see all that passed. He was not there long, before the Lights were taken away, and he heard two Persons creep into the Closet; they spoke very low, and the Night being dark, he could not distinguish whether they were Men or Women; soon after, they went out of the Closet, where the Prince thought himself alone, but the Lights being brought in again, he saw several Women, who were preparing a Bath. They hung a Canopy of rose-colour'd Sattin, embroider'd with Silver, over a large black Marble Vessel, which they fill'd with Water and Flowers, mix'd with the finest Perfumes.

Every thing being ready, a Lady came in, to whom the rest of the Women shewed much Respect, but he could not see her Face, her Head being covered with a fine Veil; this was *Felicia*, who having undressed her self to

## The PRINCE

a thin Night-Gown, ordered all her Women to retire, excepting *Zaida*; then called for her Lute, saying, Musick only can sooth my dear Afflictions. Ah! *Zaida*, *Zaida*, could he for whom I suffer, hear these Verses, how pleased should I be! Soon after she sung the ensuing Words, with so sweet a Voice, that none cou'd hear her without being inchanted.

*WHY shou'd Virtue thus torment me,*
 *Oh! unkind and cruel Law?*
*Or why shou'd fantastick Duty*
*Strike my tender Heart with Awe?*

2.

*Love, take pity of my Anguish,*
*To my soft Distress be kind:*
*Never let the fair One languish*
*When to Tenderness inclin'd.*

She repeated the last Stanza several times, and fetch'd now and then deep Sighs, which shew'd her Heart was possess'd with a mighty Passion, as well as excessive Grief. The Prince all this while perceiv'd it was not the Voice of his unconstant *Felicia*, or at least was surpriz'd, that the small distance which was between them shou'd cause so great an Alteration in her Tone, as not to know it again. Do not afflict your self, Madam, said *Zaida*; great Passions are ever influenc'd by Fortune; he whom you love, is at present inform'd of what you suffer; do you think he will attempt

nothing

nothing to evince you of his Affection? *Felicia* made no Reply, but order'd her to shut her Chamber Door, and went into the Bath. How entirely do I love you, cruel *Leonida*, said the amorous Prince to himself? But Oh, ungrateful Woman! ought not I to be ashamed of my Weakness? For let me look upon you as a Person to whom I am contracted, or as a Mistress I love to Distraction, you have equally deceiv'd me under the Titles of *Carency*, and *La Vagne*. Ah, perfidious Creature! you are now proposing to surmount all Difficulties, in order to marry *Benavidez*: Cou'd there be a Complaint more passionate, than that which you just now utter'd? But (continued he) what must I believe? Are her Designs travers'd? Here, I see her a Prisoner in a Place where she thought to find a Sanctuary; she even regrets the Absence of her Lover, and every thing seems to disappoint their Expectations.

Such were the Prince's Reflections, and in spite of his Resentment, Love still triumph'd in his Heart; but in what surprize was he, when *Zaida* opening the Door of another Closet, he drew the Curtain, and saw a Man going with Precipitation to the bathing Vessel, where he put himself on his Knees, and spoke so low, that his Voice cou'd not reach the Prince, who only heard *Felicia* cry aloud, is it you, my dear Lover; then she swooned away.

The Prince of *Carency*, seeing this, cou'd no longer refrain, but without thinking on the Consequence of the Scene he was going to open, ran out of the Closet like a Madman, and had he been capable of taking any base Advantage, it was in his power to run him (he took for *Benavidez*) thro' the Body, before the other cou'd even put himself in a Posture of Defence ; for *Felicia*'s Swoon had such an extraordinary Effect upon him, that he did not see the Prince, who was just at his Back, till hearing some body threatening him with a furious Tone, he rose and drew his Sword ; but the Prince seeing his Face, immediately drop'd the Point of his, knowing him to be Don *Alonzo*, eldest Son to the Infanta Don *Fernand* ; he had seen him at *Seville*, when he was there with his Brother, the Count of *La March* ; and the fine Qualities of this young Prince had engag'd the Prince of *Carency* to have a great Esteem for him ; he cast his Eyes on her, whom he took for *Leonida*, and knew her to be Dona *Felicia d'Ayala*, Daughter to the Great Chancellor of *Castille*, who was highly distiguish'd by his Birth, and renown'd for the Histories of Don *Pedro*, and Don *Henriquez*, Kings of *Spain*, which he had written. This Grandee being dead, *Felicia* was brought up with the two Princesses, Daughters to the Infanta Don *Fernand*. Don *Alonzo*, who saw her often, conceiv'd so great a Passion for her, that every one suspected he wou'd marry her privately, and to prevent so unequal a Match, whilst Don *Alonzo* was one

Day

Day a hunting, the Infanta his Father had order'd, that *Felicia* shou'd be secretly conveyed to *Jaen*, where she was to be carefully guarded: All the Women who attended her were at the Infanta's Devotion, and by the Death of the Chancellor her Father she was delivered up entirely to the Persecutions of those, who envy'd her. As for *Zaida*, she was a Slave, whom *Felicia* had made a Christian, and one they did not mistrust, not reflecting she had been presented to her by Don *Alonso*. This young Prince, at his Return to *Seville*, was in a despairing Condition, when he heard his Mistress was gone; and tho' he learn'd but very confusedly, the Manner of her being carry'd off, and confin'd in a strong Place, yet invited by his Passion, he Day and Night us'd his utmost Endeavour to recover her; having at last discover'd his dear *Felicia*'s Concealment, and found Means to write to *Zaida*, who answer'd his Letter, the Affair was so well manag'd, that without *Felicia*'s Knowledge, he got into her Apartment.

The Prince of *Carency* perceiving his Error, in order to repair it, presented Don *Alonso* with his Sword, the Point towards his own Breast; Punish an unhappy Man, said he, whom you will oblige, in taking away his Life. By my Words, you may judge of the Concern I am in, for having disturb'd this charming Interview, which to obtain, it's probable, my Lord, you have expos'd your self to some Danger; but be assur'd, I suffer more than

than you thro' this Miſtake. I do not reſent it in the leaſt, my Lord, (reply'd Don *Alonzo*, embracing him) and if you will promiſe to keep this Secret, you ſhall ever find me a grateful Friend. The Prince of *Carency* gave him his Word, he wou'd never take the leaſt Notice of what had happen'd, and without ſtaying till *Felicia* was come to her ſelf, he left the Chamber in ſo deep a Deſpair, that he cou'd ſcarcely ſpeak to *Gabriel d'Aguilar*, who was at the Door of the firſt Room, with *Alphonſo*, and this laſt attended him to Don *Gabriel*'s Apartment, who was oblig'd to remain in his Poſt.

The Prince having an Opportunity of yielding himſelf up to his juſt Sorrow, call'd to mind all his Misfortunes, from his firſt appearing in the World, to that Moment; on whatever Side he turn'd his Eyes, he ſaw ſo little Hopes of an Intermiſſion, that every thing became indifferent to him, and he did not even wiſh himſelf a better Fortune. All his Thoughts were fix'd on being reveng'd of *Benavidez*, which he fancy'd was the only Satisfaction he cou'd receive; but as it appear'd almoſt impoſſible, it extremely added to his Grief. Oh, *Alphonſo!* ſaid he, can any Diſappointment be equal to this? I was in Hopes to puniſh a Traitor, and recover my Miſtreſs; but that fatal Name of *Felicia* has again deceived me. What unaccountable Circumſtances have attended my Life? Fate has ſingled me amongſt all Mankind to be unfortunate.

tunate. Where muſt I go to find the Treaſure I have loſt? Alas, my *Leonida* is not here, and I diſcover too late, *Caſilda's* wicked Plot. How cou'd I believe, that ſhe wou'd have told me where her Brother was gone? If I had made the leaſt Reflection, I might have expected ſhe wou'd deceive me. Ah! Credulous Wretch that I was, I have loſt an Opportunity I ſhall never retrieve again. Juſt Heaven! my Rival is now ſafe with *Leonida*, and he peaceably enjoys a Bleſſing which belongs to me. Can I after this ſurvive my Shame and Deſpair? In ſhort, the Prince's Condition was ſuch, that nothing cou'd give him Relief; his Complaints were moving, and Love appear'd in all his Actions.

*Alphonſo*, who knew by Experience the Torments, that attend tranſcendent Paſſions, extremely pity'd this unhappy Prince; Oh Love! cry'd he, will you never ceaſe perſecuting us? You alone cauſe all our Misfortunes, and never grant a Favour that is not preceded by a Thouſand Diſappointments. Ah! Why have we no Fence againſt your Power? The Prince, whilſt he was talking, continued in a deep Silence; and *Alphonſo* finding he was not diſpos'd to converſe with him, meditated ſome time, then wrote theſe Verſes.

*L O V E, thou dear, but cruel Tyrant,
 Can nothing move thee to be kind?
Hear my Sighs and ſee my Torment,
For only Thou canſt eaſe my Mind.*

2.

*Since all are doom'd to feel thy Darts,*
*At least suspend our Pains,*
*With tender Pity bless those Hearts*
*That languish in thy Chains.*

The Prince read these Lines, and said, One cou'd have no room to complain, if, in Love, there were an equal mixture of Pleasure and Pain; but alas! I have experienc'd that all its Ills are reserv'd for me, which makes me wish a Period to my unhappy Life. Ah, my Lord! interrupted *Alphonso*, do not harbour a Thought so offensive to your Courage. 'Tis unworthy a Soul so great as your's shou'd yield to a Passion, which will divert you from the Performance of great Exploits. The Prince blush'd at what *Alphonso* said, and look'd on this Discourse, as a Reproach made him, for the time he had employ'd in entertaining his amorous Sentiments; You shall see by my Conduct, reply'd he, that my Soul is still my own: I love, 'tis true, and cannot flatter myself with ever being disengag'd from a Passion, which has so great an Empire over me; yet when Honour calls me I am ready to attend; and if I must give up my Life it shall be in so glorious a way as will do Honour to my Name.

Here they where both silent some time, till the Prince, urg'd by disagreeable Thoughts, broke out into his usual Complaints: Oh, *Alphonso*! said he, which way shall I direct my Course to find *Leonida*? I cannot hear where she is; must I then turn Knight-Errant, and run through the World, without knowing where to go? No, I have a nobler Resolution; I will return to *Seville*, and there follow my Brother's Fortune; if we engage the *Moors*, I must conquer, or bravely die.

*Alphonso* over-joy'd to hear the Prince speak in these Terms, applauded a Design so worthy of him. Consider, my Lord, said he, that all you cou'd do at present for *Leonida*, wou'd meet with no Return; for since she flies you, 'tis proable, you are the Object of her Aversion; at least, her going off with *Benavidez* is a Proof, she loves him, and is perfidious to you: What can you then expect from her? Rather strive to deface the Impression she has made, that in time you may even lose the Remembrance of having ever known her. I ought to take your Advice indeed, interrupted the Prince, but alas! how is it possible? Fortune may be inconstant, but my Heart can never change. Thus irresolute, not knowing what to determine, he conjur'd *Alphonso* not to discover who he was, nor acquaint the Count of *La March* with his being at *Jaen*, till he had fix'd a Resolution. The Chevalier promis'd him upon Honour to keep the Secret inviolably, and beg'd he wou'd not be uneasy on that Subject.

Whilst these things pass'd in relation to the Prince of *Carency*, the Count of *La March*, his Brother, neglected no opportunity of signalizing himself. He had not been long at *Seville*, when the *Moors* besieg'd *Baëca* with Seven Thousand Horse, and a Hundred Thousand Foot; so formidable an Army struck Terror throughout *Andalusia*, but as the Place was well fortify'd, the *Moors* despair'd of its Reduction, when they receiv'd Advice, that the *Spaniards* from all parts were assembled in order to relieve it; therefore they suddenly retir'd, loaded with the Plunder of the Neighbouring Villages. They were not more fortunate at Sea, where they had considerable Losses by the *Spanish* Fleet, which had engag'd their's, and gain'd a compleat Victory. This Advantage gave no small Satisfaction to the *Spaniards*, who now thought of acting offensively. The Infanta call'd a General Council of all the Officers of the Army, where it was resolv'd to besiege *Zahara*. The besieg'd defended the Town bravely, till the want of Necessaries made 'em capitulate. Soon after, he took another of their strongest Places, which so exasparated *Mahomet* King of *Granada*, that he immediately thought on Revenge; and in order to carry on his Design, put himself at the Head of Six Thousand Horse, and Eighty Thousand Foot, dividing them into several Bodies, which took different Routs for their March, and all on a sudden besieg'd *Jaen*, whilst they thought him imploy'd elsewhere.

His Approach surpriz'd the Governour, who was not prepar'd for a Siege, and wou'd have been under greater Difficulties, were he not assisted by the Prince of *Carency*, who had not yet

left

left the Town, and was rejoyc'd to have so fine an Occasion of distinguishing himself. He had been presented to *Alonzo Fajardo* under the Title of Count of *La Vagne*, and having offer'd his Services to him, the other readily accepted of 'em. This young Prince put himself at the Head of a Detachment, and by his frequent Sallies, often broke the Enemies Measures, and repuls'd 'em where ever he appear'd, carrying Death and Terror along with him. As his Neglect of Life made him expose himself to the greatest Dangers, he became dreadful to his Enemies, who knowing him by his Arms, chose rather to avoid his Blows than resist him. The Governour of *Jaen* admired his Courage, and thought Heaven had sent him to defend that City against the Infidels.

The King of the *Moors* enrag'd at his ill Success, and attributing the Cause to the Prince of *Carency*, whom they call'd the Knight of the black Arms, order'd some of the bravest of his Army, either to kill, or take him Prisoner; so immediately the Generals and most of the Noblemen made a League to be reveng'd of this terrible Enemy, or perish in the Attempt. A Detachment was sent out the next Day, much superior to that under the Prince's Command. Neverthereless he attack'd them, and his Courage surpass'd all that can be imagin'd. The *Moors* were beginning to repent their rash Undertaking, when unluckily the Prince's Horse was wounded by an Arrow; and before he cou'd disengage himself, they rush'd rush'd upon him with a Shout, and took him Prisoner. This News ran thro' the Camp, and soon found way into the Town, where it had a different Effect; *Mahomet* thought now he had conquer'd, and the Governour believ'd himself overcome. The Barbarians were resolv'd to make a general Assault, and the Christians were preparing to defend themselves, tho' most of the Soldiers were mightily dishearten'd, saying to one another, what can we pretend to? We have lost the Count of *La Vagne*; commanded by him, we might have defeated our Enemies, but his Misfortune is the Presage of ours.

At this time the Infanta omitted nothing for the Succour of *Jaen*: He assembled his Troops with great Diligence, and march'd towards the Town with the Count of *La March*, where he surpriz'd the *Moors*, who retir'd with more Shame than Glory, satisfying themselves with burning, and pillaging, wherever they pass'd. The *Spaniards* pursu'd them as far as *Malaga*, which they besieg'd in their turn. The Infanta was inform'd by Don *Alonso Fajardo*, of the young Count of *La Vagne*'s being taken Prisoner by *Mahomet*; as for his Friend *Alphonso*, he was kill'd in one of the Engagements, which was the Cause that the Count of *La March* heard nothing of the Prince of *Carency*'s being there. The mighty Character of his Bravery, and the Recital of the great Actions he had perform'd, gave the Infanta a particular Concern for his Misfortune;

he sent an Officer with Proposals for the Exchange of Prisoners, and offer'd a Ransom for the Count of *La Vagne*, being willing to purchase his Liberty at any rate; but all he cou'd do to get him out of his Enemies Power was in vain; the *Moors* made Answer, that the Count having brib'd his Guards, had made his Escape, and that were he still in their Hands, they wou'd readily send him back, to shew how desirous they were to oblige the Infanta.

The King of *Granada* in the mean time was of Opinion, that he cou'd not too strictly guard a Person, who had been very troublesome to him during the Siege; therefore Policy and Revenge having an equal share in this Design, he order'd that the Prince (tho' dangerously wounded) shou'd be convey'd to the Castle of *Solobrena*, where his Brother, Prince *Joseph*, with his two Sons, *Mahomet* and *Osmin*, were kept Prisoners; so the Prince of *Carency* found himself a second time in the Power of the Infidels; but his Sentiments were quite different from those he had at *Nicopolis*, for that which at another time wou'd have given him much Chagrin, had now very little Effect on him, all his Thoughts being only imploy'd on *Leonida*, and every thing else below his Consideration; yet it was an unhappy State, for a Man to love an Object, whom he Thought guilty of the greatest Perfidiousness.

Whilst this was the State of Affairs in Upper *Andalusia* and *Murcia*, *Celima* Queen of
*Fez*

*Fez* was taking Meafures to be reveng'd of *Abelhamar*. *Felicia* had but juft oblig'd him to leave her Chamber, when the Queen (impatient to have her Defigns executed) caus'd him to be feiz'd by a Captain of her Guards, who carry'd him immediately to a Tower adjoyning the Palace, and having pofted a Guard at every Gate to hinder People from coming near, the Queen went to him foon after.

*Abelhamar* did not appear the leaft furpriz'd at his Confinement; he faid to this Princefs, My Sentiments, Madam, are not unknown to you, fince you are inform'd of the Love I have for *Felicia*; I have not acted any thing contrary to the Allegiance and Refpect I owe you, and tho' you find me difguis'd in your Palace, it wou'd not confift with Juftice, to draw an ill Confequence from an Action, that is only the Effect of my Paffion, to which you can impute no other Crime, but that of Indifcretion. I know too well your Intentions (interrupted the Queen in a fierce Tone) to let myfelf be deceiv'd by your Wit, or Metamorphofis; No, Prince! you were here confpiring againft me; the rebellious Principles you were brought up in, cou'd never receive a grateful Sentiment, or teach you what you owe your Sovereign. Have I not preferv'd your Life, without regard to the Reafons of State, which ought to have induced me to facrifice you? Yet, ungrateful as you are! have you liv'd hitherto with the hopes of making

me

me a Victim? Cruel *Ismael* also seconds your Design, and has promis'd you Forces in order to dethrone me. You prefer a Stranger to a Queen of your own Blood, to whom you owe every thing; but Heaven that protects me, has put me in a Condition to punish you, and be reveng'd of my Enemies. Satisfy yourself, Madam, (reply'd the Prince, with a haughty Air) and don't slight so fine an Opportunity of taking away a Life, which is odious to you. Paint my Innocence in the vilest Colours, or rather, say, the legal Right I have to the Crown you wear, is my only Crime; and that, as you have ever born an invincible hatred to the unhappy Remainders of my Family, you have resolv'd to compleat, what your unjust Father had begun. Rash Man! cry'd *Celima*, do you think of what you are saying? Dare you pronounce these Words before the Queen your Mistress? Don't you know your Death waits my Command? Is it thus you endeavour to justify your self, and appease me? You don't consider the Danger you are in. *Abelhamar* made no Reply to her Threats, nor gave the least Attention to her whilst she was speaking, but rather acted like one, who despising Mercy, did not regret the Life he was going to be depriv'd of; which unconcern'd Behaviour surpriz'd the Queen, who retired full of Resentment.

*Celima* had already given orders, that *Felicia* and *Inea* shou'd be strictly guarded in their Chambers, and that none of their Companions
shou'd

shou'd be admitted to them. This new Misfortune did not add to *Felicia*'s Concern, for every thing was now become so indifferent to her, that she did not even enquire into the Cause.

The Queen being return'd to the Palace, call'd her Council, and appointed Persons to examine the Prince, because she wou'd shew some Form in an Affair, which might draw upon her the Aversion of her Relations, and particularly that of the *Maliquez Alabez*, who were also descended from the antient Kings of *Fez*, and at that time very potent in the Kingdom of *Granada*. This induc'd her to give the blackest Colours to the Crime, with which they were going to charge *Abelhamar*; and tho' she took the best Measures to conceal the Design she had against him, yet his faithful *Mula* (who was just return'd from *Tunis*, where he had carry'd Credentials to *Ismael* from the Prince, us'd his utmost Application to serve him; he had too good a Correspondence in the Palace, not to be inform'd of every thing that pass'd there, in relation to the unfortunate Prince; and as he perceiv'd the occasion was pressing, he wou'd lose no time to give immediate assistance to his Master, who otherways wou'd fall a Sacrifice to *Celima*. He went to all *Abelhamar*'s Friends and Slaves, and prepar'd them to assemble, in order to raise the City in his Favour; by which means, he hoped to restore him to his Liberty, or put all to Fire and Sword, that wou'd oppose it. These were

were his Resolutions, till he reflected, that the Queen had a great many Creatures devoted to her Service, as well as a strong Garrison, and that the People being us'd to her Government, wou'd strive to maintain it; therefore he thought it more prudent to return to *Tunis*, and apply himself to *Ismael*, who wou'd imploy his utmost Power in this important Affair; so he set out again from *Sallee*, and soon arriv'd at *Ismael's* Court.

His Grief and Affection furnish'd him with Expressions of so great a Force, that the King of *Tunis* was extreamly touch'd at *Abelhamar's* Misfortunes, and being already exasperated against *Celima*, he resolv'd immediately to assist that Prince. With this Intent, he order'd his Troops to be drawn out of their Garrisons and review'd, then sent an Ambassador to the King of *Morocco*, to renew his Treaty of Alliance with him, to prevent that Prince in his Absence from making any Irruptions into his Territories.

After having dispos'd every thing with as much Wisdom as Diligence, he open'd the Campaign, and *Mula* return'd privately to *Sallee*, to perform what he had first resolv'd for the Safety of his Master.

The young Prince being examin'd, refus'd at first to make a Reply; but when they told him, unless he answer'd to the Accusation, he shou'd receive Sentence the sooner, it oblig'd him to make a Defence, in Expectation of being reliev'd by *Ismael*; and whatever mind the Queen had to forward his Tryal, she cou'd not

not proceed to a Condemnation, without exposing herself to inevitable Dangers. The first Officers of the Crown, and Lords of the Court represented to her, that she cou'd not take too much Precaution in an Affair of this Importance, and that it wou'd be more to her Glory, to let Clemency take Place of Justice; we believe the Prince is culpable, said they, since he was found disguis'd in the Palace, which is a sufficient Proof; yet without Regard to his Youth, as he is presumptive Heir to the Crown, and of your Blood, Madam, he ought to have some Respect shewn him; therefore we beg, that your Majesty, for your own Interest, will consider these Reasons separately, and by suspending your Resentment, shew Mercy to the Prince.

The Queen was displeas'd at a Request, which shew'd, that *Abelhamar* had more Friends than she imagin'd; and fearing they shou'd take Measures to rescue her Prisoner, she wou'd no longer consult Reason, but resolv'd to do every thing by her own Authority, without taking any Advice of her Council; so having prevented those appointed to judge the Prince, she herself pronounc'd the Sentence of his Death; and to deter seditious Persons from caballing against her, she order'd, that he shou'd be executed on the Plat-Form of the Court wherein he was confin'd, that every Body might see him suffer.

In this Place they built a Scaffold hung with Mourning, and set round with Standards

and

and Scutcheons, which with other dismal Preparations drew Numbers of Spectators. The Prince was soon after inform'd of his Fate; this News at first very much surpriz'd him; his Eyes express'd an extraordinary Grief, and he was some time without speaking; at last lifting up his Hands, Oh Heaven! he cry'd, you know my Disguise was not criminal, and that this is only a pretext the unjust Queen takes to destroy me; but since you have decreed my Doom, I am ready to obey without repining; and if *Celima* grants me one Favour, I shall die with Content. Then turning himself to the Captain of the Guards, he said, go tell the Queen from me, that I beg leave to bid an eternal Adieu to charming *Felicia*; the Minutes I shall pass with her will be too short to retard the inhuman Designs of *Celima*.

The Officer went directly to the Queen, who was very unwilling to grant the Prince his Request; but her Ministers having represented to her in respectful Terms, how cruel it wou'd be to refuse so small a Satisfaction to a Person in his Condition, she at last consented that *Felicia* shou'd be brought to him. She was till then a Stranger to the Prince's Misfortune, being strictly confin'd with *Inea*; and as her Confinement did not in the least disturb her, she never enquired, why they added this new Rigour to her Captivity. Her Mind was entirely taken up with the Count of *La Vagne*, and the Tears she shed were only for his Inconstancy and Absence; every thing else that
happen'd,

happen'd, had no Effect on her; and she was in this Disposition, when she was sent for by the Queen's Orders. She follow'd the Governess of the Slaves without asking any Question; *Inea* supported her, and being very weak after her Illness, it was with a vast deal of Difficulty, that she reach'd the Tower.

The first Object that struck her Sight was the Scaffold, and a Number of Guards, which gave her room to believe, that she was going to be a Victim to *Celima*'s Jealousy. *Inea*'s Thoughts were the same, which extremely terrify'd her. *Felicia*'s Sentiments were different from hers; for tho' Death appear'd hard to her, yet she had some sort of Satisfaction, in seeing the approaching End of her Misfortunes. Take Courage, my dear *Inea,* (said she, embracing her with a great deal of Tenderness,) the Danger only regards me, and I look upon it with Indifferency; it is a Remedy my Preservation commanded me not to seek, but since it is my Fate, I receive it with Pleasure. I am going to die, and shall no longer have a Sense of my Calamities. No, Lovely *Felicia!* (cry'd the Prince, who was near enough to hear what she said,) you are not to die; this Punishment is prepar'd for unfortune *Abelhamar,* who now takes his last leave of you; I protest it less concerns me, to lose my Life in so shameful a manner, than to want Assurances of your Favour. Ah Madam! (added he with an Air full of Love and Grief) can you refuse me a Look, a Sigh, or or a favourable Word? You see I perish, and my Misfortune proceeds from your tranfcendent Charms! The Defire I had to fee you reign, made me endeavour to afcend the Throne, from which my Father fell; you infpir'd me with an Ambition, I fhou'd have manag'd better, had I been lefs in Love; You are the innocent Caufe of the Difguife I am reproach'd with, which is thought my Crime; yet I have nothing to repent of, fince my Paffion invites me to bear the Cruelty of my Fate. But at leaft, give me leave, divine *Felicia*, to believe that had my Defign fucceeded, my Refpect and Perfeverance wou'd have made fome Impreffion on you. Only approve thefe Thoughts, and I fhall not think much to purchafe fo dear a Profeffion, with the Lofs of my Life.

*Felicia* at thefe Words was fo diforder'd, that fhe look'd fome time at *Abelhamar*, without having Power to fpeak. She was touch'd with a fincere Compaffion, and deplor'd the Misfortune of this young Prince, who was going to be facrific'd fo ignominioufly. She cou'd have wifh'd, the Queen's Refentment had fallen on her; for the State of her Affairs with the Count of *La Vagne* was fuch, as had render'd Life fo infupportable to her, that fhe feem'd very willing to refign it. At laft, perceiving *Abelhamar* waited her Anfwer; fhe faid, is this Scene prepar'd for you, my Lord? Alas! why cannot I relieve you? My Tears are the only Proofs, I can give of my true Concern; yet be affured, I fhall never be so ungrateful, as to forget your Favours. This Day's Disaster will ever be before my Eyes. Ah *Felicia*! (reply'd the Prince) I thought your Compassion wou'd have inspired me with Courage, but I find it has a contrary Influence. Oh! That I cou'd now live for you. The Hopes you have given me, make me extreamly regret leaving you, since I must leave you for ever. Here, his Breast was oppress'd with so deep a Sorrow, that he cou'd only express it by his repeated Sighs. The Queen, who was impatient to have the Prince executed, had order'd, that *Felicia* shou'd be call'd away from him, when of a sudden she was alarm'd, hearing at the Gates of the Palace, the Shouts and Cries of People in Arms, who were comanded by valiant *Mula*, and had already charg'd the Soldiers of the Guard. They demanded the Prince, and threatned *Celima* with a general Revolt, unanimously calling *Abelhamar* their King, and saying, they had cause to fear a Queen, who was cruel enough to wash her Hands in the Blood of her nearest Relation; and that if she deny'd their Request, they wou'd deliver her up to the Punishment, which she had design'd for the Prince.

The Queen wou'd not have given much Attention to the Menaces of these seditious People, had she not been inform'd, that there were thick Clouds of Dust seen towards the Road of *Tunis*, and that the Centinels (who had already heard a confus'd Noise of warlike Instruments) began to discover from the Walls
of

of the Town, a Body of Men marching with great Precipitation; soon after they came to acquaint her, that there was a Herald at the Gate, who desired Admittance to her Majesty, in the Name of *Ismael.* This News struck the Queen with Terror, which she express'd by her Emotions, being divided between Revenge and Despair. Her Ministers press'd her to give Audience to the King of *Tituan's* Herald, and after being a little compos'd, she consented to see him; he brought her a Letter, which was in these Terms.

*I Am come to succour* Abelhamar, *who is a Prince favour'd by Heaven, and our great Prophet* Mahomet, *therefore you must deliver him up to me. Consider, inhuman Queen, that you have neither Arms nor Subjects to support you: I am inform'd of every thing, that passes in the Palace, which I protest, I will reduce to Ashes, unless you immediately restore the Prince to his Liberty; but if you send him to me, or Hostages for his Security, I will favour your Retreat; you may leave the Kingdom, and take with you such Attendance, as you shall think necessary.*

Ismael Sultan.

*Celima's* Fortune cou'd hardly receive a greater Change; she now saw at the Gates of her Capital an Enemy, who treated her like a Conqueror, that was just going to dethrone her. The Soul of this imperious Princess grew so furious at *Ismael's* Menaces, that instead of thinking of the Danger she was in, her Mind was only taken up with Revenge. Come, cry'd ſhe, Barbarian! Come and be Witneſs of my Courage and Reſentment; the Man you intend to redeem, ſhall be ſacrific'd before your Eyes. If Heaven and Earth ſhou'd joyn, and the Elements return to their firſt Chaos; What is it to me? I have but a Life to loſe, which has been a Burthen to me theſe many Years; let us go and ſtrike off this rebellious Head, which is ſo dear to *Iſmael*, and ſend it to him from the Height of the Tower. Follow me (ſaid ſhe, to the Herald, who waited her Anſwer;) come and ſee, how I ſlight the Threats of your Maſter. You ſhall Witneſs the Death of *Abelhamar*, and receive his laſt Sighs. Ending theſe Words, ſhe went haſtily towards the Place, where her Commands were only expected for his Execution; but, the Mufty, the Admiral, and Governour of the Town, with ſeveral of her faithful Subjects, flung themſelves at her Feet: Alaſs, Madam! ſaid they, conſider the Misfortune which ſeems to point at you perſonally; are you reſolv'd to bury your ſelf in the Ruins of the Palace? That muſt certainly be your Fate, if you irritate a King, who is before your Walls with a potent Army; this is no time, Madam, to revenge your ſelf; for in puting the Prince to Death, it may raiſe a Mutiny, and ſhou'd *Iſmael* take Advantage of it, you may loſe your Life, or become Captive to the Conqueror. Is it not more glorious, Madam, to fly and ſeek in another Country ſome Forces, who, encourag'd by by your Presence, may re-place you on your Throne?

The Queen's Women in Tears, proftrated themfelves at her Feet, and faid all that Zeal and Fear cou'd infpire; at laft her imperious Heart was touch'd, rather at the Danger fhe expos'd fo many Perfons to, who depended on her, than at what concern'd her own Perfon. Muft the Queen of *Fez* fubmit, cry'd fhe, and feek her Safety in a fhameful Flight, which will caufe her to blufh the reft of her Days? Oh Heavens! Was ever Deftiny fo wretched as mine? I fhall become a Fugitive, and banifh'd my Kingdom, be forc'd to beg Refuge of thofe whom I once cou'd have protected; I cannot think I deferve fo cruel a Fate. Here, fhe continued her Complaints, and whilft fhe yielded to her exceffive Grief, *Abelhamar* was inform'd of the agreeable Change in his Fortune.

He was entertaining *Felicia*, when they came to tell him, that *Ifmael*'s Ships and Forces were approaching. Think with what Tranfports he receiv'd this News! 'Tis now, Madam, faid he to her, that I can return the Goodnefs, you juft now exprefs'd; your Virtues have made a deep impreffion on me, and fince I am deliver'd from Death, you fhall no longer feel the Weight of your Chains. I rejoice, my Lord, reply'd *Felicia*, to fee that the Danger is paft, and conjure you, not to give your felf any Uneafinefs about me: I am born to be unhappy, and the Rigour of my Captivity is nothing, when compar'd to my
inward

inward Pain: Farewel, my Lord; you have now Affairs of greater Importance to imploy your Thoughts. Finishing these Words, she retired, and *Abelhamar* remain'd in the Tower by Order of the Queen, who sent Hostages to *Ismael*, with Assurances, that the Prince shou'd be set at Liberty, as soon as she had left the City.

Unfortunate *Celima* was now preparing a Fleet and Transports to carry away her most valuable Goods: She gave Instructions to those Persons, whom she cou'd not take along with her, and having dispos'd every Thing according to her Intention, she made all imaginable Diligence to depart, not depending on *Ismael*'s Words, and fearing the Consequences of *Abelhamar*'s Resentment. Thus the Fugitive Queen went off by Night, with her Women and Slaves, and was conducted to the Vessel, which attended her. She order'd immediately to set Sail with the rest of the Fleet, and the Wind being fair, they soon enter'd the *Mediterranean*. Nothing cou'd be equal to the Concern *Celima* was in for the loss of her Kingdom; she fetch'd deep Sighs, and in spight of all her Pride, cou'd not restrain her Tears. Fortune! Ungrateful Fortune! said she, your Capriciousness spares neither King, nor Subject. Who can flatter himself with being above your Reach? You declar'd your self my Enemy from my Infancy, and pursu'd me in the remotest Countries. Once taken by a Pyrate, I fell into the Power of *Bajazet*; soon after, you made use of *Cupid*'s Arrows to pierce my

Heart;

Heart; Alas! that Wound, I never can hope to cure; at laſt, to ſhew your ſelf more favourable, you plac'd me on a Throne, which you now force me to abandon. What muſt I expect from you next? Why don't you ſtrike me at once with your moſt poiſon'd Darts, that I may not be expos'd to new Torments. Oh, deplorable Fate! ſhall I thus be for ever perſecuted? And you *Felicia*, (continued ſhe, caſting her melancholy Eyes on *Leonida*, who was near her) you are the Author of my laſt Misfortune; it is your fatal Beauty, that has been the occaſion of this Revolution; Ah! how can you evince me, that you are innocent? Alas, Madam! reply'd *Felicia*, I had no Hand in the Prince's criminal Deſigns; for if it be true, that he had a Paſſion for me, it was contrary to my Inclination: I knew nothing of his Diſguiſe; nor did I ever flatter him with any Hopes. On the contrary, my Averſion was the only Return I made to his Addreſſes, and from the firſt Hour he declar'd his Sentiments for me, I reſolv'd never to change. I was inform'd, ſaid *Celima*, that the Count of *La Vagne*, who came to fetch away *Olympia*, had given you much Uneaſineſs; without doubt, he is the Perſon you love, but you are convinc'd, he has no longer a Paſſion for you, and ſince he has no Regard to your Affection, you ought to diſdain him. Theſe Words put *Felicia* into ſome Confuſion, who bluſhing, caſt down her Eyes, without being able to utter one Word, and her beauteous Cheeks

Cheeks moisten'd with Tears sufficiently expres'd the State of her anxious Soul. You make me no Answer (said *Celima*, fetching a Sigh) Ah! I am better able to Answer for you; I was willing to see, whether your Tongue cou'd betray your Heart, or disown a Distemper, you cannot cure. Alas, *Felicia*! I know too well by fatal Experience, the irresistible Power of Love, which unhappily surpriz'd me before I cou'd suppress its first Motions, or even think how dangerous they might prove.

If there are Torments in Love, Madam, said *Felicia*, they ought not to affect a Sovereign, whom Nature hath grac'd with such transcendent Perfections. Nothing but Death, or Absence can deprive you of the Object that is dear to you. Inconstancy, which surpasses either in Cruelty, can never make you feel the tormenting Effects of it. Ah, *Felicia*! reply'd *Celima*, there is no Pain like that, which is occasion'd by Absence, since it keeps us in continual Fears, both of Death and Infidelity. At least, Madam, said *Felicia*, there is one Comfort in it, which is, that having but an uncertain knowledge of the Truth, we are generally inclin'd to believe what we most wish. No, continu'd *Celima*, it is not as you imagine; Uncertainty in Love is a Martyrdom, which adds to all the Pains we can endure. Alas, Madam! reply'd *Felicia*, I shou'd now look on that uncertain State, as a happy one, since I might derive from it the pleasing Hopes, which my present Condition entirely destroys.

The

The Sovereign and her Charming Slave were entertaining each other with Difcourfes of this Quality ; and tho' *Celima*'s Familiarity was very great, yet *Felicia* was ever mindful of the Refpect due to her. Night was far advanc'd before they took any Reft ; but at laft their Eyes yielded to what Nature required, and *Celima* had been afleep fome Hours, when fhe was awak'd by the Noife of Seamen and Soldiers; the former were preparing againft a Storm, which threaten'd 'em, and the latter for an Engagement with *Abelhamar,* whofe Ships they had juft difcover'd.

You muft know that as foon as the Queen of *Fez* had fet out for the Kingdom of *Granada,* the Gates of *Sallee* and the Palace were open'd to the King of *Tituan,* who immediately went to the Tower, where the young Prince was Prifoner ; but the latter being already fet at Liberty, he came to meet the King with the greateft Marks of Joy and Gratitude for his happy Deliverance. After *Abelhamar* had imploy'd fome time, in giving the King as obliging a Reception, as that Juncture wou'd permit, he cou'd not forbear going to the Apartment which belong'd to the Queen's Slaves, thinking to find *Felicia* there ; for thofe who guarded him in his Confinement, had not inform'd him of her being embark'd with *Celima.*

But you may imagine how great was his Surprize, not to meet any Women there, and to fee every thing in Diforder: This giving him some Suspicion, he proceeded to the Queen's Apartments, which were open and quite empty, so that he had no longer room to doubt of the loss of his *Felicia*. He ran up and down like a distracted Man, and express'd his excessive Grief in such Terms, as extremely mov'd all that were with him. Have I then lost you, *Felicia*? cry'd he; my charming *Felicia*! have I lost you at a time, that I was flatter'd with the hopes of a perfect Felicity? The Compassion you shew'd for me, when I was expecting immediate Death, was an Evincement of the Disposition you were in to do me Justice, and had you not been compell'd to fly me, I am inclin'd to believe, you wou'd no longer refuse me your Affection. But Oh! my *Felicia*, they have snatch'd you from me, and my raging Passion is the only thing I have left in your cruel Absence. Go *Mula*, continu'd he, go tell the King, he has done nothing for me; I am ready to give him up that Life, which he has preserv'd, and I conjure him to take it from me, or restore me my Mistress; but what do I say? she is not in his Power, then let him give me his Ships to pursue her.

*Mula* obey'd his Commands, and went to *Ismael*, whilst some Persons, who remain'd with the Prince, were giving him an Account, with how much Precipitation the Queen went off, and that she had set Sail for the Kingdom of *Granada*. *Abelhamar* (whose Impatience was great,) wou'd not wait *Mula*'s Return, but ran to *Ismael*, who readily granted him all he desired;

fired; so having chosen some of the King's best Ships, and swiftest Sailers, he pursu'd *Celima*, whose Fleet he knew was neither considerable in Strength, or Number; tho' he did not reflect that his Squadron was still Inferior. Having put to Sea, he stood on the Quarter-Deck, endeavouring to discover some of the Queen's Ships, when he spy'd a Vessel, not very distant. He gave Orders they shou'd make all Sail, which being executed, and the Wind fair, it was not long before he came up with her.

The first Object that presented it self to him, was the Count of *La Vagne*; for his and *Olympia's* Sailing had been prevented by stormy Weather, which forc'd 'em back; so they chose to stay on Shipboard, and remain in the Harbour, where they waited a fair Opportunity of going on their Voyage. As soon as *Abelhamar* perceiv'd it was the Count, (whether he look'd on him as a Rival, who was the Occasion that his Passion for *Felicia* had not met with an obliging Return, or that he consider'd him as an Enemy to that lovely Captive, having behav'd himself towards her in an ungrateful and perfidious manner,) he cou'd not help conceiving so immoderate an Aversion for him, that he instantly commanded *Mula* to take the Barge, and go to the Count of *La Vagne*. Tell him, said the Prince, that I look on him as a Traytor, who deserves Death; and if he has a Mind to save Those who are with him, and have nothing to interpose in our Quarrel, he may come to me, or give me his Word of
Honour,

Honour, and I will go and decide the Affair with him.

*Mula* went on Board the Count of *La Vagne*'s Ship, and tho' he was not acquainted with *Abelhamar*, whom he was sure had no reasonable Motive to quarrel with him, yet he was so offended, to see himself suspected being a Traytor, that without entering into a Detail, which might have made up the Difference, he leap'd into *Mula*'s Boat. I will go, (said he to him, with an Air full of Pride and Anger;) your Master shall see, that such a Man as I is not to be insulted unreveng'd. Thus without reflecting on the Danger to which he expos'd himself, and even forgetting his dear Mistress, he order'd them to Row him to *Abelhamar*'s Ship.

The Boat had already made some Way, when *Olympia*'s Woman awak'd her, and gave her an Account of what was passing. Her Surprize was so great, that she just gave her self Time to take her Night-Gown, then ran upon Deck, from whence, she perceiv'd her Lover at a great Distance. Do you abandon me then, my dear Count, cry'd she, and are you going to expose a Life, which is mine? What have you to say to cruel *Abelhamar*? Oh! don't leave me so; but come back to your dear *Olympia*, or take me along with you, that I may undergo the same Fate. Whilst she was uttering these Words, the Count had reach'd *Abelhamar*'s Ship. *Olympia* seeing this, desir'd the Captain of that she was in, to let her take his Barge, which being granted, ed, she bad them pull up with all Speed towards the Prince's Ship; but she unfortunately arriv'd there too late: The Count was already engag'd with *Abelhamar*; and tho' he fought with all the Courage and Dexterity imaginable, he was forc'd at length to yield, having received a mortal Wound.

As he was making his last Efforts to defend himself, against *Abelhamar*'s reiterated Blows, the unhappy *Olympia* came up, and perceiving at a small Distance, that her Lover was cover'd with Blood, and hardly able to support himself, she cry'd out in a loud Voice, hold, barbarous Prince! hold! What have I done to you, that shou'd provoke you to deprive me of my Life? Don't you know that the Count of *La Vagne* is to be mine? Give some Intermission to your Rage, (cruel as you are,) or if nothing but a Sacrifice will satisfy you, I am here ready to receive the Blow; Come and pierce my Heart; but spare! oh! spare the Man I love!

The Accent of a Voice so dear to the Count, reach'd him, just as he fell at *Abelhamar*'s Feet. He strove to raise his Head, and turning his Eyes towards *Olympia*'s Barge, he saw his Divine Mistress despairing, who with much ado got on Board the Ship, and was no sooner there, but fell in a Swoon near the Count, and remain'd Speechless a long while. After she was a little recover'd, all she cou'd do, was to lay her dying Lover's Head on her Knees, and bath his Wounds with her Tears: Thus oppress'd with mortal Grief, she sate down without being able to complain.

The Count endeavour'd to speak to her, and taking her by the Hand, said, I die, my dear *Olympia*, I die entirely yours, and regret departing from Life, only for your sake. With these Words, his Soul took its Flight, and left his Body in the Arms of his deplorable Mistress, who said such moving things, and acted so much Despair, that even *Abelhamar* was inconsolable, for being the Author of her Affliction. He sent her half dead on Board the Ship, she was in before, and order'd the Count of *La Vagne*'s Corps to be also transported. *Olympia*, instead of going to *Genoa*, sail'd for *Sardinia*, in order to retire to her Aunt's Monastry, where (having erected a magnificent Tomb for her Lover) she continu'd the rest of her Days, lamenting the irreparable Loss she had made. Thus we are often deceiv'd, when in the greatest hopes of an approaching Happiness, which Fortune changes into the cruelest Torments.

*Abelhamar* wou'd not have left *Olympia* in this desolate Condition, had not his Passion invited him elsewhere. He impatiently desir'd to overtake the Queen, being resolv'd to force his *Felicia* from her; and he was not long in his Pursuit, before they came to tell him, that they had discover'd *Celima*'s Ships. One may judge how extremely overjoy'd he was at this News. He immediately gave Orders to make all Sail, then imploying his Wishes for Success and a fair Wind, prepar'd himself for an Engagement with the Queen's Squadron, who were also doing the same.

**This**

This unfortunate Princess knowing the Danger which threaten'd her, encourag'd her People, and having sent to all the Captains to come on Board her Ship, she call'd a Council, then Orders were given, and each Officer thought of nothing but doing his Duty. The Trumpets began to sound, and the Cannons roar'd, whilst on each side they were endeavouring to gain the Advantage of the Wind, with a Resolution not to shew any Favour. Thus ready for a Fight, *Celima* said to her Soldiers, Observe that dangerous Serpent (pointing at *Abelhamar*, who was in Armour walking on his Quarter-Deck) see that ungrateful Man, whom I brought up with so much Care, he is now meditating my Ruin; did I not spare his Life, tho' it ever endanger'd mine? yet he is not satisfy'd with my quitting my Kingdom, to expose myself on this dangerous Element. He even pursues me, and so greedily thirsts after Blood, that nothing can please him but my Death. Help me, ye brave and Loyal Subjects, to punish this Rebel, and let us by destroying him, afford an Example for other Traytors in Ages to come!

The Queen was thus animating her Soldiers, whilst *Felicia* and *Inea* were indulging their Melancholy. See my Dear! said *Felicia*; see, these dreadful Preparations; what can be the fatal Consequence of this Engagement? I fear, we shall once more be the Victims of Fortune: Oh, Heaven! cry'd she, rather let me die, than fall into the Hands of *Abelhamar*, since no greater Disaster can ever happen to me.

*Inea*

*Inea* endeavour'd to comfort and give her hopes, faying, why do you thus afflict your felf, fince nothing is yet decided? We are all preparing for a vigorous Refiftance, and the Weather begins to be fo Stormy, that one wou'd almoft believe it impoffible for the two Fleets to approach. She was ftill fpeaking, when on a fudden, there arofe fuch a boifterous Wind, with Thunder and Lightning, that on each fide, inftead of continuing their Preparation for a Fight, they were forc'd to employ all Hands to fave themfelves from greater Dangers.

Thus the Fleets were difpers'd without knowing which way to fteer their Courfe: The raging Wind rent the Sails and fplit the Mafts, and the artlefs Pilot, with Death in his Looks, was torn from his Helm: The impetuous Waves tofs'd the Ships here, and there, till at laft, unable to withftand their refiftlefs Fury, fome were dafh'd againft the Rocks, others wreck'd on the Shoar, and few efcap'd this terrible Tempeft.

*Abelhamar* (having loft Sight of the Ship wherein he thought *Felicia*, and defpairing of ever feeing her more) look'd on the Danger he was in, with fome kind of Satisfaction. No, (faid he to *Mula*, who made unfuccesful Efforts to confole his Mafter) no, fhou'd I efcape Death, which now threatens me, you muft not think, that I can ever enjoy any Pleafure, or Happinefs, without the Poffeffion of *Felicia*: My Paffion for her increafes more and more,

by

by the many Difficulties I meet with, and tho' I fee the fatal Powers, which oppofe me, yet nothing fhall make me change the Defign I have of purfuing her.

By this time the Weather grew more Calm, and Day being far advanc'd, the Prince was confulting *Mula*, which way he fhou'd fteer his Courfe to find his Miftrefs. He had already pafs'd the Streights of *Gibraltar*, in order to go to *Carthagena*, or *Porto-Real*, not doubting, but the Queen had reach'd one of thofe Harbours, to fhelter herfelf from the Storm; he therefore refolv'd for the Coaft of *Andalufia*, but they who accompany'd him, difapprov'd his Defign. Confider, my Lord, faid they, that this is the only Ship left of feveral, which *Ifmael* lent you, and that your purfuing *Celima*, may prove of a fatal Confequence: Her Sex, her Beauty and Misfortunes will plead for her, and what will the King of *Granada* think, to fee you come into his Dominions in Purfuit of an unhappy Princefs, who has abandon'd her's, and left you Mafter of them. He may detain you as an Hoftage, till he has made advantageous Conditions in her favour, with the King of *Tituan*; and it is not to be expected, that this Monarch will continue your Friend, whilft you act contrary to his Intereft; for fhou'd his generous Difpofition happen to change, he might take Poffeffion himfelf, of what he has juft acquir'd for you. Let us return to *Sallee*, my Lord, continu'd they; if the Kingdom of

*Fez* remains in your Hands, you may soon be in a Condition to ask what you please of the King of *Granada*, who will deliver up *Felicia* to you, rather than have any difference with you about a Christian Slave.

*Abelhamar* was mortally displeas'd to see, that the present Conjuncture oblig'd him to return to *Fez*; and what added to his Affliction in his way thither, was to meet on every side the dismal Fragments of Ship-wracks, which cover'd the Surface of the Sea, and made him but too sensible, that he had lost the greatest part of his Fleet.

The Queen, on her side, had not been expos'd to lesser Dangers, for all her Fleet was dispers'd; and as the Wind drove her into the Port of *Carthagena*, the stern of her Ship struck so fiercely against another, that they both had like to have sunk, which Accident shatter'd what the Storm had spar'd; but several Boats and Barges came immediately to the Queen's Assistance, and landed her safe with her Women and Equipage.

She had hardly step'd out of her Barge, but was inform'd of the great Alterations which had happen'd in the Kingdom of *Granada*, by the Death of *Mahomet*, who (being poison'd by the means of a Gown, which was sent to him as a Present) had left the Crown to his Brother *Joseph*, whom he had detain'd Prisoner many Years in the Castle of *Salobrena*. *Celima* sent an Officer of her Guards to congratulate this Prince, on his happy and unexpected
Accession

Acceffion to the Throne, defiring him at the fame time, to take Compaffion on her: She fent alfo to fome of her near Relations, who held the higheft Rank in that Court.

The Governour of *Carthagena*, hearing that the Queen of *Fez* was landed, went to meet her with all the Marks of Honour and Refpect, that were due to her Quality. She had an Apartment prepar'd for her in the Caftle, where fhe remain'd two Days to repofe her felf, after the Danger and Fatigue, fhe had undergone; and from thence fet out for *Granada*, where they were already inform'd of her Landing, and were prepar'd to receive her, being willing to give a Sanctuary to that unfortunate Queen.

*Jofeph* King of *Granada* immediately order'd his two Sons, *Mahomet* and *Ofmin*, to go and meet *Celima*, with Affurances of his Concern for her Misfortunes, and how defirous he was to ferve her in all that lay in his Power. Thefe Princes were perfectly accomplifh'd; and as the Prince of *Carency* had been confin'd by the late King's Orders, in the Caftle of *Salobrena*, whilft they were Prifoners there, they had conceiv'd fo entire a Friendfhip for him, that they refolv'd to fet him at Liberty, if ever their Condition fhou'd change; but the King their Father, being defirous to make Peace with the *Spaniards*, and knowing that the Infanta, Don *Fernand*, had offer'd *Mahomet* a confiderable Ranfom for the Count of *La Vagne*, (for he continu'd calling himfelf by that Title) thought,

thought, that in detaining him, it might be a more effectual means to obtain what he so earnestly wish'd. Nevertheless, as he had a particular Esteem for the Prince, he ask'd him if he wou'd give him his Honour, not to go away without his Consent; which the other having readily promis'd, the King took him along with him to *Granada*.

The Day he made his Entry, he sent the Prince of *Carency* a magnificent Dress, with a rich Turbant and a Scymiter embellish'd with Jewels, which shew'd it was the King's pleasure he shou'd dress himself after the *Moorish* manner, in order to accompany him to all the Solemnities of his Coronation.

But the King, who had found in the Prince a great Resemblance of the brave *Assimir* (who was a Grandee of the House of *Abanserages*, much consider'd in that Kingdom, and had been lately kill'd) us'd often to give the Prince that Name, out of a Mark of Favour, who equally receiv'd it as such; and as he was unwilling to be known, he chose rather to be called by that Name, than any other.

Tho' time had not been able to diminish the Prince's Passion, or alleviate his Grief, yet in spite of his excessive Melancholy, every Body distinguish'd him, as one of the finest Gentlemen, that was ever known. Amongst all those who shew'd him the greatest marks of Esteem, the Princes *Mahomet* and *Osmin* particularly express'd themselves his Friends. *Mahomet* had eminent Qualities, but was so presumptuous,

sumptuous, that he wou'd have sacrific'd any thing to gratify his Desires. His younger Brother, *Osmin*, was as fine a Prince, and had nobler Inclinations, which made the King have a greater Affection for him, than for the rest of his Children.

As soon as News was brought of *Celima*'s being near *Granada*, these two Princes (by the King their Father's Order, at the Head of the Noblemen of that Court) went out of Town to meet the Queen. The Prince of *Carency* was one of those, who accompany'd them in this Cavalcade, and each Cavalier had a Motto painted on his Shield: The Prince caus'd an *Apollo* pursuing *Daphne*, to be drawn on his, with these Words round it, written in *Spanish*, *Quiero y busco quien me aborece y me fuyo*; that is, I love and pursue one, who hates and flies me. This Thought express'd in a gallant Manner his disappointed Passion. The Princes understood it immediately, for whilst they were in Confinement together, he told 'em part of his Adventures, and made a Secret only of his and his Mistress's true Name, which he conceal'd for several political Reasons, especially on his Brother, and *Don John* of *Velasco*'s Account, who had both fought against the *Moors*, and defeated them in several Engagements.

So many Historians have inform'd the World, how highly the *Moors*, in those Days, distinguish'd themselves above other Nations, by their Gallantry and Magnificence, that I shall decline extending that Subject, and only say, that the unfortunate, but beauteous, Queen of *Fez* elected that Court for her Refuge, where she appear'd with such Attractives, as inspir'd Love in all, who beheld her.

*Mahomet* and his Brother (accompany'd by the Prince of *Carency* in his *Moorish* Dress, which admirably became him) met the Queen at a small distance from *Granada*. She sate alone in a fine open Chariot, and all her Women follow'd her in Chaises. *Felicia* and *Inea* were together in one, and had drawn the Curtains, to have an Opportunity of entertaining each other more conveniently. Ought we to look on our being near *Spain*, said *Felicia* to her Friend, as a favourable Change towards our better Fortune? I think, reply'd *Inea*, that the Circumstances can no ways prove to our Disadvantage. Alas! as for my part, interrupted *Felicia*, I have so little hopes of Happiness in this Life, that I cou'd now leave the World with Pleasure. *Inea* did not omit any thing, which cou'd divert her from these melancholy Reflections, tho' she herself had cause enough to be uneasy, not having heard from her dear *Don Ramire*. Whilst they were talking, the Princes alighted, and saluted the Queen with many Assurances in the Name of the King their Father; then took Horse again, and rode by the side of her Chariot, entertaining her Majesty, with what was most suitable to the Occasion of her Voyage. But *Celima* became of a sudden so pensive, that she cou'd hardly make 'em any Answer; her Eyes were entirely ly fix'd on the Prince of *Carency*, and she had not Power to turn them on any other Object: Her Joy and Surprize were equally extraordinary, and what added to both, was seeing him in a *Moorish* Dress, which gave her a Curiosity to ask his Name of one of the Guards, that was near her, who (not knowing, that the Prince was a Prisoner of War, but had only seen him with the King, in his Journey from *Salobrena* to *Granada*,) told the Queen he was call'd *Assimir*.

She immediately conjectur'd, he had some important Reasons, which oblig'd him to assume that Name, and Disguise, so did not ask any other Questions relating to him; yet what gave her some Uneasiness, was to find that he did not take any particular Notice of her. She was a good while in Expectation he wou'd have spoken to her; at last seeing he continu'd Silent, she address'd her Discourse to him, and for a pretence ask'd him the Signification of the Motto, which she had perceiv'd on his Shield. He told her the Meaning, and added, that he was the unhappiest Man in the World. The Queen imagin'd, that by the *Apollo*, he meant himself; and *Daphne* to be her, which fill'd her Mind with such Ideas, as were too pleasing to be express'd. I have sometimes had a Prophetick Spirit (said she to him smiling) and have foretold things without knowing their true Cause: Methinks I have a great Disposition to do you the same Favour, *Assimir*! Your *Daphne* neither flies, nor hates you, and you shall soon have the Satisfaction of seeing her. Ah, Madam! cry'd the Prince transported, what do you tell me? Is it possible, that the cruel fair One, who is the Object of my Sufferings, will at last vouchsafe to make me happy? Yes, (reply'd *Celima*, with a gracious Air) she is as willing as you, to put a period to your Torments, and I promise you, that as soon as I am a little at Leisure, I will tell you more of the matter. Alas, Madam! reply'd he, I do not deserve, that so great a Queen shou'd be concern'd in my Fortune, which hitherto has prov'd very fatal, and I dare hardly hope a better one for the future. *Celima* said no more to him at that time, fearing the particular Distinction, she had shewn him, might be taken Notice of, which undoubtedly wou'd have disoblig'd *Mahomet*, who had already found so many Charms in the Queen, that he cou'd not sufficiently deplore her Misfortunes; and whilst he was thus offering her his Pity, a more powerful Passion made way to his Heart.

The nearer *Celima* approach'd *Granada*, the more she admired the Beauty of that famous City, which is situated in a Plain, at the Extremity whereof is a snowy Hill, from whence spring two Rivers, the *Daro*, and *Genil*; the one often produces Gold-Dust, mix'd with the Sand, and the other pure Silver. The Air of that Climate is sweet, and refin'd, and there seldom appears any Winter; the Spring and Autumn united, afford Flowers and Fruit,
without

without being at the trouble of cultivating the Earth. There are whole Forests of Orange, Mirtle, and Pomgranate Trees; and as Nature had taken Care to embellish the Country, so no Art had been spar'd to beautify the City, which was incompass'd with a strong Wall, and Twelve Hundred Towers. The Palace of *Alhambro* (which the Kings had chosen for their Court) was so magnificent, that nothing but the Castle of *Abbaycin* cou'd be equal to it, which on every side shin'd with Gold and Azure, supported by Marble and Porphyry; besides, the *Moors* observ'd an admirable Order in Architecture, which highly recommended their Buildings; and as for their Gardens, Walks and Fountains, they were so wonderfully well contriv'd, that nothing cou'd be added to their Beauty and Agreeableness.

The Queen arriv'd at the Gates of the Town, where the People assembled in great Multitudes: But the Prince of *Carency*, to avoid the Crowd, took another way, which insensibly led him to the side of the River *Daro*, whence he continued till he came to a Fountain, whose Water was as clear as Crystal; the deep Silence, which reign'd in that Place, and the Inclination he had to meditate on what the Queen of *Fez* had said to him, invited him to alight; he ty'd his Horse to a Tree, and lay down on the Grass; then calling to mind what *Celima* had told him, by what Chance, thought he, did this Princess (who never saw me before) single me out to acquaint me, that *Leonida* still

still loves me, and that I shall soon see her. Has any one inform'd her of my Sentiments? Methinks it does not well become one of her Rank, to rally an unfortunate Man, who cannot even flatter himself with Hopes, much less with the real Enjoyment of so unexpected a Blessing.

He was drown'd in Reflections of this Nature, when the Voice of a Man, (who spoke the *Arabick* Tongue) interrupted him, asking whether the Queen of *Fez* was yet arriv'd at *Granada*? The Prince knew very well, that the Person who was coming up to him was a Stranger, and that he only spoke *Arabick* to him, because of his Dress, supposing him to be some Grandee in Alliance with the *Moors*. He fix'd his Eyes on this Foreigner, but Heavens! how great was their surprize, when they knew each other. *Benavidez* (for it was he) cou'd not help turning pale at the thoughts of his Perfidiousness, and the Prince, swelling with Anger, said to him, From whence come you, unworthy Wretch that you are? What *Dæmon* has convey'd you here to receive the Punishment of of your Treacheries? Finishing these Words, he drew his Sword, and us'd it with such Fierceness, that the *Spaniard*, notwithstanding his Bravery, was daunted and seiz'd with Terrour; till at last, calling Despair to his Succour, and seeing the inevitable Danger he was in, he fought rather like a desperate Man, than one who had a mind to save his Life. The Prince, resolving not to spare him, reiterated his Blows with such Vigour, that he soon gave *Benavidez* a mortal Wound, which made him fall at his Feet. Ah! my Lord (said he to the Prince, with a feeble and incoherent Accent) it is but just, I shou'd die by your Hand, after all the Injuries I have done you. Did I deserve such Usage, Traitor, reply'd the Prince? Since you can deceive me no longer, where have you left perfidious *Leonida*? Now is the time to convince me, that you are yet capable of repenting a base Action. I am willing to obey you, (answer'd *Benavidez*, stretching out his Hand) upon Condition, that you will forgive me. Speak, and I will even forget all, said the Prince; tell me what is become of my *Leonida*. I declare to you (reply'd *Benavidez*, whose Face shew'd the Symptoms of an approaching Death) that *Leonida* never ceas'd loving you; she no ways consented to her Flight, but almost consum'd with Grief, loaded me with the cruellest Reproaches, and her utmost Aversion was the only return she made my Passion; yet in spite of her Tears and Resistance, I took her with me on Board a Ship, and was promising myself a happy Voyage, when we were met by some of the Enemy's Ships, who engag'd, and took ours: I was so dangerously wounded, that— Farewel, my Lord; I can say no more, I am dying. His Eyes instantly clos'd, and his Soul made its Exit, whilst he was lying in the Prince's Arms.

*Benavidez*'s Death touch'd the Prince of *Carency*'s generous Soul, who forgetting all his Ingratitude,

Ingratitude, began to pity him, saying, that he wou'd never have been guilty of the Crimes he had committed, cou'd he have defended his Heart from *Leonida*'s Charms; and looking on him as an unhappy Rival, and a reconciled Enemy, his Compassion took Place of his Resentment: He reflected on what *Benavidez* had just told him, relating to his dear *Leonida*, but he was perfectly inconsolable, not knowing the Enemies, who had taken her. Fatal Death! cry'd he, thou hast snatch'd away the Life of a Man, who was going to inform me of a Circumstance, which is of the greatest Importance to me. Where must I fly to seek the Object of my Love, and how can I tell into whose Hands she is fallen? Oh Heavens! am I not more unfortunate than ever? The Thoughts of her being inconstant, gave some Intermission to my Passion, for which I was endeavouring to find a Cure; but now the Case is chang'd; I am concern'd for a Mistress, to whom I am contracted; she has ever been true to me, and perhaps, has found a Lover and a Master, in the Man who has her now in his Possession. Oh unparallel'd Fatality! How tormenting will these Apprehensions be to my afflicted Soul? Which way shall I go to find her? The Prince was so deeply involv'd in these anxious Reflections, that he did not immediately perceive a Wound he had receiv'd in his Arm; but finding himself grow weak by the great Loss of Blood, he thought fit to retire.

Just

Juſt as he enter'd the Town, he met *Zulema*, who was a *Moor* of the Family of *Abenſerages*, to whoſe Guard he had been committed by Orders of the late King, whilſt he was Priſoner in the Caſtle of *Salobrena*. The Prince having a Confidence in this *Moor*, thought he cou'd not chuſe any one more capable of ordering *Benavidez*'s Burial; therefore he deſired *Zulema* to oblige him in this Occaſion, who without delay, tho' the Night was far ſpent, took ſome Slaves with him, and went to the Fountain, in order to execute the Prince's Commands.

As he came near the Place, he heard a Perſon lamenting grievouſly, which at firſt ſurpriz'd him, not diſtinguiſhing what he ſaid; but having alighted from his Horſe, he perceiv'd a Man, who was embracing *Benavidez*'s Body, and bemoaning his Misfortune in the *Spaniſh* Tongue. Ah! my dear *Benavidez*, ſaid he, how unlucky it is, that I was not here to defend you againſt the Traitors, who have murder'd you. Alas! my Uneaſineſs and Fears had already foretold your Death. Here *Zulema* interrupted this Stranger, and being compaſſionate, told him, *Benavidez* had not been kill'd by any treacherous means; and that he, who fought him, was ſo generous an Enemy, that he had even deſir'd him to come and ſee the Corps interr'd. The *Spaniard*, who was very young, expreſs'd his Concern by his Tears, and ſaid, Oh Sir! Nothing can alleviate my Affliction, ſince I have loſt all, in loſing my dear Maſter. *Zulema* endeavour'd to comfort him, then order'd his People to take the Corps, and bury it in a little Wood, not far from the Fountain.

This being perform'd, *Zulema* (who was naturally generous, and then mov'd with Pity at the repeated Complaints of this Servant of *Benavidez*) ask'd him, if he wou'd go along with him to *Granada*. You shall be safe in my House, said he, which is a Favour your Countrymen cannot well expect in this Kingdom. Don *Sanche* (for that was the *Spaniard*'s Name,) hesitated some time before he made an Answer, but at last, whether Fear or Prudence prevail'd with him, he told *Zulema*, that since he was pleas'd to offer him his House for a Sanctuary, he was very willing to wait on him. *Zulema*, who was uneasy about the Prince's Wound, went directly to see him, and the mean while sent the *Spaniard* to his House, to wait his return.

The Prince was in Bed, and the Surgeon, who had dress'd his Wound, found it somewhat dangerous, which soon occasion'd a Report in the Town, that he had had a Rencounter, tho' the Particulars were not known; and when *Zulema* enter'd the Prince's Chamber, he found the King's two Sons sitting by him, who were much concern'd at this Accident. *Mahomet* thus continued the Discourse he had already begun; I must tell you, it is unkind, to make a Mystery to us of your Enemy's Name. I owe you, my Lord, reply'd the Prince, too much Gratitude and Affection, ever to do that

which

which might deserve a Reproach from you; I shou'd be very willing to tell you who was my Enemy, if there were Cause to apprehend any farther Consequences, but I am entirely easy on that Score; besides, I am oblig'd to keep a Secret, which I was sworn to, before I thought you wou'd have ask'd me the Detail of this Affair, so beg leave to be silent.

*Osmin* fearing this Conversation might create some Uneasiness in the Prince, obligingly wav'd the Discourse, and said to him; You have lost very much by not attending the Queen of *Fez*, for (laying aside the honourable Reception the King my Father gave her, and the extraordinary Lustre which the Ladies of our Court appear'd in) she commanded all her Slaves to pull off their Veils, and I must confess, we were both astonish'd, and charm'd, to see so many beautiful Creatures. Their Praise was the chief Entertainment of the Court, and I am persuaded, they will cause many a Lover to be guilty of Infidelity. That is already your Case, Brother, reply'd *Mahomet* smiling, and you cannot deny, but the Eyes of that *Felicia* (whose Name you were so desirous to know) have made such an Impression, as may endanger your Liberty. I own to you, said *Osmin*, that I prefer her to all the rest; her Beauty is not to be parallel'd; and I am surpriz'd, Brother, that you escap'd falling her Captive. No, answer'd *Mahomet*, my Heart is not so easily wounded.

ed. Alas, my Lord! interrupted the Prince of *Carency*, perhaps your Time is not come, but you will find your self as sensible as any of us, when you meet with the Object, whom Destiny has decreed to inspire you. As for my part, I dread that fatal Moment, as much as a Pilot does a Rock in a Storm. Why don't you bestow your Inclinations on a Slave like *Felicia*, reply'd *Osmin*? At least, you wou'd be free from any cruel Torments. Who can tell, my Lord, said the Prince, whether that Slave will like the Man, who has a Passion for her? Love is capricious, and ever guided by Fancy, therefore a Slave may look with Indifference on the greatest Monarch in the World. How can you thus oppose my Satisfaction with your Reflections, cry'd *Osmin*? Wou'd you have me cease loving *Felicia* out of groundless Apprehensions? Indeed, Brother, reply'd *Mahomet*, it's strange you shou'd say, you love a Person, whom you hardly know. Nay, you may stile it as you please (said *Osmin*,) but what I can affirm is, that the Perfections of this young Captive have already engag'd me: Nothing in Nature can be more beautiful! no, nor even comparable to this lovely Creature; and I impatiently wish *Assimir*'s Recovery, that he may be able to make his court to the Queen of *Fez*; he will then be judge of what I advance.

It will not be so easy to see her, as you imagine, my Lord, interrupted *Zulema*, (who had been silent all this while) I have been at *Salee*, where

where I stay'd a considerable Time, and the Negotiations I was imploy'd in, by the late King, gave me frequent Opportunities of having both private and publick Audiences with the Queen; yet, whenever I was admitted, I found her surrounded with the oldest, and ugliest Women in the World. She us'd to set a strict Watch on all her pretty Slaves, and keep 'em so conceal'd, that unless her Humour be much alter'd, I am sure you will find some Difficulty in paying your Courtship to *Felicia*. That Sex is very unjust, cry'd *Osmin*; I suppose *Celima* will not let her Slaves be seen, for fear they shou'd eclipse her Charms. 'Tis you that are unjust, reply'd *Mahomet*, why shou'd you attribute to any other Cause, a Custom which has been long establish'd, only for the safety of Slaves? Every one must agree, that *Celima* is endow'd with too many Excellencies, to apprehend any thing from other Beauties. Ha, Brother! said *Osmin*; you were boasting a while ago of your Insensibility, but I find by the passionate Air, with which you express yourself in the Queen's Defence, that you are not so very indifferent, as you wou'd make us believe. *Mahomet*, who had no mind to satisfy his Brother on that Subject, made no Reply, but rising up, addres'd himself to *Afsimir*, (meaning the Prince of *Carency*) whom he embrac'd; and after having desir'd him to take Care of his Health, he and his Brother took their leave of him. *Zulema* retir'd at the same time, without acquainting him, that he had met *Benavidez*'s Servant. The Prince on the other Hand was impatient to entertain him, but there was no poffibility of doing it, till the next Day.

One may imagine, the Prince pafs'd but a very ill Night. What the Queen and *Benavidez* had faid to him, ftrangely perplex'd his Mind, which, being added to the Pain he fuffer'd by his Wound, threw him before Morning into a violent Feaver. *Zulema*, who had a particular Concern for the Prince, rofe early, and went to enquire after his Health; they told him he had not repos'd all Night, and if he pleas'd, might go into his Chamber. As foon as the Prince perceiv'd him; Ah my dear *Zulema*! faid he, I was wifhing to fee you: All that pafs'd Yefterday, has put me into fuch a diforder, as I fhall not be able to overcome, without your Affiftance. The Queen of *Fez* fpoke to me, as if fhe knew me, and I remark'd in her Air and Eyes, fomething more obliging, than is ufually exprefs'd for a Perfon one has never feen; befides, fhe affures me, that my Miftrefs neither flies, nor hates me, and that I fhall have the pleafure of feeing her foon. Who cou'd have inform'd her of a thing fo pofitive? I fhou'd be inclin'd to think, that Chance was the only Caufe why fhe entertain'd me fo agreeably, were it not for the Rencounter I had Yefterday near the Fountain. He whom I fought was my Rival, the fame *Benavidez*, who carry'd off my *Felicia*: He told me with his laft Breath, fhe had ever lov'd me,
and

and that her Sentiments for me were still the same; it is not probable, he wou'd have utter'd an untruth, in so dismal a Condition. But just as he was going to tell me where he had left her, he was depriv'd both of his Speech and Life. You cannot imagine, how this grieves my Soul; *Felicia* loves me, can any Happiness be greater? Yet Alas! I have lost her, and know not where to enquire after her: What Misfortune can be equal to mine? Here he was some time silent.

*Zulema* told him, that a more favourable Fortune wou'd certainly disclose a Secret, on which depended his Felicity; and that he did not doubt, but he might receive some Information from a young Man, he found weeping near *Benavidez*'s Body, whom he had detain'd at his House for that purpose. Oh! I conjure you, send for him immediately, cry'd the Prince; I remember, his Master in approaching me, ask'd whether the Queen of *Fez* was yet arriv'd at *Granada*; perhaps she knew him, and that in relating his Adventures to her, he mention'd something concerning mine. I ought not to neglect any means in my present Circumstances; for if that young Man was with *Benavidez*, when he ran away with my Mistress, and can tell me what is become of her, I shall be bless'd above Mankind.

I perceive so great an Emotion in you, my Lord, reply'd *Zulema*, that I am sorry for having acquainted you with a Particular, which may be prejudicial to your Health. No, said the Prince, do not fear any thing; but if you have either Love, or Pity, relieve me in this urgent Occasion. Shall I tell you then what I was thinking, answer'd *Zulema*? *Osmin* spoke to you Yesterday very much in Praise of one *Felicia*, who is a Slave of *Celima*'s; it is probable she may be the Person you love. I began to suspect the same, interrupted the Prince, but was not willing to harbour such a Thought; for there are many *Felicias* in *Spain*, and after the Adventure I had at *Jaen* with Don *Alonso* by a Mistake, which that Name occasion'd, I have room to fear the like Disappointment; I only beg you will send for the young Man, you spoke of.

*Zulema* commanded one of his Slaves, in whom he confided, to give a *Moorish* Dress to the *Spaniard*, and bring him immediately along with him: This was the Precaution he us'd to prevent his being taken at *Granada* for a Sranger. Don *Sanche* was a little unwilling at first, to go out of *Zulema*'s House, not knowing where they intended to carry him; but the Slave having told him, they were going to an intimate Friend of his Master's, whose Name was *Assimir*, he readily follow'd him, believing *Assimir* was a *Moor*; and he continued in the same Opinion, even when he enter'd the Prince of *Carency*'s Chamber, who was in Bed, and the Windows clos'd. Come nearer Don *Sanche*, said *Zulema* to him, and tell us sincerely, what you know concerning *Felicia* of *Leon*.

This unexpected Question surpriz'd the *Spaniard*, who was some time without making any Answer. What! said the Prince, do you hesitate? Tell me immediately what is become of her. Were you not with your Master, when he carry'd her away? Heavens! What new Astonishment did this Voice create! Don *Sanche*, or (to explain myself in a clearer manner) *Casilda*, Sister to *Benavidez*, (for it was she, who was thus disguis'd) was suddenly struck with such a violent Trembling, that had not the Chamber been very dark, it wou'd have been impossible to conceal her Disorder: Her Eyes were endeavouring to see the Person whom her Heart already knew, whilst the Prince on his side, was in the utmost Impatience to be inform'd of his Mistress's Fate. What (said she to her self) shall my Rival for ever be ador'd, and cou'd her Absence no ways extinguish the Prince's Passion? Was ever Misfortune equal to mine? Then resolving at once, not to mention any thing, which might discover *Leonida's* being with the Queen of *Fez* ; 'tis true, my Lord, said she, I was with Don *Fernand Benavidez*, when he ran away with the fair Lady you nam'd, and we shou'd have had a prosperous Voyage, were it not for the fatal Rencounter of two *Turkish* Ships, who engag'd ours, and took it, my Master being the only Man, that resisted with undaunted Courage. The Captains of these Ships were so charm'd with *Felicia's* Beauty, which had receiv'd no Injury from her Affliction, that they resolv'd to carry

Y 3          her

her to *Constantinople*, in order to present her to the Grand Seignior; therefore having given her a very Rich Dress, they brought her to that Emperour, who was so mightily taken with her, that he immediately plac'd her in his *Seraglio*. As for my Master and I, good Fortune wou'd have it that we were sold to the *Bashaw* of *Morea*, who knew Don *Fernand Benavidez*, to whom he was indebted for some considerable Service, he had render'd him in *Spain*. This *Bashaw* was a famous Renegado, which was his only Crime; for he was very generous, and so grateful, that he restor'd us to our Liberty without requiring any Ransom. Thus we return'd to *Andalusia*, where we were just landed, when my Master heard that the Queen of *Fez* was coming to *Granada*, which determin'd him to come hither, in order to pay his Court to her.

The Prince, during *Casilda*'s Relation, was seiz'd with an unspeakable Affliction, when he heard, that *Felicia* was among the Grand Seignior's Women: The Anxiety of such a cruel Thought over-power'd his Senses, and his Wound opening, so great a quantity of Blood gush'd out, that it flung him into a Swoon.

*Zulema*, surpriz'd at the Prince's Silence, spoke to him, but as he made no Reply, he took his Hand, which was in a cold Sweat; this startled him, and calling for a Light, he saw the Picture of Despair painted on the Face of this unfortunate Prince, who was without Motion, and his Paleness wou'd have persuaded ed one, that his Soul had already left his Body. But how shall I represent here the deplorable Condition of *Casilda*, whose Passion was rais'd to such a Transcendency, that having no Regard to her Honour, she fram'd a false Story, to destroy the Prince's Hopes of ever seeing his divine Mistress; at another time she wou'd have sacrific'd a Thousand Lives to have sav'd his, but at this Juncture had he died, one might have accus'd her with being the Cause of his Death.

Had not *Zulema*'s Concern been so great, he wou'd have easily discover'd that of the Counterfeit Don *Sanche*, who without Restraint, shed a Deluge of Tears, and express'd a more than ordinary Care in assisting the Prince, who at last receiving a little Strength from the Cordials they gave him, open'd his weak Eyes, which he fix'd languishingly on his Friend and Don *Sanche*, whose Face he thought he knew, yet did not take much Notice of him; then turning to *Zulema*, Ah, pity me! cry'd he, since my Misfortunes can never be greater; they are come to their last period. I had lost my *Felicia*, and thought her false, which in some Measure suppress'd my tormenting Passion; but now I am informed, she is Living, and that her Affection for me is still the same. Had that Tyrant, Death, snatch'd her from me, I shou'd doubtless have been inconsolable for her Loss, yet methinks I shou'd be free from those tumultuous Fears, which now rack my Mind. Oh! What dismal

mal Objects appear to my distracted Imagination! *Felicia* in the *Seraglio*, and belov'd by the Grand Seignior! Heavens! What greater Cruelty can ever be inflicted on a Man, so passionately in Love? I have lost her, and shall never see her more; I am even jealous, and I fear her Heart will at last yield to the barbarous Laws, which ill Fortune has impos'd on her. Here his disturb'd Thoughts interrupted his Discourse, whilst *Zulema* was using all his Endeavours to mitigate so violent a Grief. *Felicia* had too sincere a Passion for you, said he, ever to change in favour of a Prince, who is no ways agreeable, and is too proud, to give himself the least Trouble towards obtaining the Favours of a Lady; he thinks all must submit to his Authority, and I am persuaded, that as she will neither relish his Addresses, nor make any Return, her Resistance and Coldness will soon render her indifferent to the Emperour. Suppose I were free from these Apprehensions, interrupted the Prince, by what means shall I hear from her? Is she not in the Grand Seignior's *Seraglio*, and absolutely lost for me? Oh, 'tis too true! I cannot flatter myself, no, not even wish to see her more, which Misfortune compleats my Despair.

*Casilda* was in no small Confusion, when she heard him speak in such passionate Terms. She was several times tempted to make herself known, that she might address herself to him, in the tenderest Expressions, Love cou'd inspire; but calling to mind what pass'd between 'em, when

when she acquainted him with *Leonida*'s Flight, it made her apprehend, that if she spoke to him at this Juncture, it wou'd be as ill timed, therefore thought proper to wait another Opportunity; in the mean time, she affected an extraordinary Concern for the Prince, who remark'd it, and was not slow in shewing his Acknowledgments; for he told her (thinking he was speaking to a Man) that altho' his present Fortune (being then a Prisoner) did not permit him to bestow great Favours on those who were in his Service, yet if he was willing to stay with him till he cou'd be better provided for, he wou'd take Care of him. *Assimir* little knew the Effect this Proposal created in our disguis'd Lady, who immediately accepted it, with all imaginable Marks of Joy and Respect, assuring him, that no Body wou'd serve him with more Zeal and Fidelity; but before we see how strict she was to her Promise, let us be inform'd by what Chance she came to *Granada*.

*Abelhamar* and the Admiral of *Fez* having taken the Ship *Leonida* was in, it was thought *Benavidez* cou'd not recover of the Wounds, he had receiv'd in his vigorous Resistance, so was left for Dead; but after *Leonida* had been conducted on Board the Admiral, they found in *Benavidez* some Symptoms of Life, which made 'em take care of him, till they were landed at *Sallee*, where he continued a long time extremely ill. *Leonida* knew nothing of it, being strictly guarded in the Palace; but as soon as he was recover'd, he resolv'd either pay her Ranſom, or carry her off by Stratagem. With this Deſign he wrote to *Caſilda*, who having receiv'd his Letter, loſt no time in preparing for that Voyage; and as her Paſſion for the Prince of *Carency* had met with no Return but Diſdain, ſhe was meditating on ſome deſperate Enterprize, in order to act a Vengeance proportionable to the Injury; ſhe thought this might be a favourable Opportunity, therefore taking her Jewels, with a conſiderable Sum of Money, ſhe diſguis'd herſelf in Man's Apparel to prevent her being known, and embark'd for *Sallee*, where ſhe arriv'd ſoon after, with the Reſolution of taking away *Leonida*'s Life; and to ſucceed in her wicked Deſign, ſhe had brought with her a Box of the ſubtileſt Poiſon.

*Benavidez* was not a little overjoy'd at *Caſilda*'s Arrival, and after he had paid his Ranſom to the Admiral, he only thought of recovering *Leonida*: But the Queen, having an extraordinary Friendſhip for her, hardly ſuffer'd her to be out of her Sight, which made him fear his attempt wou'd be in vain. This was the State of his Affairs, when the King of *Tunis* invaded the Kingdom of *Fez*, which oblig'd *Celima* to abandon *Sallee*; and at the ſame time that ſhe embark'd, *Benavidez* and his Siſter in diſguiſe took their paſſage in one of the Ships, which were bound for *Granada*: During their Voyage, they often ſaw *Leonida* aboard the Queen's Ship, whoſe Sight only inflam'd *Benavidez*'s Heart with Love, and *Caſilda*'s *filda*'s with Rage; but the dreadful Storm which arofe, difperfing the Fleet, their Ship was driven fome Leagues beyond *Carthagena*, where they landed, and fet out immediately on Horfeback for *Granada*. *Cafilda*, who was of a weak Conftitution, and already very much fatigu'd with her Voyage, was left a great way behind, which was the Occafion of her not arriving, till after her Brother's Rencounter with the Prince of *Carency*, which was then too late.

I have already told you with what Marks of Honour and Diftinction the Queen of *Fez* was receiv'd at her Arrival at the Court of *Granada*; but I did not mention the magnificent Entertainment the King gave her at the Palace of *Alhambro*; after which, the Princes and moft part of the Noblemen conducted her to the Caftle of the *Abbaicyn*, which was prepar'd for her, and there took leave of her Majefty.

As foon as fhe was at Liberty to give fome time to Reflection, fhe went to take the Air on a Terrace Walk, adjoyning her Apartment, which had a Profpect over the River *Daro*; there a thoufand hurrying Thoughts ftarted from her Mind: What Courfe fhall I take, faid fhe to herfelf, and whom fhall I truft with my Secret? Muft I once more (to the Shame of my Sex and Glory) make my Weaknefs known to this lovely Stranger? Heaven has fent him to me again, and I am inclin'd to believe he is thinking on me. Yes certainly!

certainly! The *Apollo* pursuing *Daphne*, which was painted on his Shield, with his Motto; nay more than that, his languishing Looks and Distractions; in short, every thing persuades me, he is in Love; yet if it were with me, ought not he to be inspir'd with some Motions of Sympathy, which wou'd have told him that his Unknown of *Nicopolis* and the Queen of *Fez* were the same? Why does he not discover as many Charms in my Person, as he did in my Wit and Generosity? Alas, he was then too young to feel the Effects of Love; Gratitude was the only thing that mov'd him to make a Return, and I now fear, some softer Care imploys his Thoughts: But, continu'd she, I cannot perfuade myself that Fortune has brought him once more in my way, only to add fresh Afflictions to those I have already undergone: I am rather dispos'd to look on this, as the beginning of a Happiness, which will end by the Destruction of my Enemies. This Prince is nearly related to the King of *France*; I will make myself a Christian, and in giving him my Hand, present him with my Crown: He may head an Army and invade the Kingdom of *Fez*, which he soon will be Master of. The People, by my Example, will submit to his Laws; and after being an unhappy Fugitive, destitute of all Hopes, I shall see myself Crown'd with unspeakable Felicity. *Celima* thus indulg'd her Imagination, till it grew so late, that she thought fit to retire to her Apartment, where she

she pass'd the Night betwixt soft Repose, and a Thousand agreeable Ideas, which made her appear the next Day in all her Charms.

But before the Queen wou'd admit of any Visit, she sent for *Felicia*, to whom she spoke in these Terms; I am desirous to know, whether your Sentiments for the Count of *La Vagne* are still the same; therefore, *Felicia*, confess ingenuously the Truth. Has not his Perfidiousness been capable to extinguish the Affection you had for him, when you were persuaded of his Constancy? Search well into your Heart, for I have some Reason to enquire about it; and whatever Answer you make me, I shall not love you the less. These Questions caus'd some Surprize in *Felicia*, who at first, had a mind to disguise her Sentiments; but having consider'd, that she had not long before confess'd her Weakness to the Queen, she was of Opinion, it was better to speak her Thoughts without any Dissimulation. Madam, reply'd she, since they are your Majesty's Commands, I cannot refuse obeying; I own with the utmost Confusion, that till now, it has not been in my Power to banish from my Heart the fatal Idea of the Count of *La Vagne*. I daily entertain myself with the Cause I have to hate him as the cruellest of my Enemies: Yet alas! it is past my Skill, and I dare not even hope, that time it self will ever be able to effect my Cure. You do love him then, interrupted the Queen? If Love consists in often thinking of a Person, reply'd *Felicia*, I

am

am convinc'd I still have an Affection for him. I may now confide in you, reply'd the Queen, therefore hear me, and be secret.

I was hardly out of my Infancy, when my unlucky Stars decreed I shou'd fall into the Hands *Bajazet*, whose Passion for me only increas'd my Aversion to him, and I thought nothing cou'd be more deplorable than my Destiny.

These were my Sentiments when he went into *Missia*, and compell'd me to go along with him, where after a Victory over the Christians, he was desirous to see the Prisoners of Distinction, who had been taken; and as out of a politick Motive he endeavour'd to inspire me with Cruelty, and inure me to Tragick Scenes, he order'd, I shou'd be placed at a Window which was grated, and look'd over the Court, where the Christians were to suffer Death, and several Noblemen of *France* had already been executed, when I saw a young Prince appear, whose Beauty surpass'd that which we attribute to the God of Love: He seem'd to be about Fifteen or Sixteen Years of Age; he was tall, well-shap'd, and had fair Hair, which hung in fine Curls on his Shoulders, and in spite of his careless Air, he had something so great and noble in his Mien, that the other Princes were not to be compar'd to him. Oh, *Felicia*! cou'd you but imagine what I felt in that Moment; a quick Emotion seiz'd all my Soul, I was troubled without knowing the Cause, and in a Word, had
like

*of* CARENCY.

like to have died, for fear *Bajazet* fhou'd have taken away a Life, which was already dearer to me than my own. I began to think what I cou'd do, to deliver this lovely Prince from the immediate Danger which threaten'd him; whether to fling myfelf at *Bajazet's* Feet, and beg his Life, or to offer myfelf a Victim in his Room, for I cou'd have done any thing to fave him; but whilft a Thoufand fuch Thoughts were torturing my Mind, the Emperor refolv'd on accepting his Ranfom, which News fo tranfported me, that my Joy was inexpreffible.

This young Prince was Prifoner in the Tower of *Nicopolis*, and as my Apartment had a Profpect of it, I us'd to pafs whole Days at my Clofet Window in fruitlefs Sighs and Wifhes; but one Evening, as I was endeavouring, with the help of a Telefcope, to difcover the Object I fo dearly lov'd, I perceiv'd him walking on the Leads of the Tower, and he appear'd to me fo melancholy, that it threw me into the deepeft Concern. I immediately refolv'd on writing to him, notwithftanding the Danger to which I expos'd myfelf, if *Bajazet* had known it: But Love is often more lucky than wife, and Chance on that Occafion is a much better Servant than Reafon. When I had ended my Letter, I confided it to an Eunuch, who had attended me a long time, and fhew'd a particular Affection for my Service. What did I not fay to perfuade him to be faithful? which having promis'd me,

even

even at the hazard of his Life, he convey'd my Letter to the Top of the Tower by means of an Arrow; and the Prince having receiv'd it, sent me an Answer, which entirely vanquish'd me. I was inform'd that his Ransom was not come, and the more I consider'd how dear he daily grew to me, the greater Cause I had to fear equally for him and myself. I was perfectly acquainted with *Bajazet*'s inhuman Temper, and too sensible of my own Weakness, to believe that it wou'd be in my Power to fly a Prince, who so entirely possess'd my Thoughts. These Considerations oblig'd me to take Measures for his immediate Departure; but alas! What Torments did not I endure, thro' the Necessity of so cruel a Resolution?

To this Effect, I was forc'd once more to confide in my Eunuch, who brib'd one of the Prince's Guards, by whose means a strong Box was convey'd into his Chamber, wherein I sent him a considerable Sum to pay his Ransom, and a Letter, which was the last I wrote to him, being bereft of the hopes of ever seeing him more. Imagine, *Felicia*, how many anxious Hours I have pass'd, since that unlucky Day!

Soon after, *Bajazet*'s Fortune met with an unhappy Change; for *Tamerlane* having engag'd him, gain'd a compleat Victory, and took him Prisoner. It was with no small difficulty I made my Escape, and return'd to my Father's Dominions; where I was no sooner arriv'd, but several Kings and Princes made their Addresses

dreſſes to me, ſome out of Ambition, and others out of a ſincere Love for my Perſon; but I was ſo entirely prepoſſeſs'd with the Idea of him, who had charm'd me at *Nicopolis*, that nothing at *Sallee* was capable of making an Impreſſion on me; ſo in ſpight of myſelf I was in Love, without Hopes of a return. This was the State of my Mind at my Arrival here; but how can I expreſs the Surprize and Agitation I was in, when amongſt the Noblemen, who came to receive me out of the Gates of the Town, I perceiv'd the Man I love. This Chriſtian Prince (under the Name, and Dreſs of a *Moor*) appear'd to me as charming as ever; no, it's impoſſible for you to comprehend what I felt at ſo unexpected a Rencounter. My Heart was ſeiz'd with ſo many different Motions, that I was not able to ſpeak; and whilſt I was endeavouring to recover myſelf, *Aſſimir* (for that is the Name he goes by at this Court) approach'd, and gave me an Occaſion to ſee the Motto that was painted on his Shield, which perſuaded me, the Memory of his Unknown of *Nicopolis* was dear to him. I muſt confeſs, I was equally ſurpriz'd and overjoy'd, for I cou'd not flatter myſelf, with being ſtill in the Thoughts of that young Prince, who had not the ſame Motives to inſpire him. I had ſeen him, and was inform'd of his Name and Birth, but he had neither ſeen me, nor knew who I was; therefore what had touch'd him, was either Gratitude, or the obliging Expreſſions of my

Letters,

Letters, which I muft fay are no fmall Attractives to a generous Soul.

In fhort, *Felicia*, I have a mind that you fhou'd talk with him, and endeavour to difcover his Sentiments. The Management of this Affair, which I intruft you with, is of a nice quality; but as you are very difcreet, I cannot imploy any one, who will give me lefs Sufpicion; tho' I muft own my Weaknefs to you, I am naturally of a jealous Temper, and a Confidant fo beautiful as you, with *Affimir*'s Merit, might give me fome Apprehenfion, were it not that you are entirely prepoffefs'd in favour of the Count of *La Vagne*. *Felicia* threw her felf at the Queen's Feet, and kiffing her Hand with great Refpect, faid to her; I have fo true a Senfe, Madam, of the Honour you do me, when you are pleas'd to confide in me, that I cannot eafily exprefs my Acknowledgments for fo high a Favour; but whatever Ambition I have to ferve your Majefty, I am ftrangely diffident of my Capacity, for I know that in fo important an Affair, one cannot act too prudently, which makes me fear I fhall not anfwer the good Opinion you have conceiv'd of me. What, reply'd the Queen, wou'd you yield to another, the advantage of doing me a piece of Service? Is not your Affection for me great enough to prevent you from acting thofe Faults, you forefee? *Felicia* underftood by what the Queen faid to her, that her Majefty wou'd be highly difoblig'd, fhou'd fhe neglect fo fair an Opportunity

portunity of ſerving her, therefore conſidering the unhappy State of her Captivity, ſhe made no other Reply, but that ſhe was ready to obey her Commands. You muſt then write to *Aſſimir,* ſaid the Queen, and deſire him to meet you on the Terrace adjoyning my Apartment, where you ſhall entertain him with ſome Particulars relating to me.

*Felicia* immediately retir'd, in order to write to *Aſſimir,* and finding *Inea* in her Chamber, ſhe gave her an Account what had paſs'd between the Queen and her; then wrote her Letter in theſe Terms.

*THO' I am unknown to you, my Lord, and you alſo a Stranger to me, I have a mighty deſire to entertain you, which perhaps you may think very extraordinary. If you will be pleas'd to meet me this Evening on the Terrace Walk, next to the Queen of* Fez's *Apartment, I ſhall there explain my ſelf more at large.*

Felicia.

This Letter *Felicia* ſhew'd to the Queen, who call'd for one of her Pages, and charg'd him to go and deliver it to *Aſſimir,* who (as I told you before) was extremely afflicted at what *Caſilda* (under the Diſguiſe of Don *Sanche*) had ſpitefully intimated concerning *Felicia.* The mean while *Zulema* (who had ſtay'd by the Prince) was ſaying all he cou'd to ſoften his Diſtreſs; and as he was talking to him, they came to tell *Aſſimir,* that one of the Queen

Queen of *Fez*'s Pages had a Letter to deliver to him. This caus'd some Emotion in the Prince, who looking at his Friend; Can you conceive, said he, what may be the meaning of this Letter? If I may believe my Thoughts, reply'd *Zulema*, they persuade me, some agreeable News is coming to you, my Lord. Whatever it be, said the Prince, I desire you will speak to the Page; I am unwilling to see him for fear he shou'd discover the Disorder I am in.

*Zulema* readily satisfy'd the Prince's Impatience; he took the Letter, and brought it to him, which he no sooner open'd, but knew the Name and Writing. Heavens! How great was his Surprize! He cou'd not conceal his Transports, but giving the Letter back to *Zulema*, said, am I in a Dream, or must I believe what I see? Is my *Felicia* in *Granada*, whilst I am bemoaning her Absence, and bereft of all Hopes of ever seeing her more? *Zulema*, my dear *Zulema*! how can I outlive so unexpected a Felicity? Indeed, my Lord, reply'd his Friend, I am sensibly touch'd at your good Fortune, and heartily congratulate you; but am afraid, you will go to the Palace of *Abbaicyn*, before your Wound is heal'd, which may prove very dangerous to you. Were I to hazard my Life, answer'd the Prince, I wou'd not defer the Pleasure of seeing her, and as I am not able to write, I desire you wou'd do it for me. I am assur'd, said *Zulema*, that she does not know the Condition you are in,

other-

otherwife fhe wou'd be very much concern'd at the little Care you take of a Life, which ought to be dear to her; but I am ready to do any thing, my Lord, to oblige you; fo the Prince dictated thefe Lines.

*YOU are not fo great a Stranger to me, as you imagine, adorable* Felicia. *I do not doubt, but you will be convinc'd of it, affoon as I have the Pleafure of Saluting you. I have had the Misfortune of receiving a Wound, which very much difcompofes me, yet nothing fhall prevent me attending your Commands.*

Whilft the paffionate Prince was abandoning himfelf to a Thoufand Tranfports of Joy and Impatience, the Page deliver'd his Letter to the Queen, who having read it, was feiz'd with the deepeft Chagrin. Was any Fatality like this, cry'd fhe? *Affimir* is acquainted with *Felicia*, and fays, he will attend her, tho' he is wounded. What Accident cou'd have happen'd to him, fince Yefterday? Sure there muft needs be an intimate Underftanding between *Felicia*, and him, tho' fhe has conceal'd it from me. I thought her Sentiments for the Count of *La Vagne*, wou'd have left me no room to apprehend any thing from her: But alas! How deceiv'd have I been? Well, I am refolv'd, fhe fhall neither fee him, nor fpeak to him. As *Celima* was thus reafoning with herfelf, *Felicia* enter'd her Chamber. *Affimir*, faid the Queen to her, has receiv'd your Letter, and is very much indispos'd, therefore cou'd not write to you. *Felicia* seem'd concern'd at his Illness, thinking by that means to pay her Court to the Queen; but she cou'd not have taken a more indirect Step towards it, for *Celima* was so prepossess'd with the Opinion of *Felicia*'s having a Correspondence with the Prince, that the most innocent Actions of this young Slave, in her Eyes appear'd Criminal.

The King of *Granada* (being now indispos'd,) sent his two Sons to visit *Celima*, whom they invited to take the Air in the Forest; this Queen accepted the Invitation, and as *Assimir* Illness had been confirm'd to her by the Princes, *Mahomet* and *Osmin*, she did not in the least imagine, that he wou'd venture to go abroad; besides, *Celima* had observ'd, that *Osmin* was mightily taken with *Felicia*, which extremely pleas'd her; for she wou'd not have cared, had all the Monarchs of the Universe ador'd that lovely Captive, so the Prince of *Carency* had but look'd on her Indifference.

Thus the Court set out from the Palace of *Abbaicyn*, follow'd by a great Number of musical Instruments. All the Ladies were seated in little open Chariots, each of them having a Cavalier to drive them; *Mahomet* drove the Queen of *Fez*'s Chariot, and *Osmin Felicia*'s. As they were going by the Palace of *Alhambro*, the Queen desired she might stop a little to enquire after the King's Health.

*Zulema*

*Zulema* hearing that *Celima* was coming to the Palace, told the Prince she shou'd pass under his Windows, and that if he was able to rise, perhaps he might see *Felicia*. Heavens! cry'd the Prince, what wou'd not I do for so dear a Satisfaction? With that, he leap'd out of Bed, and having put on some Clothes, went and sat in one of the Balconies of his Apartment, where soon after he saw *Celima*, and *Felicia* attending her. *Osmin* perceiving the Prince, desired this beauteous Lady to take Notice of him; but how shall I express the Motions which seiz'd her Soul, when she knew him to be her Lover? The Prince of *Carency* on the other side, was so transported, that he was just going to speak to her, had not *Zulema* persuaded him to the contrary.

*Felicia* was in such a disorder, that at first she knew not what to say; but being extremely desirous to be inform'd by what Chance her false Lover happen'd to be in *Granada*, for she took him for the Count of *La Vagne*, she recover'd herself a little, and told *Osmin*, that the Person he had shewn her appear'd to be a Stranger. You judge right, Madam, reply'd he, for he is a *Genouese*, of the noble House of *Fiesques*: The late King having besieg'd *Jaen*, took him Prisoner, and sent him to the Castle of *Salobrena*, where my Father, my Bother, and I were confin'd. There I contracted an intimate Friendship with the Count of *La Vagne*, (that's his Title) and after *Mahomet's* Death, my Father coming to the Throne, conceiv'd so particular an Esteem for this illustrious Count, that he gave him his Liberty, upon Condition, that he wou'd not part from *Granada* without his Consent; therefore he still remains with us, and we are daily charm'd with his noble and polite Behaviour.

These Encomiums, which *Osmin* gave to the Count, were very acceptable to *Felicia*, notwithstanding the Reasons she had to be dissatisfy'd with his Conduct. She then ask'd him, when the Count had been taken Prisoner; but nothing cou'd astonish her more, than what *Osmin* told her on that Subject; for either the Scene, which pass'd at *Sallee* between *Olympia*, the Count, and her, was a Vision, (which she had no room to believe) or what *Osmin* was saying to her, cou'd not be sincere. This made her impatient to be with *Inea*, to entertain her with this surprizing Adventure; and she grew of a sudden so pensive, that she cou'd not make any Reply to the obliging Terms, in which *Osmin* address'd her. What is it that troubles you, divine *Felicia*, said he to her? You seem very melancholy; do but confide in me, and I will use my best Endeavours to deserve so great a Favour. Alas, my Lord! (reply'd *Felicia*, with a dejected Air) what Secret cou'd I impart to you? I am an unfortunate Captive, and perhaps I repine at the Cruelty of that Destiny, from whence flows the Sorrow, which you perceive. Vouchsafe, Madam, said *Osmin*, to accept of my Service; I may procure you your Liberty, and soon remove the Cause of your Uneasiness; but you must at least give me leave to pay Homage to your transcendent Charms, since they have inspir'd me with such Sentiments, as do not merit a disobliging Return. I conjure you, amiable *Felicia*, to be favourable to me, and let me feed my Passion with the Hopes of your Affection. I cannot answer your Request, my Lord, interrupted *Felicia*; I have too great a Regard for you, and as an Evincement of it, I declare, that I am neither desirous to be belov'd, nor dispos'd to receive an Impression: It is a Resolution I have made, which nothing shall induce me to change, therefore I intreat you, my Lord, never to think on me more. This Confession extremely surpriz'd *Osmin*, who wou'd rather have met with more Dissimulation, and less Cruelty: But as Love is always deluding, he did not doubt, but in time he shou'd conquer an Indifference, which he thought unreasonable.

The Court being return'd from the Forest, *Celima*, (whose Thoughts were entirely imploy'd on her Rendezvous with the Prince of *Carency*) retir'd to her Palace, and *Felicia* went to her Chamber, where she found *Inea*, whom she embrac'd tenderly, and said, How shall I express to you, my Dear, the Agitation of my Mind? The Count of *La Vagne* is here; I have just seen him in the Palace of *Alhambro*; it is no Imagination; for he saluted me so respectfully, that I cou'd not help returning the Civility, and I am even asham'd of having discover'd cover'd my Weakness to a Man, who has deserv'd my Aversion: But alas! when Love commands, Reason must obey. I have something yet more surprizing to tell you, continu'd she; I am inform'd, he has been some Months in *Andalusia*, and by the Relation I have heard, I find he was taken Prisoner, about the time that I had a Dream at *Sallee*, which represented him to me engag'd with the *Moors*, and vanquish'd. *Osmin* told me, the Count had been ever since in the Castle of *Salobrena*, or at *Granada*; but I fancy he desired him to speak to me in that manner, with a Design to screen his Offence; for who knows whether he does not repent his unworthy Behaviour towards me; moreover, I am surpriz'd not to see *Olympia* here, which makes me believe, the *Moors* took the Count at Sea, and that he has not been long in these Dominions. It is very probable, interrupted *Inea*; for what pass'd at *Sallee*, is not to be contradicted, and perhaps he is now sorry for having disobliged you; therefore you must resolve to pardon him. No, my dear *Inea*, reply'd *Felicia*; I shall never forget his Ingratitude; he is still dear to me, I confess; yet I hope in time to banish him from my Heart. Oh Heavens! added she, weeping, what a Series of Misfortunes attend me? I must tell you something more; young *Osmin* has declar'd himself my Votary, and you may judge how favourably I receiv'd his Addresses.

Whilst

Whilst *Felicia* and *Inea* were discoursing together, the Queen of *Fez* sent for the Governess of the Slaves, who (as I told you before) was an ugly old Woman, and commanded her to wrap herself in her Veil, and wait on the Terrace for the Prince of *Carency*'s Arrival; she charg'd her at the same time, not to discover herself, but to appear overjoy'd at seeing him, in case he took her for *Felicia*. It was a Moon-Light Night, and the amorous Prince, leaning on *Cafilda* (whom he took for a young Man) was making as much haste towards the Place appointed, as his Strength wou'd permit him; and perceiving at a distance a tall Person walking on the Terrace, he did not doubt, but it was his charming *Felicia*; therefore approaching her, he said: Ah, Madam! has Fortune brought you to me again, after having so long bemoan'd your Absence, and spent Days and Nights endeavouring to find you? I can hardly believe my Eyes: Is it you yourself, my divine Mistress? Here transported with Love and Joy, he went to throw off this Woman's Veil, who not being quick enough to take hold of it, let it fall on the Ground, and discover'd a Face, which was as Ugly, as *Felicia*'s was Beautiful.

His Astonishment was so great, that he cou'd not help crying out aloud, and any one might have perceiv'd, by his Emotion, the strange Disorder he was in. The Queen being in a Closet, that look'd on the Terrace Walk, easily saw the Prince's Action, and knew his Voice, which made her guefs what had pafs'd; therefore approaching him with a Majeftick Air; I am come to your Affiftance, Prince, faid fhe, (taking his Hand and fmiling,) follow me, I have fomething to tell you, which is of too great a Confequence to be conceal'd from you any longer.

The Queen went in firft, but *Cafilda* being oblig'd to wait without, was mighty uneafy concerning what might pafs between *Celima* and the Prince. This inquifitive Creature ftay'd till the Governefs of the Slaves was retired, then plac'd herfelf near the Clofet, where fhe cou'd eafily hear their Converfation. The Queen looking at the Prince, who was not well recover'd from his Surprize; I have been imploying my Skill for you, my Lord, faid fhe, and by the help of my Books, and the Figures I have caft, am already acquainted with fome of your Adventures; moreover, I can affure you, that I intereft myfelf very much in what concerns you, and if you will be fincere with me, I do not in the leaft doubt but I fhall be able, by the Affiftance of my powerful Art, to put you in a way of overcoming your ill Fortune. I am perfuaded, Madam, reply'd the Prince, that a Sovereign, who has fo great an Influence as your Majefty, may eafily change my Deftiny, without confulting the Stars; yet I cannot flatter myfelf with deferving fo extraordinary a Favour. As an Evincement of the Progrefs I have already made, faid *Celima*, I know, *Affimir* is not your Name,
and

and that by your Birth, you are nearly related to a great King.

The Prince of *Carency* was amaz'd to hear the Queen expreſs herſelf in theſe Terms, and before he cou'd make her any Anſwer: Nay, continu'd ſhe, you will own my Knowledge is no Fiction, when I tell you, that you was in *Miſia*, and taken Priſoner by *Bajazet*; beſides, whilſt you were in the Tower of *Nicopolis*, did not you receive very paſſionate Letters, and a conſiderable Supply from a Lady, who, to this Hour, is unknown to you? The Prince ſigh'd, and ſeeing *Celima* waited an Anſwer; It is, as your Majeſty ſays, reply'd he, and ſince you are ſo well inform'd of what has happen'd to me, I beg, Madam, you will tell me who was that charming Unknown. This Requeſt extremely pleas'd the Queen, who concealing her Satisfaction, ſaid to him, Out of what Motive, do you deſire to know this Lady, perhaps you may never ſee her? That is a Misfortune, I fear, Madam, interrupted the Prince; yet I often flatter myſelf, that ſome lucky Chance will convey me were ſhe is. But (added the Queen, in an Accent which diſcover'd part of her Sentiments) is it poſſible, that the Memory of a Perſon can be ſtill dear to you, who had no other Attractive to engage you, but her writing a few obliging Letters, and ſending you a Sum of Money to pay your Ranſom? Ah, Madam! reply'd he, there are Impreſſions, which never can be effac'd, and cou'd you conceive the Torments I have
endured

endured for that Unknown, you wou'd soon be convinc'd, that one may feel the sharpest Darts of Love, without seeing the influencing Object. Is it then really true, said the Queen, that you are impatient to see her, and that she often imploys your Thoughts? I declare it is sincerely so, Madam, answer'd the Prince, and there is nothing I wish more ardently, than an Opportunity of making my Retributions to a Lady, who has conferr'd so high an Obligation on me. Well, Prince, said *Celima* smiling, I will consult with some favourable Genius in order to compleat your Desire. Come to me to Morrow at the same Hour, and you shall be farther inform'd of this Subject. The Prince return'd his Acknowledgments to her in a most grateful Manner, and retir'd to the Palace of *Alhambro* with the disguis'd *Casilda*, who was waiting on the Terrace.

*Zulema* (impatient to know what had pass'd at the *Abbaicyn*) repair'd soon after to the Prince's Apartment, and *Casilda* (who perceiv'd, they had some matter of Importance to communicate to one another, feigning to withdraw) went and hid herself in a Place, where she cou'd hear their Conversation. You think, perhaps, said the Prince to *Zulema*, that I have seen *Felicia*, and am going to inform you of the Particulars of an agreeable Rendezvous; but instead of that, my dear Friend, I must tell you, some *Dæmon* appear'd to me in the Shape of an ugly old Creature, and that I was in the greatest Astonishment, when the
Queen

Queen of *Fez* came upon the Terrace, and defired me to follow her into her Clofet; where I no fooner enter'd, but fhe endeavour'd to perfuade me, that fhe had acquired an extraordinary Knowledge, by correfponding with good and evil Genius's, and in reality fhe told me every thing relating to my Adventure at *Nicopolis*, which very much furpriz'd me; for fhe certainly muft have been inform'd of it, by the Unknown herfelf, whom, I believe, is now amongft her Slaves; and I cannot put it out of my Head, but *Felicia* wrote to me by the Queen's Orders.

Here the Prince was fome time filent, and *Zulema* fpoke to him in thefe Terms: I begin to have a Thought, which appears to me very probable, and you may judge of it your felf, my Lord, when I have inform'd you, that *Celima* herfelf was at *Nicopolis*, at the time that the Chriftians were defeated by *Bajazet*: As you were of the number of the Prifoners, it is likely fhe faw you, and receiv'd an Impreffion; befides, if you confider the Prefent, which was fent you in the Tower, it cou'd not come from a Perfon of an inferiour Rank, and——You give me fuch a Light into the matter, interrupted the Prince, as opens my Eyes at once. I cannot call to mind what the Queen faid to me the Day of her Arrival, and the Converfation we have juft had together, without being convinc'd, that fhe is my Unknown of *Nicopolis*. Alas! into what a Labyrinth am I fallen? *Felicia* is with her, and

and if she discovers my Passion for that lovely Creature, I fear she will make her feel the Effects of her Revenge. Ah, cruel Destiny! cry'd he; am I born only to pass my Days in a continual Series of Woes, and have you decreed, that I shall never be happy? Here, the tormenting Thoughts of his past Disappointment, came fresh to his Mind, and interrupting his Discourse, threw him into so deep a Melancholy, that even his Friend *Zulema* endeavour'd unsuccefsfully to divert it; therefore as it was late, he took his leave of the Prince, tho' extremely concern'd at not having it in his Power to give him some Relief.

Whilst the Prince and *Zulema* were entertaining each other, *Casilda* heard their whole Conversation; and finding she had no hopes left of ever touching the Heart of a Prince, for whom she had already acted many Extravagances, she resolv'd on some desperate Undertaking. Her Revenge against her Rival was more predominant, than either the Passion she had for the Prince, or her own Honour; so that nothing less than the Death of the unhappy *Leonida* cou'd satisfy her raging Spirit.

The Queen of *Fez* (extremely overjoy'd at what the Prince of *Carency* had said to her) was forming a thousand agreeable Projects, not doubting but his Passion for his Unknown of *Nicopolis* was very sincere, and that he wou'd be equally transported to find she was the Person; yet as her Jealousy of *Felicia* gave her much Uneasiness, she thought it prudent

dent, firſt to clear her Suſpicions on that Subject; for, ſaid ſhe, if the Prince has ſeen that beautiful Captive, he muſt needs love her; therefore I will contrive, they ſhall meet in a place where I may hear their Diſcourſe, which will give me ſome Inſight into the matter.

*Celima* immediately ſent for *Felicia*, and being alone with her: I command you, ſaid ſhe, to be ſincere with me. Conſider, you are my Slave, and that your Deſtiny is in my Power; I can make you happy, if you will confeſs the Truth. Read this! (continu'd ſhe, ſhewing her the Letter, which the Prince of *Carency* had deſired *Zulema* to write) do you know the Writing? *Felicia* read it, and having examin'd it ſome time, told the Queen ſhe ſincerely cou'd not tell whoſe Hand it was, which in ſome Meaſure ſatisfy'd *Celima*; yet to be thoroughly convinc'd in an Affair, that ſo nearly concern'd her; Tell me, ſaid ſhe, have you ever heard of the Houſe of *Bourbon*, related to the Kings of *France?* *Felicia*, at this Queſtion, did not doubt but the Queen knew her, and without being any ways out of Countenance, reply'd, that the Name of ſo illuſtrious a Family was not unknown to her. And are you acquainted with any one of that Name, ſaid *Celima*? Did not you ſee the Count of *La March*, or the Prince of *Carency*, when you were in *Spain?* No, Madam, anſwer'd ſhe, I never ſaw thoſe Princes; they are intire Strangers to me. Know then, *Felicia*, interrupted the Queen of *Fez*, that the Perſon

I spoke of, and who appear'd so charming to me, is of the House of *Bourbon*, and is call'd the Prince of *Carency*: I have a mind you shou'd talk with him, and endeavour to penetrate into his Sentiments; he came here last Night, when I order'd the Governess of the Slaves to entertain him; but she managed the matter so very ill, that I must wholly depend upon you. Had the Queen's Thoughts been less prepossess'd with her Project, she might have discover'd *Felicia*'s Surprize, when she heard, the Prince of *Carency* was the Person whom the Queen lov'd, and that he was actually in *Granada*: But her mind being otherways employ'd, this young Slave had time to recover from her Disorder, and said to *Celima*; Your Pleasure, Madam, is so dear to me, that I fear I shall not be able to effect your Majesty's Commands with Success; for I have but very little Experience, and shou'd I miscarry in an Affair, which requires so much Prudence, I cou'd never forgive myself. No, reply'd the Queen, do not let that give you the least Uneasiness; I know you better than you know yourself, and am persuaded, you cannot do any thing amiss: But as the Moon shines very bright, I do not think it proper you shou'd meet the Prince on the Terrace, because I saw many People walking there last Night, and it wou'd not be convenient I shou'd be seen with him; therefore I will give Orders, that he may be convey'd to the Grotto in the Wood, where you may entertain him till I come to you. *Felicia*

*Felicia* having receiv'd her Instructions, retir'd to her Chamber, very much troubled, which *Inea* peceiving; Lovely *Felicia*, said she, do not conceal your Thoughts, but tell me the Cause of your Pain. Ah, my dear *Inea*! (cry'd *Felicia*) nothing but fresh Afflictions attend me. The Prince of *Carency* is in *Granada*, and goes by the Name of *Assimir*; 'tis he, whom the Queen loves, and by her Command, I am to have an Interview with him this Evening. What! interrupted *Inea*, can that give you any Uneasiness? Do you consider, that Heaven has sent him here, to put a Period to your Miseries? He will procure you your Liberty, and carry you back to your native Land, where all your Wishes will be crown'd with Felicity, whilst unfortunate *Inea*, absent from her dear *Don Ramire*, must pass the Remainder of her Life in Tears and Captivity. You bewail your Destiny, reply'd *Felicia*, and you think, that my being united to the Prince of *Carency* will make mine happier; Alas! you are very much deceiv'd, for we have conceiv'd a secret Antipathy for each other, and must never expect a perfect Satisfaction in our Alliance: Besides, do you imagine, that I can so easily banish the Count of *La Vagne* from my Thoughts? In spite of his Infidelity, he is still dear to me, and it's probable he is now sorry for having offended me; at least, his Eyes tell me so, and his Repentance may deserve Pardon. In short, *Inea*, I believe he loves me; but let it be as it will, the Prince shall not know who I am: As he has seen my Picture, he may call to mind its Resemblance, therefore I will hid my Face so well, that he shall not see it. *Inea* finding *Felicia* was fix'd on that Resolution, wou'd not any ways oppose it, tho' she was of a contrary Opinion.

The Prince of *Carency* was now thinking on means to convey a Letter to *Felicia*, in order to know, how he might have an Opportunity of entertaining her. He told his Design to *Zulema*, who advis'd him not to write, for fear his Letter shou'd fall into the Hands of the Queen of *Fez*, but promis'd him, he wou'd contrive some way to speak to her. By this time, the Hour of the Prince's Appointment was near, yet he made no great haste to go to the Palace, for he began to reflect, that a Second Interview with *Celima* wou'd only puzzle him, because he believ'd, she was his Unknown of *Nicopolis*, and that, were she inform'd of his Passion for *Felicia*, it might prove of a fatal Consequence.

*Zulema* put him in mind to repair to his *Rendezvous*; at last taking the suppos'd *Don Sanche* with him, he went with some Reluctancy to the *Abbaicyn*, where he found a Mute waiting on the Terrace, who convey'd him to the Grotto; *Felicia* came soon after, so entirely hidden from Head to Foot, in a large white Veil, that it was impossible to know her. The Prince did not doubt in seeing her, but it was the same old Woman he had

had met the Night before; which made him resolve not to have any discourse with her. *Felicia* on the other side (who felt strange Emotions, finding her self, at that Instant, with the Prince of *Carency*) was some time without speaking; but she had scarcely broke Silence, when the Prince, knowing the Voice of his lovely Mistress, went and flung himself at her Feet. *Leonida*, Charming *Leonida*! said he, what a Blessing is this? Have I found you at last, and have you still the same obliging Sentiments for me, which you had, when I was in the House of the Traitor *Benavidez*? *Leonida*, calling to mind what had pass'd at *Sallee*, was griev'd at this Discourse: Go, said she! (breaking out into a Passion) go, ungrateful Man! have you forgot the Cause, you have given me to upbraid you? The Prince thinking she was angry, that he had conceal'd his Name from her; I am guilty, Madam, I confess, reply'd he, for not having confided in you; I ought to have told you, that I was the Prince of *Carency*, and not have appear'd under an other Title; but the cruel Designs of *Leonora* (by whose Orders I was pursued, when I parted from *Villa-Real*, and wounded in the Forest, where you found me) was the Occasion I chang'd my Name, and took that of the Count of *La Vagne*, whom I very much resembled. This is my only Crime, divine *Leonida*; sure it is not so enormous, as to be unpardonable. Whilst the Prince was talking in this manner, *Leoni-*

*da* (whose Surprize was great) had a thousand different Imaginations; and cou'd not tell what Judgment to make: At last the Prince, impatient to hear her speak; Ah, Madam, said he, how much do I dread, that you are no more the same for me? Here, you see me at your Feet in Transports of inexpressible Joy, whilst you, my Beauteous Mistress, are indifferent and melancholy. What disobliging Sentiments have you receiv'd for a Man, who adores you, and whom Destiny has decreed to be yours? Do you consider, that I am going to offer up to you the Remainder of my Life, and that, from the fatal Moment I lost you, no Torment cou'd be equal to that I endured? Be assur'd, Madam, that the Prince of *Carency* has a Passion for you, no ways inferior to that, which you found in the Count of *La Vagne*. I must own to you, my Lord, reply'd *Leonida*, that I cannot believe what I hear; for when you were at *Sallee*, you even treated me with Disdain: What greater Offence cou'd you give me, than to abandon me as you did, and go away with *Olympia Doria*, whom you passionately lov'd? Do you think, my Senses cou'd deceive me, or that I am not capable of resenting the Perfidy? I cannot tell to this Hour, whether you are the Prince of *Carency*, or the Count of *La Vagne*; but what I am certain of, is, that you are the Person, who has highly injured me, and it wou'd be a shameful Weakness in me to pardon you. These Words strangely confounded the Prince, who

who believ'd his dear *Leonida*'s Mind was difcompos'd; and what confirm'd this Opinion, was his being perfuaded, that the Count of *La Vagne* perifhed at Sea, in his Return from *Nicopolis*, and that *Olympia Doria* died in her Father's Houfe at *Genoa*. Thefe were Circumftances, he cou'd no ways doubt of; and as for his Voyage to *Sallee*, he had never been there; fo that he look'd on all her Reproaches as Vifionary, which threw him into a defpairing Condition; yet he wou'd not let her perceive the Trouble he was in, nor what occafion'd it, but continu'd fpeaking to her in a very obliging manner: You do me a great deal of Wrong, Charming *Leonida*, faid he, to her fighing, and I fhou'd not find it a very hard Task to juftify myfelf, tho' I fancy, I have the moft Caufe to complain. What muft I judge of the Letter you writ to *Cafilda*, when you and *Benavidez* contriv'd your going off, which was a thing, I cou'd never have believ'd you guilty of? And what fhall I conjecture from your being at *Conftantinople*, and the Grand Seignior's Paflion for you? *Leonida* heard the Prince with Aftonifhment, and thought likewife, he knew not what he faid; fhe cou'd not imagine how a Man of fo good Senfe cou'd talk after fuch an extravagant manner; and as her Affection was more predominant than her Refentment, fhe was fenfibly griev'd at his Misfortune. Who I! my Lord, cry'd fhe; did I write to *Cafilda*, or give my Confent to *Benavidez*'s infolent Behaviour; and was I ever in *Turkey?* These Things are so new to me, and so far from being true, that I cannot bear to hear 'em: How long have you entertained these Chimeras? Here she took the Prince's Hand, and cou'd not restrain her Tears; which proof of her Tenderness, with the other Circumstances, so thoroughly touch'd him, that he was soon convinc'd of her Sincerity. Let us do Justice to each other, most amiable *Leonida*, (said the Prince, printing an ardent Kiss on her fair Hand;) be assur'd I never was false to you. I shou'd be willing to satisfy you, interrupted *Leonida*, cou'd I forget the Adventure, which happen'd to me lately at *Sallee*: She then recited to him her whole Story, with so much Wit and Coherence, that he perceiv'd, what he had taken for an Effect of Lunacy, was supported by solid Appearances; therefore having explain'd matters, they came to a right Understanding, which created unspeakable Transports in these two Lovers.

One may easily imagine the Consternation of *Casilda*, who had heard their whole Discourse, and was distracted to see so perfect a Sympathy between *Leonida* and the Prince. All her Perfidiousness, as well as her Brother's, was laid open, and seeing herself frustrated of those hopes, which had flatter'd her till then, she had like (in her excessive Despair) to have enter'd the Grotto, with a full design to stab *Leonida*; but as she consider'd, that the Prince wou'd prevent the Blow, and disappoint her revengful Attempt, she deferr'd her wicked Action,

till

*of* CARENCY. 361

till she found a fairer Opportunity of executing it.

After *Leonida* and the Prince of *Carency* had given each other reciprocal Assurances of their Joy and Affection, they consulted, how they shou'd behave themselves towards the Queen of *Fez*, till they cou'd find an Opportunity of going off. While they were on this Subject, the Queen came to the Grotto; but I must tell you, what prevented her from repairing thither sooner.

As *Celima* was coming out of her Apartment, they told her, that *Mahomet* was in the Palace, and had something of the highest Importance to communicate to her: She had given Orders, that no body shou'd be admitted that Evening; yet as that Prince's Visit seem'd to import some weighty matter, she wou'd not refuse seeing him. *Mahomet* addressing the Queen, told her, that *Mula*, Favorite to *Abelhamar*, was just arriv'd from *Fez*, with a Letter to her from his Master, and that being a particular Acquaintance of his, he had apply'd to him for a private Audience, which if she was pleas'd to grant, he wou'd immediately send for him. Tho' *Celima* was very impatient to be at her *Rendezvous* with the Prince of *Carency*, yet on this Occasion, she was forc'd to yield to her Politicks, fearing, that if she shou'd defer this Affair till the next Day, *Mahomet* might suspect she was imploy'd in some more agreeable Occupation; therefore having assented to *Mula*'s Admittance,

tance, he came and threw himself at the Queen's Feet, and presented her with a Letter from the Prince his Master, which was written in these Terms.

*THO' I have an indisputable Right to the Kingdom of Fez, and am now in the Possession of it, yet I am willing, Madam, to yield up one half of it to you, upon Condition, that you will give me Felicia. Before I had seen her, nothing cou'd be equal to my Ambition; but now her Charms have made so deep an Impression in my Heart, that all other Passions have submitted to my transcendent Love. I can never be happy without her, and if I am indebted to you for the Possession of that lovely Creature, half my Kingdom will be too small a Return, for so high an Obligation; therefore grant me but your Slave, and I will acknowledge you for my Sovereign.*

Abelhamar.

*Celima* having read this Letter in the Presence of *Mahomet*, they both admired *Abelhamar*'s Passion for *Felicia*; and as *Mahomet*'s Vows were already dedicated to the Queen of *Fez*, he was overjoy'd to find, that this Occasion afforded her sure means of recovering, at least one part of her Dominions. He joyn'd with *Mula* in his Proposals, and offer'd to go himself with *Felicia* to *Sallee*, in order to bring back with him such Hostages from *Abelhamar*, as shou'd warrant the performance of the Treaty. *Celima*, with a gracious Air, return'd turn'd *Mahomet* Thanks and assur'd him, she shou'd never forget the generous manner, in which he espous'd her Interest; but as *Abelhamar*'s Proposals requir'd some Consideration, she desired, her Answer might be suspended till the next Day; then *Mula* withdrew, and left the Prince there, who took so great a Pleasure in entertaining the Queen, that he did not retire till it was late, which gave time to the Prince of *Carency* and his Mistress, to take some Measures relating to their particular Affairs.

*Mahomet* having taken leave of the Queen, she immediately went to the Grotto, where being enter'd, *Leonida*, out of Respect retir'd, and left her alone with the Prince of *Carency*. This lovely Captive was walking in the Wood, with her Thoughts entirely imploy'd on the Happiness, she propos'd to herself, thro' the means of her faithful Lover: but alas, Fate was preparing a New Tragedy; *Casilda* (still under a Man's Disguise) distracted with Jealousy, at what she had just heard, and seeing her Rival walking alone, thought she might easily pierce her Heart, before any one cou'd come to her Assistance; so running up to her like a Fury, she drew out her Poinard, and plung'd it into *Leonida*'s Breast, who fell with the Blow, crying out for help, and calling the Prince of *Carency*; at which Name, *Casilda* was possess'd with such inhuman Rage, that she repeated her Blows. The Grotto not being distant, the Prince was struck at the mournful Accents of his wounded Mistress,

and

and leaving the Queen fuddenly, he made hafte toward the Place where he heard *Leonida*'s Voice; he faw her lying on the Ground bath'd in Blood, and perceiv'd *Don Sanche* running away, which convinc'd him that he was the Murderer; he immediately purfu'd him, and with his Sword run him through: After he had thus reveng'd unfortunate *Leonida*, he came up to her; but oh! what a lamentable Condition did he find her in? She exprefs'd herfelf with painful Sighs, and had fcarce Strength enough to take her Lover's Hand, which made him fear, her beauteous Eyes were going to yield up all their Charms to that univerfal Conqueror, Death.

How fhall I here paint the difconfolate State of our unhappy Prince; he was refolv'd not to furvive fo great a Misfortune, and had already turn'd the Point of his Sword to his Breaft, when the Queen (who had follow'd him out of the Grotto) interpos'd, and prevented him from acting his own Death: She repeated her Shrieks in fo prefling a manner, that the Guards immediately came up to her, and foon after, moft of her Attendants, with a great Number of Flambeaux, which fhew'd all the Horror of this Tragick Scene. It was not long before they were inform'd of it at the Palace of *Alhambro*: The two Princes, *Mahomet* and *Ofmin*, came to the *Abbaicyn*, with *Mula* and another Gentleman, who had accompanyed him in his Voyage from *Sállee;* In fhort, the Wood was full of People, who were in a strange Consternation; *Leonida* wounded, (lying in the Arms of a despairing Prince, who was near losing his Mistress) mov'd all Hearts with Compassion.

On the other hand, *Casilda* (that wretched Creature) was tearing open her Wounds, to hasten her deserv'd Death: *Zulema* approach'd her, and still thinking she was a Man; Ah Barbarous Villain, that you are, cry'd he to her; what *Dæmon* urg'd you to commit a Crime so black? Tell me, what had innocent *Felicia* done to you, and how came you to murder her in this cruel manner? I am *Casilda*, (reply'd she with a furious Air) and she was my Rival; go to your Friend, and he will tell you the rest. These were the last and only Words she pronounc'd with her expiring Breath.

Tho' *Leonida*'s Life was despair'd of, yet the Surgeons were sent for, who us'd all their Skill to stop the bleeding of her Wounds, which they dress'd, and having assisted her with proper Remedies, her Spirits began to revive: She open'd her weak Eyes, then fix'd them on the Prince, who held her in his Arms, and appear'd in as great want of Relief, as his dying Mistress. At last they took her from him, and carry'd her by the Queen's Order to her Chamber, where she was laid in Bed, and *Inea*, who had a tender Affection for *Leonida*, staid by her almost inconsolable for the unlucky Accident, which had happen'd to her illustrious Companion. She was so sensibly touch'd at it, that even the Presence of *Don Ramire* cou'd not mitigate her excessive Grief. He was just arriv'd from *Fez*, where he had been, in Expectation of finding his dear *Inea*, who had sent him a Letter whilst he was at *Morocco*, to acquaint him with her Captivity: But before he cou'd reach *Sallee*, the Queen was embark'd, which oblig'd him to wait there for a favourable Opportunity of coming over to *Granada*; and as about this time *Mula* was setting out for that Kingdom, he took his Passage in the same Ship.

*Osmin*, who had a real Passion for *Leonida*, was thoroughly concern'd at her Misfortune; and as for the Queen of *Fez*, she cou'd not help being mov'd at this dismal Adventure, tho' she prudently conceal'd her Thoughts. The Prince of *Carency*'s mournful Complaints, too well confirm'd her Suspicions in relation to his Sentiments for *Leonida*; and she saw him possess'd with so violent a Despair, that she had no room left for any hopes, no not even to come to an Agreement with *Abelhamar*; for in the first Place, she was convinc'd, that shou'd *Leonida* die of her Wounds, her Death wou'd render his Proposals of no Effect; and on the other Hand, she foresaw, that if she recover'd, the Prince wou'd claim her as one, perhaps, he had lov'd a long time, and whom he intended to marry.

As for *Mula*, he was so amaz'd, that he cou'd scarcely believe his own Eyes; for tho' he was present when his Master fought the
brave

brave Count of *La Vagne*, and kill'd him, and that he saw him give up his last Breath in *Olympia's* Arms, yet he cou'd not be perfuaded, but the Prince of *Carency* was that same Count; so great was their Resemblance.

The Prince, all this while, was like a Man whose Senses had abandon'd him, and in that Condition, the Queen of *Fez* gave Orders, that he shou'd be carry'd into one of the Apartments of the *Abbaicyn*, where being laid on a Bed, his Wound open'd afresh, and there gush'd from it a great Quantity of Blood, which alarm'd all his Friends, particularly *Ofmin*, who look'd on him as his Rival, and notwithstanding, shew'd a sincere Trouble for his Misfortune, as well as his generous Friend *Zulema*.

No body cou'd now tell who was in the greatest Danger, the Prince of *Carency* or *Leonida*; they both continu'd extremely ill: His excessive Grief for the Condition of his beloved Mistress, retarded his Recovery, till they assur'd him, there was Hopes of her Life; which agreeable News caus'd so wonderful an Effect in him, that his Wound was soon heal'd, and in a few Days he was able to visit her, who was also in no small Concern for the State of her Lover's Health. The Presence of this lovely Prince had so great an Influence on her, that it contributed likewise to her speedy Recovery: His daily Attendance and tender Care gave her more Relief than all the Remedies, which

the

the Surgeons apply'd to her Wounds; and it may be faid, that as Love was the Author of the Pains and Difafters of thefe conftant Lovers, he was alfo their Phyfician and Comfort. No Satisfaction cou'd be equal to theirs, nor is it poffible to conceive the endearing Expreffions, they mutually exchang'd, during their Illnefs.

By this time it was known, thro' the means of *Inea*, that *Leonida* was Daughter to *Don John* of *Velafco,* and *Zulema* having mention'd *Cafilda*'s Name, fhe alfo inform'd the Court of her being of the Family of the *Benavidez's*, and related to them the whole Story, as fhe had heard it from *Leonida*.

As to the Prince of *Carency*'s Name, it was not long kept a Secret; *Celima* told the King of *Granada* who he was, which added fo much to the Efteem, he had already acquir'd, thro' his perfonal Merit, that he receiv'd all poffible Marks of Honour from the King, who went often to fee him after this unhappy Adventure; and endeavouring to confole the Prince, amongft other obliging Expreffions, he told him, he reftor'd him to his Liberty, for which, he defired no other Ranfom than his Friendfhip, and that had he known fooner of his being of the Houfe of *Bourbon*, he wou'd have fhewn him all the Diftinction, that was due to fo illuftrious a Family

The Prince, who now faw *Leonida* out of Danger, was very willing to retrieve his Liberty,

berty at any rate: He readily accepted of the King of *Granada*'s generous Offer, and return'd him Thanks for that, and the many other Favours he had confer'd on him, since the time he was taken Prisoner.

*Celima*, notwithstanding *Leonida* was her Rival, extremely pity'd her, and order'd that all the Attendance imaginable shou'd be given her: She also visited the Prince, who laying aside the Respect due to her Rank, receiv'd her with so much Indifferency, that she resolv'd never more to speak to him of his Unknown of *Nicopolis*.

The mean while the King of *Granada* (who was desirous to compleat the Prince of *Carency*'s good Fortune, and had a Design, at the same time, to oblige the *Spaniards*) thought on means to procure *Leonida* her Liberty; he therefore address'd himself to the Queen of *Fez*, offering her whatever Sum, she wou'd please to demand for the Ransom of that young Lady: But *Celima*, whose Greatness of Spirit was equal to her Passion, resolv'd no Sovereign shou'd surpass her in Generosity; the Prince of *Carency* being a Christian, and in Love with her Slave, was enough to make her determine never to think of him more. She told the King of *Granada*, that far from requiring any Ransom for *Leonida*, she desired, he wou'd accept and dispose of her, as he thought fit; and that not only *Leonida*, but all the rest of her Slaves were at his Command if agreeable to him. The King heard with Pleasure *Celima*'s Answer, and in his Turn, gallantly

B b  presented

presented *Leonida* to the Prince of *Carency*, who receiv'd her with inexpressible Marks of Joy and Gratitude, but cou'd not find Words to make a Retribution suitable to the Present.

The chief and only Care of these happy Lovers consisted now in giving each other daily Proofs of their tender Affection. Their long and cruel Disappointments made their Felicity the greater; and tho' they were not as yet Perfectly recover'd, they were proposing Means to leave *Granada*, in order to perform the Promise which their Parents had made for them in their infant Years. The Prince wrote to *Don John* of *Velasco* at *Villa-Real*, acquainting him with the Particulars of his and *Leonida*'s Fortune, and withal, that he hop'd soon to be the happiest of Mankind.

*Mula* (seeing his Master's Designs were render'd impracticable through this Adventure between the Prince of *Carency* and *Leonida*) went back to *Sallee*, and gave *Abelhamar* an Account of what had pass'd; which News so cruelly affected him, that the Loss of his Mistress had like to have made him act his own Death; but as an Evincement of the Greatness of his Passion, he took a Resolution proportionable to it; for having renounc'd to the Crown of *Fez*, he retired to a Castle on the Sea-side, where he consecrated the Remainder of his Life to the dear Memory of his *Felicia*. *Celima* soon receiv'd Advice of this unexpected Change; and as *Mahomet* was extremely sollicitous to serve her in so favourable a Conjuncture,

Conjuncture, he intreated the King of *Granada*, his Father, to give him a Fleet and some Forces, in order to reinstate the Queen of *Fez*; which being granted, he took the Command entirely upon himself, and convoy'd her to *Sallee*, where, far from meeting with any Opposition, she found all Things in a perfect Tranquility. By this time her Mind was more at Ease; for having consider'd that she cou'd no longer hope to receive an obliging return to the Passion, she had for the Prince of *Carency*, she thought nothing wou'd sooner effect it's Cure, than approving *Mahomet*'s Vows; therefore being of too haughty a Temper to bear with the Disdain of the one, and Gratitude pleading in behalf of the other, she at once resolv'd to give her Hand, and all her Affection to *Mahomet*, who by this Alliance saw his Love and Ambition satisfy'd.

*Celima*, before she parted from *Granada*, restor'd *Inea* to her Liberty, and *Don Ramire* took her with him to *Toledo*, where these two Lovers, by a happy Union, receiv'd the Reward of their Constancy.

What I have farther to add relating to the Prince of *Carency* and *Leonida*, is, that as soon as they were in a Condition to set out on their Journey, they took leave of the King of *Granada*, who made them considerable Presents, and order'd several Noblemen with a strong Detachment of his Guards to conduct them as far as the Frontiers of *Spain*; whence they proceeded to *Villa Real*, where they were receiv'd with